PRAI

Above

D0370736

"A twisty tale with an otherworldly setting that readers will happily revisit."

—Kirkus Reviews

"Though reminiscent of beloved fantasies—think *A Wrinkle in Time* meets *The Princess Bride*—*Above the Star* is a magical rendition of a wholly creative tale. Chute imagines unheard of lands, mythical characters, and irresistible folklore, weaving all the magic together with what we know to be true: everyone is searching for something. Her sympathy for the characters—both human and not—is palpable, leaving even the most despicable anti-heroes with room for redemption. And while the story is relentless in its conflict, there are enough moments of tenderness to keep the reader from being overwhelmed. *Above the Star* is as fanciful as it is grounded, and as gritty as it is fantastic. Chute's visual, visceral storytelling will pull you into a reality you never saw coming and a world you'll be sad to leave behind."

—Lee Lee Thompson, publisher of *The Perpetual You* magazine

"*Above the Star* is one weird and wild ride full of memorable characters created by an imaginative writer. A mesmerizing and other-worldly read that kept me off-balance from beginning to end. Think of *Star Wars*, *The Lord of The Rings* and Homer's *Odyssey* all wrapped up together in a gift box called *Above the Star*. A spellbinding tale of a hero's quest to save his daughter from the clutches of illness and evil."

—Raymond Gariepy, editor of *WestWord* magazine

"Chute's debut fantasy novel takes you on an exhilarating trip to an enchanting, dangerous world where adventure, discovery, and the cure to a young girl's illness awaits . . . *Above the Star* is the enticing first installment to *The 8th Island Trilogy* fantasy series."

—Naomi Maharaj, Masters of Library Information Studies

Above the Star is a creative tour de force from the wildly talented author/artist Alexis Marie Chute. Part adventure, part fantasy, part family saga, part quest, the novel leads its heroines and heroes—some human, some extra-human—into peril and redemption, love and loss, and terrors generated by both illness and magic until they finally emerge into a world where courage makes everything possible. The first in *The 8th Island Trilogy*, *Above the Star* ingenuously incorporates Chute's own drawings as important clues that keep the tale racing forward. Her images help to create a strange new world so thoroughly real that when you put the book down—if you do—you won't remember where you are.

—Pamela Petro, author of *Sitting up with the Dead*
and the artist's book *AfterShadows*

"Alexis Marie Chute's vivid, descriptive passages transported me into a fantastic yet dangerous world. But this is more than an incredible voyage; this is a story about family—it raises the question: How far would a parent go to save the life of a child? You will cheer for Ella, as she transforms from helpless victim to savvy heroine, spurred to greatness by her strange new allies. This is a book that combines adventure, mysticism and also offers a worthy character study."

—Steven Sandor, editor of *Avenue Magazine*

"In this endlessly inventive fantasy, Alexis Marie Chute handles a prismatic but utterly compelling plot with the skill of an expert storyteller, effortlessly blending the magical and the matter-of-fact. Chute's imagination evokes a dazzling, sometimes scary, world—a world both enchanted and cursed—but her deepest strength may be her gift for creating indelible characters. The more we get to know the book's three intrepid heroes, the more time we want to spend with them. *Above the Star* is a wild ride indeed, and we gratefully go along for the ride, not just for the adventures, but also for the company we keep."

—Steven Cramer, author of *Clangings* and *Goodbye to the Orchard*

"Infused with the mysterious and the fantastical, *Above the Star* is both a page-turning story of a young girl's coming-of-age and a gripping tale of a family's journey through illness, grief, and healing. Chute is writer of psychological acuity whose language and images transport the reader into this fascinating world filled with heart. *Above the Star* will leave readers reluctant to leave this magical world and breathlessly awaiting more."

—Laurie Foos, author of *Ex Utero* and *The Blue Girl*

"*Above the Star* is a fantastical fast-paced quest, anchored in the familial—in this case, a father's desire to find his missing son and to care for his teenaged granddaughter. It is parental love to the extreme, beyond all bounds, even into the next dimension. Chute's experience as an award-winning artist brings *Above the Star* to life with her visual storytelling, clearly crafting an entirely new world, and through the thought-provoking ink illustrations. *Above the Star* shows readers that there is a power within all of us to change the world, right where we are."

—Jessica Kluthe, author of *Rosina, The Midwife*

"*Above the Star* is an adrenaline-charged ride that grips you tight! Just when you think you know what's coming next, you're hit with a new twist! With relatable characters (some that are out of this world), expressive description, and an attention-grabbing premise, book one of *The 8th Island Trilogy* leaves you breathless in anticipation of what's to come in the next installment."

—Adrianne Baker, Librarian

"Get ready to be lost and then found in a world of intrigue, suspense, and love. Time will stand still as you travel through dimensions to the far-off land of Jarr-Wya and engage in a battle between good and evil. You may just discover Naiu inside of yourself as you fight alongside the heroes of *Above the Star* to find a cure and a way back home."

—Donloree Hoffman, author of
If I Die, Please Bring Cheesecake to My Funeral

"Fasten your seat belts and break out the life preservers. *Above the Star*, the first book in Alexis Marie Chute's *The 8th Island Trilogy* sucks the reader, as well as a cruise ship, through a dimensional portal into a world filled with compulsive stony beings, fiery philosophers, and deliciously dangerous and horrifyingly sentient crushed shell people. Propelled by a grandfather's determination to save the life of his dying teenaged granddaughter, Chute's exquisite prose powers a rollicking roller coaster of a tale filled with the kinds of twists and turns that will leave even the most stalwart of armchair adventurers breathless."

—Mindy Tarquini, award-winning author of *The Infinite Now* and *Hindsight*

"In *Above the Star*, a regular family with heartbreaking problems enters a world of epic adventures and the possibility of extraordinary solutions. Alexis Marie Chute manages to tell a fantastical tale that is also deeply human."

—Todd Babiak, author of *Son of France*

"*Above the Star* is a debut fantasy novel by Canadian author-artist Alexis Marie Chute. Like Alexis Marie herself, this novel has unexpected corners and charmingly quirky characters. This piece would be just another adventure-fantasy, were it not for the main character of Ella, a 14-year-old girl who doesn't speak. Ella is seriously ill and deteriorating, and the novel's quest is for her family (grumpy grandpa Archie, strong-willed mother Tessa) to find her a cure by whatever means possible. Including a journey to a planet-world that no-one has ever heard of in company with Zeno, a yellow-eyed mystic who sports stones on his face, and various other strange beings who inhabit the world of Jarr-Wya. This imaginative tour-de-force is outstanding for the sensitive treatment given to Ella, who despite her illness shines quietly as an emerging character. Highly recommended for Middle Grade and their parents."

—Cynthia Sally Haggard, author of *Thwarted Queen* and *Farewell My Life*

An amazing novel that easily transports you to another world. Filled with excitement and adventure, *Above the Star* is a must read!

—Maya Breen, grade 11 student

Centered around a magical underworld in the sea off the west coast of Africa, *Above the Star* is a lively tale of hope, loss, and love written with layers of visual detail to draw a reader in to Jarr-Wya where sand, fire, glass and water take on political dimensions as the Wellsley family seeks a cure for their 14-year-old daughter Ella's terminal illness. Naiu, the life force of the world of Jarr-Wya, combines with desire to permit earthlings and Jarr-Wya natives to cross over between realms using a magic tool, the Tillastrion. The intermingling of mythology and imagination fuel this exploration of good, evil, and the unintended consequences of risky choices. Fast-paced and engaging, *Above the Star* will fascinate readers.

—Casandra Goldwater, word-and-image photographer, writer and professor

Above
the
Star

Above the Star

the

Star

The 8th Island Trilogy

BOOK 1

BY

Alexis Marie Chute

Published by SparkPress, a BookSparks imprint,
A division of SparkPoint Studio, LLC
Tempe, Arizona, USA, 85281
www.gosparkpress.com

Published 2018

Printed in the United States of America

ISBN: 978-1-943006-56-4 (pbk)
ISBN: 978-1-943006-57-1 (e-bk)

Library of Congress Control Number: 2018931875

Illustrations by Alexis Marie Chute
Book design by Stacey Aaronson

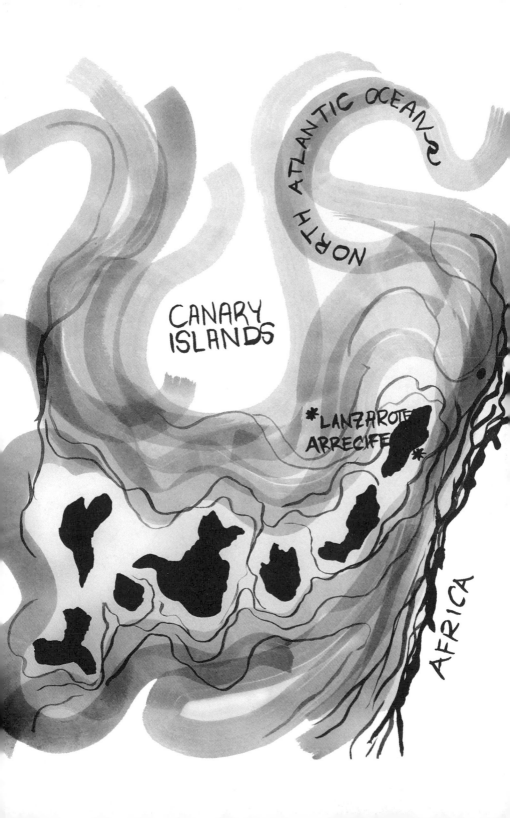

Dedication

For Aaron, Hannah, Zachary, Eden, and Luca.
My inspirations and fellow adventurers.

chapter 1

The *Atlantic Odyssey* awaits its passengers at the mainland of the Spanish harbor, sitting stoic and stable in the water like the architecture that grows out of the sea along the coastline. "It'll be okay," Tessa says to herself, shading her pale-green eyes against the ship's reflection of the smoldering Barcelona sun. "The cruise ship isn't even rocking." The breeze threatens to billow upward Tessa's turquoise, gingham-checkered circle skirt that she grips tightly to her legs. She swallows hard and plants her feet wide on the dock, attempting to calm the motion sickness already curling in her stomach at the sight of the unsettled water, which cracks indignantly against the weathered wood of the harbor's jetties and splashes up the side of the ship. Its foam reaches for the portholes. The distant horizon is shadowed with a faint though expanding darkness.

Fourteen-year-old Ella stands beside her mother, her drawing-journal and artist pens clutched in one hand and her school library's stained copy of an anatomy guide for illustrators in the other. Ella pays no attention to the weather—in her colorful leggings and oversized black t-shirt—but for the wind's bending and crinkling the pages she studies. She snaps the book shut and taps Tessa's bare arm, her mother's goosebumped skin exposed in her fitted white tank top tucked into the high waist of her skirt. "What is it, Ell?" Tessa smiles and gathers Ella's long, honey-blond bangs behind her ears, but it's no use. The wind, gentle at dawn, is now tipping over the wide-brimmed hats of the tourists studying their cruise itineraries and maps, and braiding the hair of women shifting their weight from one sandaled foot to the other, impatient to board.

"Exciting, isn't it?" Tessa adds.

Ella swings her backpack around her shoulder to her chest and tucks away her book and drawing tools, then begins to gesture with her hands, signing a word from American Sign Language. Her palm faces her forehead, her fingers fanned, and in a downward swooping gesture, ending at her chin, she closes her fingers to her thumb, also shutting her eyes. She repeats this several times. Her midnight-blue-painted nails complement her icy-colored eyes that quickly flick open to ensure her message is received.

Tessa recognizes the sign and answers, "Sleeping."

Ella nods, then points first to herself, then to Tessa, and finally to an old man sitting on a splintered wooden bench a few paces away. His weathered face and drooping nose are nearly wedged between the pages of a scuffed leather book that he reads intently, protectively, his shoulders hunched in his khaki coat to block the view.

Ella finishes her thought by raising her index finger and pivoting her hand side to side, signing the word *where*. She scrunches her eyebrows together, the language's method for communicating a question.

"Sleep. You. Me. Grandpa . . ." Tessa says, piecing together her daughter's question. Ella had not spoken in six months, ever since a seizure had spasmed through her petite body. It confirmed the worst: Ella's brain tumor had grown.

Tessa brightens with understanding. "Where will we sleep

on the cruise? Well, you and I are going to share a cabin. It'll be like a long sleepover. That'll give us plenty of girl time. Grandpa Archie will have his own cabin." Tessa looks over at her father-in-law. Her smile slowly fades.

ARCHIE moved in with Tessa and her husband—the ever-optimistic, studiously handsome Arden—when Ella was seven years old. Arden had worried about his father's wellbeing after his mom died. "It won't be permanent; just a few months while Dad finds a smaller place and adjusts. I'll make sure he behaves," Arden promised.

Not even a week had passed before Archie's wool socks were tucked into every crevice of the couch and his stained mouth-guard lay forgotten in his cup of Earl Grey after breakfast. The walls of their boxy 1960s Seattle bungalow were not thick enough to muffle Archie's lionlike snores, which woke Ella and sent her from her princess bed to snuggle under the covers with Tessa and Arden. Ella was a wiggler. She would root herself in the center of the bed between her parents and for half an hour rest still before rotating her legs and eventually her torso ever so slightly, like the long and short arms of a clock marking the passage of time.

It was a sleepless spell for all but Archie, who shuffled out of his room every morning stretching, scratching, yawning, and grinning, while offering a "Good mornin', everybody!" on a gust of rank breath.

One week turned into two, two months turned into three, and the years began to multiply. Arden did his best to tidy up after his father and ensure Archie's robe was fastened after his morning bathroom ritual with the *Seattle Times*.

"He's forgetful, that's all," Arden would say, pushing his chunky frames up his nose and brushing aside his dark hair from his forehead, his endearing nervous habits.

"How did your mom put up with this?" Tessa complained.

"I'll talk to Dad." But Arden never did, for that was the time Ella's headaches and vomiting began. MRI and CT scans confirmed the presence of the tumor, which was greedily expanding in Ella's ten-year-old brain and spinal cord. It coiled itself at the base of her skull, so horribly entwined that not even the most skilled pediatric surgeon could extract it.

The radiation oncologist began external beam therapy to shrink the tumor, but Ella did not understand. The medical team strapped her small body to a chair, so she couldn't fidget. Her feet dangled an inch above the floor and her chin rested on a plastic oval ledge swung over on a metal arm. The machine that delivered the high-energy x-ray was aimed at the soft, flush-pink skin of Ella's neck. Tessa could only watch from an attached room where her tears dampened her long blond hair as she pressed her forehead and hands against a pane of glass, her breath fogging the view of her screaming, terrified child.

Years passed.

Arden would come home from Seattle University, where he worked as a historian and professor of ancient Egyptian dynasties, only to find Archie pacing on the front steps. "We've got to do something, son. I don't know what, but we need a miracle." Archie clutched Arden's shoulders so tightly that his fingertips turned white, until Arden shrugged hard out of his father's grip. Archie and Ella, his only grandchild, had developed a playful and protective bond in the five years of sharing a hall bathroom and a host of inside jokes.

Father and son would stand without words on the front steps for what seemed like hours. Arden removed his glasses and ran his fingers along his eyelashes, brooding silently. Archie wrung his handkerchief between his deeply creased palms until its fibers frayed and fell to the ground. The younger of the two men would cross the threshold first, only to find a pale Ella asleep on Tessa's lap where they sat on the dated kitchen tiles, with whatever dinner his wife was cooking burning in the pot. The whole house reeked of vomit and charred food. Tessa simply looked up at Arden with hollow eyes.

A chipper young woman in a white skirt and blue blazer, with a gold crest embroidered on its breast, switches on a portable microphone and speaker. It shrieks loudly. "Welcome to Constellations Cruise Line!" she begins, attaching the mic to a flimsy stand. "My name is Valarie and I am your cruise director. Our team is full of nautical knowledge—and insider tips on the local landscape and culture—so don't be a stranger! We will board in a moment—please excuse this brief delay—but while we wait, it is my immense pleasure to introduce Captain Nathanial Billows, who will be guiding us through Spain's Canary Islands on this proud vessel, the *Atlantic Odyssey*." Valarie gestures to the tall, broad-shouldered man beside her—in his early forties Tessa guesses, maybe only five years older than herself—before clapping ardently, cuing the crowd on the waiting platform.

The captain approaches the microphone. He is dressed in the classic brilliant white seaman's suit, its ornamental black epaulets decorated with gold lines and the executive curl of the captain's insignia. "Thank you all, and thank you, Valarie," he says as he scans the passengers with a confident gaze, bowing his head ever so slightly, his free hand holding the black brim of his stiff white hat up to his chest. "Valarie is our cruise director and leader of guest services. She is more than happy to assist you while on our voyage, both day" —he smiles cheekily at Valarie— "and night." Valarie blushes and toys with a strand of her shoulder-length brown hair. Her pale face flushes with color. She smooths the front of her blazer.

"Please, call me Captain Nate," he continues as he swings his hat back onto his ash-blond crew cut and rubs his palms together. "You folks are in for a scenic treat! For the next eleven days, we will explore the seven main volcanic Canary Islands. One legend says the islands are the mountaintops of sunken Atlantis. Another tells the tale of a mythical being who kidnapped the sun and hid it inside one of the volcanoes. Still, another myth speaks of an eighth island." Captain Nate's voice slips into a whisper, and he widens his brown eyes and spreads his hands wide. "Only the setting sun will reveal the location of the mystery island—but don't blink, or it will vanish as quickly as it appeared!"

With the captain's words, a low screech slips out of Ella's mouth as she tries to laugh or speak—Tessa does not know which—as the tumor tears through the normal sound like a deeply scratched record. The curiosity on Ella's face morphs to embarrassment, and she drops her sunglasses from the top of her head to her nose, hiding her eyes behind their reflective lenses, and she crosses her arms. Tessa puts a comforting arm around her daughter while glaring at the passengers that turn with disgusted expressions to see where the noise originated.

Valarie, back at the microphone, announces, "Our first stop: the port at Arrecife on the island of Lanzarote." Her two-way radio chirps in her hand and she listens. "Wonderful news, folks! We are ready! Welcome aboard!"

chapter 2

Tessa, Ella, and Archie ride the elevator in silence. After the safety briefing on the promenade deck and a tour of the life preservers and rafts on the quarterdeck, where sunbeams streaked in long lines between the cracks of angry clouds, the passengers had been released to find their cabins on one of the eight expansive levels. From deep within the ship, they can hear the *Atlantic Odyssey*'s horn blast. The engines growl as the vessel leaves the dock to shrink from view behind them.

Ella looks up at her grandpa, fumbling through an awkward gesture.

"What is it, sweetie? Hmm." Archie watches Ella intently as she repeats the motions in a loop, pleading for understanding with her eyes. Archie's white eyebrows are raised, deepening the creases on his forehead.

The family had begun sign language lessons months before, but while Archie's arthritic fingers were near useless, Ella was merely resistant. Thus, beyond the fundamentals, the family had resorted to a frustrating game of charades to express more complex ideas and emotions.

"Hmm, Ell. I'm not sure." The old man exhales deeply. "I'm sorry, sweetie."

Tessa steps in closer. "I don't know that sign, Ell," she says and pulls out her ASL pocket dictionary. She is still flipping back and forth between pages when the elevator doors open. Ella gives up, her arms falling limp as she walks out into the hall.

Archie deposits his luggage in his cabin around the corner from Tessa and Ella's room, then raps on their door. "You ladies decent?" he hollers.

Ella waves her grandpa in to the small cabin—number 251—which contains a queen bed, a wardrobe built into one wall, and a narrow bathroom. Ella shows him the continuous blind contour drawing of the *Atlantic Odyssey* she had made before boarding. "That's great work, Ell. Hey, guess what I saw? A cabin with a tiny circular window," Archie says, sitting down on the edge of the bed. "Those folks can look out to the sea." Ella looks impressed. "Maybe next time, my sweet Ell." Archie pulls Ella in close, ruffling her hair—which she quickly tidies back into place—though she releases a happy squeak, what Archie has recognized over the last months as his granddaughter's giggle.

"Want to go up top?" he asks Ella, before swiveling to catch Tessa's gaze as she hangs a creamy-white cotton dress in the wardrobe. "Can I take her up? For a look around, just Ella and me? You know, grandpa bonding time?"

"Is that what this trip is all about?" Tessa barks, searching Archie's face for answers.

"What d'you mean?"

"I don't have you figured out, Archie. Is it quality time you're after? I have never seen you spend this kind of money. And out of the blue!"

"Always harking on me for being a penny pincher! I couldn't afford a cabin with a window."

"You know what I mean."

As Tessa stares at Archie, she sees Arden's face: her husband's smile lines, exaggerated; and the curve of his cheeks and forehead, though the face before her is freckled with sunspots from Archie's career as a roofer. The old man is bald on top, with a half-halo of coarse, silvery hair reaching from ear to ear. Archie's features have their own quirks, distinct from Arden's, but Tessa recognizes her husband's eyes and even his build in Archie's slouching frame. Tessa unconsciously shakes her head and a thin line deepens between her eyebrows at the thought of Arden Wellsley.

"All right, Tessa. You got me." Archie raises his hands in the air. "I do have a motive for this trip. I want my granddaughter to be happy. Does that make me a bad guy?" He looks over at Ella, who shakes her head and pinches her pointer and middle fingers together with her thumb, signing the word *no.* "That's my girl," commends Archie with a chuckle.

A deep sigh escapes between Tessa's teeth. She pushes the last two years of struggle as a single parent out of her mind. She had been distrusting of Archie since Arden's abrupt disappearance, though her father-in-law had proved dependable, even on their toughest days. *That is the one difference between Archie and Arden,* Tessa reflects. *Archie is still here.*

ARCHIE and Ella stroll along a hallway below the quarterdeck, passing expensive gift shops, a beauty salon, fitness center, and a grand entrance to the ballroom and theater at the base of a broad, maroon-carpeted circular staircase. A chandelier of crystal petals dangles above the stairs in a wide skylight, three floors above their heads. The daylight catches the curve of the petals, which cast rainbows in every direction. Ella touches each bend of color along their path. She curls her arm backward and pulls her phone from a side pocket of her backpack and posts a photo of the rainbows on Instagram.

The pair head up the staircase and Ella runs her hand along the rich oak railing. "Awwweeek—" Ella says, forgetting her vocal limitations. She drops her head and grits her teeth, though peers at her grandpa through the corners of her eyes. A few passengers pause on the stairs.

"It's okay, sweetie. Don't care what anybody thinks, you hear me? I know you've been having a rough go in junior high—but high school, and the real world, can be even rougher. You need to toughen up."

Ella nods but her jaw remains locked. She clumsily signs her thought but her fingers trip over themselves. Her eyes swim behind instant tears and she looks away.

"This is our secret, Ell," Archie whispers as he pulls a pen and creased receipt out of the pocket of his oversized pleated pants. "Now don't get me in trouble and tell your mom about this. She'll report me to the sign language teacher and get us both in heck. You're on vacation, sweetie. Now tell Grandpa Archie what you want to say."

Ella beams at her grandpa, tears still on her cheeks. She scans the stairs to ensure her mother is not within sight before taking the paper and pen. Ella developed an expansive vocabulary in the years she carted books to every doctor and radiation appointment. When she lost her ability to speak, in the peak of awkward adolescence, she retreated between the hardcovers in her school's library.

Ella scribbles on the flimsy receipt: *This place is lovely. Like a dream.*

When they pass through the sliding glass doors into the dense salty air on the quarterdeck, the speed of the ship becomes apparent. Ella's bangs are again swept from behind her ears and tickle her freckled nose. She and Archie explore, discovering a kidney bean-shaped pool carved out of the deck, surrounded by wooden patio chairs, their pristine white canvas slings blowing erratically in the swiftly traveling air.

"Look! There, Ell!" Archie points at the sea. "Is that a dolphin jumping? Or a whale?"

They jog to the railing, but startle at the loud thumping of many feet crossing the deck behind them, led by Valarie, the cruise director, who is calling out above the wind, "This way! Port side!" Archie and Ella find themselves at the most desired section of railing, surrounded by nearly forty eager men and women wearing vests with dozens of bulging pockets and cameras slung around their necks, their fingers poised on their release buttons. Shutters begin snapping open and closed with a whir like a swarm of insects.

Archie is undeterred, a trait he learned from years of working with tradesmen. He gently pushes back on the encroaching mob. When one zealous photographer wields a pudgy elbow while jockeying for a better view, Archie pipes up. "Come on, fella! Let the young lady see!" Ella ducks for the camera men and women, crouching low against the railing. A look of awe paints across her face as she watches the black shape emerge as smooth as a knife from the unsettled water, then flop back in on its side. An eruption of foamy spray blasts into the sky, glittering in the waning sunlight, before the great dark form slaps its tail in one final disturbance—and is gone.

"Many apologies," says the round-bellied man when it's clear the whale will not reappear. He smirks with self-importance, his words patronizing. Archie scowls. The breeze carries the pungent cologne unsuccessfully masking the man's body odor into Archie's nostrils, for a moment overpowering the dense, briny air.

"What is this anyway, a camera club?" Archie grumbles.

"Yes, that's exactly right. We do a cruise this time every

year," the man bats his eyelashes proudly. "Our photographs are often featured in *National Geographic*."

"Any of *yours* been printed in there?"

"Well, no." The man looks annoyed.

"That's all right, champ." Archie pats the man square on the back. "If only old men and girls got out of the way, right? Then you'd get your shot."

"Our whale is on the move, folks!" Valarie yells. "Starboard side!" And with that, the feet pound the deck again as the camera club stalks its subject. As quickly as they came, the group—and the fat man—are gone, leaving Archie and Ella alone once more.

"That was neat, huh, Ell? You did see the whale, didn't you?" Ella nods without looking away from the water. Archie slowly crouches down beside her and follows Ella's gaze toward the sharp horizon, where towering clouds and a deep blue-black shifting sky loom over the equally turbulent ocean.

"It might be a rough night," says Archie, wiping a raindrop from his forehead. Ella holds up her index, middle, and ring fingers, spreads them, and touches the three to her chin, signing *water*. She brings her hands side by side, palms down, and rolls them forward, as if following the arches of angry waves.

"You know what, Ell?" Archie wets his lips. "Your dad is a good man. It may not seem like that, but it's true." Archie scratches the white stubble on his chin. "I got somethin' to tell you, Ell, but you can't tell your mom, all right? Another Grandpa Archie secret, okay?" He looks at Ella with a stern face and she nods.

"I think I know where your father is." Archie pauses. "It's not like my son to up and leave, especially when you're having such a rough go with this . . . this tumor. Your mother is not very happy with Arden—Dad—right now, and that's fine. I understand.

These last two years have been one heartbreak after another, and I'm afraid I'm not the help I should be. But your dad is good, Ella. And I'm going to find him. We Wellsley men may seem like loons most days, but we know more than we let on. Your old Grandpa Archibald Wellsley is going to make things right."

Ella leans in and hugs her grandfather around the waist and Archie bends his back to share the embrace. The ship hits a wave and the two tumble over, onto the deck. They laugh; Archie's voice deep and gruff, Ella's a squawk.

Archie rolls to his knees to stand, but his expression suddenly darkens. He pats the front of his trousers and tunnels his hands deep into his pockets. Standing upright, he pivots, his eyes dilated, his breath held, his neck jerking to and fro. "The notebook! Where's the notebook?" he moans.

Ella, who pulls herself up beside Archie, looks for the brown leather book she had seen her grandfather reading at the harbor. She spots it and points. Archie follows her finger and spies the book a few paces away, the cover freckled with rain. As Archie lunges forward, a camera club member steps into his path, once more tracking a mammal beyond the railing. The thunder of footsteps fills Archie's ears, but he continues forward. He shoves men and women out of his way, his eyes locked on the book. His tan coat flaps and snaps in the gritty breeze, its metal zipper slapping painfully against his abdomen. One word escapes his lungs, drawn out and desperate: "No!" But it is too late. The toe of the fat cameraman connects with the notebook and punts it overboard to be gobbled up by the sea.

chapter 3

"*Y*ou all right, Tess?" Archie asks but Tessa does not answer. Instead, she throws-up her breakfast over the bow of the ship, which affords the trio extra shoulder space as the encroaching passengers quickly back-step.

Captain Nathanial Billows appears beside them and passes Tessa a small pill bottle. "Oh, Nate," Tessa chirps, covering her mouth to shield her breath. "I didn't see you coming."

"I could have heard your heaving a mile away," the captain chuckles. "I hope these'll help. They're the best motion sickness medication I've come across."

"Wow, thank you. That's so thoughtful of you," says Tessa. Archie elbows his daughter-in-law. "Oh, sorry. Nate, this is my daughter Ella. She's in grade nine. And this is Archie. My father-in-law."

"Pleased to meet you, Captain," Archie says as he shoots forward his hand. Nate shakes it firmly.

"The pleasure's mine. Well, I'd better be off. Someone needs to steer this beast into the marina. You all have a great day. This is one of my favorite places on earth. I'm sure you'll understand why very soon." Nate touches Tessa's arm, lingers, smiles at her, then turns toward the captain's bridge. At that moment, Valarie, the cruise director, passes them on the deck.

Valarie's shoulder connects squarely with Tessa's. Without stopping, Valarie apologizes with only a slight turn of her head. "Slippery deck this morning. We all best watch our step."

"What was that about?" Archie huffs.

"I don't know, it seemed a bit mean spirited," Tessa answers, rubbing her shoulder.

"No, Tess, not the cruise director. The captain. Do you know each other?"

"Nah, not really. We chatted, that's all."

"Uh huh. Does he know about Arden?"

"Yes, Archibald. He does. God, Archie! Can't you give me two seconds to be happy? You are obsessed with Arden. I get it. He's your long-lost, only child. But he's gone. He left us. Do you see me going out, Archie? Do you see me having friends or going on dates? No. So, can you give me some space? To figure this all out? Don't I deserve a little bit of happiness?"

"Thank you."

"What?"

"Thank you, Tess. I don't think I say it enough."

"I appreciate that, Archie." Tessa pauses, takes a deep breath. She turns to Ella. "I'm sorry, Ell," Tessa begins. "For everything. I know this is hardest of all on you—for so many reasons." Ella makes no sound and does not raise her hands to sign in reply. The three, each defeated in their own way, turn back to stare at the sea without saying another word.

The air is like hot breath exhaled off the unseen coast of Morocco as their voyage traces parallel to the western coast of Africa. All passengers grow quiet under its spell, inhaling its rich, earthy scent. Archie, Tessa, and Ella watch the straight edge of the horizon as their destination grows from a speck, taking on form, almost as if the myth of the eighth island were manifesting before them.

Marina Lanzarote—and the island's capitol, Arrecife—
would be a colorful, vibrant sight with its red and orange roofs
and palm trees, but for the storm that continues to stir and
charge the atmosphere overhead. The family of three lean
against the railing as the *Atlantic Odyssey* approaches the port, the
hub of the fishing city, flanked on either side by rock reefs beneath electric-blue water. The shadows of the low clouds darken
the whitewashed buildings with their cobalt-colored doors; the
reds and golds of the sailboats rocking helplessly; the quaint
patio cafés; and the Gran Hotel Arrecife at the lip of the island,
southwest of the harbor.

"Give it a rest!" Archie grumbles as a camera clicks near his
ear. He swats it away like a fly.

"Are you sure you need that big bag, Archie?" Tessa asks.
"It'll be a pain to carry around the park."

"I'm stronger than I look, Tess. Maybe Ell will find an ex-
otic rock for her collection at the Biosphere Reserve—or some
other treasure."

"The bag's already full."

"Nah, just old person stuff. You can't be too prepared—no,
Ella, don't!" Ella wriggles her hand into the opening where the
zipper is not fully fastened. She pulls out the object that had
caught her eye: a worn royal blue notebook, similar to the one
lost the day they embarked. Archie snatches the blue book from
her hands and shoves it back in the bag.

"What've you got there?" Tessa takes a step toward Archie.
"I've seen that notebook before. Where'd you get it?" Tessa's
hand shoots into the bag as Archie struggles with the zipper. Her
fingers stroke the smooth cover of the notebook she retrieves, her
breath growing thick in her throat. "Arden . . ."

"I found it in the attic," Archie admits, reaching for the
notebook, but Tessa steps away, bumping into another passen-

ger, as she folds open the pages. The spine is soft, and it flops to an entry near the back cover. "Please, Tessa," Archie begs.

She glances at the bag. "How many books have you got in there?"

"All of them."

Her wide eyes meet his. "All of them?"

"All but one." Archie briefly catches Ella's gaze.

"'Once on the island, the Tillastrion is within reach,'" Tessa reads. "'The portal-maker is there, in our time and realm . . .'"

"Tessa—"

"What is this? Was Arden writing a story?" Tessa shakes her head, her brow scrunched. "Why does he have notes on the Canary Islands? And magic?"

Archie steps aside as passengers line up to disembark. He fidgets with the bag, though watches for a moment when he can pluck the notebook from his daughter-in-law's grasp. "I'm not going to lie to you, Tessa. It's complicated."

Tessa snaps the book shut and fishes Ella's phone from the side pocket of her daughter's backpack. She plugs in her earbuds and passes them to Ella. "You've been really patient. Here." Ella is engrossed in her device as the three join the line. Tessa slams the journal against Archie's chest, leaning in so close that her nose is almost touching his.

"Is he here?" Tessa breathes, her jaw clenched tight. "Is Arden here?"

"I don't know . . ." Archie fumbles. "No. I don't think so."

"Then why are we in the Canary Islands? Tell me the truth or I will fly Ella and me home this minute! And you, Archibald, will be relocated to the *Seattle Seniors' Center!*"

"Fine, Tess." Archie throws his hands up in surrender as they continue to shuffle along with the line, their feet now treading on the marina platform. Shoulders slouched, he confesses, "I found Arden's notebooks and wanted to come here—for all of us to come here—to feel closer to him somehow. He was studying this place. Who knows why. And I . . . I miss him."

The fierce edge fades from Tessa's expression. "I get that," she says finally. "But please, please don't let Ella see those notebooks. I don't want her to be reminded of him. *I* don't want to be reminded of him."

"I understand."

"And you be careful, too. I don't know why Arden did what he did—and I'll never forgive him—but we need you, Archie. Ella needs you. I can only guess that whatever is in those notebooks is trouble."

Archie is about to speak, but the cruise director's high-pitched voice interrupts him. "Ready to explore the Biosphere Reserve at Timanfaya National Park?" she says. Valarie smiles with her lips but not with her eyes. Her enthusiasm is thick, insincere. Archie and Tessa realize they have reached the front of the line.

"Let's go and have a nice day, okay, Archie?" says Tessa. "I really don't want to talk about this anymore." She gently taps Ella and signals for her to remove her earbuds, then helps Ella up the steep first step onto the bus.

Archie shifts on the spot. "You know what, gang? I'm a little tired."

"You're not coming?" Tessa asks. "Why, Archie? What are you up to now?"

"Cool it, Tess! I'm beat from these last few days at sea. You're right, I shouldn't have brought this bag. It's too much. I'm going to have a coffee at that café over there." Archie points. "Read the paper. If it's in English, that is. Don't worry about me. And I promise, I won't get into trouble."

"I don't know . . ." Tessa bites her lip, but takes another

step onto the bus, looking over her shoulder for Ella, who has already claimed a seat, though not at a window. The camera club members have swiftly slid into all the best spots. "I really think we should stay together."

"A day watching the boats is just what I need. Go! Enjoy yourself. I'm a stone's throw to the *Odyssey*."

Valarie taps her foot firmly though her painted smile does not waiver. "Are we about ready, folks? Tick, tock."

"Ready," Tessa says. She climbs on and squishes in beside Ella.

Archie waves as the ancient motor vehicle takes a wide turn before groaning into gear and chugging away. He strolls toward the café.

Once the black exhaust dissipates and the bus has tipped out of sight, Archie straightens his back, his weary gait transformed into a deliberate hustle. He digs into his bag, retrieves the blue book, flips to a dog-eared page, and traces the handwriting with his finger. He steps out onto the curb beside the road and hails a cab.

"To the artisan market! Mercado Artesanal in the plaza of Haria. Here is your tip. Now, drive fast, man!"

chapter 4

*A*rchie studies the notebook intently, bracing himself with one arm as the cab races around pedestrians milling in the streets. A small pen drawing illustrates the appearance of Archie's destination: a shop called Treasures pinched between two larger storefronts. The sketch shows a flat-roofed structure with a distinctive, broad crack beginning at the foundation, splitting the façade. The wooden sign is cut in the shape of an island with a steep volcanic mountain at its center.

"Do you know this place?" Archie asks the driver, holding the book out toward him. The driver glances at it, frowns, and shrugs.

Archie heaves himself out of the cab at the mouth of the artisan market, which clogs the narrow street with stalls capped in weathered green canopies that swell in the wind. The local vendors anchor their wares with fat stones and tarps over their produce, as tourists hold tight to their hats. A light rain begins to fall. Archie tucks the notebook inside his bag and turns up the collar of his jacket. A scooter toots its horn at him as he stands in the middle of the road, feeling immediately frail and helpless.

"Dear god, how am I to find it?" Archie wheezes. As the words pass through his lips, the sprinkling rain turns torrential and pounds down on the square-cobbled street, splashing up to Archie's knees. The old man shivers and shelters his bag as he watches the vendors parcel their jewelry, hand-sewn purses, and woven hats, tossing their tubs and boxes into the backs of cars that wait, already running. Dark-haired boys in sneakers and tank tops, younger than Ella, disassemble stands and crank the handles of shop awnings as tourists seek shelter within their doorways.

Archie begins a slow, wet march up the now vacant roadway. His bones quiver in the damp breeze, his hair is blown ragged and water trickles down his neck. "Nope, that's not the one," he says to himself, studying the buildings along his route. "I know you're out there, Arden," Archie tells the rain. "I will find you, my boy."

Water droplets catch in Archie's bushy eyebrows—once the same shade as Arden's: deep chestnut brown, Archie recalls. Arden had always been a kind and thoughtful boy. "You only came home with a black eye and bloody lip for stickin' up for some other kid," Archie remembers aloud. "And you always wanted me to get out of my recliner and have adventures with you. To travel to the places you read about in your history text-books. Well, looks like you've got your wish," he mutters as he nears a bend in the road.

"Now, wait. What do we have here?" Arden's drawing stands before Archie in three dimensions, from the low flat roof to the crack, now a gaping fissure where two scraggly cats find refuge from the storm. "Treasures! By golly! It's real!" Heat surges through Archie's fingers and toes. The shop sign is faded and splintering, but unmistakable.

Archie ducks beneath the low doorframe and enters the dimly lit shop. Haphazardly placed lamps send out flickering light that illuminates the curling smoke of multiple sticks of earthy-smelling incense. Beneath the perfumed air is another, distinct smell that abruptly halts Archie mid-step. "That fragrance . . . what is it?" he wonders, lost for a moment in half-thought, half-memory. "Fresh and wispy, warm, floral, spicy even—I can almost taste it . . ." but before Archie can place the smell, a strange voice breaks through his trance.

"Is there something you are looking for?" the voice asks innocently enough, yet with a resentful inflection.

Archie's eyes, which he hadn't realized he'd closed, snap open and he is back in the immediacy of his body, weighed down by damp clothes.

"I recognize you," the voice continues.

"Wh—where are you?" Archie stutters, peering around at the aged cabinets and dusty displays. "I'm looking for something, yes, something I believe you may sell." Archie weaves his way toward the back of the shop, where a child sits on a stool. He wears a camo-patterned fishing hat and rests his chin against his Adams apple.

"Your son was here." The sound comes from the boy, but it is an old voice, raspy and curt.

Archie's chest tightens. *Arden!* he screams in his head and nearly bursts out smiling, but his thudding heart suddenly pierces him with fear. *If everything I have read is true, then that is not a boy sitting there.* Archie slowly considers his words before speaking. "You remember my son?"

"How could I forget?" the boy taps the glass counter he sits behind with a long, pointy silver-white nail. The counter is lit from within, displaying oxidized metal jewelry. It highlights the boy from his collarbone to his nose, revealing sickly gray skin, but still the boy's eyes are downcast and in shadow. His black lips move, as if replaying a long-rehearsed conversation of which he is loath to speak. As the moments pass, the boy taps the glass harder and harder.

"Your son came looking for something. I assume it is the same something that you are after," the boy hisses, finally, after a tiny crack appears in the glass countertop.

Archie nods. "Yes, the Tillastrion," he pronounces slowly, his trembling voice a pitch higher than normal. The word is etched in his mind. Finding the Tillastrion has been Archie's mission, his sole preoccupation since he found Arden's notebooks thrown roughly into a box and stuffed between the rafters in the attic.

Archie did not blame Tessa for purging their home of all reminders of Arden. His departure from their lives was sudden and jarring. Even Archie had silently questioned his son, wondering why he would give up on his family like a coward. It took Archie months of reading to discover where Arden's notes had taken him. Now, Archie stands where his son last ventured. This shop was the final clue. Archie's heart flutters at the thought of reuniting his family, though he masks the feeling with a throaty cough.

"Do you have it?" Archie asks when the boy does not respond. "The Tillastrion? Do you have one I can buy?"

"I may, or I may not," says the boy. "First, do you know the purpose of the device?"

"I do, or I believe I do," Archie hedges. "But you may not believe me if I tell you."

"Oh, I would believe you. Yes. And it is your lucky day," the boy snaps, jumping from his stool and wrenching off his hat. The light from beneath the cracked glass casts light on the boy's face, though he is not a boy at all. The grey skin on the creature's face and bald head are split open with white protrusions. His eyes are immediately blinding like the sun, glaring in the dim shop. Archie stumbles backward. "I am Zeno, the maker of the Tillastrion."

Archie had prepared himself for this moment, knowing that who he would meet would be beyond the realm of anything he had ever known—anything of this world. Yet, the presence of Zeno is far more terrifying than Archie anticipated from reading Arden's research. The old man immediately brings up bile in his mouth. He sucks it down and swallows hard, biting his fist to abate the nausea. Archie wobbles on his feet. The sickly taste rises again and he chokes on it. Vomit drips from his bottom lip but he does not wipe it away. All of a sudden, Archie's vision turns blank, seeing grey-black as if he stood up too quickly, and all that he can think of is to escape from the constricting walls of Treasures, sprint to the *Odyssey* as fast as his tired legs will carry him, and sail to the other side of the world from Lanzarote.

Unsure of the creature's malice—and winded by the shock and terror that claw at his sanity—Archie backs up on wobbling legs, his trembling hands feeling for obstructions at his sides. Still, his hip connects with the corner of a table. A blown-glass vase tumbles to the floor and shatters. The sound is so startling in the presence of Zeno that Archie covers his ears. His lungs burn for air. Archie's mind swirls with delusions from which he cannot tell what is real and what he has conjured, as if he actually has gone mad with dementia as Tessa frequently asks him when he forgets to shut off the gas stove or misplaces his wallet at the petrol station. Archie turns to run.

The creature does not flinch at the crash or at the old man's retreat, but continues speaking. "I have made the Tillastrion once before, but it was stolen from me."

"Arden," Archie says, pausing before crossing through the doorway back out into the rain. He whispers to himself, "Archibald, be brave. You're so close. Everything Arden wrote was true. You can find him. Don't give up!" Archie slowly turns back to face the creature. There, dripping rain on the wood floor of the fragrant shop, surrounded by treasures of magnificent color and mysterious origin, Archie feels his son's presence, like a shadow at his feet. "I will find Arden. I will find Arden," he whispers to himself before speaking up.

"I'm sorry for what my son may have done. But, but is there—by any chance—another Tillastrion here? Could I . . . could I pay for them both?" Archie fumbles over his words as he projects his voice to the back of the shop, which is dark but for the glowing case and even brighter yellow eyes, like two floating suns.

The creature chuckles. "It is not as simple as that. What is your name?"

"Archibald Wellsley."

"As I have already told you: I am Zeno. You would do well to show me respect, as I am the bearer of Naiu in this pitiful dimension, and heir to the kingship of the Bangols. As for your questions, Archibald: the price . . ."

"Please, I am a man of little means. I spent near all my savings to bring my family here . . ."

"Your family?" Zeno repeats, his eyes bulging. "The child? I must know. Do they travel with us?"

Archie realizes he has said too much. "Oh, they're not here; not with me, exactly." He backtracks. "They're on the continent. Not on the islands. I'll go to them after I use the Tillastrion, you see. They are waiting for me—in hiding. But, but of the child, who exactly do you mean?"

Zeno appraises Archie with narrowed eyes, reading the truthfulness of the old man's words. "Your son spoke of a girl, but pay no mind to my question. If she is not here, she is of no concern to me," Zeno replies slowly. "Now, we must proceed in the manner I see fit. First, tell me what you know of the Tillastrion. I must ensure you are not a fool—or a thief."

"I only know what I have read," Archie begins. "The Tillastrion is a portal-jumper, from one world to another."

"Close," Zeno replies, "but not quite. It only transports from this wretched place to my world. To Jarr, to the island of Jarr-Wya. That is all."

"Jarr-Wya?" Archie gulps.

"Are you afraid, Archibald Wellsley?" A hungry smile spreads across Zeno's pointed face.

"Yes. I am scared," Archie admits.

"Good." Zeno looks thoroughly pleased and climbs back on his stool. "Don't you want to know what happened to your son?" he asks.

"He went to your world."

"Again, so close," Zeno nearly sings. "Arden came here looking for the Tillastrion, just like you. But he was greedy and untrusting. He stole from me. He agreed to my terms and then broke his word."

"What are your terms?"

"All I ask is that you bring me with you. I have unfinished business on Jarr-Wya."

"Why wouldn't you use the Tillastrion yourself? To go back anytime?" probes Archie.

"It doesn't work that way," Zeno snaps. "Maybe you *are* a fool! I am from there, thus I can make it, but I cannot use it myself, you see. Someone from here must help me operate the device. Our two worlds are connected, Archibald. Mine is of course superior, yours the derivative with no magic. If one wishes to transport from Jarr to earth, a person from earth must build the Tillastrion and operate it with a Jarrwian traveling companion. And vice versa. To travel from earth to Jarr, someone from Jarr must build the device and operate it with an earthling companion. Do you see? There must always be two."

"Then how did Arden use it?"

"He didn't."

"I'm confused."

"Arden tried, you are right. But he changed his mind about keeping his word. He soon discovered that I am much more powerful than I may appear."

"What did you do to him?" Archie chokes out, running to the counter and smashing his fists upon it. The crack spreads.

Zeno smiles and leans in closer to Archie. "It's not what I did to him. It's what he did to himself. He lied to me, tried to jump portals, to my dimension, without my company and thus the curse of the Tillastrion transported him to ageless, immortal, torturous black; the space between worlds from which no one can return."

Archie gasps and his eyes fill with tears. He covers his mouth and falls to his knees, on top of the broken vase, but there is no physical pain like the stabbing ache of finality Archie knows in his heart. He can no longer hear or see—or chooses not to. Lost in sorrow, Archie struggles to regain his breath. His blood seems to fill and pulse in his head, drowning out his ability to think.

Suddenly, Zeno's voice is in Archie's ear, so close that the Bangol's stench, like decaying flowers, fills Archie's nose and the coarse hairs on the old man's skin stand erect. "Your son was right, Archibald. About my world. About Jarr-Wya. He was right, you know."

"What do you mean?"

"There is a cure for the child, your granddaughter. What was her name again?" Zeno pauses. "Ella."

Archie's damp clothing clings to his skin and feels suddenly suffocating. He searches his mind, straining to remember if he mentioned Ella to the creature, or if, in all of Arden's notes, he had read something about a cure in this parallel world that Zeno speaks of. So many of the notes are cryptic and scrawled in Arden's messy penmanship. Archie reminds himself to look later. *If I have a later.*

"That's why he left us," Archie finally says. "To find a cure for Ella. It all makes sense. Ella's tumor was growing and untreatable. All the doctors said she would die." Archie shakes his head. Sweat trickles down the side of his face. "Arden was pale and reclusive, working long hours at the university, returning to the library after reading Ella books at bedtime. But I remember. The week before Arden disappeared, his spirits were up. He smiled more, laughed from his gut. Oh yes, and he brought Ella a gift! It was a potted plant. Tessa—my daughter-in-law—was furious."

"He knew," Zeno interjects.

"You're right. Arden told Tessa that Ella wouldn't die. That he had hope. Then he was gone the next morning. His clothes were missing too. And his boots and backpack. There was not even a note, which made me wonder: maybe Arden hadn't intended to be gone as long as he was. Then the days added up."

"You can save her. The girl. The cure is in Jarr-Wya, as Arden knew, and I can take you to it."

"How can I know you're telling the truth?"

"You can't. You have two choices. Leave my shop, enjoy the islands, and travel home. Your granddaughter will die in a matter of sunsets. Tessa will despise you for your son's actions and you will die alone. Or—" Zeno emphasizes the word, leaning forward with both palms on the glass "—you trust me. Simple. You are near death yourself, Archibald. What do you have to lose? You have even more to gain. A healthy grandchild. A daughter in Tessa. Happiness."

"You really only see this going one way, don't you?"

"To me," Zeno rests back on his chair, "the answer is clear. What does your intuition tell you?"

Archie thinks for a moment. Even though he dreamed of reuniting his family, Arden set out on an even greater mission. If Archie can trust this creature, maybe he can finish the work his son began.

"How will I get back with the cure?" Archie finally asks.

"Simple. Like I told you, only someone who has been displaced to a world other than their own can make a portal to return home."

"But you said that person cannot also operate it."

"True. I know one of my kind, a Bangol, who desires this world, or at least I desire it for him. You two will transport back here together; Ella will be saved, and all will be right."

"Will we be gone long? In this world's time I mean?"

"Time in my world is fluid, water over rocks. It moves sometimes slower, often quicker; it is hard to tell. We must be off. Do you have something of your granddaughter's?"

"No." Archie searches the bottoms of his pockets, but knows he has nothing. "Why?"

"I thought you would at least come with the child, as I had told your son was ideal if not necessary. Must I always repeat myself? To locate a cure, you need the ailing one, or at least an article of her clothing or another belonging. This possession becomes a talisman, an object which evokes the power of deepfelt emotion, an instrument of desire to succeed in bridging worlds, an aid for channeling your focus in transporting a remedy to one unable to journey to it themselves"

"The ship! We must hurry to the *Odyssey* before Ella and Tessa return from their tour!"

"You said they were on the continent."

"I'm sorry, Zeno. No more lies." Although Archie wonders at the truthfulness of even these words. He also begins to question why Arden broke his promise to take Zeno with him to Jarr-Wya. Maybe his son knew something that he does not.

"I shall retrieve the Tillastrion," Zeno croaks, hopping down from his stool.

As Zeno walks from the counter and through a floral back-curtain, Archie studies him. Zeno is about four feet tall, with short, stubby legs supporting a long torso and disproportionately gangly arms. "If anything, I outweigh him by about a hundred pounds," Archie says under his breath.

Oh Archibald, what have you gotten yourself into? Run now while there is time! he scolds himself in his mind and slaps his thighs to stimulate the blood flow, to prompt his legs to bolt, but he finds his body disobedient. Archie senses he must follow through with what Arden had intended, though everything in his well-worn nature screams in protest. *There's a reason—you daft fool— that you like your routine, your comfortable chair, your corner of the city, your safe life! This isn't you. You're no hero.*

Zeno emerges from behind the curtain wearing a camouflage jacket that matches his hat, which is also back on his bald, bumpy head. A sack is slung over one shoulder and his hands hold a simple pine box sealed by a rustic brass clasp. "Is that it?" Archie asks, startled by the simplicity of the object. "What's inside?"

"No time. No time. We must be off!" Zeno protests. He brushes past Archie and walks out the door. At the last moment before he disappears into the swirl of the storm, which has torn leaf from branch and chases each through the currents, Zeno turns back to stare at Archie with his radiating, buttery eyes. Zeno opens his mouth, usually twisted in a menacing sneer, and says, "The happenings on Jarr-Wya are never truly as they appear. Be careful who you trust, Archibald—even me, though for now our fates are aligned." Zeno disappears into the rain.

chapter 5

*a*rchie stares into the perfectly round yellow eyes and they stare back. They betray no emotion, and cast their own light even when closed, glowing beneath the thin layer of rough, dirty-gray skin. Zeno has no eyebrows or eyelashes, maybe no hair at all except for the thick brown matted patches on his chest and on the tops of his hands. Archie refrains from imagining what is concealed beneath the human clothing the Bangol wears with the discomfort of scratchy wool. There are silver-white mounds growing out of Zeno's face along his cheekbones and beginning again at his temples, arching down the back of his neck.

"They are stones," Zeno says. "My race, the Bangols, are of the earth. Clay and stone and soil."

"Does it hurt?"

"Only when young. The stones grow outward like teeth, breaking the skin, slicing it from the inside. For some, the stones never stop their conquest. They grow and grow until their hosts resemble massive, unmoving flowers. Inwardly they destroy the brain, crushing it as if it were ripe fruit."

Archie and Zeno sit on a torn seat in a derelict cab, which scrapes along the angled roads of Arrecife. Zeno speaks freely, ignoring the driver who slid shut a plexiglass window after Archie's instructions, muffling him to his passengers though providing little actual protection from the creature he stares at in the rear-view mirror. The Bangol clutches the wooden box. The muscles in Archie's fingers tingle, aching to touch the object he has read so much about in Arden's notebooks. "Every Tillastrion is unique, fashioned with desire by the hands of its maker," Zeno says. As if knowing Archie's thoughts, Zeno croaks again in a coarse voice, "Not yet, Archibald Wellsley. Don't you want to save her? Then do what I say and only what I say."

Turning to look out the fogged window, Archie sees his own reflection. His white hair is damp from the downpour and worry deepens the wrinkles creasing his skin—and yet his eyes sparkle with the possibility of hope, though not hope itself.

On the other side of the island's rolling hills, with orange and shrub-freckled flatlands, floats Marina Lanzarote, where the *Atlantic Odyssey* is moored. "Almost there," Archie says, not looking back at Zeno, though he can see the creature's lemon-colored light illuminating all the filthy crevices of the cab better left in shadow.

"Your son did not listen to me, so he died," Zeno tells Archie. "If you want to save her, I will bind us together by the wrists before we operate the Tillastrion. It would not be worth sacrificing your hand to cut us loose. Soon we will see Jarr-Wya. Even now I can feel it."

chapter 6

The cabbie grumbles in Spanish when he unfolds the twenty Euros Archie tosses in his direction. The complaints are abruptly silenced as Archie swings shut the taxi door and hustles to catch up to Zeno, who already approaches the *Atlantic Odyssey*. "Stay behind me," Archie warns the creature as they ascend the plank to the main deck. A ship attendant greets the passengers a few paces ahead of the suspicious pair. Archie nods as they pass the unsuspecting young man who welcomes them aboard. "This way," Archie directs Zeno into a set of sliding doors toward the maze of inner hallways.

"Oh, good heavens!" a portly woman wails, steadying herself on the glossy railing of the grand staircase. Nearby passengers and busy cruise staff turn curiously toward the commotion where Zeno has mistakenly bumped into the opera singer, Lady Sophia, as he surveys the ship. "Dear sir!" Lady Sophia shrieks at Archie, her jowls jumping as she speaks, "please keep your grandchild in tow!"

Archie looks around for Ella, confusion wrinkling his brow, before realizing the woman is referring to Zeno. Standing nearly two feet taller than the creature in her soaring high heels, all she can see is the top of Zeno's hat.

"Someone, keep this woman in tow!" Zeno retorts loudly in his deep, raspy voice.

Lady Sophia's face morphs from injury to shock. "*¡Madre*

mía! Good heavens—your eyes!" she yelps in her Spanish accent and faints onto the wide staircase.

The cruise director, Valarie, recently returned from touring the Biosphere Reserve at Timanfaya National Park, runs up the stairs two at a time to kneel, panting, beside the groggy singer. "Oh my, Lady Sophia! I am terribly sorry for whatever has transpired here. I will address this promptly!" To the gawking passengers, she adds, "Nothing to see here folks! Have a lovely afternoon!"

Archie and Zeno withdraw from the crowd and slip silently away, just as Lady Sophia lets out an impassioned moan and exclaims, "*¡Hostia!* I have never, never in all my life been treated so poorly!"

Archie peeks over his shoulder as they slink away. Valarie is scanning the passengers for the instigators and Archie hurriedly shoves Zeno into an intersecting corridor before the cruise director spies them.

"Here, gentlemen," Valarie calls to nearby staff. "Please, help me escort Lady Sophia to her suite." The workers drop their errands and heave Lady Sophia's meaty arms over their shoulders as Valarie lifts the train of the singer's sequined gown.

"Did you see those eyes?" Lady Sophia rants. "Those eyes! Those huge yellow eyes!"

"I do hope this upset will not affect your performance tonight . . ."

Valarie's voice fades as Archie urges Zeno down the hallway and into another, longer corridor.

"You understand why I remain in the darkened spaces of this world," Zeno says when the pair are finally tucked away in Archie's cabin.

Archie leans against the door, catching his breath, one hand resting on his wildly beating heart.

"You are close to death?" Zeno asks without concern. "At least wait till we travel." He hoists himself up on a corner of the bed.

"I believe death *is* near, as long as I'm in your company!" Archie huffs. Man and creature surprise each other with laughter.

Their grins disappear quickly, however, at the sound of firm, persistent knocking at the door. "It must be Valarie!" Archie whispers. "She recognized me!" He crouches and runs his hands over his bald, freckled head.

"Who's there?" Zeno demands, perfectly mimicking Archie's nuanced Pacific coast accent.

"It's me, Archie. Tessa! Are you all right?"

Archie's shoulders slump. "It's Tess," he sighs, and peers through the small eyehole. Tessa and Ella stand in the hall, Ella looking bored and Tessa irate. They hold dripping-rain tunics that dampen the floor.

"Should I bring Ella?" Archie wonders aloud.

Zeno answers, "She is ideal, as I told your son."

"Archie? Are you okay? Let me in!" Tessa demands, banging loudly again.

"Let her in before she draws more attention!" Zeno warns.

"Quick, in the bathroom!" Archie points at the narrow door and Zeno slips inside.

Archie opens the cabin door and Tessa barges in. "I'm relieved you're here," she says. "But from now on, we stay together! I've been worried about you all day! Are you okay?"

"What? What do you mean?"

"Your face. It's all red and splotchy—and you're sweating through your coat. Were you exercising?"

"Me, exercise? Pah! I just returned from a brisk walk along the coastline. Lovely island, really. Quite damp out there, though. And, as you can tell, I'm a tad bit out of shape, that's all." Archie turns to Ella before Tessa questions him further. "How was the reserve? Did you take any good pictures?"

Ella nods, pulling out her phone. She leans her head on Archie's shoulder as he flips through her photographs. "Oh, these are great! Well done, Ell!" Archie pulls off Ella's Mariners cap and kisses her forehead. "I love you, sweetie, you know that, right?" Ella wraps her arms around Archie's waist. "I would do anything for you, Ell."

"You sure know how to make my girl happy. Thank you for that," Tessa says.

"She is my world, this girl."

"Mine too." Tessa turns to Ella and smiles weakly. "Can you give me and Grandpa Archie a sec, hon? Here's our room key. I'll be two minutes behind you."

Once the door closes after Ella, Tessa turns to Archie. "At the park today, Ella nearly lost her balance on the path. She bent over, clutching her head. The headaches are getting worse. I worry we shouldn't have come on this trip."

"You heard the doctors. We're out of treatment options. So, what do we do? Hole-up at home and let her suffer in the shadows? Or show her the bright beautiful world while we still can? I haven't seen her this happy in—I don't know how long."

"You're right." Tessa smiles faintly. "Thank you, Archie."

"You know, I am feeling chilled from the rain today. I think I need to call it a night."

"Do you need your blood pressure meds? I'll get them for you." Tessa puts her hand on the bathroom knob but Archie shuffles between her and the door.

"No!" he says too hastily. Deliberately lowering his voice an octave, he adds, "I just need a rest. I promise I'll be in tip-top shape for our stop tomorrow on that island . . . oh bother, whatever it's called."

"But you're going to miss the cruise show tonight. Lady So-phia! The world-renowned soprano! The 'darling of the stage' as she's been called."

"Oh brother, that old cow?" Archie waves his hand dismis-sively. "For as big as her voice may be, her ego is even bigger. I saw her earlier on the staircase. Someone bumped into her and she made a huge fuss, as if she were the queen of England. I'll pass. I'd rather order dinner into my room and read my Canary Islands guide book, if it's no bother to you."

Archie latches the deadbolt behind Tessa when she leaves, then steps into the bathroom. Zeno is sitting on the floor, sur-rounded by the contents of Archie's toiletry bag. "What on earth are you doing?"

"Why do you have so many pills? Really! Your doctors merely guess at what people in my world learn from infancy." Zeno tosses a pill bottle he failed to open into the sink, where it clatters to rest near the drain. "Let's proceed." The Bangol jumps up and leads the way out of the bathroom. "You let the girl go," he adds.

Archie stares at Zeno a moment before answering. "I can't put Ella in danger. She is so pale. I will risk my life, but not hers."

Zeno pulls the Tillastrion from under the bed. "Your grand-daughter is fading quickly," he says. Archie nods thoughtfully. "Her spirit is strong and blue, like busy streams, dancing and jumping and crackling—but her body! It is gray, like ash rising on the breath of fire. It soars now but soon it will fall."

Archie feels his age in every corner of his body. "What I wouldn't give to change places with her. Ella deserves a life. A good long, full life." Archie shrugs off his wish for Ella to expe-rience milestones, mistakes, crossroads, heartaches, and all the joys of living, as he focuses on his mission. *One day at a time,* Archie tells himself. *Let's get through today and see what the Tillastrion may bring tomorrow,* he repeats in his head.

"Tell me, what makes this child so special that she has such a hold over you?"

"Where do I begin?" Archie smiles, looking off as if he does in fact have a porthole to stare through. "She is a thoughtful girl. She listens, really listens, and hears more than the words you say. After my wife died—Ella's Grandma Suzie—I said I was okay, but I wasn't. Ella knew. Though she had no idea how to ease my grief-stricken heart, she helped in the only ways she knew how. One time I told her mom that my pillow was too flat, it was hurting my neck. Of course, Tessa told me to fold it in half and that I'd be fine, but when I went to bed that night, something was different. I didn't know what at first, but then I found Ella's pillow, still in its pink floral pillowcase, beneath my own. She was eight then. She has always taken care of me, that girl." He shakes his head fondly.

"And her laugh—oh, if you had heard it! It was the kind of laugh that makes your heart feel lighter, actually physically lighter, and you cannot help but to smile with your whole face all lit up. I hope I will never forget the sound of Ella's laughter." Archie wipes tears from his cheeks with his thumb.

"I peered through the door. She looks like your son, apart from her hair. That feature belongs to that Tessa woman, in all certainty." As Zeno says these words, his eyes begin to radiate more brilliantly and Archie squints. Zeno unlatches the wooden box. "We're almost ready, Archibald Wellsley. Do you have something of the girl's?"

"Yes!" Archie announces proudly, a grin tugging at the corners of his lips. Bending low, he picks up an object lying on the floor beside the bed and holds it up: Ella's Mariners hat. "I tossed it there when she wasn't looking. I hope this will work."

Zeno nods. "Now, join me here, and let me bind our wrists."

Archie hesitates, hoping Zeno doesn't notice. Suppressing

the alarms flaring in his head, Archie quickly sits on the duvet beside the small creature, who pulls fraying twine from the breast pocket of his jacket and loops it around their two wrists, tying a triple knot at the end. Then Zeno places the Tillastrion on his lap, the lid now open, and Archie peers inside.

"Is that all? A bowl and a ball?"

"Imbecile! Never presume such simplicity!" Zeno barks. "This clay vessel I fired myself, in a kiln as hot as the sun, and imbued with the enchantment of Naiu, the magic of my world, which possesses the soul of the elements." Zeno removes the sphere and hands it to Archie. "Hold this—be careful!"

"Whoa, heavy!" Archie exclaims. "What's it made from?"

"Glass," Zeno answers. "With precious metal—rhodium—at the core."

Archie cups the sphere in his hands and marvels at its warmth, as if a fire smolders within it. "Now what?" he says.

Zeno strokes the lip of the clay vessel, exhaling long, with a whisper, into the pine box. As he taps the center firmly but delicately with one sharp nail, he sends the bowl spinning. It revolves so quickly that all imperfections in the terracotta blur into irrelevance. Not once does the clay graze the inside walls of the box; instead it spins perfectly balanced on an invisible axis. Archie leans in. He can feel the breeze from the vessel's revolutions caressing his cheeks. The bowl maintains its pace, never decelerating, never increasing its rhythm.

"It's mesmerizing," says Archie, without thinking.

"You will see even greater beauty in Jarr-Wya," Zeno replies without looking up. "Now, pass me the sphere."

Archie is reluctant to release the glass ball. He covets it like no other object he has ever desired in all his life. Once he slips it into Zeno's waiting hands, Archie stretches his fingers wide. He stares at his thick, wrinkled palms in awe. "They feel new." Archie laughs. "Like they are agile young roofer hands again!" Zeno stares at him, but Archie understands the look to be pride, not irritation.

Zeno clutches the sphere above the spinning vessel, then allows it to slip into the rising current. Archie expects the ball to hit the bowl with a clatter, but the sphere hangs, suspended on the calmness at the epicenter of the animated device. The sphere begins to cloud and evolve, altering in color from a clear, silvery gloss to a milky cream, then to a brilliant white. With a flash and clap of air that is both blinding and deafening, the sphere deepens to a pulsating sapphire hue. With that, the electricity in the cabin crackles and sparks fly from the surging outlets. Then the lights go out.

chapter 7

*C*umulus clouds swiftly float, trapped, within the radiating blue sphere. Archie leans back on the mattress, his eyes imprinted with the afterimage of the galaxy within the glass. His wrist is still bound to Zeno's, and throbs at the contortion as the creature runs his hand, and Archie's, through the air. As Archie's sight clears, he sees that the black cabin is illuminated in sapphire—and emerald, where the light from Zeno's yellow eyes refracts through the blue. The clouds within the sphere are projected on every wall, but as Archie's fingers, mirroring Zeno's, reach for one, he startles at its density and dampness. The wind begins to pour out of the box in every direction. Archie feels it creep inside the sliver of space beneath his eyelids.

With a brash snap of the lid, Zeno closes the box and seals the latch. "Embrace the device, Archibald!" Zeno orders, and Archie lays his hands on the rough wooden lid, which is astonishingly, blisteringly hot to the touch; it takes all his will to resist recoiling. The cyclone of air rushes out the seams of the box, along with the mutating sapphire light, which is at once peacock blue, then indigo, and finally a dull oxford denim color that only slightly brightens the black room, like a nightlight, but for the direction of Zeno's gaze. A lemon-green aura radiates around the creature.

Together they steady the device, which balloons in girth yet decreases in mass.

"My hands!" screams Archie. "They burn!"

"Steady yourself, Archibald!" Zeno cries. The wind blasts Zeno's canvas hat from his head, pinning it to the art poster hanging on the wall behind them.

Archie's vision warps as the device enlarges—his hands with it—then shrinks to the size of a pin prick, and again, morphing as if its angles, its very form, is undecided. It is all Archie can do to steady his grip on the Tillastrion as it channels unseen energy in a spasmodic battle for equilibrium. Archie cries out and feels his strength wane. Zeno's presence disappears to him but for the creature's two glowing eyes, which also appear in flux, separating and rotating around the box in a peculiar orbit.

The shifting focus—magnifying and exaggerating, then diminishing, and again but in new slants—dissects the old man's mind and his brain throbs freely, extracted from his skull, with his skin floating loosely like a scarred canvas. "Am I going mad?" Archie yells into the vacuum of wind both sucking inward and thrusting out from the Tillastrion. Hours seem to have passed when Archie's voice returns to his ears and answers, "Mad indeed, my man, mad indeed!"

Suddenly, everything halts. The cabin is midnight-black, starless, and still. Archie is no longer clutching the Tillastrion. He touches his face and the back of his head; both are intact. Silence plugs his ears and grows louder, into a vibrational hum that electrifies his heartbeats. He curls his body, bringing his knees to his nose, and rocks back and forth. "No more, no more!" he screams. He presses his eyes closed, though he sees blackness either way.

The hum stops. The pounding in his mind instantly ceases. Archie opens his eyes slowly, and they take a moment to adjust to the lights now shining through the cabin's lamp and out the bathroom door. He pats the duvet he still sits on, as if his reality was in fact the dream. He snaps into awareness when he notices Zeno is no longer perched beside him. The twine has been burned from their wrists.

Archie rises to his feet, wobbles, and collapses as he takes a step. He pulls himself into the chair beside the desk, reminded of the renewed strength in his hands from the sphere. He squints around the room as a moan rises from the far side of the bed. Steadying himself on the furniture, Archie rounds the mattress to find Zeno lying prostrate on the floor. The creature's gray hands tremble. The box is gone. All that remains are shards of pine, shattered clay, and orange dust. The glass sphere has vanished entirely.

"Zeno?" Archie demands. "Zeno, talk to me! Are you all right? What happened?"

"Where are we? Am I home?" Zeno gasps, staring at the ceiling. "The air . . . the air does not smell right. Help me up!"

Slipping his hands beneath Zeno's arms, Archie hoists the creature like a child, plopping him down on the bed. Zeno looks altogether puny and weak. His eyes, now dull, scan the cabin. "It did not work." He trembles. "It did not work!" His thin eyelids fold over his protruding eyeballs. His mouth gapes and his head tilts back in what Archie can only liken to the silent scream of a toddler. He pats Zeno's back, feeling compassion for the homesick creature.

Zeno composes himself and his eyes pop open with a flash of yellow. He straightens and slides off the bed to collect his canvas hat, which he tugs over his stony skull. Without a second glance at Archie, the creature slowly trudges to the door.

"Where are you going?"

"I must make another. Build a Tillastrion and wait for some other human from this world to take me to Jarr-Wya."

"Let's go together. I will help you. We can try again!"

"No. There is not enough magic in you. The Tillastrion is fueled by Naiu and desire. It seems your love for your grand-daughter was not enough," Zeno whispers.

The little creature lets the door bang loudly behind him.

chapter 8

Weeping overcomes Archie and he buries his face in the bedcovers. In his mind, Archie watches Ella—when she was a little girl, before the wicked caress of cancer—run through the green space by her elementary school, crickets singing as the warmth of the setting sun reddens her bouncing hair as she twists and twirls. He can hear Ella's laugh, a melody that plays in Archie's heart greater—he feels—than a hundred songs performed in harmony by the greatest orchestras. Then he sees Ella in her creaking-metal hospital bed, her head shaved smooth, her cheeks sunken, her eyes vacant. There is no sound there.

"Ella!" Archie cries, "I'm sorry! I am so sorry, Arden. I failed, like I knew I would!" Archie rises from the bed and beats the pillows till they split. His arms do not ache with the weariness of age. He tears the art from its hook and hurls it across the room, where it dents the opposite wall and its frame cracks. Energy, anger, and despair coarse through his muscles in spasms. He flings the covers from the bed and stomps on them as he marches to the bathroom.

Breathing hard, he leans on the sink, looking at his face in the mirror. He does not like what he sees: a feeble, powerless man who has accomplished nothing of meaning in his life. Scooping up the pill bottle Zeno had tossed into the sink, he throws it hard at his tortured reflection. The container bursts and red-and-white pills erupt around the bathroom, bouncing off the walls and ceiling before settling on the floor.

An earsplitting shriek interrupts Archie. Then another. "Now what?" he grumbles, ignoring the pills beneath his boots as he walks to the door and peers through the peephole. Passengers are sprinting through the hall, smashing into each other in their panic. Wide-eyed parents carry frightened children. There is a familiar rumble of footsteps on the deck overhead. "What is the camera club moaning about?" Archie wonders.

"Zeno!" he blurts, realizing that the creature must have been spotted. Archie races out of his cabin and joins the mob squeezing through the clogged hallway. He turns down the corridor toward the *Odyssey*'s grand staircase. "He's probably been captured trying to leave the ship," Archie says to himself. When he reaches the bottom of the stairs, however, Zeno is not there, nor at the top.

The fat cameraman leans on the upper railing of the staircase and yells down to his group, "This way! Follow me!" He then sprints outside through the sliding glass doors.

"Oh dear," Archie frets, "this is going to be a circus!" He imagines Zeno pinned to a corner of the railing, being photographed like a zoo animal. Hopping up the stairs as fast as his rickety legs will carry him, Archie charges out onto the deck, which he realizes is tilting significantly to the port side. What he finds there are three hundred passengers crowded painfully against the railing, standing motionless, blubbering, and clutching one another. Archie struggles to look beyond them, to what they are watching on the ocean.

What he does see, in the brilliant orange of the setting sun, is the absence of Lanzarote. "Where's the port?" he asks the people beside him, but they only whimper. The ship had not been scheduled to raise anchor for another three hours after he and Zeno had returned with the Tillastrion. "How much time has passed?" he ponders. "I didn't feel us leave the harbor."

Archie shoves his way closer to the railing. "What is everyone looking at?" he asks a young couple. They are clearly not jeering at a scared creature. The woman points. Archie scans the sea in the fading light of the sun that paints the ship. Footsteps grow louder behind him as the camera club jockey for the best portion of the deck, pushing their way into the crowd, but Archie is unmoving.

"Is the sun on fire?" he whispers. "No . . . but how?" A lump wedges itself in his throat, silencing him. The sun is not only on fire, but is bursting and sizzling with flames.

"What is happening?" an elderly woman shrieks behind Archie. All eyes watch as the flames reflect and dance on the eerily still water.

"It's getting closer!" yells a man. "Run for cover!"

Archie finds a spot against the railing as hysterical passengers retreat from the deck. He holds his breath and refuses to blink, keenly watching the horizon. A moment before, the red glow had emanated from the divide between sky and sea, but now that is not the case. The glow takes form and rises like flaming daggers into the amber-tinged atmosphere. It continues to alter in shape from round to angular as it approaches, though Archie guesses it is still many miles away.

"Is it . . . ?" Archie's eyes grow wide.

"Yes, Archibald," Zeno says calmly beside the old man. "A ship."

"With sails of fire!"

"I owe you an apology, Archibald Wellsley," Zeno says. "It turns out your desire was more than enough."

"What do you mean?" Archie asks slowly.

"Your love for your granddaughter is so great, you brought the whole ship with us."

chapter 9

"I brought the whole ship? All these people? And now a boat of fire is heading right toward us?" Panic rises in Archie's voice. "What have I done?" he cries, shaking his head. "Oh no! Ella! Tessa!" Archie runs to the tail end of the crowd pushing their way through the ship's sliding doors, looking for safety. He is blocked at the first set of doors, and the second, and the third. He gives up and rejoins Zeno.

"It is the ship of the Olearon warriors. They hunt us."

"Olearon?"

"They are the guardians of my world, of Jarr-Wya."

"Are they evil?"

"I grew up believing so. But I do not fear them. The Bangols have had dominion over the Olearons for many generations, although I do not want to be seen by these." He gestures to the boat that is shrinking the distance between them. "They will take advantage of finding one of my kind alone and vulnerable—let alone the rightful king of the Bangols!"

"I can smell it. The fire. The burning," Archie whispers as the flames devour the damp salty air. Archie and Zeno watch the fire and its curls of smoke that twist, bend, and fold, slipping upward. "But not only that," Archie continues. "There is also something sweet now. Or floral-smelling? I can't put my finger on it."

"Your nose is better than mine, Archibald. I must be off!" Zeno scurries around the bow of the ship and slips between banging knees, disappearing from Archie's view.

The only people remaining transfixed by the hellish apparition, unwavering at the cruise ship's railing, are the camera club members. Telephoto lenses poised at attention, they cackle greedily as they photograph the approaching ship. The fat cameraman gives his friend a high five.

Not only is the approaching boat so close that its smell grows stronger by the minute, Archie can also decipher its black mast, proud and menacing. Beneath its puffing—always burning but never consuming—sails of fire, tall, thin, shadowy forms hustle around the deck. They too are robed in flame.

"Look," a passenger hollers.

Archie stares hard and then understands what the fire-creatures are readying. He backs away as he yells, "Run! Run, everyone!" He finds an opening between bodies and squeezes himself through the crowd toward the doors.

A ball of fire—the size of a small car, Archie guesses—is catapulted toward the *Atlantic Odyssey*. It sizzles and pops, launching sparks like fireworks to the left and right. It arcs, rolling through the air, picking up speed, transforming into a wild inferno. At first, no one screams, no one flees. Then—as Archie imagines the brevity of life and the reality of its immanent end blankets the passengers' minds—terror rips through the crowd. The people's cordiality turns savage as they shove and kick and flight each other for escape through the doors. Families are separated. Children's screams pierce the air, above the holler of angry men and the wail of women who plead, "Please, please," over and over again though no one is listening. The weak and the timid are trampled underfoot and blood dampens the deck.

When the sliding doors jam, and people are crushed within

their entryways, the movement on the deck—bottle-necked and blocked—slows to a dizzying halt. All eyes turn back to the fireball, which, for a moment, eclipses the sun, though is no less blinding. As the fireball descends like a shooting star, people narrow their eyes at its light. They hold their breath. They hold tight to whatever or whomever is nearest.

The *Odyssey*, with the crew and Captain Nate at the helm, had begun a retreat as soon as the flaming boat was spotted. The Captain had accelerated the ship in a sharp turn away from its pursuers. Thus, when the fire ball hits—with a thundering clap and a jarring crash downward—it ricochets off the rail and plummets into the sea with a fifty-foot splash. The impact tips the ship 135 degrees into the air at one end, the other sinking deeply into the tepid water. More than one hundred passengers stumble and slide overboard before the vessel rights itself in the water. The fireball does not fail, however, to mortally wound the ship, tearing a gaping hole in the stern and through three full floors, which remain enveloped in flame despite the partial immersion. The *Odyssey* also surrenders a broad section of portside railing and, along with it, every member of the camera club.

chapter 10

*A*rchie runs through the carpeted halls, turning sharp corners in unfamiliar corridors without slowing his gait. He had entered through a less congested door, far from his cabin, and now must navigate his way to his family. "Ella!" Archie huffs, winded. Children cling to the backs of their parents, who run like Archie; men throw punches for life preservers; others loot the gift shop display fridge and shelves. Weeping is the constant sound—echoing from every corner of the ship—so that Archie no longer hears it at all, but for the shrill screams that break through the noise every minute, like a metronome. Each pained, bloodcurdling wail into the crowded hallways makes the throbbing lump in Archie's throat grow larger, wedged there, unable to be swallowed.

Archie pauses, leaning against a wall, and watches as passengers either barricade themselves inside their cabins or carry their hurriedly collected belongings toward the life rafts. The hall is littered with dropped clothing, broken laptops, sneakers, and toothbrushes. The air conditioning has stopped functioning. Heat quivers Archie's vision. The odor in the hall is thick. Acidic vomit. Excrement. The metallic scent of fresh blood.

"What if the lifeboats on the starboard side are destroyed too?" a crying woman asks her friend. They cling to each other as they run, panting through shallow breaths.

"I guess we swim," the second woman responds. Blood oozes from a flesh wound beneath her right eyebrow.

Archie watches them jog down the hallway, which is when he notices the smoke. It is lilac in color and slinks along the floor, creeping—as if intentionally—up the walls on both sides and merging on the ceiling. As before when he was on the deck, Archie notices the sugary quality to the smoke, which is not altogether unpleasant. "Is that vanilla bean," he wonders, "or cotton candy?" His words, like his thoughts, begin to slur.

As Archie watches the smoke, a figure with red skin steps out of the haze—walking on two feet—fifteen doors down from where he pauses to rest. The shape is familiar; two legs, two arms, a torso, and a head. It wears a royal blue jumpsuit. The figure takes another step toward Archie, then another, growing in clarity. Archie is frozen in place. His visceral reaction to the Bangol, Zeno, is instantly paled to the horror that now courses through his body in sickening convulsions as the sight of this new, more incomprehensible creature.

Flames fan out from the back of the red figure's head. The eyes are a solid, ruddy black. Passengers scream, and Archie becomes entangled in the throng withdrawing from the creature, which Archie believes to be an Olearon, as vaguely described in Arden's notes. Archie, never having been one to express extreme emotions, opens his mouth like those beside him. He whimpers and pleads for safety. Still, he is overcome by something, slowly, dulling his distress, making him sluggish and increasingly groggy.

"Ella," calls Archie as he knocks his head with the heel of his hand, trying to jar his mind into alertness. He runs, his shoulders skidding against the walls and his feet tripping over debris. He struggles to focus his eyes. The drunken fatigue of his youth—after nights spent partying, fracturing his memory into oblivion—descends upon him. "What is happening to me?"

Cabin 248 . . . 249. Archie pulls himself along by the door-frames, his feet unbending and as heavy as concrete. *250.* "Almost there." His tongue trips over the words. "Must save Ella. Must save Ella," he repeats, but his lips are tender and swollen so that his nostrils are blocked, and saliva trickles out of his mouth and drips off his chin. The fog is upon him and its sweetness has turned sickly. He brushes away its lilac clouds in a futile effort to see, but still Archie trips over a man, then a woman, collapsed along the hall. Archie cannot decipher if they are dead or only wounded. "Finally—251," he blubbers.

Each breath is a wheeze and Archie's head bobbles. His forehead bangs against door 251 before his hands can reach it as he tumbles forward. The hinges swing the door wide and Archie lands on his chest, his teeth cutting through his bottom lip. The blood is immediate.

"Ella? Tessa?" he moans, raising the collar of his shirt to pinch the wound on his lip. He can hear the crackle of hungry flames and the thudding splash of waves against the wall of the cabin as the boat rocks forcefully. Smoke fills the room and Archie bats at the air once more, struggling to clear it. A vehement wave slaps the *Atlantic Odyssey* and Archie tips and rolls across the floor. He grabs a leg of the upholstered chair, but it tips over on top of him. His hand finds the edge of the wooden desk, which is fixed to the floor, and he pulls himself beneath it. By how he hangs from the leg, Archie surmises the ship had tilted near ninety degrees

When the vessel rights itself, people and furniture tumble back into new configurations of disorder. The rocking is stable long enough for Archie to crawl to the bed. His mind tricks his eyes. The walls drip water. The bed is a pool of distorted faces. "Where am I? This smoooke . . . it makin' me sweeee tings . . . Ello? Tessn?" Archie's words are nonsensical and he gives up on speech. *This must be what it feels like to be Ella,* he thinks coherently, and that one clear thought cuts through the delusion.

"There, there they are!" Archie gurgles. The women lay on the bed. His puffy, bleeding lips do not reveal his smile. Tears of relief run into his mouth. He tries to rouse the women, but they do not stir. Tessa wears a pale pink jacket over her pearl-colored cotton dress—the one Archie saw her hang in the closet the day they boarded. Ella is in sheer-paneled black leggings, which Archie knows her mother would have grumbled over, saying they were not appropriate for Lady Sophia's concert that night. Ella also wears the baby-blue satin bomber jacket Archie gave her for her fourteenth birthday. "Blue to match your eyes," he had said. Tessa's blond hair lies on the comforter like a halo around her head and tangles with Ella's equally golden mane. They appear peaceful to Archie.

He uses the last of his strength to pull himself onto the bed. He drops his head near Ella's feet and closes his eyes. "At least we die together," Archie murmurs as he fades away.

chapter 11

Tessa hears before she can see. A firm, feminine voice speaks above her, repeating, "Rise and fall in line." The voice is like that of a mother who cares for children not her own. Tessa tries her eyes but they feel smeared with a translucent gloss. She pinches her forefingers and her thumbs to her pupils, and pulls. A thin film slides away from each eye then wriggles on her fingers like hyper slugs. The one on her left hand begins to crawl down her fingers. Tessa shakes her fist furiously, but the little creature suctions to the back of her hand. Tessa tears it away with a pop of flesh and flings it across the room before it can re-adhere to her skin. She does the same to the second glossy creature that has made its way down her wrist.

Tessa can now see that the fog in her brain is in fact a dense haze of smoke that engulfs the tiny cabin. Her first instinct is to cough, but she quickly realizes that this cloudy whiteness is unlike the smoke she knows. Tessa passes her fingers through it and marvels at its swelling density. What before was wispy, Tessa now pulls aside like curtains. She peers through the vapor to see who spoke.

A woman who towers eight feet tall Tessa guesses, nearly to the ceiling, stands at the foot of the bed. She has coral-red skin, jet-black eyes, and a matted weave of raven-black fire-engulfed hair. She is dressed in a faded blue jumpsuit that clings to her feminine curves, and is rolled up at the sleeves and legs to reveal more ruddy, muscular skin. Over her one shoulder, is a large decorative patch with stitches in a rainbow of colors, though they dull in comparison to the brilliance of the woman's vibrant face.

"Rise," the fire-woman repeats, her body unmoving.

There are heavy footsteps out in the hall, and screams. The red shadow of fire illuminates the door of 251, which hangs ajar. Tessa shrinks back on the bed, never breaking her stare with the black eyes. She pulls Ella with her.

"Ella, wake up," Tessa begs. "Wake up!" Ella stirs and panics when she cannot see; pained squawks escape her lungs. "Wait," Tessa orders, and she clears her daughter's eyes as she had done her own. They are huddled at the head of the bed when Ella notices Archie at the foot. The teenager lunges forward, out of Tessa's grasp, and pulls her grandfather toward them as far as she can manage. Tessa yanks her back.

"Rise!" The fire-woman's impatience borders on irritation. When Tessa and Ella do not budge, the woman shakes her head. "My command is in your tongue, is it not? The young one's language is not familiar to me."

"Who are you?" Tessa demands, her breath stirring the purple smoke, allowing her to see the bizarre woman more clearly. Her dreadlocks are molded into a wide mohawk and though not fire itself, it is blackish—like coal—with highlights of burnt sienna and ruby hues when ablaze.

"Ah, so you do understand! I am the Maiden of Olearon. Now rise, or I will burn you where you lie." With her words, a flame erupts out of the back of the Maiden's spine, beginning at the curve of her neck. It curls around her cheeks and reaches for Tessa, Ella, and Archie.

Archie snaps awake with the heat. He rubs his face roughly,

scrubbing his eyes free of the living obstruction. The first words out of him are the defeated drawl, "We die together." Suddenly aware of everyone in the room, Archie turns toward the Maiden, raises his hands in a gesture of surrender he often uses when Tessa is angry, and steps from the bed. His skin flushes in the heat radiating in waves from the fire-woman. "Please don't hurt them," Archie says, as calmly as he can manage.

The Maiden of Olearon tilts her head, regarding him suspiciously. Her thick locks of hair fall onto her sharp cheekbones, distinct peaks beginning beneath her eyes and arcing out above her pointed ears. "You are the one, aren't you?" the Maiden asks.

"Wh-what do you mean?" stutters Archie.

The Maiden pauses, studying Archie's face with her bottomless black eyes. "It was you! The one who brought this vessel to Jarr-Wya?"

"Hold on! Jarr-Wya?" Tessa whispers furiously to her father-in-law's back as he faces the fiery woman. "I saw that word in Arden's notebook this morning, Archie!" she continues. "What's going on?"

"Do you really not know?" The Maiden looks at Tessa in disbelief, tilting her head sideways. "This human," she points a long, narrow finger at Archie, "brought you to Jarr-Wya. For what motive, we have yet to learn."

"Please! Please do not hurt these women." Archie takes a step toward the Maiden. "What do you want?"

Her flame broadens, though her expression is fixed. "Ah, yes. I am sure of it. You are the one. We saw your face in the sky—with that Bangol. What business do you have with him, human?"

"I don't know a Bangol. I don't know what you're talking about."

"Deception will cost you your life—and the lives of those you love!"

"Okay, okay!" Archie slouches. "The Bangol, Zeno, helped me get here."

The Maiden nods slowly. "And are your purposes aligned?"

"What? No! I barely know him—it. He helped me, that's all. Yes, I admit, I did accidentally bring this ship—and all these people—to Jarr-Wya—"

"Archie!" Tessa shrieks, forgetting herself. The Maiden's fire sparks and Tessa cowers again, blocking Ella.

"But I didn't mean to! Can't we simply send them all back now, easy-peasy?" Archie feigns a smile.

"Zeno was banished by his kind, which is of no business to the Olearons, but for our pact with the Bangols, and our desire for peace on Jarr-Wya."

"Archibald, what have you done? I don't understand what's going on," Tessa hisses, unsure which emotion—fear or anger— takes precedent in that moment.

"I wanted to find my son, to find Arden."

"Arden?" Tessa exhales as if the air has been beaten out of her.

"But he's not here, Tess. Zeno, the Bangol, he told me. Arden is dead."

Tessa's face falls. Her eyes blossom with tears that she quickly blinks away. Ella's gentle cry transforms into sobs and her quivering body trembles violently against her mother's. Ella's lips part in a wail that cuts through the air like a slow, painful death. Tessa wraps her arms and legs around her child, but she is not strong enough. The muscles in Ella's neck—dropping from the area behind her ears to a V at her jugular—are defined and flushed, her skin turning a patchwork white and pink. Her gag reflux nearly chokes her. Ella throws up all over the bedspread, narrowly missing Tessa's dress. Archie turns his back to the fire-being and struggles to comfort his thrashing granddaughter.

The Maiden watches coolly before speaking. "You see? Evil!" The Maiden of Olearon says evenly as she radiates with renewed heat.

"I came here to help Ella," Archie whimpers, his eyes downcast. He turns and continues, pleading to the Maiden, "To save this child. Now, I see. My actions have hurt many. Do what you want with me, but please—send my family back to our world, unharmed."

"Rise! Now!" The Maiden disregards Archie's words.

Tessa, Ella, and Archie stand and huddle together on the narrow cabin floor. Ella is weak, pale, and Tessa supports her weight. With a foreboding dread, they shuffle forward, following the Maiden through the door.

"Was the Bangol successful in reaching Jarr-Wya, or was he thwarted?" the Maiden asks over her shoulder.

Archie sighs. "He's here," he replies, ashamed.

Archie whispers to Tessa, instructing her to keep Ella behind him, but Tessa won't meet his eyes. The trio hasten to keep pace with the long-legged Maiden, who weaves through groups of people. The cooperative passengers are herded along the hall, while the ones that fight are incinerated by nine-foot-tall male warriors, their red chests bare and steaming through their unfastened jumpsuits that they wear as shorts with the tops tied by the arms around their waists. Their jumpsuits, unlike the Maiden's, are not decorated with the embroidered patch. The hall is deafening with weeping, screams and the crackle of stinking, burning flesh. Blood, vomit, and feces cover the ornate hall runner and squish out from beneath the family's shoes as they follow at a generous distance behind the Maiden.

"Eaww akeeeawww," Ella cries, but Tessa cups her hand over Ella's mouth.

"Shhhhh, please, my love. If they think we're talking, they'll burn us. Watch me, all right? When I see an opportunity, we'll run for it." Tessa squeezes Ella's hand and her daughter nods. She scans the hall to make sure that no Olearon—especially the Maiden—had witnessed her exchange with Ella. Tessa's palms sweat as she looks for a vacant corridor to escape through. "The moment's got to be right," she says to herself.

They pass by a long line of fearful, wide-eyed passengers with bawling children. A man steps in front of his wife and young children, barricading himself between them and an Olearon warrior, who looms over him. The man punches the Olearon across the face. The warrior cracks his neck but says nothing before blue fire consumes his red body from dreadlock to black boot—even the jumper is ablaze, though unsinged. The warrior pulls the passenger into a snug hold and the human ignites instantly, shrieking, his skin bubbling and splitting before he crumbles to a mound of ash on the carpet runner. The man's wife stumbles backward, curling her body on the floor and hollering "NO," again and again, while her children bury their faces into her clothes like baby birds.

Ella releases a pitiful gurgle of sounds as she cries along with the widow, with the fatherless boy and girl. She covers her own mouth this time and leans deeply in to Tessa, nearly tripping her. Tessa wants to whisper, "It'll be okay," and she starts to speak it, but the words catch in her scratchy throat. Instead, Tessa strokes her daughter's tangled, singed hair. She finally meets Archie's eyes, and scowls at him with a rage as hot as the flames that curl the wallpaper and char the doorframes. Fire burns on every side of them and finds the seams in the drywall, leaking heat in intervals and spewing ash across their path.

The Maiden of Olearon nods to her fellow warriors as she glides by them—a foot shorter but with the confidence of unconditional authority—and they bow their heads at her. She is rail-straight, yet womanly and graceful with every gesture, every word. All remaining groups of passengers deliberately, though hesitantly, follow the Olearons out onto the upper deck. The boat continues to sway stubbornly in the water though it is severely tipped after the impact with the fireball, and now water battles flame in a war for the stern. Tessa pauses to vomit at the wall beneath a melted oil painting of the Canary Islands that drips like rain down a window. Ella pulls her mother's long tresses clear and helps her to stand.

The ship is traveling at a reckless pace. The sliding glass doors, jammed open and smashed by the fleeing crowds, funnel rapidly flowing air into their faces. Archie, Tessa, and Ella follow the Maiden out a dented and misshapen hole in the *Odyssey's* flank and into the penetrating light. "It must be tomorrow," says Archie. "I wonder how long we were knocked out."

"There was no land in sight—not Lanzarote or any other island—when Ella and I ran to our cabin. And now, look!" Tessa points overboard to where a landmass, as tall as it is wide, weighs down on the water with sharp cliffs and a triangular glass city to the west; gold beaches ahead; and mammoth stone arches to the east. The island is abloom with emerald greens, pops of fuchsia, and tangerine hues. A carved, twisted mountain cuts upward from the island's core. From it, many smaller fragments of land jut sideways, either supported on precariously narrow rock chutes, or appearing to float on their own, anchored to the mountain by the creeping vines and tangled tree roots.

"Stay close," whispers Archie as they walk past ordered lines of roughly a hundred passengers, detained in pairs on what is left of the deck. Olearon warriors, with no weapons but their own bodies—though on their belts hang glass daggers in fabric sheaths—steer the humans. They are broad-shouldered and narrow-hipped, their red arms muscular and their backs erect and unflinching. The tallest of these, towering a foot above the other male Olearons, has the fullest weave of black and blood-red hair, braided in eight strands mixed with strips of colorful leather and rope the full length of his back. Jewels adorn his mane.

"My Lord," the Maiden of Olearon says, bowing slightly, "I have found the one from the sky. He knows the Bangol, Zeno."

The Lord of Olearon smolders like hot coals. "Is he here?" he asks. "Is the Bangol here? If Tuggeron lays eyes on Zeno, his madness will propagate. The stone king may choke out what health still remains in Jarr-Wya."

"I agree, my Lord."

"Tell me." The Lord of Olearon turns to Archie. "Where is he? Where have you hidden Zeno?"

"I don't know! I would tell you if I knew. I'm sorry! Please," Archie begs, "please, leave my family out of this."

"Detain this one. We'll use him to draw out the Bangol," the Lord orders. "Get Olen and Azkar. They are to stand guard immediately."

The Maiden wraps her long fingers around Archie's arm and jerks him forward.

"Eewooah!" Ella shrieks and dashes for her grandfather, skirting around an Olearon's tall legs. Another huge red hand grabs her by the shoulders and yanks her back. Ella falls. She lands on her back and is winded. Tessa shoves a warrior aside to sprint to her daughter's aid.

"Olen! Azkar!" the Maiden hollers above the breeze created from the moving vessels. Two massive Olearons appear and immediately their flames bloom and dart toward Tessa and Ella, who cower on the ash-covered deck. Archie witnesses a flash of fear sweep across Tessa's usually brave and guarded countenance, but Ella only glares at the red bodies.

"No!" Archie wrenches his arm free of his sleeve and twists out of his coat, away from the Maiden, and darts toward his family. He throws his body on top of theirs. Olen's and Azkar's flames ignite Archie's filthy polo shirt, charring it, and he screams in agony.

chapter 12

"We go together, or I'll jump into that fire!" Archie threatens, pointing at the seething flames at the back of the ship. "Or I'll... or I'll jump over the rail! Drown myself. If you want what I know—and believe me, you do—then we three stay together!"

Olen and Azkar calm their flames at the Lord's order and Archie drops to his chest and rolls on the deck. His shirt is badly burned but his skin is only reddened, like a sunburn. The Lord nods to the Maiden, then in the direction of a wooden gangplank bridging the gap between the *Atlantic Odyssey* and the flaming ship, which is towing the ocean liner toward the island of Jarr-Wya. The Maiden shoves Archie's coat into his hands and gestures for the trio to cross.

"What kind of magic is this?" Archie gestures toward the black ship with its flaming sails blowing in an invisible wind.

The Maiden of Olearon looks at him suspiciously, "Do you not know Naiu?"

"I don't," Archie lies.

"Naiu is the life force of this world, the soul of the elements. It created this island, this world, and everything in in. It lives on, though weakly because of the Bangols. Naiu is sacred. You'd be wise to revere it," the Maiden warns.

Archie says nothing, weighing the evil of Zeno as cautioned by the Maiden against the cruelty of the Olearons he observed in the ship's hallways. "Zeno can't be all bad if he used Naiu to bring us here," Archie says under his breath.

They are guided into a small room below the black-glass deck, where they quickly realize the entire ship is formed with the seemingly fragile material. To both an outsider and someone inside looking out, it appears as a murky, obscure surface—until the outer walls of the ship are touched. Then the glass distortion swims away in an iridescent sparkle for a moment only before swimming back to obscure the view once more. In that moment, you can see the world beyond as clear as if you stood on the deck above.

The inner walls and floors are flawlessly clear, as if only air partitions the space. Movement on their left draws their eyes to a group of Olearons discussing an aged and delicate map in a neighboring glass room. On their right are vaults holding huge pieces of coal—for the fireballs, Archie surmises. He counts forty vaults housing the carbon boulders that wait patiently for deployment. "I don't think we stood a chance," he says, reassessing the malice of the Olearons. For the time being, at least, the passengers that cooperate are still alive.

Ella kneels on the floor with her hands pressed to the glass. She peers downward into what is obviously a kitchen. A dozen red-skinned beings count food reserves and wield mops. Below them, two more Olearons shovel ash into large barrels. Farther beneath them still, several levels lower, the ocean swirls, lit by some mysterious golden-bluish-greenish hue, as if the core of this bizarre, unfamiliar world is a sun itself.

"Wait here," the Maiden commands, and abruptly leaves.

They are in a room furnished with a small glass table and bench, where Archie plops down. Tessa paces, watching the

Maiden navigate along a labyrinth of intersecting corridors and up onto the deck.

"Hello?" Tessa yells. The Maiden of Olearon does not stop. "Hey you!" Tessa screams again, watching the map-readers, but their heads do not pop up from their worn papers, from their glass nautical instruments, as they discuss matters silent to the humans' ears. "Good," she says, turning to Archie. "We need to get out of here. Do you think we could make it to the island if we swam?"

"Not before they do," Archie says of the Olearons' vessel hurtling toward its target. "Tess, can I explain?"

"Don't, Archie." Tessa raises her finger to silence him. "Just don't. You are more like Arden than I have let myself admit and that scares me, almost more than anything else. Apart from getting us outta here, we are done. Do you hear me?" Archie nods sadly. Ella's cheeks are streaked with tears. She runs to Archie's side and wraps her arms around him, turning her face to her mother and shaking her head and mouthing the word *no*.

"Why Ella? Why do you always take his side? Don't you see that I do everything for you? Everything? I work so hard and yet Archie has your eternal affection! I sacrifice my own happiness for you, for what is left of our family—"

Ella pinches her index fingers and thumbs together, her middle, ring, and pinkie fingers raised and creates a circle with her hands. She points to Tessa and to Archie.

"Yes, we are family," Tessa retorts to Ella, "but family are supposed to take care of each other—not walk out on them, not take them to dangerous places following crazy obsessions . . ."

Ella signs the word *stop* and Tessa snaps her jaw shut and releases a deep-chested sigh through her nostrils in place of words. Tears fall from her eyes. Her shoulders slump in defeat.

With one hand, Ella laces her fingers between Archie's, and with the other raises her thumb, pointer, and pinkie fingers, her palm towards her mother, and smiles weakly.

"I love you too, Ell." Tessa crosses the glass floor and embraces her daughter, though avoids touching her father-in-law. When a moment has passed, she pulls away from Ella.

Tessa turns to Archie and speaks slowly, though her words cut the air. "Think, Archibald. You got us into this nightmare. You'd better get us out of it—alive." Tessa steps backward as her words linger in the room. She turns and tiptoes to the glass door and tugs gently. "Locked."

One of the Olearons reading the map looks over at Tessa and gestures with a long red hand in their direction. Suddenly, the transparent glass on every side sparkles with distortion. "Fine!" Tessa screams. She runs to the external wall and touches it with a tentative finger. The darkness briefly dissipates, revealing a small section of ocean. "Ha!" she yells again.

Ella joins her and together they press their hands, fingers fanned wide, against the glass. The area that opens is significantly larger. "Oh, I can barely see the *Odyssey*," says Tessa, leaning so that her cheek is squashed against Ella's hand. Ella chuckles in an awkward croak. "Archie, come help," says Tessa. "We need to know what's going on out there."

Archie, sitting motionless as he stews over his "tragic fantasies," as he decides to call them, does not hear Tessa the first time. Finally, when Tessa's voice breaks through his inner noise, he rises sluggishly from the glass bench to join the women. His mind replays the hundred deaths he witnessed that day and his neck feels tight, strangled by guilt.

With Archie's touch, the darkness retreats far enough that the trio can watch the happenings beyond their smooth cell. The *Atlantic Odyssey* is not far behind them, towed by a mammoth rusting chain near the footbridge connecting the two ships' decks. The stern is blanketed in flame that creeps toward the ship's midsection. The passengers, still in their lines and lorded-over by the Olearons, are crammed at the bow, struggling to avoid being burned to death or drowning as the *Odyssey* floats dangerously low.

Ella lets out a caw when the door abruptly swings open behind them. Tessa steps in front of Ella, who leans around her mother to peer at the two male Olearon warriors that enter. Their chins are tipped low to their chests and they glare from under ruddy eyelids. When they see Archie, however, their black eyes widen. Their flames quiver. They stare at him with the peculiar gaze of familiarity—and not only from nearly burning him to death on the deck moments before. The Olearons exchange an unreadable glance before approaching Archie.

"Who are you?" one asks, leaning in close.

"Uh, Archibald Wellsley?"

"Wellsley?" the other warrior repeats.

"Yes." Archie shrugs at Tessa. "Who are you?" he asks boldly, shoving his quivering hands into his pant pockets.

"I am Azkar," says the Olearon with a smile—or sneer—distorted by a jagged black scar slicing from his left eye to his collarbone. "This is Olen." Archie recognizes the names of the guards called by the Maiden on the *Odyssey*—and he recoils at the close view of Azkar's grotesque, cauterized wound.

The Olearons whisper to each other in their own language, their flames joining. "Who's she?" Olen finally asks Archie after studying Tessa.

"My daughter-in-law. She is my son's wife."

"Was," Tessa adds in whisper.

"Your son?" Olen asks. It is more of a statement than a question.

"Look there," he says to Azkar, pointing to Archie's head. He looks at Archie. "It was once . . . ?"

"Brown, dark brown," Archie replies. "Yes, you saw me in the clouds. Yes, I am the one who caused all this hullabaloo. All this death." Archie exhales deeply. "Tell me, do you have a Tillastrion? Please, I'll give you whatever you want, as long as you get my girls back home."

The Olearons ignore him. "The strong jaw," Olen says, taking one step toward Archie, who backs two steps away. They maintain distance in this way until Archie is pressed against the outer wall, which blurs at his back. He stares at the black eyes and the steaming form towering above him. Olen stretches his burly arm toward him and Archie closes his eyes.

"Make it quick," Archie wheezes. But Olen's flames do not broil his brain, heart, and lungs, as Archie expects, as he feels he deserves. Instead, Olen traces Archie's jawline with one elongated finger, leaving a warm, rosy streak on Archie's skin.

"We must report," Olen says as he walks to the door. Azkar bobs his dreadlocks in agreement and turns to follow.

"Report what?" Archie barks. "Why don't you let us outta here? I don't know anything; I was lying before," he pleads, but the Olearons close the door securely behind them. In that instant—as Archie, Tessa, and Ella watch the guards tread the same route the Maiden walked not long before, in the fraction of a second before the shimmer returns to the smooth surface—the boat runs aground with a crash of glass and sand.

Archie tumbles backward and knocks his head on the lip of the table. He falls to the floor and does not move.

ELLA and Tessa, holding hands, flip painfully into the corner of the room. "Awwwk!" Ella whimpers, clutching her left arm.

"Oh no!" Tessa feels Ella's forearm and agony creases the teenager's features. Tessa purses her lips, not wanting to admit there is a break. She pulls her daughter in close. "I'll take care of you, Ell. It'll be okay." Ella cries into her mothers' filthy pink jacket.

Without warning, Olen and Azkar barge back into the room. Olen rushes to Archie, Azkar to the outer wall, where he peers out. "I must go to the battle line," Azkar fumes. "Guard this one," he says to Olen. "Do not let him out of your sight." Tessa and Ella follow Azkar's black eyes to Archie.

The humans and Olearons barely make out what happens next through the fluttering translucent glass. The *Atlantic Odyssey* skids along the Olearon vessel, which is already lodged on the shore, and slips sideways onto the gold-sand beach.

"Oh no." Olen gulps, then leaves Archie as he runs to watch at the glass. "The Millia . . . Prepare yourself for an ambush," he barks at the women. "I cannot carry Archibald and the two of you!"

"Millia?" Tessa repeats. The name does not evoke dread but for the way that Olen had said it: as if it choked him, and once it left his lips, he wished to forget it forever. Tessa watches Olen with suspicion, but the Olearon picks up Archie kindly and hoists him over his shoulder.

Tessa jumps to her feet. She tears a strip of fabric from her calf-length skirt and loops it around Ella's arm, knotting it behind her neck. "How about that, Ell? Not too shabby." She smiles quickly, for her daughter's sake, while adrenaline thuds through her body in nauseating waves. She swallows hard. Ella looks to her with wide eyes, silently begging for safety and Tessa feels the weight of the stare in every muscle of her aching body.

She pulls Ella in close, wrapping herself around the replica of her teenage self in both appearance and naivety. She mutters a near faithless prayer for strength.

"What language does she speak?" Olen asks cautiously. He tips his chin toward Ella.

"She cannot speak," Tessa admits as she struggles to hoist the bench and—before Olen can stop her—hurls it through the cracked glass wall toward the beach.

chapter 13

*I*t's beautiful." The words roll out of Tessa's mouth without a thought, as she and Ella stare at the sparkling gold village at the far edge of the beach. The structures are spherical on one side, and droop in miniature shimmering avalanches on the other. They have no sharp angles of any kind, but mimic the curve of the sea and the ripples it carves into the shore. To one looking inland from the deep sea, the village would appear as mere sand dunes, short slices of earth and its shifting gold, rising and falling carelessly beyond the tide's reach. From the beach, however, the intelligible design is evident.

Curved stairs lead to misshapen doorways, without doors. Raised tunnels—that look to Tessa like the feeding runways of the moles she exterminated from their yard in Seattle—curl between and connect the buildings. Small windows are formed in the outer walls of the gold village where sections of sand have given way, resulting in unexpected shapes. Every window faces the sea.

"The homes look carved," Tessa continues, "like the walls of a gorge. They remind me of the sculpted sandstone of the Grand Canyon, where your dad and I hiked before you were born, Ella. Hundreds of years of a river rushing against it, caressed by it."

"It may appear alluring, as you say," Olen begins, "but its occupants are treacherous and bloodthirsty. They have no regard for the beauty of any life other than their own."

"Who are they?" Archie asks. He had woken when Olen slid his limp body down an angled twenty-foot fragment of the shining external structure of the Olearon's ship. The sheet was lodged in the hull of the now extinguished glass vessel, six feet below the section of the outer wall that Tessa shattered. She and Ella had flung themselves out the yawning opening to slip down the smooth surface to the ground; Olen had resigned himself to follow, keeping his watch. Now the four stand on the divide between sea and shore among a graveyard of broken, still shimmering glass.

"They are the Millia sands," Olen answers in a whisper.

"Sand?" Archie repeats, rubbing the back of his head where a protruding welt and small cut dampen his white hair with crimson.

"I should not speak to you beings—humans as you're called—so freely, however you are the Wellsley family . . ." The Olearon pauses in thought before continuing, answering Archie's question and the inquisitive expressions on all three pale faces. "The Millia are formed of crushed seashells. Their name means 'soul of the shell.'"

"Sand people?" Tessa says.

"Yes, sand and selfishness." Olen puts a hand on Archie's chest before the old man takes a step closer to the *Odyssey*. "Hold back. We are safer here, beyond sight for now."

"Will you let us go, now that we've reached the island?" Tessa demands as she trudges closer behind Olen, kicking up silt. "We could slip under the cover of those trees over there—"

"You do not want me to let you go on these corrupt shores," Olen says vehemently.

"Sand people don't sound all that dangerous," Tessa scoffs.

"The life of the sea creatures is a difficult one. They are summoned by the Star at the center of the sea—beneath Jarr-Wya—but the Star is too bright, too warm, too wicked. The sea creatures never reach it. They spend their lives diving, but it cannot be done. They perish, wretched and unfulfilled, but their encasements remain and crash on the coral and break into countless pieces, more numerous than all the worlds together. They wash up upon this shore. The souls of the shells contain the bitter unfulfillment of their past masters. Many sunsets before, the broken fragments decided to unite and make their golden village, as they could not reach Jarr-Wya's sea-Star."

Ella signs *star* and then *sea*—as a question—which Archie recognizes. "I was thinking the same thing, Ell," he replies, and Ella offers a pained smile, clutching her limp arm. "Olearon, uh, Olen—"

"Yes, Archibald Wellsley."

"My granddaughter wants to know, I want to know: why is there a star under the sea? Where we come from, stars are up in the sky."

"Five thousand sunsets past, the midnight hour erupted with lightning and fire. The blaze was blinding and the crash shook Jarr-Wya; trees split and their topmost leaves burst into flame. The Star . . . it started as a black spot amidst the light, but it grew till it encompassed the sky. I kissed my mother and brothers then, knowing that our flames would soon fail to burn, never to be relit. I bowed low to the Lord and the Maiden. They have been good to the Olearons, leading with wisdom and protecting Jarr-Wya with courage for many ages.

"Our flames burned blue that night—but the Star had mercy on us, its only mercy. It plummeted into the sea, where it now dwells, below Jarr-Wya."

"That's a relief." Archie chuckles.

"Yes and no, Archibald. The Star changed much on the island. The birth of the Millia. The black flyers grew claws from their wingtips. The voice of the trees, when the wind plays upon their branches, now sing a foreign melody. We lost the rain, but for the fewest of days; some places of Jarr-Wya turn from forest green to desert nothingness. The sunlight grows weaker and the nights more treacherous.

"And the Bangols' minds—" continues Olen, his flame flaring up behind him.

"Zeno," Archie whispers.

"They have grown mad, wild! They conspire against their own, crushing their leaders to blood, rubble, and bone dust. They are of the earth, but forsake their very nature, poisoning the soil and clay, corrupting the fruit of Jarr-Wya. They starve their kin, hungering only for dominion."

"That doesn't sound like Zeno, from my experience of him," Archie reflects. "He's going to lead me to Ella's cure and help us return home."

"Is that what he told you, Archie?" Tessa says and grits her teeth. "Oh, you are more foolish than I thought! How could you do this to us?"

"I do believe she is right, Archibald. You have been deceived." Olen acknowledges Tessa for the first time by meeting her eyes with his own twin black voids.

"Is it all a lie? When Zeno mentioned a cure, I didn't recall reading it in the notebooks. I had hoped Arden's motives were good, but instead I now see—for the first time—he really did walk out on us."

"As I have been saying for years, Archie. You've got to let him go. We have, right, Ell?" Ella does not look up from her feet, half buried in the sand. When she does raise her face, her expression suddenly changes from forlorn to fear as she notices movement out of the corners of her eyes. She points without making a sound.

Tessa gasps. "Where did the village go?"

"The Millia are the village. They are this beach. They are coming for us."

chapter 14

Tessa grabs Ella's good arm and yells, "*Run!*" They sprint through the sand toward the lush, shadowy tree line, but Olen lands on them. He crushes his heavy, steaming body onto theirs, pressing their flesh into the sharp sand.

"You will not make it that way, by running. They already know. The Millia. You would be dead before your toes touch the forest floor. If you wish for death, fine, I will let you run; but if you desire life, be still. I will protect you, as long as I am able."

"Why? Why protect us? Because of Archie? Why do you care so much about him?" snarls Tessa, spitting sand.

Olen ignores Tessa's question; he stands and returns to their lookout among the twinkling shards of glass. Mother and daughter struggle to their feet in the slippery golden sand, brushing it from the corners of their eyes, their lips, and their frayed clothing.

"The Millia are every fleck of sand you see down this shore. They become whatever they wish, or value most, though they are solidly shell. When we meet them, they'll likely come as yellow beasts or birds, hoping to tear us to pieces for trespassing. Their bloodlust is born from their unfulfillment; now they seek to destroy."

Archie wrings his hands. "I am so sorry, Ella, Tessa. I never meant for any of this. I only wanted to help." Ella rests her petite hand on her grandfather's back.

"You haven't helped. You've killed Ella. You've killed us all!" Tessa turns to Olen. "So, what are we going to do? Wait here to die?" she hollers.

"Wait and hope the Millia may need something from us. Something we can exchange for our safety. If not, then hope that our warriors can hold them off long enough."

Tessa whispers, "Long enough for what?"

"For you to run, human. Their attention must be elsewhere for us to make it. Right now, they are watching and listening—in many places. Aggressive movements will provoke them. Wait now. I will tell you when. You have a heat all your own, daughter-in-law. I have seen this heat in one of your kind before. It must be harnessed. For now, we watch. The Olearon warriors are ready, but our surest path to safety is that our alliance with the Millia will allow for negotiation."

Off in the distance, beside the *Atlantic Odyssey*, the Olearons create lines of the disheveled cruise passengers as they scramble over the side of the ship. Half of the roughly one hundred people left alive whimper and plead. The other half scowl angrily and look resigned to fight, maybe even to die. Yet, all the humans—from their short time since meeting the fearsome Olearons, the *Odyssey*'s shipwreck on the mysterious beach, and their capture—appear drunk with shock. The people huddle near the flank of the dented, scarred vessel. Another group of red-skinned warriors stands guard, some moving out in units as they search the beach.

"Look," Archie says and points. "The couple we sat with at breakfast yesterday. And the school friends. And the mom . . . but where is her second child?"

"The Captain is there too," Tessa adds brightly. "At least he's alive."

Olen displays little concern for the mixture of distress and relief of the humans in his charge. "Olearons protect the western land and the sea-face from intruders to Jarr-Wya and the sea creatures—now the Millia—defend the breadth of this southern shore and the evils that lurk beneath the water," he discloses. Olen holds a book-sized shard of glass from the Olearon ship. His skin glows and yellow-orange veins throb through his arms to his fingertips. The glass slowly melts and Olen shapes it into a translucent dagger, which he passes to Ella. She stares at it for a moment before gingerly slipping the weapon into one pocket of her bomber jacket.

"This alliance with the sea creatures, which was preserved through their transformation into the Millia thousands of sunsets ago—has allowed us mutual peace through many generations," Olen continues. "Both races are interested in the preservation of our coexistent way of life. The Millia stay on this shoreline and beneath the sea, and we do not venture onto their beach. Unfortunately, hauling your ship has quickly depleted our fuel reserves. We were unable to sail farther around the island to our port among the cliffs to the west. The Millia will see this as an insult."

An Olearon runs from the front line in the distance toward Archie, Tessa, Ella, and Olen. "Azkar!" acknowledges Olen, and the two Olearons converse in whispers, though what the humans do hear of the melodious language is beyond their understanding.

Tessa leans in to Archie. "I can't believe I'm saying this . . . Was there anything in Arden's notebooks about how to get home?" A grin spans wide across Ella's face as she listens.

Archie shakes his head. "No, but Zeno told me that someone from our world—like one of us—" he looks at Tessa and Ella, "can make a device that can transport us back. We would need someone from here, from this dimension, to operate it, though." Archie pauses, stroking the white stubble on his chin. "But it could be lies," he adds, defeated. "I don't know what to believe anymore."

"There's got to be a way," Tessa huffs. Ella nods emphatically. Tessa cracks her knuckles and continues. "We got here, didn't we? And Zeno was somehow living on the Canary Islands."

"Right. I never thought about that," says Archie, but before he can continue, Azkar and Olen turn to them and order the trio toward the *Odyssey*.

Tessa leans again to Archie and murmurs, "We've got to find Zeno," before she is shoved forward by Azkar. Archie nods, their eyes locked over Tessa's shoulder. He takes a deep breath and hurries along through the loose sand, summoning what lingering strength resides in his thudding heart, which outruns his feet.

As they walk nearer to the *Atlantic Odyssey*, the sound of screaming passengers reaches Tessa's ears and she gasps. Then she sees why. The clothes of the men and women are torn, bloodied, and whatever color they once were is obscured by a film of ash and the black caress of smoke. Blood—damp and fresh or dry and muted—obscures faces, chests, and limbs, revealing wounds. The people cling to each other, some with broken or dislocated arms like Ella's, others limping or clutching oozing gashes, their faces pale from trauma and loss of blood.

"There's the singer! Lady Sophia," says Tessa. The opera performer shuffles to and fro in the sand, wearing her ball gown and jeweled necklace, and clasping her gloved hands to avoid them flailing in hysteria. "She's standing by Nate. And the cruise director—wait, what's happening?"

The sand begins to rush around at the passengers' feet, as if pulled by an intentional wind, though the air hangs still. The gold flecks rise in waves around the pitiful ship, some a foot tall and others like monstrous rip tides. The passengers, despite their condition, follow the Olearons' orders, queueing and huddling together, cowering behind the wall of fiery warriors.

"The Olearons are protecting them," says Tessa.

"You sound surprised," Azkar huffs.

"It's just that, well, after watching people I sat and ate with, talked with, just one day ago, burn to death. . . yeah, it doesn't quite make sense."

"Does everything need to make sense to you?" Azkar puts a warm hand on Tessa's back to keep her moving. Tessa wrenches free of his touch, frightened by his undeniable strength, despite his tall, willowy build. Azkar looks back at Archie. "We are negotiating," he offers, flashing a scowl at Tessa for her defiance. "The Millia will not continue until all people have disembarked both the Olearon boat and your vessel."

Tessa, Ella, and Archie join the cruise passengers beside the *Odyssey*, but the wounded humans glare at the trio suspiciously and shuffle a few paces away. Azkar returns to the apex of the Olearon barricade, which blocks the view of whoever owns the bitter voice that snarls and snaps at the rose-red warriors, whose flames curl vehemently. Tessa squeezes Ella's hand and they inch closer to the Olearons to peer between their arms and narrow torsos.

The Millia stomp around in human form, mimicking the silhouette of the *Odyssey*'s passengers, though they lack detail and are made of solid sand. One sand-shape, as tall as the Olearons, bears down on the Lord and Maiden without fear. It gestures to the people with disgust. With every swoop of its hand, its fingers crumble and spray sand in the Olearons' faces. Tiny trickles of crushed shells climb up the Millia leader's legs, chest, and arms to reform its hands, which it continues to flail.

"They're negotiating in our language," remarks Tessa in whisper to Ella. "Why would they want us to understand?"

An Olearon overhears and tips his head back to clarify. "The Olearons and Millia do not share a language, but this," he says. "We do not know how your tongue traveled to our island many ages ago, but it has become the common expression between Jarr-Wya's distinct races."

"Senior Karish, please do understand," the Lord of Olearon implores, speaking in an even tone. "We have not intentionally nulled our alliance. We were simply fulfilling our agreement to protect the sea-face, but this vessel"—he gestures to the *Atlantic Odyssey*— "proved heavier than we had anticipated. Our fuel was insufficient to return us to the west. Because of the Bangols, our supplies are exhausted."

"But why haul it to Jarr-Wya in the first place? Hmm? Why spare these? That's what I want to know!" Senior Karish demands, gesturing to the passengers. On his sandy head, he wears a tall crown of what looks to Tessa like oyster and lion's paw scallop shells, all still housing their living hosts. Growing up in Seattle, near Elliott Bay—which connects, by the Strait of Juan de Fuca along the Canadian-American sea boarder, to the North Pacific Ocean—Tessa had a natural love for seafood. However, the crown, decorated with cowie and bonnet shells in a fanning pattern, with crabs peeking out of their curled casings and pinching in the direction of the Olearons, makes Tessa's stomach grow sour.

"Is the boat of value? Are these—this race—are they sweet? Maybe we too are hungry!" Senior Karish continues. The sand shapes behind him constantly shift forms; the Millia spike up into the air like geysers, hissing and cackling at Senior Karish's mention of a meal. The people cower and cry out, backing farther toward the *Odyssey* until they bang their heads against its warped steel.

The Maiden answers. "The Olearons are weakened by lack of crops; the poison spell of the Bangols wiped out more than half the vegetation of our land. We wish these, here, to work. And to fight for us. Let us cross to our lands and collect fuel and food. We will return and remove our boat and this vessel from your shores in less than twenty sunsets."

"Too long! Too long! Unacceptable," Senior Karish rants, sand flying as he shakes his head in protest. He strokes the breastplate of shells and barnacle-encrusted rope he wears across his chest. As he thrashes around, the shell-creatures on his crown and at his chest reveal their legs and torsos, readjusting themselves into position. "Remove these vile vessels—and all of you—from our shore immediately. Or we will do it for you!" Senior Karish snarls through yellow teeth, glaring with similarly colored sandy eyes.

"Ten sunsets! Can you give us ten?" the Maiden pleads. "We need our boat, though it requires repair. We cannot sustain our people without it."

Senior Karish continues to wildly shake his head, his granular nose and ears loosening from his face in a shimmering spray before quickly reforming. His patchy beard, dense with flecks of gold, reflects the light of the dazzling foreign sun into the human's eyes.

"You must feel the malice of the Bangols' poisoned clay beneath your beach, do you not?" the Lord of Olearon asks. "You must know it is only a matter of time before it leaches into your shell fragments and threatens your very dominion of Jarr-Wya's south. The poison worsens by the day. We must work together to remove it from our lands."

"Now that," Senior Karish hisses, pointing and twisting with one glittering finger, "now that is an altogether different issue!" What looks to Tessa like a wicked grin is carved across his rough, sandy face. "We agree, purge the Bangols! Let me discuss with my . . . my advisors; maybe some future course—alongside the Olearons—can feed our" he gestures the full breadth of the beach, "our distinct cravings." With a sandy tongue, Senior Karish licks his golden lips. He reaches down to the sand at his feet, snaps his fingers, and a conch shell rises out of the beach. He lifts it to his mouth and blows.

At the end of his breath, the shape of Senior Karish crumbles from the top of his head to his neck and shoulders, then lower and lower, until nothing more remains than a mound of shifting sand. The conch is sucked back into the beach from where it came. The mound of what had been the leader of the Millia, now creeps a few feet away from the Olearons' barricade of warriors, amalgamating with the smooth beach around it before simultaneously rising and narrowing, stretching upward into a tall, sandy shaft, extending higher and higher—thirty feet into the cloudless blue sky. Other shafts grow near it, all reaching, shifting, and spilling themselves.

Tessa's left cheek warms as she inadvertently brushes it against the back of the Olearon who had spoken to her a moment before. She leans around him to watch with dread as the thinning funnels form a perfect octagon of eight points. A fierce wind cyclones out from between the shafts, though it is mostly contained within them. Increasing in speed, the force sucks the shafts into the gale, spinning flecks of gold from the core and into the air mass of low atmospheric pressure. The Olearons are like statues, never flinching or blinking, though the wind slaps out at them unpredictably. The *Odyssey*'s passengers cover their eyes and turn away as tiny granules blast forcefully out like vengeful sparks.

Voices emerge from the dazzling cyclone, though the swoosh of the laborious wind—weighed down beneath the density of the crushed shells—deadens the Millia's argument to a low rumble in a strange dialect. Their voices are turbulent at times, both deep as thunder and discordant as smashing cymbals. Ella ducks behind Tessa, and the Olearon in front of them breaks the line to shelter both women. At first, Tessa cowers back from the warrior, confused at the changed red beings who at first gave little regard for the *Odyssey*'s passengers. Since Archie was recognized, the Olearons exhibited restraint and even compassion. In that moment, amid the sand storm, Tessa surrenders to the Olearon's protection, banking her nagging questions.

With a final explosion of silt, the cyclone halts in mid spin, and the sand collapses to the shore in a brilliant splash that blasts low, then crashes back on top of itself. The Olearons and passengers are peppered with dust and grit. Ella coughs and scratches her nails along her lips and tongue, cleaning away sand. Tessa wipes her face with her sleeve, which drags the shell fragments across her cheeks, leaving tiny white lines on her skin. The passengers slowly turn their eyes back to the beach, where the Millia again grow out of the sand to mimic their human form.

Senior Karish approaches the Lord and Maiden of Olearon with steps that raise his golden legs but never disconnect him from the shore. "We have reached a consensus," he says. "We will allow—allow—these vessels to remain on our shore for ten sunsets. No more, no more."

"Thank you," says the Maiden. "That is very honorable of you."

"Ah, ah, ah! I am not finished! We grant you that time for your warriors to challenge the Bangols, restoring our lovely island to health!"

The Lord inhales deeply. "What you ask requires more time, Senior Karish! As we stand, now, I do not believe it is possible," the Lord objects.

"Then you had better get moving! Get moving! The faster you accomplish this task, the faster you reclaim your boat and feed your young flames." Senior Karish interlocks his wilting fingers. "And, one more thing."

"What is it?" demands the Maiden, her dreadlocks radiating like fiery embers. The Lord turns to his partner, but his eyes read blank to Tessa, though, after a moment, the Maiden's fire calms.

"Blood must be spilt today. We want the people," hisses Senior Karish.

Ella squeezes her mother's arm, her breath catching in her throat. Tessa—her face twisted in distress—clings to her daughter so tightly the muscles in her hands ache, their veins bulging. She and Ella stumble back from the warrior. Tessa, thinking quickly, is about to whisper to her daughter and father-in-law, "run," but as she turns the word never forms—for Archie is gone.

chapter 15

*A*s Tessa and Ella are corralled in the direction of the Olearon barricade, instead of following obediently, Archie slowly retreats backward through the crowd. No one notices him, as all eyes stare, nearly without blinking, at the animated sand beyond their wall of protection.

Archie's head throbs as he searches for a way into the *Atlantic Odyssey*. Finally, he spots a manageable entrance up high, and, thankfully, out of direct view of the commotion on the shore. He wades out into the sea until it reaches his thighs and the salt water stings in the cuts he didn't know were hiding beneath his pant legs.

Hoisting himself upward over the torn steel of the hull and the splintered wooden portholes with cracked and missing glass, Archie reaches the warped railing and climbs it like a ladder, higher and higher. He tumbles to his knees on the ship's deeply tilting deck, tripping over the remains of a charred pool chair and slipping in the water that drips from his trousers. Lying prostrate on the deck, he shimmies up the forty-five-degree angle, gritting his teeth against the pain at his singed chest.

"I'm too old for this," Archie wheezes as he pulls himself through a burned section of wall into the darkness beyond the promenade deck. He straddles the divide between floor and wall, one foot on each. "Now, where am I?" He scrunches his forehead in concentration and looks around, then runs down the first corridor to his left. He pauses when the path forks. The signage, wallpaper, and cabin numbers are blackened, melted, or missing entirely.

Archie chooses a path to his right, then to his left, stepping around a curling iron, a lonely shoe, and a door broken from its hinges. His jog slows to a slink and it's all he can do to lift one heavy arm to put a hand on his chest to calm his breathing. "I'm not going to make it . . ."

Picturing Ella and Tessa, down on the shore, caught between flame and an even greater threat, Archie shivers. "Arden, wherever you are, help me. If there is something in your notebooks that could get the girls and me outta here, please guide me to my cabin . . ."

"Da da?"

Archie holds his breath. "Arden?"

"Dad?"

Archie follows the sound of the soft voice to another door, busted from its frame and leaning against the corridor wall.

"Arden?"

"Da da?"

Archie flips the door and it tumbles and slides down the slanted floor. There, at Archie's feet, is an African boy around four years old. "Hey there, little fella," says Archie. He looks from side to side, but there is no parent looking for the child. The ship is silent but for the steady dip of water and the sizzle of filament in lightbulbs about to dim. "I guess you're coming with me."

The little boy stands and reaches for Archie's hand. "We do have to hurry, little fella . . . er, what's your name?"

"Dad? Where's Dad?" the boy asks again.

"I hear ya, kid. We're all looking for someone. And right now, I'm looking for some*thing*."

Archie and the boy aimlessly wind through drenched and darkened hallways until the old man's eyes suddenly widen. "There!" Archie chirps, and points. The little boy—whom Archie has decided to call Duggie-Sky because of the child's Pacific Aviation Museum T-shirt of a cartoon superhero riding a 1950's Douglas A-3 Skywarrior aircraft—smiles and matches Archie's pace.

Archie shoves aside the cracked door of his cabin, where he and Zeno had operated the Tillastrion. The secured furniture remains in place, though the pillows and mattress—plus the contents of Archie's toiletries bag, which Zeno had riffled through; and the stack of tourist books about the seven Canary Islands Archie had left in a tidy pile on the desk—lie mangled on the floor. The toilet steadily overflows. Archie and Duggie-Sky step in with a splash, and glass from the bathroom mirror crunches beneath their shoes. The room that had once been illuminated with sapphire clouds from the whirling sphere is now dim and Archie struggles to see.

"Where is my bag, Duggie-Sky? Look for a shoulder bag! Oh bother, where did I leave it?" Archie gropes around in the ankle-deep water. Duggie-Sky too lifts waterlogged articles of clothing with his tiny hands and peers beneath the desk. "Ah-ha!" Archie cheers. He twists the fractured chair out of the corner and heaves his bag from the water. He again struggles with the zipper and curses under his breath.

"Where's Dad?" Duggie-Sky asks quietly.

Archie peers into the bag, which is half full of soupy black water and paper pulp. He tips it and drains as much as he can without dumping the notebooks, using his fingers as a strainer.

"Dad?"

Archie pries open one book but its pages wilt and tear. The old man groans. "They need to be dried! Maybe even one can be salvaged, but I'll never be able to read them like this. All I need is one page, just one clue of how to get Ella's cure and then get out of here. . ."

"I want my dad!" the boy cries.

"Yes, Duggie-Sky, you're right! We must be off!"

chapter 16

The Lord and Maiden of Olearon are silent for a moment. "No," they disagree with Senior Karish in unison. "These humans are ours. You cannot have them," the Lord refuses.

The sand howls and sneers. "You cannot possibly care for all these humans, if indeed the Olearons struggle as you say. What will you feed them?" Senior Karish laughs. "Who knows how much they eat—or what!"

"They are our concern," the Maiden responds calmly.

"Fine, as you wish!" The golden shapes twirl and morph, taking on the silhouettes of thrashing four-legged creatures with long fangs that drip sand. Again, Senior Karish rises two feet above the rest. He pounces toward the Olearon barricade. The red beings ignite, their flames reaching twenty feet above them. "You are wasting precious time!" Senior Karish growls and leaps over their fire. The sand that falls from his feet melts into shards of glass within the heat of the flames. The Olearons break their line as they shimmy and shield themselves from the deadly raining slivers.

Senior Karish lands with a spray of yellow and pins a nearby woman. Tessa recognizes her from the Constellations Cruise Line staff. The woman looks to be twenty-five. She has no time to scream before the creature steals her voice in one bite of his broad jaw, tearing away her flesh. The *Odyssey* passengers shriek and cower, shoving and climbing over each other as they withdraw toward the water. The sand glistens with the woman's blood.

Turning back to the Lord and Maiden, Senior Karish snarls through crimson teeth, "Return, return to your glass houses! To your glass city! Send a company to deal with the Bangols. Another to harvest your fuel. Once we Millia sense a healing beneath our beach, then you may take your boat, and our alliance will thrive in peace—or, shall I continue here?" He snarls menacingly, though playfully.

The Lord and Maiden shift where they stand. "The people must be spared," the Lord huffs, though with failing resolve.

"Ahh!" screams an Olearon on the far end of the barricade as another sandy creature fans his claws through the warrior's chest.

The sharp sound of a crack, then a crash, turns every head in the direction of the Olearons' boat. A panel of glass, like the one Tessa broke along the bow, sends an eruption of twinkling, silvery fragments in every direction. Tessa gestures with a tip of her head to Ella, then drops her eyes to her daughter's protruding Bomber jacket pocket. Ella slips her good hand in and clutches the dagger from Olen. Ella bites her lip, but Tessa nods reassuringly.

"I don't need to say it, Lord, Maiden; we Millia can crush your boat in an instant. Our shore can gobble you up. The Olearons at your houses will never know why their rulers and warriors fail to return. But they will not be left to die in peace. Oh no, no, no! We will sweep inland and blast through them. They will weep that they do not die quickly enough!"

"You would break our pact and enter our land?"

"It would seem that you have already broken our pact, no?"

"Enough, Karish!" the Maiden demands. "Enough!"

"It is true, we cannot care for all these," the Lord of Olearon admits slowly. "We will do as you say—defeat the Bangols, collect our fuel. Return for our ship. But—"

"Ah, ah, ah!" warns Senior Karish.

"But you cannot have them all."

"Half," Senior Karish demands. "Half or nothing."

The Lord leans toward the Maiden and whispers, "We are defenders, not murderers—but Karish is right. We cannot feed the humans and let our own perish. We can still do right by saving the few we can."

The Maiden turns to gaze at the frightened *Odyssey* passengers with her unchanging, charcoal-black eyes. She raises a red hand to touch where Tessa guesses her heart must be, in a similar place to humans. The Maiden bows her head in a silent gesture before facing Senior Karish. She nods slowly.

"We give no further concessions," the Lord of Olearon breathes, his flames roaring around him.

Senior Karish changes with a flash back into the form of a man and claps greedily. "Of course not, we wouldn't think to ask anything more, anything more, of our great friends, the Olearons! We Millia are very happy to continue this wonderful alliance that has kept our races in peace these many sunsets." He turns to the snarling gold beasts and gestures with his sandy spray. "Divide the captives!" To the Olearons, Senior Karish says, "Kindly step aside, friends." The pleadings of the humans grow, but none of the two races—Millia or Olearon—pay heed.

The Olearons begin the long trudge to the forest and allow the sneering Millia to approach the begging, weeping humans. The Millia force a line amid the group and one shouts, "You fifty, over there!" pointing to the Olearons who watch without emotion as they retreat. Those passengers, realizing they have been saved, bolt inland on the wavering sand. Azkar looks back toward Tessa and Ella and, seeing they have been spared, continues his march. Captain Nate and his cruise director, Valarie, along with the opera singer, Lady Sophia, are also driven forward, to the forest.

"No! Wait! Please let me go!" a man yells. Tessa recognizes him from the ship; another passenger. He rushes and shoves people aside to join the saved and begins to run. A wall of sand erupts in front of him. The man hits it hard and flips onto his back. His skin has been shaved from his face by the quickly rising fragments of broken shell. He lies thrashing, hands bloodied, before he is buried beneath the sharp sand and is silenced.

Tessa clutches Ella as they run toward the Olearons. Ella's eyes search the passengers. She signs *Grandpa*—her outstretched fingers and palm, bouncing away from her forehead—but Tessa does not see. She too frets about her father-in-law. Tessa yells over her shoulder, "Archie? Ar-chie?"

"Tessa!" Archie yells from behind the slithering wall of sand. He is holding a little boy in his arms and has his bag slung over his shoulder. Archie raises a hand, though not in a wave for help, but in a gesture of goodbye. Tessa clenches her teeth, regretting every harsh word she had ever spoken to the man. She reads his lips: "Go! Go!" he repeats.

"GOOD," Archie says to himself as he watches Tessa hasten her pace, towing Ella along, not letting her daughter fall behind. Archie holds Duggie-Sky close to his chest. The boy whimpers. They had not found his father among the living, though those that cower around them will not live much longer. "Snuggle in

close, Duggie-Sky. You don't deserve this, little fella— but I do."
Archie tucks Duggie-Sky inside his jacket. "No need to watch.
Close your eyes," he says, rubbing the boy's back.

The sandy figures—their forms flickering from two-headed
serpents to monstrous winged bulls to human shapes to malicious
bulging shafts—begin to slowly close in on the passengers—
taunting them—and roaring with laughter at the deafening
screams.

chapter 17

Tessa does not break her pace when she reaches the joyous humans spared by the Millia. Still suspicious of the Olearon warriors, the people trail a few paces behind their fiery protectors who lead them toward the forest. Tessa shoves her way through the *Odyssey* passengers approaching the red bodies. The Captain calls to her but Tessa only waves to him to wait, and continues. Valarie has her arms wrapped around Nate's waist, though the captain lumbers forward without embracing the woman at his side. Searching the Olearon's stoic faces, Tessa sees the scar. "Azkar! Azkar!" she cries.

Azkar drops from the line. "You call for me?" he asks with bent head, his chin tucked, his eyes narrowed.

"You looked at my father-in-law like you knew him," Tessa says. "Archibald Wellsley. His white hair, his jaw . . . remember? Please—he's not here! He's with the other group, by the ship. Please, Azkar—please save Archie!"

As Tessa speaks, another Olearon warrior approaches from the line. He is as tall as the rest, but his flaming hair is shorter and his gait not as graceful. "What is it?" he says. "What's wrong?"

"The Lord warned you about revealing too soon, Ardenal," Azkar huffs. "I'm sure he will speak with you about stepping out of our barricade to protect the humans."

"What is wrong, Azkar! Tell me now!" the other warrior barks back, ignoring the reprimand.

"Look, Ardenal!" Azkar points to Tessa and Ella. The warrior sees the women and reaches out his hands in their direction. Azkar steps between them and shoves the warrior's arms away. "No time! The third human, the one the Maiden saw in the sky, Archibald Wellsley—he is with the others to be sacrificed to the Millia."

Ardenal's black eyes widen. "I thought you were on guard! I never should have listened. I never should have let them out of my sight! Guard these two now, Azkar—or I'll beat you to embers!" Ardenal looks back at Tessa and Ella one last time before he sprints away, his long legs stretching the fabric of his warrior's jumpsuit as he runs. Sand sprays up from the toes of his boots and his fire flares wildly from his neck.

"Ardenal?" Tessa wonders at the name, but she is herded onward.

"Let's move," Azkar barks at Tessa and Ella. "We need to cover much ground this day." Tessa protests but Azkar again shoves her forward with his broad hand.

WHEN finally, Ardenal reaches Senior Karish, the Olearon is breathing heavily. "What now?" sneers the leader of the Millia. "Is our deal off? Have you come to die?"

"There is one in this group that I must have," Ardenal wheezes. "We have given many concessions. Now I ask for one from you."

"I bore of this," Senior Karish says dismissively. "Take the one—and only one—and remove your stinking Olearon feet from our beach, or it will bring me much pleasure to remove you myself!"

"Thank you, Senior Karish."

"See? None can say that I'm anything but merciful. Merciful. You'd better hurry; your kin already cross through the trees."

Ardenal turns to see the last of the passengers slip into the forest at the start of a path that leads to the foot of the tall mountain. He pivots back to the group of weeping cruise passengers who scream at the taunting Millia and cower on their knees in the sand. He winds through them and they cling to his blue jumpsuit, staining him with their blood. Ardenal pulls humans off of him as they cling to their last hope for safety, whispering, "I'm sorry. I'm so sorry." Then he spots him: Archie, slouched on the perimeter.

"Come with me," Ardenal orders, grabbing the old man by the arm. "You can trust me. My name is Ardenal. I will explain later, but for now, hurry!"

"Careful now!" Archie yelps. He opens his jacket just enough so that Ardenal can see the little boy cradled there. The child's head and torso are concealed, but for his scrawny legs that dangle in the open at Archie's waist.

"We can't!"

Archie plants his feet. "I'm not going without him." Duggie-Sky peeks at the Olearon while clinging to Archie. "I can't bare for the child to die alone."

Ardenal clenches his fists and stands as stone for a moment before relenting. "Fine! Stay in front of me. Wrap your legs around him," Ardenal orders to the boy as he tears Archie's bag from his shoulder and flings it over his own. "Faster!" He implores Archie as they weave through the desperate crowd.

"You have the one you require?" a mound of sand asks as it shoots up an inch in front of Ardenal's face. The Olearon wipes his hand through the sand as if parting a waterfall and continues to march for the trees.

"Yes, I have the one," he answers over his shoulder.

"Leave. Leave. Leave," moan the Millia.

"Take me with you!" the people scream to Ardenal, but he does not regard them. Archie watches his feet as they plow through the sand, avoiding the eyes of the pleading humans. They beg and barter for their lives. The angry few throw their belongings at Ardenal and Archie, calling them cowards. Duggie-Sky ducks his head below Archie's collarbone, his body trembling from forehead to foot.

The wails of the passengers turn shrill behind them. Archie looks back as Ardenal grips his arm and hurries him forward. The Millia have surrendered their forms and are no longer jeering. They rise on a wind of their own conjuring. Sand, shell, and powder lacerate the air and slices through the people one by one, shredding them to pieces of exposed flesh and bone, sending sprays of hot blood back onto the white ship. Ardenal grabs Archie and helps him run.

Instantly, the beach is eerily silent. Not one person is left standing. The shore is blanketed in crimson, which leaches into the sea in graceful curls. Then, a slurping, sucking sound replaces the hushed stillness.

Tears fall from Archie's eyes as he pauses to stare at the massacre. With each shallow breath, his shoulders and head jut up and down. His tongue grows dry from panting. His forehead is pinched with the deepest of creases and Archie's mind spins dizzily in his head. More tears. His body spasms, his muscles contracting, flaring, throbbing erratically. Archie sets Duggie-Sky down to stand on his own two tiny feet, as he steadies himself with arms outstretched at his sides.

Archie—overcome by the carnage of death, and the guilt that his actions sealed the tragic outcome for so many innocent lives—moans finally, "What . . . what's that sucking noise?"

"It's the Millia. They are drinking the blood."

*a*rdenal releases Archie's arm once they cross into the forest and put distance between them and the beach. Duggie-Sky slips off Archie's hip once more, from beneath the flap of his coat, and crouches on a dry rock to watch Ardenal with both curiosity and guarded apprehension. Archie stumbles and topples over. He kneels on the muddy path freshly pressed with footprints. His forearms and fingers tremble from carrying Duggie-Sky. He presses them against the ground, using his weight to calm himself as he rocks from knees to palms. His breaths wheeze painfully.

"Are you injured?" Ardenal asks.

"Fine, fine," Archie murmurs. "Thank you for saving me—" is all he can make out. The throbbing at the back of Archie's head surges toward the front of his skull. He sits back on his heels and jams his fists into his eye sockets to counteract the pain, but it is no use. It blackens his vision and he feels himself falling.

The second before Archie collapses, he winces as Ardenal cauterize the flesh wound and he hears the Olearon say, "You need rest. The others are not far, and they will move slowly." The burning pain subsides and Archie feels Ardenal's warm hands lay his limp head on his coat in the crook of a tree root. Ardenal continues, "Rest now, Dad . . ."

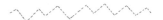

ARCHIE startles awake and sits up. "Dad?" he says aloud, confused, but he is alone. "Dad . . . I must've misheard." Archie
shivers, and realizes that the sun is gradually setting and the
land cooling. The trees paint crooked shadows across the forest.
A creature watches Archie from a high branch. Archie compares
the size of it to a small terroir. It has the body of a lizard,
though the head and hard wing-covers of a flying beetle. The
creature clicks and shrieks through a black pincher. Archie
blinks hard at the sight of it. The bizarre lizard-beetle stares
back at Archie with the compound eyes of a fly, divided into
hundreds of diamond-shape receptors, each receiving its own
set of visual stimuli. The creature's color shifts like the rainbows
of a gasoline slick. It clicks again defiantly and slithers around a
broad tree trunk of bluish, reflective bark, slipping out of sight.

"What have you gotten yourself into now, Archibald?" he
asks himself. "This place will be the death of you."

Archie rolls to his knees, looking around. He is alone and
there is no path, not even a clear direction he can recall of the
journey from the beach. The thought of the golden shore makes
Archie shudder and he pulls his coat on and zips it to his chin.

"You have been tricked again!" Archie stands and looks
around. "Why am I so stupid? Of course, he ran off! Of course,
he is not my son." Archie stumbles on a rock, which he picks up
and hurls into the misty dusk. "Arden is dead, you old fool," he
rebukes himself angrily.

A haunting caw echoes overhead. The white hairs on Archie's
arms bristle. Critters in the trees scurry into hiding with the
swoosh of shifting leaves and scratching feet against the bark of
the looming trees. Archie peers upward but sees only the forest
canopy and rays of dull light. Suddenly, he hears the patter of

tiny beating wings and notices a group of delicate emerald-colored birds twisting and spinning through the slow musky breeze. The caw so obviously did not originate from these merry creatures. The birds play together happily and fly to Archie, pausing, their wings still clapping the air, while they peer at him through thick eyelashes.

"Hello, little ones," Archie laughs. The birds look at him as if understanding. Their flapping wings spin fading threads of lemony-colored wind that curls around them. Their eyes are human-like, Archie reflects as he beholds the creatures closer than any other wild animal he has seen outside of captivity.

The birds chirp in answer to his greeting, serenading him, the melody like a lullaby. Very slowly, Archie extends his arm, then his fingers toward the whirl of green. In a chaotic flutter of wings and chirps and bumping bodies, the whole bevy charge him, and soon find a spot to perch on Archie's fingers, out-stretched arm, and shoulders. Of the twenty or more birds, Archie guestimates, five balance on the top of his head. He can sense their smooth feet shuffle about, though their toes do not scratch his skin with any kind of nail. Instead, their touch is gentle and silky.

Afraid to make a sudden movement, Archie stands motionless, and says, "Well, what are we going to do now?" His amusement is soon silenced, however, when a second piercing caw rains out above him. The emerald birds flutter wildly once more and rush away, flying in every direction. The light is darkened for a moment as a huge black bird descends. It's broad wings swiftly stir the air as it hunts. With a slapping gesture of both feathered arms, it pierces ten green bodies through their hearts with claws that retract from their wingtips like curled daggers.

Archie back-steps quickly till his shoulders collide with a tree. He holds his breath. The black form flaps once, with powerful ease, and is gone. *Gone for now*, Archie worries, *though it may return*. The hunt leaves behind tiny drops of the green birds' blood on the forest floor.

A yellow light in the distance catches Archie's eyes, drawing his gaze away from the leafy branches above him. "Zeno?" Hope surges and Archie sprints away from his safe tree toward the glow, hopping over roots and ducking under branches. The light radiates from yellow to red and dances from tree to tree, darting this way and that, disappearing and then reappearing around the waists of the peculiar trees. As Archie draws closer he whispers again into the night, "Zeno?"

The response is the hoot of a child's laughter. Archie pauses. "Duggie-Sky?"

"It's me!" The boy's voice bounces back into Archie's ears like his own echo.

Out from behind a thicket bounds Ardenal with Duggie-Sky in his arms. "The boy was hungry and you were sleeping so deeply."

"Wake me next time, all right? This place is unnerving."

"We need to go, Dad. The others may be half a day ahead now. I need to see my girls. There is so much I want to tell them. Eat as we travel." Ardenal tosses Archie a green fruit that, when he bites into it, is smooth like a banana but with crunchy seeds.

"Why do you call me Dad?" Archie asks cautiously, his mouth full of fruit. His skin tingles with hyper-awareness. He does not dare disagree outright with the red being, not wishing to offend the Olearon and cause trouble for himself and Duggie-Sky. "You must be mistaken, my son died two years ago."

"That's not the truth."

"Who are you, really?"

"It's me, Arden, Dad, but on Jarr-Wya they call me Ardenal.

They're funny like that. They like to bestow complicated names—I'm constantly corrected."

"And if I was to believe you, how did you become like this? Do all people eventually turn red in this world?"

"No, not everyone. Jarr-Wya is magical, Dad. There is so much I need to tell you, but right now we must save our breath till we make up ground."

"Won't you burn him?" Archie asks as Ardenal changes the position with which he carries Duggie-Sky.

"I'm thinking coolness into my hands and arms and core, drawing my heat up into my neck at the base of my skull. I must control my emotions, not grow angry or suspicious. When the effort of this focus becomes too great, I'll give you the boy, Dad. To be safe, let's wrap your jacket around him for an extra layer."

Archie reluctantly agrees to jog, struggling to maintain Ardenal's pace, as they find the trail of the Olearons and *Odyssey* passengers. They share the work of carrying Duggie-Sky, passing the four-year-old back and forth, giving the other's arms a chance to rest as they travel the jagged path. The moonlight reflecting on the bark twirls like pond ripples, an inch here and an inch there. The whole forest hums a melancholy vibration, like the sound of fingers and a thumb slowly rubbing together beside the ear.

"How is Ella, Dad? Tell me about her," Ardenal asks, but stops when Archie bristles at the question. "You don't believe it's me, do you?"

"I don't know what to believe," Archie replies. "Can you blame me?"

Ardenal nods. "I understand. Let's lay it all out there. My name is Arden Eugene Wellsley. I guess I have you to thank for that horrible middle name." Ardenal chuckles. "I love history.

I'm a professor, or, I was a professor. Egypt was my fascination. I grew up in Seattle. Played basketball as a kid. I am a diehard Sonics fan. Dark brown hair. Blue eyes. I married my college sweetheart, Tessa. We have a beautiful daughter together . . ." Ardenal's voice trails off. They walk for a few moments in silence.

"I don't understand it, but I *feel* it," Archie whispers to himself. It is Ardenal's voice and the way he speaks, more than anything he had said, that makes Archie's arms goose-bump. "I know you," Archie says firmly, finally, breaking the quiet lull that had both man and Olearon lost in thought. "You are my Arden."

"Dad—" Ardenal begins.

"This is strange for me, all right?" interrupts Archie. "You looking like this. I didn't expect it, although I haven't the foggiest of what I did in fact expect to find here. My gut tells me that it's you, Arden. Maybe it's dementia, like Tessa says, or the strange air in this world, but I do believe . . ." Archie stops trekking and hugs Ardenal, Duggie-Sky cradled between them.

The human and Olearon embrace until Archie's skin tingles with heat and he must pull away. Duggie-Sky, who had fallen asleep, wakes and stretches. Archie welcomes the boy's arms around his neck as he snuggles onto the dirty shoulder of Archie's shirt. The clicking of the lizard-beetle begins again, echoing off in the distance. It screeches violently. Then clicks. The pattern repeats. Ardenal scowls in the direction of the creature, which he informs Archie are called *carakwa*. The clicking of the carakwa unnerves Archie and he shakes his head as if the sound originated between his ears. He refocuses on what the Olearon—Arden—had said.

Archie brushes dampness away from the wrinkles around his eyes. "Arden, I thought I'd lost you forever—" Archie begins, "but here you are. When the Bangol told me you were dead, I believed him. Still, I couldn't let you go."

"Zeno . . ." Ardenal pauses. "I should start at the beginning—although, since you are here, I presume you already know about my research."

"What bit of it I understand," Archie admits.

"I came upon a piece of information in my historical studies that spoke of another world, a place that sailors had heard rumors of for decades, a place they'd written stories about, stories that were dismissed as myths. Legends of a place among the seven Canary Islands. It all started there.

"I continued to uncover more accounts of this other world—this island—Jarr-Wya. Not all the sources were reputable, mind you. I visited every post-secondary library in the city, not to mention hole-in-the-wall antiquity collectors, new age shops, and even spiritual mediums, but every little detail I learned became a puzzle piece in my understanding of what I needed to do."

Archie stubs his foot against a mangled blue root but Ardenal catches him, and Duggie-Sky, as he stumbles. The boy climbs across into Ardenal arms, slipping Archie's jacket between them, and his eyelids flutter before closing once more. "I have no idea what day it is; the poor kid's exhausted!" By habit, Archie slides up his unfitted wristwatch to check the time. "Strange," he says. "It appears to have stopped."

"Time moves differently here, Dad. Even I have not found logic in its rhythm."

"Hmm, well!" Archie shrugs and replaces his sleeve. "Go on, Arden," Archie continues, panting. "Tell me more about your research."

"I guess it all began when I was studying the Fifth Egyptian Dynasty and came across a terrifying, though beautiful goddess named Isis—in no way connected with the terrorist group. The name of the goddess first appeared in the temple of King Nius- erre and was also connected to the high priest—Pepi-Ankh—at the beginning of the Sixth Dynasty. The goddess wears a collar- piece decorated with jewels and a fitted sheath gown. Isis is often pictured with broad, fanning wings growing out from beneath her arms and spreading wide beyond her fingertips. The historical records show Isis with a variety of headdresses; one popular depiction portrays her crown rising upward with cow horns that support a blood red solar disc.

"The goddess's name means 'throne.' Some artistic depic- tions show her headdress marked with the hieroglyphic sign for *throne*, with her body literally bent at the hips and knees, as if she was the seat of royalty herself. In this way, she was inti- mately connected to the pharaoh, who was painted or sculpted as a child who sits on her lap. In these representations, Isis nurses the tiny pharaoh.

"Isis was worshiped as a mother-fertility figure, and as a goddess of magic and medicine. Her deity spread beyond An- cient Egypt and she is still worshiped by modern pagans. As the stories go, her father, Geb, was the god of earth, and her mother, Nut, the god of sky. The Isis mythology tells of the murder of her brother, Osiris, by another ancient figure named Set, who washed Osiris' body down the river Nile in a coffin."

Archie shudders. "That's morbid," he says.

"It gets better, Dad: During the Greco-Roman period, peo- ple attributed the flooding of the Nile to the tears Isis shed for Osiris. Isis collected Osiris's body parts from the river and brought him back to life. Then she married him. The story goes that, together, they had four sons."

Archie interrupts Ardenal. "Why are you telling me all this?"

"That's just it, Dad. In the suspicious records I uncovered, who I thought was Isis was depicted very differently."

"How so?"

"In those documents—almost as if they had been hidden in university libraries—I saw images of a beautiful Amazon woman, like Isis, but she wore no crown or jeweled collar. She had on a piece of gold armor that looped from her neck to one shoulder. In the back of it she stored for easy access two long blades with curled gold handles decorated with metal leaves. Her wings grew out of her back instead of beneath her arms, like Isis. Her gown flowed softly, and was braided in parts, not fitted or stiff. This mystical figure also had antlers growing from her forehead—elongated with golden thread—and a serpentine tail. In all my investigations, the Egyptian goddess never had a tail of any kind, despite the ancient artists occasionally portraying the character of Isis with the attributes of their sacred animals, like cows, scorpions and snakes.

"Plus, this mysterious winged woman, and her race, do not give birth to children. And especially not to boys. They were all women and their little ones grew from the earth, plant-like, from within a flower, not from the womb."

"So . . ." Archie begins. "What does this all mean?"

"As I began to dig deeper and deeper, I realized that I was not looking at images or reading passages about Isis at all, as I had first suspected. The woman-creature is called a Steffanus. They transport to our world from Jarr using a magical portal jumper—"

"The Tillastrion."

"Yes. Apparently, from what I read, the Steffanus have been sneaking between worlds for hundreds if not thousands of years. I never discovered why. What I did learn, however, is that the Steffanus' magic—Naiu—has many peculiar qualities, one of which is the ability to heal. I read about a glowing orb that must be cracked open. The records were vague, but the writing spoke cryptically of a child and a 'life-wilting illness;' those exact words."

"Ella . . ."

Ardenal nods. "That was my first thought too, Dad. I felt Jarr calling to me through the aged, brittle pages I studied. Isn't that weird? I felt that I was meant to read them. To see what I saw in the illustrations. I'm just so terribly forgetful that I had to take notes. At the same time, I didn't want Tessa to find my notebooks; I didn't want her to think I was crazy.

"The home of the Steffanus—Jarr—is this place. The island of Jarr-Wya. Learning about Jarr-Wya became an obsession for me. Before work, after work. The weekends. You know, Dad. I wasn't around much. I met many bizarre individuals in my research, people gone mad in search of the next Steffanus to appear on earth. All this mystery proved a great distraction from what was going on with Ella. I could never do enough for her, I could never take her pain away, and Tessa—" Ardenal sighs deeply. "She probably hates me." He looks over at Archie, who grimaces and shrugs.

"I'm not going to lie," Archie says. "You disappeared. You walked out on her, on all of us."

Ardenal continues down the trail for a moment without responding. "I did think about it—but that's not what this was about."

"Tessa is a different woman now. Harder, judgmental."

Ardenal runs his free hand through his flaming hair. He cradles the sleeping boy in the other, the heat of his body keeping the child warm as the deep night settles a damp cold over them. "Every day since I arrived in Jarr-Wya, I have worried about Tessa and Ella—"

"Ella hasn't been able to speak in months . . ." Archie's voice trails off. "I know I'm a fool most days, but—but—there always seems to be the tiniest molecule of hope left in me. And I believe it. Being here—the existence of this place—it's proof, to me at least, that you didn't walk out because life got too hard."

"Right, there's a reason. Why I left in the first place . . ."

"Ella's cure," Archie finishes Ardenal's thought.

"Now I see that she needs it more than ever. But I couldn't return without it—especially looking like this."

"What happened to you?"

"It's a long story, Dad. A frightening story. Let's save it for another day."

Archie tries not to study the Olearon's features but he fails, and Ardenal clears his throat. Archie looks away. "So, no luck on Ella's cure I suppose?" the old man asks.

Ardenal's flame blazes, though he says nothing at first. "My last night at home, when I rushed to pack for this trip—to find that yellow-eyed creature, Zeno—I must have misplaced the one notebook I intended to bring, the one with the map and instructions. When I got here I tore my gear apart, but the book wasn't in it. I've searched every day since then for the object I must break open, but I can't remember the details—they've grown murky in my mind—and I've forgotten the way . . ."

"Look here, son," orders Archie. "I don't know why you look the way you do—there is a lot I don't know—but I do believe you—I believe it all." Archie yanks his bag from Ardenal's shoulder, careful not to wake Duggie-Sky. "These belong to you."

"What? Oh! My notebooks!" Ardenal passes Duggie-Sky to Archie before digging through the bag. "The cover is green, the texture of leather . . . Ah-ha! I can't believe this! Dad, this is exactly what I was missing . . . but—wait—what happened?"

"Is it still wet?"

"Soaking! All the writing . . . it's . . . it's illegible." Ardenal shows Archie the pages, no longer white but stained like an ocean of blue ink. He backs away from Archie and Duggie-Sky, his flame sizzling. The book in his hands explodes with blue fire and crumbles into flakes of ash that are sent upward in the Olearon's blaze. He whirls and marches off into the woods.

"Arden—"

Ardenal doesn't slow. His flame is tall, doubling his height, and it withers the low-hanging leaves along his path.

"Arden—" Archie jogs as fast as he can while holding Duggie-Sky.

Before he can say more, Ardenal halts. "Look!" The Olearon's face is transformed by a smile. "Do you see that light?"

"Yes, faintly."

"We are not far behind now! Maybe only a hundred yards." As the words leave Ardenal's mouth, the clicking—which had been constant, yet distant—rings in their ears, followed by a piercing shriek. The lizard-beetle—which Archie notices too late—leaps from the tree cover above them and lands on Duggie-Sky, clawing and slicing at his face with its pinchers and forearms.

chapter 19

*A*rdenal struggles to control his flame while wrestling the carakwa that digs its half-moon claws into Duggie-Sky. "Dad, you've got to knock it down! I don't want to burn you two!" As Archie thrashes, Ardenal thrusts his thick fists beneath the creature's clicking pincer and thousand eyes. It loses its grip, and Ardenal smashes it to the forest floor, immediately sending unforgiving flames upon its shell. Ardenal rips the charred shell from the creature's back, but it swings around and lunges at him, cutting his shin with the serrated edge of its forelegs. Stumbling back, Ardenal falls, his head striking hard against a protruding tree root with a sickening *swack*.

Archie, seeing his son lying unmoving, hollers until his throat is raw, calling to the glow in the trees. When Archie thinks the flicker will slip into blackness for good, it stops. Then grows brighter.

Tall, flaming Olearon warriors appear in the forest as if their bodies are a part of it. They run for Archie, Ardenal, and Duggie-Sky. Their shapes are silhouettes against their cracking, bursting fire, their faces as black as their eyes. Little flames hiss at their feet, sucking oxygen from the air until they've exhausted it and they die in a tiny puff of smoke.

Azkar is first to arrive, his long strides covering two yards at a time, though he is quickly followed by the Lord and Maiden, and the rest of the Olearon warriors. The humans trail behind. Azkar spots the wounded creature limping toward the base of a tree. "What vengeance do you have here, carakwa? No? No answer?" Azkar's red fingers quickly find the curve of the creature's neck. He burns through the flesh and tears its scaly head from its squirming, oozing body.

The carakwa's blood is thick and iridescent. The decapitated body sends a polychromatic spray of the shiny blood over the faces of the Lord and Maiden, over the already stained clothing of the cruise passengers who arrive at that very moment, and over Archie too, as he cradles a whimpering Duggie-Sky dripping with crimson.

"Filthy carakwas!" Azkar spits. He wipes his hands on the front of his jumpsuit as he turns to Ardenal.

"Awake Ardenal! Awake!" Azkar cups Ardenal's neck and its tiny flame in his broad hands. Ardenal's eyes open slowly, like the dusk that night giving way to the weight of its shadows. Slowly, Ardenal's black eyes appear. He sits up and inhales deeply, steadying himself.

"The carakwa is a vessel for evil, Archibald," Azkar says when he sees that Ardenal can stand to his feet. "They have no soul, and thus there is a vacancy in them that is easily filled. One cannot be sure if the carakwa that attacked the child—attacked you, Archibald—was possessed by another, but since you are a foreigner to Jarr-Wya, we can presume this onslaught was coincidence only."

"Archie!" Tessa yells. "Archie!" She rushes to the old man and—once she sees that he is uninjured—Tessa cups Archie's face. "I am so relieved that you're okay. Oh—" Tessa says, startled as she observes the boy who shifts into the light. Tessa lifts Duggie-Sky onto her lap, tearing another piece from her skirt and applying pressure to the boy's wounds. "Oh, little one; you will need stitches, or you'll scar badly, but you'll be okay. We'll take care of you. Shhh, honey, shhh . . ."

"A nurse is never off duty," Archie chuckles awkwardly, feeling childish to have said something so common in his normal life, which sounds so very out of place on the island of Jarr-Wya.

"Where's Ell?" Archie asks, scanning the passengers that look to him at the center of the commotion.

"Oh, Archie . . ."

At the sound of Tessa's voice, Ardenal bolts through the crowd of passengers that surround Tessa, Duggie-Sky, Archie, and Azkar. He frantically searches the faces of the humans, who freeze with dread. "Where is she?" Ardenal hollers. "Ella?"

Tessa turns to glare at Ardenal. "What do you want with her?" she snarls, her countenance morphing from forlorn to ferocious.

Ardenal's voice rises. "Why are there so few?"

The Maiden answers. "The Bangols were waiting for us—"

"The Bangols?" Ardenal notices the dampness of blood on the *Odyssey* passengers' clothing and the burnt stain of it on the warriors' skin. "When? How many died?"

"An hour past," Azkar replies. "They were hiding in the tree canopy, and jumped on our heads. They killed some of ours, some of them," he gestures to the humans, "and took others prisoner. Only half remain."

"Tessa," Ardenal pleads. "Not Ella? Tell me not Ella?"

Her red-rimmed eyes reveal the helplessness beneath her anger. "They took her," she chokes out, "and these beasts would not let me follow."

"They went to the air, Ardenal. We could not pursue on foot," growls Azkar.

Archie scrunches his brow. "Bangols can fly?"

"They had clay baskets in the trees tied to huge patterned balloons, weighed down with stones," Tessa answers, her voice thin. "They dragged people away, threw their bodies in sacks so we couldn't tell them apart. They didn't care who they hurt. They climbed up, flung the people in. Cut the ropes. Their stones rained down on us. Ella . . . I knew she was in the basket of one balloon because of her scream. All the balloons floated up, but still I could hear her . . . ."

"Tessa," Ardenal whispers, wrapping his long arms around her shivering body, Duggie-Sky also surrounded in the hug. Ardenal kisses Tessa's neck without regard for his appearance, lost in the heartbreak of the moment. "Tess, I'm so sorry."

"Ardenal, no—" Azkar begins.

"Get off me!" Tessa hisses. She fights free of his arms. "Don't touch me!"

"Back up now!" Captain Nate yells, stepping forward and shoving Ardenal hard.

Valarie leaps from the crowd of passengers. "Be careful, Nate!" she screams. The captain ignores her as he stares at Ardenal with unwavering resolve.

Archie steps between Ardenal and his daughter-in-law. "Tessa, it's okay, it's Ar—"

"Nothing is okay. Nothing!" Tessa shrieks.

"Come here, Tess," Captain Nate whispers protectively. Ardenal and Archie stare with bewilderment as the captain puts a muscular arm around Tessa's shoulders.

"Tessa—it's me, Arden—"

The Lord of Olearon steps forward. "Ardenal, we commanded your self-control. To wait until the human has calmed. Wait till we reach our city."

"I cannot wait. I listened before and now my daughter may never know me. Never know I love her, that I did all of this for her." Ardenal turns his black eyes to Tessa. "I need *you* to know . . . I never meant to leave you. Believe me. I love you, Tessa."

"We should be moving on, Ardenal," growls Azkar. "You endanger us all with this delay. Remember our agreement with the Millia?"

Tears swell in Tessa's eyes, though she scowls at Ardenal with a clenched jaw. "It doesn't make sense . . . how could you possibly be my good-for-nothing husband?"

"Tessa," Archie interrupts. "It's true—"

"People, please," the Maiden interjects. "Quiet! There may be another possessed carakwa nearby. They are easy hosts for the dead and much loss has bloodied this day. There will always be questions, but their answers are worth our patience"

Tessa ignores her. "If you really are my husband, why did you leave me—leave Ella? What kind of a man leaves his family like a coward?"

"He's not a man, Tessa," says Captain Nate.

Ardenal's flames burst into sweltering flowers around his head. He inhales, exhales. "Who is this, Tess?"

Tessa steps out of Nate's embrace, with Duggie-Sky still straddling her hip. "Don't you call me that. Who are *you?* Just a—a fiery freak! What's your angle anyway? What reason can you possibly have to pretend to be my husband?" Her hips sway as she rocks Duggie-Sky, covering his ears with her hand and shoulder. Tessa turns to Archie and grumbles, "How could you bring us here?" The tears in Tessa's eyes become a downpour on her cheeks and reflect the orange glow of the Olearons' flames.

The Lord of Olearon says coolly, "Ardenal. Human one. Please calm yourselves. The Bangols are not far off. They may hear your ravings and return. Come." He turns to the Olearons and cruise passengers. "Let us be off. We walk through the night guided by our light. We will reach our land in the dawn, then rest will greet us all. Sleep is the revealer of many truths. Let us be off."

"You are right, Lord . . . the Bangols," Ardenal whispers, mulling over that single remark, "they are not far!" He turns to bolt, but instead collides squarely with Azkar's chest—the taller, brawnier, and unyielding warrior—before Ardenal has taken even one step.

Azkar envelopes both he and Ardenal within his flame so they may whisper in private. "We are all weary. You as well—I can see it, Ardenal. Let us return home. Replenish. Then we will pursue. We will find your daughter. I promise you this. We will slaughter the Bangols. Have you ever known a time where you could not trust me?" As Ardenal nods in agreement, Azkar absorbs—as if inhaling—his fire back into the tamed flame at the crook of his neck.

"Thank you, Azkar. My daughter needs me."

Ardenal startles at Tessa, who had approached while he was unaware. "Ella needed her father when she was being bullied at school," she snaps. "She needed her father when she wanted to go to art camp in the summer, but I couldn't afford it on my own. She needed her father a year ago when she had her first boyfriend and he broke her heart. She needed her father six months ago when she lost her voice from a seizure! You—" she spits, "are not Ella's father."

"You may never forgive me—I will never forgive myself—but let me do what I can now, while I am able."

Tessa studies Ardenal. Her breathing is sharp and quick, until she takes one long suck in of air and her shoulders sag, relenting. "You are not my Arden—let's be clear on that one point—but, I will take whatever help I can get."

"Thank you, Tess. That's good enough for now." Turning to the Olearons, he continues, "We need to strategize as we walk.

Join me Azkar—and where is Olen?" Ardenal asks and calls, "Olen?"

"Olen perished defending these humans," the Lord answers, his words laced with disdain.

The Maiden of Olearon gestures to a stretcher made of fresh-cut wood, bound with curling vines, and mounded with boughs. "He must be lit and his spirit freed to the smoke," she says.

Ardenal rushes to the stretcher and pulls away the leaves to reveal the body. He beats his chest at the sight of Olen. Ardenal traces the broad nose and full lips of the Olearon with his fingertips. He touches his forehead to his friend's. "He's cold," Ardenal says as he straightens. He pulls the branches and foliage back over Olen's bloodied face and stands beside the stretcher, his shoulders slumped and his head bent.

"When I came here, to the world of Jarr, it was Olen that found me," Ardenal tells Archie and Tessa. "I was lost in the blue woods, hurt and growing weaker—and was terrified of everything. Olen spoke with me, when he should have burnt me up upon sight. He brought me back to the glass city, where we are headed now. He and his brother, Eek, shared their room and blankets with me, and called for the healer. That first week, Eek and Olen fed me with their food portions when you, Lord, were uncertain of my trustworthiness—but Olen always believed. He taught me to hunt the cradle bird. He became a dear friend, as close to a brother as I have ever known as an only child. Olen searched for Ella's cure with me, by the sun and by the moon, putting himself in danger, repeatedly, when he had no need to. We shared many adventures. You, and all your siblings—" Ardenal gestures to Azkar— "have shown me incredible kindness. Olen was tender-hearted and brave. He must be honored," Ardenal finishes, imploring the Lord and Maiden.

The Olearons speak among themselves and agree that it is best to return Olen's body to their homeland, being within a reasonable distance from it, for a proper scorching ceremony. The Lord and Maiden of Olearon urge everyone forward. "Let us go now," orders the Lord. His warriors begin the trudge through the forest. The Maiden, dragging the stretcher as an act of tribute, falls in line. She does not struggle and the muscles in her arms are tight and defined.

"Dad," Duggie-Sky cries to himself from within Tessa's arms.

"Come to Grandpa Archie, little fella," says the old man.

"Keep the pressure there, on his forehead," instructs Tessa.

"Got it." Archie pauses. "It's him, Tess. It's Arden."

"I don't care who he is. All I care about is Ella—" her words hang, her sentence unfinished. When all have passed her by, she finishes in a whisper, "and if no one will help me now, I'll go after Ella myself."

chapter 20

Tessa—seeing an opportunity to slip away in secret as the remaining *Odyssey* passengers and Olearons pass through the trees toward the glass city—dashes as quietly as she can to her right into the trees, off course. She heads in the direction the Bangols' balloons had floated; a slight eastern trajectory compared to the route directed by the Olearons. Tessa hikes her skirt with one hand and deflects tree branches out of her face with the other. A piercing caw slices through the night overhead. Tessa ducks but continues to run.

There is no sound of thudding feet or cracking branches behind her. "This may work!" Tessa smiles. "I need to see for myself. Maybe I can do this on my own. If I can't catch up to the Bangols, I'll circle round, back to Archie and the Olearons. Then I'll join whatever plan they're concocting."

The gloom under the trees is as dark as midnight and Tessa tumbles over an unseen root. She pushes up onto her knees and cradles one hand that is deeply scratched and wet with blood. She does not cry in pain, though it would not have mattered how much noise she made, for in that instant there is a loud flap and stirring of air. Prolonged, curling claws encircle her left bicep and jolts her up, off the ground.

"Help" Tessa shrieks in terror of what unseen monster lifts her higher, and higher still. Before she can call out again, warm hands seize her ankles. She feels her shoulder slip out of its socket with the weight.

"Help me! Please! I'm so sorry—" Tessa stammers. The warm body climbs up her bare legs and disheveled dress. The other clawed foot of the black fowl reaches for Tessa and the Olearon, slicing the air, but the warm body stabs at it with a glass knife. They are dragged through the leaf canopy, which scrapes and slaps their bodies. Tessa winces in pain and clutches her arm above the shoulder. The Olearon reaches high and cuts straight through the bird's tarsus, an inch above its toes.

"No—" Tessa screams as she plummets—the claws still clutching tight—before she lands with a thud in Azkar's arms. His large palm covers her mouth, stifling her cry. Unable to breathe, Tessa bites his hand and immediately falls to the carpet of moss. She is again grabbed, but this time less gently. Azkar hoists Tessa into the air where she thrashes and kicks hard before her limbs are restrained. Tessa begins to weep.

"We will pry off the claws when we arrive at the glass city. The postmortem spasm of the foot will not release you on its own," Azkar declares as he tucks Tessa firmly under his arm.

"Let me go!"

"I no longer trust you to follow orders," he retorts, carrying her with ease as he follows after the withdrawing group that illuminate the blue trees in the distance. "The Bangols are evil but also curious. They will not kill your daughter. We have time to prepare. It is the only way we can defeat them; otherwise all is lost."

"Put her down!" orders Captain Nate when he bursts through a leafy plant, breathing hard after tracking Azkar and Ardenal into the woods, but Azkar only snarls at the tall man, who looks petite in comparison. Nate brushes his fingers against Tessa's as she is hauled past him. Tessa abruptly quiets her sobbing when

Ardenal drops to his feet from a tree branch he had caught on his fall. They lock eyes. He clasps his mangled forearm, which is bleeding with three parallel gashes. Tessa and Ardenal watch each other until Azkar carries her beyond view. Captain Nate follows the warrior and Tessa into the darkness.

Archie, with Duggie-Sky perched on his shoulders, appears at that moment, drenched with sweat. "Am I too late? I see Tess is all right, and you—" Archie wheezes.

"I'm fine." Ardenal cauterizes his wounds with a burst of flame. He wraps Duggie-Sky in Archie's coat and carries the boy. "No time to catch your breath, Dad," he says, before adding, "She didn't even say thank you." Ardenal huffs off.

For a moment Archie is left alone in the darkness. He sighs deeply. "All your plans have unraveled, Archibald," he scolds himself. "All I wanted was to slip into this world with none the wiser. Find Arden. Find Ella's cure . . . At least we are all in the same place again, though, in some ways, we are further apart than ever." Archie sprints to Ardenal's side, where they catch up and march with the Olearon rearguard. Ardenal's flame is a weak flicker.

"We'll make all this right," Archie whispers to Ardenal, who angrily stomps over the uneven terrain. Archie acknowledges to himself that death is a journey, which, he supposes, there is no Tillastrion to bridge the space between. Archie knows that Ella's tumor may divide them further—a greater distance than even worlds apart—but he grows in his resolve. "I don't know how, Arden, but we will make it right."

---

chapter 21

The Bangols remind me of a cross between the short boy in my math-nine class, a pudgy performance wrestler, and the lemur-like tarsiers I studied during science in the sixth grade. The tarsier looks like a small monkey, but that's not why they remind me of the Bangols. Their eyes are the same. They take up most of their face—with a two-inch diameter I estimate—are almost marble-round, and have the same small black pupils—like the dots of cats' eyes—at the center.

I think this is the longest I have been without my phone since I was eleven. So much for posting photos of the cruise on Instagram. I wonder if I would've gotten cell reception out here anyway. If I had, I bet anything I posted would've skyrocketed my followers.

When the Bangols first attacked us in the woods, Mom used my phone as a weapon. It was amazing seeing her like that, all superhero-like. I only wish she had used *her* phone instead of mine. I heard the screen crunch when she fell. I told her not to wear skirts so often, that you don't need them to be feminine— if you want to be ladylike, anyway.

"Agrahhhh." That sound scared the Bangol guarding me. Look at him back up. Yeah, keep walking! That was true terror in those big yellow eyes; I love it!

At home, everyone thinks I'm weird and stupid, just because

I can't talk. They treat me like I'm broken and need extra help. I was starting to believe it myself. Well, here in this weird world, I'm powerful. "Eerockwwwwa!" See? Watch that stone-head cower! The Bangols don't know me. I can feel the difference. It's like I'm taller. I'm braver. More myself, whoever that may be.

Finally. He's out of sight! It's unnerving to be guarded, to be held hostage. I've got to figure out how to get my foot out of this chain. Maybe I can lift the boulder it's attached to. Darn. It's way too heavy.

Let's examine my body. My shoulders are definitely bruised. That sucks. And my arm . . . Well, at least I still have the sling Mom made. Yep, knees are still there, but totally scratched up. Getting dragged hurt more than I imagined it would. They slipped a sack over my head, wrenched it down over my shoulders too, and kept on going till my feet were also gobbled up in the course-textured weave. The claustrophobia of being unable to stretch to my full length nearly drove me insane. I screamed and screamed, even when they chucked me into something. Even when I hit my head hard, which rattled me, and I felt like I was floating. Everything looks different this morning.

The Bangols are loud. I wonder what they're yammering about over there. I wish I could see what they're up to. Stupid little hill in the way. I'm still in the blue forest, I know that, but I can hear waves off in the distance if I hold my breath. The air is salty too, but I think we're curling away from the Millia's beach. My inner GPS is pretty smart. We definitely headed east after the attack, from what I remember of Olen's navigational directions.

What is that? This uncanny tingle. Hmm. Is someone watching me? Let me slip my hand onto the dagger from Olen. Oh no! It cut through the pocket of my bomber jacket! And it's broken. Shoot, well at least I can still use one of the larger shards as a weapon. Be careful not to cut myself. There's the rustling again! It's coming from that huge root. How long have those eyes been peeping on me? The rocks growing out of their heads are small. They must be young. The big fat Bangols, the ones in charge, are totally top heavy. These two are looking around with funny expressions on their faces. I know that look! It's the same face I make when I'm checking to be sure Mom isn't nearby when I want to read my favorite fanfiction horror stories on the internet.

They are still staring at me, but closer now. I feel like I'm at a wildlife park, and I'm the animal. I'm orbiting this heavy stone like a planet. What do we have here? This is the perfect stick to draw with in the dirt. I might as well put on a show while I've got a captive audience, except I'm the captive.

I draw an old woman. I keep an eye on the two Bangols. They of course don't recognize my grandma, Suzie, and her long blond bangs—like mine—that used to hang in her eyes. Red scarf. Grandma always wore a red scarf, but the color is impossible to draw in the dirt. I don't know why I feel calmer when I doodle her. There. Round cheeks, check. Bright smile, check. She's dead. Like I probably will be soon.

Now they're staring at me again. Is that their thing? Don't the Bangols know it's rude to gawk at someone?

Their language sounds horrible.

"Hello?" the girl one says.

Now that's English. I nod in response, and they understand. They're figuring it out. The boy one is kind of cute—for an alien, I mean. Oh, I have an idea! There. Fourteen lines. Point at the lines. Point at me. Point at the lines. Point at me. I think they're getting it!

"She's telling us her age," the boy one says. "See, she's nodding at us. I'm Luggie. I'm sixteen."

Wow, he's older than me, if their years are the same as human years. But I'm bigger. He has a nice smile, even if his skin is dead-looking. All right, girl, how old are you?

"And I'm seventeen."

"Her name's Nanjee. She's my sister."

I lift my stick again. There. That's my name. Look at the ground!

"E-l-l-a." The girl's got it.

Awkward silence . . . Another thing that's the same between Earth and this place. What else can I draw? What about Nanjee? She's pretty in her own way. Let's find a new area of dirt. There. Okay, let me draw her eyes. Does she have eyelashes? Nope. Okay, her blackish-gray lips. Her stones are like a tiara. Luggie and Nanjee wear the same sort of outfit as the rest of the Bangols; a sleeveless top and trousers made of fur, animal hide, and warm brown and grey fabrics. It's a wonder they're not constantly sweating in this jungle-heat. Okay, there. Not my best drawing . . . Yes! She likes it!

"Are you hungry, Ella?" Nanjee asks.

Yes! I'm a bobble-head. I hope they are getting exactly how starving I am. Let me sign eat and drink. Huh. Apparently, those sign language gestures are universal. Even in weird places like this.

Oh, okay—bye! I wonder what they are going to bring me . . .

Uh-oh, the guard is coming back. So much for my secret meal. Hold up—Nanjee just ran out of the trees. What is she saying to the guard? She's pointing and he's going with her. That fat, reeking Bangol . . .

"Ella?"

It's Luggie!

"Ella, here."

This bag is heavy! What does he want me to eat, rocks?

Luggie is gone. The guard is nowhere to be seen, either. Oh well . . . let's open this thing up. Now, what kind of food is this wrapped in paper? It's kind of like bread . . . Yum. Spongy and sugary. And a jug. Blech. Sour wine, I think. Yuck. What is this stuff? It's black!

And what's this? A book? But it's empty. Nice smooth, creamy pages—and it's sewn together so beautifully. What do they want me to do with a blank book? Oh wait, what's that at the bottom of the bag? A pen? No. A paintbrush! Well, where is the paint, Luggie? Oh. The black drink. Yes!

Look at those lovely lines! Oh, Luggie!

The guard is coming now. Shoot! Eat up the bread stuff. I need water, bad! Come on, swallow Ella! Throw the bag behind that tree. Now where do I put the sketchbook? Ah, bras were invented for this very reason, right? Ouch.

Oh, hello there, ugly guard. What? Nah, I've only been sulking here while you were gone. Don't smile, Ella. He'll notice your black teeth. What have you got there? Oh no . . . I know that big, scratchy sack. No, please—NO!

"Agreakhhh!" No—

Ella

The land of the Olearons sits at the far end of a vast emerald pasture. A delicate breeze animates the landscape from the smallest leaf to the smoke that rises from the glass city built on the side of a low hill. On its west, the ocean glints and sways.

The bases of the Olearon's homes, shops, warrior training paddocks, and edifices for large gatherings are cut into the earth with every conceivable shape; octagons, quadrants, diamonds, concave squares, cyclic rectangles, isosceles trapeziums, obtuse and scalene triangles, and many other shapes for which humans have no words to describe. Some structures are built of millions of triangles. They are fused together perfectly at every edge, forming hexagons, which connect and amalgamate into shimmering glass domes that remind Tessa of bath bubbles in the sunshine. The domes are anchored precariously to the sides of other erect, laser-cut structures.

The building-faces glow azure as they reflect the heavy sky, the thick topiary landscape bulking up against the pastureland, and the sea on the western edge. The sea, which Ardenal informs Tessa and Archie, has a reputation for being nefarious waters. It is called the Sea of Selfdom, of personalities, Ardenal tells them; because those that venture toward its horizon never return, except in hollow whispers on frigid winds.

Ardenal clears his throat, and adds, "The Olearons do not sail beyond sight of Jarr-Wya. The island must always be within their vision."

"So, what's out there?" Archie gulps.

"Are there other islands—or a mainland?" Tessa probes deeper. She holds her limp arm, still encircled by the black bird's sharp claws.

Ardenal clenches his fists. He drops his voice to a murmur. "Either they don't know or they're not telling me," he answers.

"What are those things?" Valarie asks Azkar, gesturing to the pasture where lofty crystal pillars stand proudly, radiating a rainbow of light in every direction.

"As our flames flow like lava through our veins, so too do our crystaliths imbue the heat of our sun into the roots of our crop," explains Azkar.

"Crystaliths?" Archie repeats, shuffling nearer.

"The triangular prims, there," Ardenal points and Azkar continues, "They penetrate our field in segmented spirals. Channeling the sun. Once inside the crystals, the sunbeams are reduced into Naiu."

"Magic!" Duggie-Sky calls, then ducks behind Archie's legs where he trots to keep pace, now rested and hyper.

"This place sounds like the gardener's dream!" Donna says, beaming. Donna and her husband, Harry, are *Odyssey* passengers; senior citizens with matching short white fringe-cuts and tropical cruise wear. They look to be a similar age to Archie, who deliberately avoids the couple. Donna reminds Archie of Suzie, and her presence accentuates the pang of his wife's absence. Donna's cheery disposition, her care of the wounded, her flushed vein-lined cheeks. Archie shifts he and Duggie-Sky to the far side of Azkar, away from Donna.

Azkar scowls and continues. "The harvest was brought in

only five sunsets past. It is pathetic what miniscule supply the land did offer since its poisoning. Six-thousand sunsets ago, the Naiu would trickle into our crop from the crystaliths. The herbaceous plant life would radiate, like the blue forest. Olearons were braver then. Now," Azkar spits, "the crystaliths are merely ornamental, haunting statues, a testament to our failing birthplace."

"Mind your words, warrior," the Lord commands. Azkar frowns deeply, then tips his head in apology, and is silent. "As the twenty-ninth Lord of Olearon—"

The Maiden interrupts her partner by laying a hand on the Lord's back and gazing at him wordlessly, intentionally.

"Ah, yes. Excuse my forgetfulness. As the thirtieth Lord of Olearon, it is my duty to honor our homeland, protect it, and renew it to its original glory."

"You will, Lord," says Azkar gruffly. "With my dying breath, you will."

"Yes, Lord," the Maiden echoes. "Together, we will." The Lord takes the Maiden's hand as they lead the disheveled humans toward the glass city.

The Olearons and *Odyssey* passengers shuffle through the knee-deep grass of the pasture toward the glimmering structures. Every step is exhausting, yet they are charged with anticipation. The passengers, though still leery of their flaming hosts, chat with the lanky beings at their sides, telling them of the human Earth, of their homes on every distant part of it, and of boat rides for pleasure rather than purpose. They ask about the blue bark of the trees, which the Olearons explain is imbued with the stardust of ten thousand sunsets; and of the world beyond the island of Jarr-Wya, though it seems none are certain of those details.

"There is much now in the shadows of mystery," a female Olearon says to Valarie. The Olearon's shape is rounder in places than that of the males of her race; her nose is also shorter and her eyes wider. "We have endeavored to stay firmly within the realm of peace, though Jarr-Wya has changed. I fear that if we do not change with it, the Star will be the ruin of us all."

"I get that, I guess," says Valarie. "I often have to change, depending on who I'm with or what I'm doing. It doesn't seem fair, though, does it?"

"For us, the Olearons, it is less a matter of fairness than of survival."

"I see, I see. What was your name again? Junin?"

"Yes, you are right human. Valarie."

"Junin, from my experience, it's all about survival. Everything. As a kid, I worked hard at school, glued my eyes to the textbooks so I didn't have to see Alissa Smith and her popular gang gawking at me, poking fun at my hair or acne or weight. As an adult, I've learned how to play the game—"

"The game?" Junin asks.

"Yes, it's all a game. Dress this way. Act that way. Weigh this much. Work harder than everyone else. Figure out what people want from you. Who they want you to be. It's a game, see? And I've learned to survive by beating them at their own game. Love them less so it hurts me less. Unfortunately, I'm not great at that part. Anyway, maybe things aren't so different here. Maybe you need to beat the Star at its own game." Valarie pants as she struggles to match Junin's pace.

"I will tell you truly, Valarie, I must reflect on your words. Your perception on life is unfamiliar to me."

"Speaking of unfamiliar!" exclaims Valarie, her frown transformed to childlike wonder. "What amazing butterflies!" A violet insect flutters near her shoulder, then lifts off higher, circling, swooning. "Each wing is the size of my whole hand," Valarie observes.

"Wait, human. The awakins will change soon. They possess two pairs of wings—two sets of forewings and two sets of hindwings—so they have no need to land for rest. One pair for day, the other for night. That is why we call them awakins. They are always awake." Thousands of the purple insects hover in playful ribbons above the tall grasses. Their wings flap sleepily, rhythmically stirring the humid, misty dawn air.

"See," Junin nearly sings, "the awakins are crossing over!"

Valarie—and all the humans who overhear Junin's merry words—stare at the butterflies as they unfurl the full breadth of their brilliant yellow-orange wings. The sunny pair are twice the size of the violet wings, which the awakins curl and stow away like sheaths around their thoraxes and abdomens. Their bodies now shine deep purple.

Junin begins again. "There is a flower here, on Jarr-Wya, that disorients and makes delusional those that touch it. Or those—in the case of the awakins—who land on it. Many of their fragile winged family—after contact with the plant—were devoured by the black flyers—the hunting birds that were fierce even before they mutated following the Star's arrival—as the awakins were a lazily caught meal. You can see by the size of the claws around Tessa's arm what damage the black flyers could inflict on these delicate creatures. As beautiful as they are, the awakins are careful now who and what they trust. For that reason, many sunsets ago, they chose to expend their Naiu on wings. For self-preservation."

Valarie nods. "They're beating the flowers and the black flyers at their own game."

"True, though they now live a lonely existence and are often captured by those who would wish to exploit the strength of their wings, however tenuous they may appear."

"The Bangols balloons. That's what keeps them afloat."

"Yes, Valarie," Junin sighs. "There is much sadness in the awakins. Which is why it is remarkable if one would ever choose to land. I hope, however, to see it one day, with my own eyes, before my end."

Walking a short distance ahead of Valarie and Junin, Tessa leans over and whispers to Nate, "Do you think we can trust them?" Azkar had allowed her to walk after she complained that his grasp burned her skin through her dress. She had acquiesced to the Olearons' demand to return to their city, but secretly despises them for restraining her. Tessa's hair twists into subtle curls in the damp heat and falls in her eyes.

Nate leans in, brushing aside a golden strand, and whispers close to her ear, "I'm hesitant. They seem friendly—for now. Stay close to me. I'll do whatever I can to keep you safe. I'm a man of my word—and I plan on keeping my promise of visiting you in Seattle." Tessa smiles. Nate rests his hand on her back as they approach the glass city. "I am sorry that we are here, for the loss of lives," Nate continues, "but I am thankful for one thing."

"What's that?"

"You beside me, that we have this time; as corny as that may sound. It doesn't make sense—we've known each other a short time—but everything has changed for me, Tessa. And I'm not only talking about our surroundings. It's uncanny. It feels warm, like a spot of sunshine on a windowsill, even with these devils walking in our shadows." Nate tips his chin in the direction of Azkar and Ardenal.

Tessa notices Valarie glaring at her as the cruise director listens to Junin. Tessa bites her lip and looks up at Nate. He grins at her and she feels the warm spot too. His eyes are a deep chestnut color, like the bark of the Seattle redwood forest. *Kind eyes*, Tessa thinks. Nate's skin is tanned and firm, his arms muscular, strong, and tattooed with a ship of billowing sails and other nautical symbols. Tessa does not step away from Nate's touch, instead enjoying his warmth—different from that of the Olearons—that sets off firecrackers through her skin. Her cheeks grow rosy, but not from the sun or the heat radiating from the ruddy-colored warriors. She looks away.

Valarie kicks up dirt as she and Junin pass Tessa and Nate. "Sorry," Valarie mutters.

Without warning, Junin darts ahead of the group, running gracefully, her fire hair streaking out behind her and sparking, the tiny bursts of flame sizzling as they are consumed in the damp air. "My love!" the female Olearon calls, beaming.

Tessa looks in the direction the red woman sprints. Several short Olearons stand at the edge of the field bordering the city. One of them turns at Junin's call, exclaims in a little girl's voice, and runs toward the adult that Tessa guesses is the child's mother.

Tessa cannot look away from their embrace. She leans in to Nate, so close she can smell him, and whispers, "I know this is a lot to ask—and she's not even your child—but, will you stay by my side and help me find Ella?"

"I will," Nate responds without hesitating.

Tessa removes Nate's hand from her back and squeezes it once before letting go. She increases her pace to a jog and approaches the Lord of Olearon. "We are here now, at your city, and I cannot wait any longer. My daughter is unwell. I have to find her now, before—I can't even say it."

"Our duty is to purge Jarr-Wya of the Bangols. Heal the land. Then, we may save your child."

"I knew it! You lied to me!"

"Let's go, Tessa," Nate growls, catching up. He glares at the Lord of Olearon.

"Wait!" Ardenal also approaches swiftly, with Archie close behind, now carrying Duggie-Sky. "There are dangers here you know nothing of, Tess. Listen to the Lord. Give me a day to prepare and we will set out together."

Tessa shakes her head. "I can't—who knows what they will do to her, or where they will take her. I don't trust this place, and I obviously can't trust these people, whatever they are, whatever *you* are. Ella is sick. She's getting worse by the day. Whatever happens, I don't want her to die alone."

"You're a great mom, Tess. I admire how you love and care for Ella, and never give up—and I'm with you—" begins Ardenal, searching his mind for a solution. "Will you give me one hour? I'll gather what I can, as quickly as I can, and then we'll go? With your permission of course, Lord."

"Tessa, it's your decision," Nate cuts in. "But I will go with you right now if that's what you need. These fire-people are looking out for themselves. We—" he points to Tessa, then to his own chest, and gestures as well to the rest of the humans, "—we must take care of ourselves. We don't need these others, the Olearons. Maybe we shouldn't have come to their city in the first place. Who knows the real reason they saved us. I've done my fair share of navigating through unmapped waters. We'll eat what we scavenge. I've got a knife." Nate pulls a blade from his boot and flips it open by the handle so the razor-sharp edge flashes in the morning light. He conceals it again. "We'll sneak up on the Bangols. Rescue Ella. Make a plan for how to get home."

"Folly from the mouth of a fool," the Lord of Olearon sighs.

The warriors and humans stare at Tessa. She pauses and looks between Nate and the Olearon claiming to be her husband. Her mouth is chalky and her tongue sticks to her palate. *Who can I trust?* she asks herself, wringing her hands behind her back. Her shoulder screams out with a pain that cuts through her thoughts.

Archie's voice chimes in from amid the Olearons as he wedges his way through them to stand at Tessa's side. "Trust Arden," Archie whispers, as if reading her mind. "If anything, trust me, Tessa. I have stuck by you. The one thing I know with all my being is that this—" Archie points at Ardenal "—is my son."

"One hour—" Tessa begins, but she is cut off.

"Halt, you!" The Maiden of Olearon shouts. A boy with a wide-brimmed hat is slinking away from the group toward the forest on the far side of the pasture. "Human, there are many dangers. Return for safety!"

"I am no human!" the boy shrieks and turns, pulling the hat from his head.

Archie recognizes the voice immediately. "Zeno!"

"Zeno . . ." Ardenal's chin tips to his chest and he charges at the little creature, who is by now a fair distance away. "How dare you—how can you show your nasty face here?"

"Same as the rest of you. I am on a quest." Zeno looks proud and indignant, and not the least bit intimidated by Ardenal as he nears. The creature laughs. "Oh Arden—yes, I know it's you—have you forgotten? This is my world and my powers. Though I am rusty, the strength of Naiu remains in my blood." With these words, Zeno thrusts his hand down toward the pasture. A gush of air and a swoosh rumbles the ground, spitting up dirt. Ardenal halts abruptly on the edge of a deep-forming chasm.

"How did he do that?" Valarie asks the Maiden. The humans huddle behind the Olearons.

"The Bangols can control rock and clay," the Maiden answers. "It is a part of them, where they came from in the beginning. Like the coolness of stone, such is the heart of a Bangol."

Ardenal backtracks, then charges Zeno again. His long legs stretch across the gaping abyss as he jumps. Zeno lunges down once more. The exposed soil and clay ripple and rise like waves, propelling the creature skyward. He crashes against Ardenal in midair with such force that the breath is smashed out of their lungs. Zeno lands with a thud on the far side of the chasm. Ardenal, knocked off his trajectory, fails to reach the edge with his foot. His right hand snags an exposed root and, for a moment, he swings wildly. The root shifts, strained by his weight. Dirt sifts down, peppering Ardenal's face. He spits and gags.

"Zeno's running!" Archie yells.

Ardenal hoists himself out of the chasm in one swift contraction of his biceps, his toes finding a solid edge of earth to leap from. His breathing is loud.

"Should we help him?" Tessa asks whomever is near.

The Maiden slowly shakes her head. "He will catch the Bangol. This is what he has been trained to do, primed for since he swore his loyalty to the Lord, and discovered his true identity on Jarr-Wya, as an Olearon."

Ardenal races after Zeno, who is running for the edge of forest, far to the east of the glass city. As Ardenal runs, his dreadlocks grow into a ball of flames that he separates from himself and juggles like a child's ball before launching it at Zeno, who is nearing the rocky ground dividing the pastureland and the starlight-blue forest. The flames erupt at Zeno's feet, instantly igniting the grass and sending up a wall of fire ten feet tall beneath Zeno's nose. The Bangol leaps back, patting at his smoldering camo-jacket. He turns to face Ardenal and sends another swoosh of white wind down, blowing skyward the clay beneath the pasture, rocketing clods of dirt and chunks of grass into Ardenal's path.

The Olearon plucks an airborne blade of grass and hurls it

toward Zeno. The blade ignites and glows reddish-yellow, like a slice of fire. It elongates, arrow-like, before curling around Zeno's ankles.

"Curse you! It burns! Get it off! Please!" Zeno screams as he drops to the ground, thrashing. Tessa can feel the pasture quiver where she stands, watching helplessly.

"Enough of this!" demands the Lord. The clay calms as Zeno surrenders. "Ardenal, bring the Bangol."

Ardenal sends another burning blade to coil together Zeno's wrists. The creature flinches but no longer wails. "Is that really necessary, Arden, my old friend?" Zeno hisses.

Lifting Zeno by the foot, Ardenal carries him dangling upside down over the shoulder of his blue jumpsuit, filthy with earth. Once they reach the rim of the chasm, the Lord asks, "If we loosen the cords that bind, will you talk with us a moment, Bangol?"

Zeno nods. "Please."

The Lord of Olearon points one long finger and the fire cords relax and crumble to ash.

Azkar is at the edge of the crevasse. He launches himself across. Without Zeno to deflect him, Azkar lands solidly on the other side. Ardenal takes one of Zeno's arms, Azkar the other, and they leap back over the gap.

"Do not drag me farther into your wretched lands," Zeno jeers. "This is as far as I go."

"So, should we kill you here?" Ardenal growls through clenched teeth.

"Arden, don't," Archie says. "He helped me transport to Jarr-Wya, to reunite us. We owe him something for that."

Ardenal pivots to face Archie. "We owe him nothing. Do not be deceived. This Bangol is trouble. When I traveled to the Canary Islands, to Lanzarote, it was almost as if Zeno was waiting for me. I had been warned about the Bangols and I soon learned why. He was banished by his own. He used you, Dad, to get here. He was not helping you, only helping himself."

"Zeno knows about Ella's cure," Archie protests. "He explained to me that I needed something of Ell's, like her hat—which I forgot on the cruise ship of course—to help me channel my focus, to help me transport her remedy."

Azkar sneers, "What does a Bangol know of aiding others?"

"The Scar is right, Archibald, though I'm loath to admit it." Archie's face slowly twists with anger at Zeno's confession. "Your granddaughter's headpiece, it gave you hope, it fueled your desire, which is what I required to operate the Tillastrion, to bring me home."

Zeno struggles against Ardenal and Azkar but they tighten their grip. "So what if I was helping myself? What do you care? You're here. I'm here. No harm done. It's true—my mission is to murder the king of the Bangols, Tuggeron. There you have it! He killed my father, the last ruler, and exiled me in your pitiful world." Zeno points at the passengers. "Such a sad place, with no magic."

"Your presence will start a war between factions of the Bangols—and anyone else in their path. That puts my people in danger," the Lord retorts, his dreadlocks swaying as he shakes his head.

"You could kill me," the Bangol hisses, his eyes pulsating with renewed malice. "But I may be of use to you."

"And what might that use be?"

"I heard your vow to Senior Karish, to the Millia sands. If you wish to purge the evil from beneath Jarr-Wya, I know the one who poisons it."

"Who?" the Lord steps forward.

"The same one who killed my family—Tuggeron." Zeno spits. "I know his weakness. Let me help you find him and rip the stones from his skull."

"What is your price?" asks Azkar stiffly.

"My life. Freedom. Peace for us all."

"The Bangols have never been peace-loving," Ardenal growls. "How will you atone for the innocent lives stolen by the Millia? You do not deserve to be a king."

Zeno turns to Archie. "As I told Archibald, his love for the child was too great. The *Odyssey*'s presence in Jarr-Wya is his doing, not mine."

"Let us gather what supplies and stores of food we can spare. And glass weapons for the humans," the Lord commands. "We make two parties. One that travels east tracking the balloons, to save the child, with Ardenal and these two." He points at Tessa and Archie. "The other will consist of Olearon warriors who will march north with Zeno to defeat Tuggeron's army at their primary fortress."

"Unfortunately, I cannot agree," Zeno counters. "You see, I have no guarantee that your warriors will not slaughter me on the spot once we venture beyond your lands. I do, however, believe that this human would not harm me." Zeno stares at Archie with wide, willing eyes. "For my compliance, Archibald Wellsley must be at my side at all times." Zeno leans in and whispers to Archie, "I will help you build a Tillastrion to get back to your world, once you've helped me. Agreed?"

"I need your word, Zeno," Archie whispers. Zeno nods. Turning to the Lord, he says, "I agree to the Bangol's wish. I will be by his side on the quest."

"Dad!" Ardenal fumes.

Tessa paces on the spot.

"It is done, Arden," Zeno declares.

"One company it must be." The Lord nods. "You have much to accomplish. One hour may be too long. You must leave and move with haste!"

chapter 23

"*N*o!" Duggie-Sky screams. "Don't leave me! Daddy!" he wails. "I want my Dad!" the boy pleads to Archie and then calls out into the expanse of pastureland beside them, his eyes budding with tears. No one answers his call. The billowing smoke from Olen's scorching ceremony—teal and smelling of sunrise dew on newborn roses—floats from the glass city to dissipate over the field.

"I'm sorry, little fella, but Grandpa Archie has to go soon. I am glad, however, to hear you using your words. I knew you had more to say than you were letting on." Duggie-Sky frowns. "So now that we're talking, man to man, why don't you tell me your real name?"

The boy crosses his arms. "I like Duggie-Sky," he pouts.

"All right, Duggie-Sky it is," says Archie as he ruffles the child's curly ebony hair, which instantly reminds him of Ella. Archie and the boy sit on one of the glass steps of the staircase leading into the Olearons' citadel. They sit in silence for a time, watching the preparations below. "These nice people—er, fire-folks—will take good care of you. I promise," Archie says finally.

"No, they won't," Duggie-Sky whines. His bottom lip juts out.

Archie pulls Duggie-Sky into an affectionate squeeze. He remembers the cries of the passengers before the Millia cut through them, and shudders. Duggie-Sky wipes tears from his face on Archie's shoulder.

"You don't have to leave him," says the Maiden from below as she walks by with a satchel of food.

Archie frowns at her. "Don't say that! You'll get the kid's hopes up." Duggie-Sky stops whimpering. "I wouldn't put his life in danger again. He needs a safe place. It's nice here, peaceful." Archie takes in his surroundings. Olearon children skip along the grassy paths that weave around their angular glass homes and peculiarly shaped gathering places. There is a sleepy quality to the city, as if Archie finds himself in the fog between dreams.

"The boy needs a family." The Maiden smiles faintly. "It is as dangerous here as anywhere in our world. The safest place is in the arms of love."

Archie nods at the Maiden. "I just now came from the infirmary," she adds. "The healer has successfully reinserted Tessa's shoulder, and the warrior Eek has pried her arm free of the black flyer's claws."

"Thank you."

The Maiden nods and walks on. *Did I see a hint of emotion on her face?* Archie wonders. Her eyes had been somber—but also merry. *How could those two emotions exist simultaneously? Has the ability to express feeling been there all along, or am I seeing these creatures anew? Maybe there is hope for Arden!*

Archie considers Duggie-Sky's eager face. "Do you want to stay with Grandpa Archie?" Duggie-Sky laughs and jumps to his feet. His round cheeks spread wide in a toothy grin. "You're a handsome young fella, aren't ya! Well, if you're going to come along, you've got to walk more. Deal?"

"Deal!"

Duggie-Sky, satisfied that he will not be left behind, points to a rowdy group of warriors preparing satchels of supplies—and goofing off. Archie recognizes them. Azkar and his brothers, Nameris, and Kameelo—as they had been introduced to Archie—argue over the contents of their bags and elbow each other out of the way. Their youngest brother, Eek, joins them from assisting Tessa.

"Just like human brothers," Archie chuckles. "Pestering each other to no end—but don't mess with one, or look out! The others will getcha."

"I'm gonna go see," says Duggie-Sky, his tears forgotten. "Please, Grandpa Archie, please!"

"Eh, I don't know . . . I guess it can't hurt—only be careful, all right?" says Archie as he watches the little boy smile mischievously and dart away. "I'm too old to do this little-kid-thing again," Archie says as he leans back on the steps of the citadel. The sun is warm on his trousers and flushes his face. Archie nearly falls asleep, but rouses himself and stands. Stretches. "That's funny. My arthritis, it's nearly gone. May well be completely gone," he marvels aloud. He signs the alphabet he learned in Ella's American Sign Language class, finger lettering fast and fluidly, which had always defeated him. Now, his fingers form each letter so quickly that his mind is only saying one while his gestures are onto the next.

Archie turns away from the pastureland—where Olearons and humans prepare—and looks up to the tall glass doors of the citadel. They are clear and reflect the sunlight into his eyes. He squints and takes a deep breath, then sprints up the twenty-five steps to the flat landing at the top, where the angled triangular dome begins.

"Huh," he says and shakes his head. "Barely winded."

Archie peers over his shoulder to ensure none on the ground below are watching him before he steps beyond sight of the preparations and approaches the citadel's doors. He leans in so close that his nose presses up against the warm glass. A foreboding, tingling sensation seizes the muscles in his shoulders and neck, but he shrugs it off, his curiosity greater than his fear. "I've made it this far . . . For Arden's sake, let's see how peace-loving these Olearons really are," he whispers. The building appears deserted inside. Archie knocks quietly, then loudly. When no one arrives, he pulls open one of the two angular doors wide enough for his body to slip through, then shuts it quietly.

Colorful glass sculptures—of a ship on a tumultuous sea and an ever burning, never consuming flame, which rises from an island as tall as it is wide—greet Archie on either side of the doorway. Sharp tables are piled with maps and large, dusty, ornately-decorated books. The citadel reminds Archie of a greenhouse. The heat is thick and Archie takes off his jacket and folds it over his arm.

A clear fountain on his right pours water in a delicate swoosh without ever splashing. Above him, the friendly green birds—and the butterflies Archie saw in the pastureland, the awakins—flutter around the upper curve of the dome and land on the branches of the blue trees that the structure is built around. Archie uses the collar of his shirt to wipe his damp forehead.

As he continues to venture into the citadel, Archie approaches rows of glass columns that reach from the smooth floor up to various heights as the dome arches and peaks at the center. Archie listens, past the chirping birds and flowing water. When he hears nothing—no sound of steps or doors or voices—he walks in farther. Archie notices that the first column on his left, within its inner space, is veiled in a misty, shifting cloud-cover. As he nears, the clouds in the columns part and the hot face of an unfamiliar Lord becomes defined—Archie recognizes the being's status by the Olearon's lavishly braided and bejeweled dreadlocks. When the face in the column suddenly speaks, Archie nearly loses control of his bladder. He stumbles backward and drops his jacket. He is about to run, certain now that the tingle of danger he felt on the other side of the doors was an omen—but the voice does not address him directly. It repeats itself, saying:

"I, the first Lord of Olearon, honor those who follow after me."

The image in the column dissipates and zooms out to a wide view of the field Archie recognizes, which the *Odyssey* passengers had crossed not an hour past, but beside it there is no glass city. In the vacant, lightly treed space, the first Lord stands, fans his flame across a smoothed section of sand, then erects the inaugural cut of glass, then another, building the wall of the original structure of the city.

When Archie approaches the next column, it says, "I, the second Lord of Olearon, honor those who follow after me." The shape of this Lord's face is rounder than the first, but his braids and jewels are similar. When the second cloudy column shifts, Archie sees the glass city—which has grown from one to many triangular homes—with the second Lord leading a group of Olearons to cull the minuscule harvest pilled at the edge of the pastureland.

The third column also speaks into the silent citadel with the words Archie by now expects. "I, the third Lord of Olearon, honor those who follow after me." This time, the ghostly historical records portray a greater harvest and more sophisticated tools. Archie turns and counts the columns. There are twenty-nine in total. Each one—but for the 29th, still under construction it appears—shows the evolution of the Olearon race; their architecture, language, seafaring vessels, other inventions, apprenticeships of the young, and nuptial rituals.

The Maidens—partners of each Lord—are pictured in the columns, standing a step behind their counterparts, working the fields, creeping through mountain tunnels and twisted patches of forest—places the Lords were too large to squeeze through—and caring for the wounded, along with the Lord's attendants. In the moving three-dimensional histories contained within the columns, it is only the Lord—Archie notices—who sits on the glass throne at the center of the citadel, the same throne which Archie has now reached.

Archie tiptoes closer to the throne, constantly looking over his shoulder toward the citadel's doors. "Oh gee, I'm sure I shouldn't do this, but . . ." Archie climbs the ten steps and hoists himself up onto the narrow seat. He rests his back against the throne, which is broad at its base and spikes upward sharply into a needle-fine point eight-feet above where Archie rests. "Ah! So, this is what it feels like to be a king!" He laughs and smiles, pretending to speak to his invisible subjects below. He acts as though he has been given dire news. Archie scrunches his already wrinkled brow, leans one elbow onto a smooth armrest and strokes his stubbled chin with his fingers. "That is a difficult matter," Archie muses, mimicking the formal speech of the Olearons. He is about to continue with the charade when he notices something.

A thin slit has been cut into the armrest—not visible to any unless sitting on the throne—and inside it is a hide-sewn envelope which has been delicately concealed. Archie uses his dirt-lined fingernails to prod the envelope out of the slit. It is square and pristine, not a mark or scuff across its tan face. As Archie studies it, he notices a tiny flap along one seam, which he unfolds and slips his hand inside.

"You are over your head, old chap," Archie says to himself as he tenderly slides out the contents of the envelope. "Never lived a day anywhere other than Seattle, same job since I was sixteen, married my childhood playmate, and now—look at yourself—sitting on the Olearon throne! And what do we have here?"

Archie holds a square cut of glass, decorated around its border in rubies, sapphires, emeralds, amethysts, garnets, and diamonds. "Wow," is all Archie can whisper. The rainbow of sparkling colors reflects the dome's glow and dance upon his face. Archie runs his fingers across the jewels, then over the surface of the glass. "Oh no!" Archie breathes. The fragment begins to cloud, like the columns had done, but this time with dark, billowing storm clouds. Archie rests the glass on his knees and covers it with his hands, afraid an old Lord—or a living Olearon—will look through it, like a window, to discover him in a place he should not be and touching an object so obviously meant to remain a secret. The glass morphs further into darkness where—from between his fingers—Archie sees white letters slowly appear into clarity.

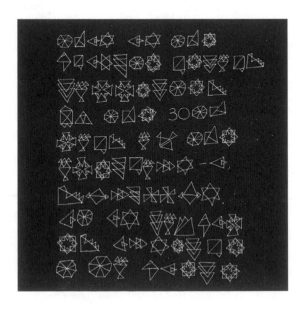

"It's the language of the Olearons! I'm sure of it," says Archie, looking up to a section of columns where he had watched generations of old Lords begin to form their symbols on the earth, gradually converting their sounds to forms and long strokes. Their language, like their buildings, are graphic, patterned, angular, and sharp. "I wish I could read this . . ."

Archie taps the face of the glass, and mumbles to himself, "This one looks a tad bit familiar." The second Archie's finger touches the glass so purposefully, the white language melts into black. "Oh, great. You've done it again, Archibald. You've gone and broke the thing!"

Ever so slowly, white begins to appear once more, but this time the message is clear to Archie. He begins to read.

This is the private record collected by the 30th Lord of the Olearons —I, Dunakkus. It is compiled in secret to piece together disparate fragments of knowledge and events of Olearon history, searching for clues. All elders and public records from which this history is sourced have been successfully burnt. Soon, as to plan, none will remember.

Archie's breath clouds the glass he hadn't realized he'd raised close to his face. His mind reels with the significance of the object he holds in his trembling hands. Archie swiftly tucks the glass back into the envelope and as he is about to replace it in the armrest he pauses. "I wonder what the Lord wants everyone to forget. Maybe Arden is in danger . . ."

Archie retreats from the throne, tucks the envelope beneath his coat, and runs from the interior of the citadel. "I need to read more," he tells himself, panting now though not from exertion. His mind races and he bursts through the doors of the citadel.

Bang! Archie crashes into the Maiden.

"Oh! I'm terribly sorry," he exhales, dripping with perspiration.

"What do you have to be sorry for, Archibald?" she answers. Archie suspects the Olearon knows what he has been doing, that maybe she had indeed seen him through the glass object. As he searches for an excuse, and is about to retrieve the envelope, the Maiden continues. "You obviously recognize that you should not have passed through these doors."

"Yes—" Archie says as he sighs.

"Did you go more than a step within?"

"No more than a step, Maiden."

"We must speak truth to each other, Archibald. Our mission ahead is perilous. Only honestly will unify us against our enemies."

"Right, totally agree, Maiden. Well, thanks for the reminder. And good talking with you. I'm off to find my bag. I must have left it with the other preparations."

Archie can feel the Maiden's black eyes watch him as he skips down the glass steps. When he reaches the ground, he turns back, smiles, and waives up at her. The Maiden turns and enters the citadel.

"If what I saw in the glass columns is correct," Archie whispers through his teeth, "I'll be all right. My guess is that the Lord is the only one allowed up those steps to the throne. I bet the Maiden has no clue this glass exists, and she'll soon forget I ventured inside the citadel. When the Lord eventually discovers his magical tablet is missing, I won't be his first suspect. Hopefully—by that point—my girls, Arden, and I will be a world away."

chapter 24

"**W**e gather for a noble purpose and shall part for the greater good," begins the Lord of Olearon. "These are not simple times, but love is simple, love is good. We fight for that which we hold dear: our land, our lives. Remember: above all, that is our quest. Let there be peace amongst us and peace we shall find." The Lord bows to each warrior and human before ascending the steps to the citadel and pausing on the landing to watch the company depart.

Archie gulps and feigns his composure, wondering if his new possession will be discovered stolen from the throne sooner than he had hoped. He swallows down his fear and takes Duggie-Sky's hand as they turn from the glass city, walking near the front of the group.

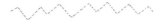

"DAD is loving this," Ardenal says to Tessa with a chuckle. She smiles, watching Archie's white head bob in front of them.

"It's amusing now, but what happens when the black flyers hunt us, or the trail grows treacherous?" Nate smacks Ardenal's shoulder. "I've trekked through harrowing conditions, but I'm sure nothing of our world will compare to this. One twisted ankle and we may have to carry him." Nate's eyes flash to Archie.

"My father will be just fine. Don't concern yourself." Ardenal's flames betray the emotion he otherwise succeeds in masking.

"Sorry, man, only trying to help." Nate turns to Tessa and adds, "I'll keep an eye on Archie."

Leaving Tessa alone with Nate, Valarie in tow, Ardenal accelerates to walk beside Azkar, who nudges Zeno along with a stick. "I hate that guy!" Tessa overhears Ardenal growl, his flames coiling around him.

Azkar continues to prod Zeno. "Ignore him. If your woman is smart, she will know before long what kinds of men she has to choose from."

Tessa scowls. "He acts like I'm the one who left Arden," she huffs under her breath.

Valarie too must overhear the Olearons' conversation. She brushes up against Nate and says, knowing full well that Tessa is within earshot, "What do they know? I've experienced what kind of a man you are." She softly tickles his neck with her fingers.

"Please, Valarie," Nate whispers. "We've been over this." He arches his body away from her touch. Valarie masks her feelings behind a smug grin.

The sole company, tasked with finding Ella and defeating the Bangols, consists of eight humans: Archie, Duggie-Sky, Tessa, Captain Nate, Valarie, Donna and Harry, and the Spanish opera singer. Lady Sophia refused to remain at the Olearon city while also demanding, "Keep those yellow eyes away from me!" after claiming Zeno terrorized her on the ship. The *Odyssey* passengers are surrounded by Ardenal, the Maiden, and Azkar, with his three brothers—Kameelo, Nameris, and Eek—plus the stubborn Bangol, who ridicules Lady Sophia's story and trails Archie, darting a step beyond Azkar's reach.

The *Odyssey*'s passengers had been invited to join the company at will, the Maiden declaring, "Bravery can be found in the largest and the smallest alike; in man, woman, and creature; in fire, stone, water, and sun. We all must choose our moment to be brave."

The group of fifteen cross the pasture and descend into the forest on the east side, heading in the direction Zeno had fled. Beneath the dense forest canopy, light is scattered and the shadows yearning, though it is just past midday. Tessa shivers. Nate puts an arm around her and she smiles half-heartedly. *If only Ardenal and Valarie weren't here,* Tessa muses. *Then I could enjoy this.* Valarie's expression is miserable, and Tessa notices the cruise director watching her with hawk-like focus.

"La, la, la, la," Lady Sophia sings. "Listen to those songbirds! You know, this is not an altogether horrible place. The air is sweet-smelling and the humidity—well, I'm sweating like a waterfall. I'm sure I've dropped two dress sizes already." She pats her portly midsection. "If I didn't know any better, I'd set up a fancy resort here and make a killing."

"We do not joke about killing." The Maiden lays a hand on Lady Sophia's forearm. "Yes, we must take lives, or let them be taken, but it is a rite of honor and reverence."

"Are you telling me you Ole . . . uh, fire-people destroyed my ship and let hundreds of faultless people die, yet don't want *me* joking about killing?"

"We must protect our waters." The Maiden removes her hand. "If we do not uphold our part of the peace agreement with the Millia, their sands will blow into our lands and suck the lives out of our children, our elders. We did not know, at first, that you were innocent passengers of the Tillastrion."

"I am a passenger of Constellations Cruise Line and hope to one day get back there, or to some other ship, I suppose," Lady Sophia replies. "My fans need me."

"Your fans?" the Maiden asks.

"Yes, I am something of a singing celebrity in my world."

"I had never heard of her," Tessa whispers to Captain Nate, who chuckles and meets her eyes. Overshadowing the giddy-school-girl feeling, Tessa is hit with a pang of worry. She can sense the heat from the fire-incarnation of Arden and the hate of jealous Valarie watching her. Tessa shrugs Nate's arm off her shoulders. "Thanks," she says quickly. "All warm now!"

"One of my favorite roles to play is Lucia di Lammermoor of Donizetti's score," Lady Sophia continues. "I have been singing since I was in diapers, with the most beautiful cries my mama has ever heard—and that's saying something. I have seven brothers and sisters. I would sing as I skipped to school. Sing when heartbroken—or in love. But my parents did not understand. They shunned me for learning Russian, French, and German, filling my mind and my mouth with their long histories of opera; songs that would rattle your bones and send shivers across your skin. When I told them my hero was Anna Renzi, the seventeenth century opera performer, they looked at me with blank eyes.

"My family believe in hard work," Lady Sophia continues, her voice so commanding that it dominates the entire company and all fall quiet to listen. "Hard work, dirty hands, change in the pockets, and full stomachs. That's what matters. To them, singing is a frivolous, girlish pastime."

"You have a lovely voice!" Valarie beams. "It reminds me of—"

"Why thank you. I quite agree!" laughs the singer heartily, cutting off Valarie mid-sentence. Lady Sophia's voice is rhythmic and passionate, especially when she dithers on about herself. "I would sneak out of school for auditions, but my town—Grado, not far from Oviedo, in the northwest of Spain—was not a hub. The roles were pathetic and people's appreciation for finer music unimaginable, simply unimaginable! Old women would shush me as I walked circles around Plaza la Cruz, singing my heart out as if I was Donna Anna in Mozart's *Don Giovanni*.

"So—what else could I do? I snuck out in the night and ran. Some people say they run and never look back. I looked back a hundred times as I carried my heavy bag to the bus, and every day of my first ten years in Madrid. The life of a soprano may seem all glitz and glamour—and believe me; now that I've made it, it surely is—but a career in opera never starts out that way."

Lady Sophia raises her arms wide, fans her fingers, and drops her jaw, doubling her chin. As she begins to sing, even Archie—Tessa observes—appears impressed with the lyrical beauty of Lady Sophia's tone. The Olearons, too, do not ask her to stop, only to quiet the amplification of her highest notes. As Lady Sophia walks, she nearly dances, as if the forest is her stage and the company her audience of a thousand twinkling eyes in the flare of stage lights. As she continues to sing, in a language Tessa does not recognize, each member of the company grows lost in the tangle of their own unspoken desires. Fears. Memories.

THE Olearons easily discover the skyward trail of the balloons, intersecting with the Bangols' trajectory not far northeast from the place of their initial attack, where Ella had been captured. The company track the littered debris of discarded Bangol foodstuff along the forest floor—stale yet spongy bread crusts, gnawed bones, and impatiently peeled fruit skins—and the line of busted branches overhead. Zeno collects every peel, filling his cheeks and sucking loudly before spitting the fruit skins sideways, spraying saliva carelessly. After a few hours spent walking

through the azure woodland, Azkar declares, "There! The blood
of the fallen! And the footprints of the Bangols!"

"Blood?" Tessa repeats. Her breathing is suddenly loud and
shallow. "Hurry!" She bursts into a sprint and passes Azkar and
Ardenal. At the foot of a small hill, Tessa stops so quickly that
she tumbles. "Archie, look!"

Archie's eyes grow wide. He confirms Tessa's excitement,
saying, "Ella's drawn her Grandma. My Suzie. And a Bangol, too."

"Ella!" Tessa says, smiling, though frantic. She searches the
area, finding nothing, before running over the hill. Ardenal is
beside her. "She's not here. And this blood . . ."

"It's Bangol blood," sighs Ardenal, relief easing the tension
on his face. "She must still be alive."

"They've been gone six hours, at least, judging by what's left
of their fires," Kameelo reports, studying the cracks in the
charred-black timber.

Mounds of coal and ash are spaced around the clearing in a
lopsided circle. There is broken clay, displaced moss, and splat-
ters of thick blood where it appears that at least three of the
Bangols' aircrafts had crash-landed. Zeno walks tentatively, unsettled by the blood of his kin.

"And wherever they're headed, they'll get there faster than
us in their balloons," adds Nameris.

Azkar and Eek kick at the ground, but there is no debris to
follow beyond the camp. Nameris turns his eyes upward to sur-
vey the leafy canopy for clues. Azkar pokes Zeno. "Where would
they have gone from here, Bangol?"

Zeno frowns at Azkar before clearing his throat and answering,
"I suspect they journeyed east. There they may regroup on the
long-abandoned rock arches, bridges from land to prison cells
above the water of the reckless, sleepless sea. They were built when
a shallow tide surrounded the stone shoals, though since the

Star's arrival—around the time of my exile—the saltwater runs high and most are flooded, to my knowledge. They used the cells many sunsets past to imprison the sprites they captured in the fairy vineyards, torturing them for their Naiu and their secrets.

"Or . . ." Zeno continues, "the Bangols take the longer journey north to the stone castle-fortress in the bedrock badlands. My home near the northern shore. Where my throne awaits me. There, the Bangol army is the strongest and our weapons abound."

"If they go north, why fly east first?" the Maiden asks. "Not straight over the mountain?"

"The weight," Harry chimes in. The senior, and civil engineer, wears thin-rimmed glasses that frame the wrinkled valleys around his eyes and slide down his nose as he calculates the scene. Harry re-tucks his Hawaiian golf shirt and straightens the cardigan tied by the arms over his shoulders. "It's the people, that's my estimation," he says. "They weigh down the balloons."

"That may be to our advantage," the Maiden reflects. "They will be slower—as long as they keep all humans alive. Knowing the Bangols—though I am not acquainted with Tuggeron—I suspect they fly to their northern fortress. As Zeno alludes, there the stone-heads can prepare for battle from a position of strength. Since we are beneath the mountain, Baluurwa the Doomful, and we must either turn back to the southwest, which is the safer route up the western coast past the sprites, or continue to the east around the mountain's sharp ridges, I suggest we maintain our swifter northeastern trajectory. The greatest factor being time."

The company sets off at the Maiden's command, keeping the great Baluurwa—that rises steeply at the center of Jarr-Wya— beside them. The Olearons guide the humans, who marvel as the blue forest thins and they begin passing lavender vines winding up slim, white-bark trees unique to the east quadrant of the island. The intense light shines through their enormous, carrot-colored leaves in beams of caramel. Flowers bud proudly between cracks in the thick carpet of patchy emerald and lemon-hued moss.

"I'm inspired to garden! I do love visiting new places and learning about their people through their horticulture," says Donna, her white hair glowing blond in the sunlight. She reaches down to pluck a flower at her feet.

Kameelo quickly stills her hand. "Do not touch the pink flowers," he warns. "They contain a hallucinogenic that will have you lost, yet happy, in a breath."

"Well," declares Donna, retracting her creased fingers. "At least if you are lost, it's better to be happy than fretting." She places her hand in Harry's and squeezes.

Harry chuckles. "You always see the good in everything."

"They're a cute couple," Ardenal says to Tessa. "I pictured us like that. I still do."

"If you are really Arden, what does Ella wear every day?" Tessa asks as she continues to hike through the vines and dangling foliage. Tessa has begun to suspect that the Olearon answering to the name Arden is, in fact, who he claims to be. True, he saved her from the black flyer and says all the right things that one who is impersonating another would say in such circumstances. However, it is Ardenal's mannerisms that are most compelling to Tessa. She watches him as he brushes his dreadlocks away from his forehead. Sometimes he even pushes up his chunky black glasses, though he wears none on Jarr-Wya.

"That's easy—" Ardenal answers. "If it hasn't changed in the last two years, that is. I hope I'm right. Ella wears my mother's locket with a picture of Archie—Dad—on one side and me as a baby on the other."

Tessa's pace slackens as she looks intently at the red profile, the matted hair, the strong, slender build of the Olearon beside her. Dry branches crack under her shoes.

"Look out," Ardenal blurts, pulling Tessa in close to him with one hand as she narrowly misses a low-hanging branch that would have caught her across the forehead. Ardenal keeps his arm around her as they continue, walking slowly, falling behind the others.

The conversations of the company fade and the woodland sounds grow bold. Wings flap. Something scurries across crisp leaves. The breeze sings through the trees. Ardenal plays with Tessa's hair, brushing it away from her shoulder. He gently kisses her neck, then her lips. They linger together. The forest breathes deeply around them. Tessa knows this mouth, the way it pulls at her skin, its taste.

"Hot," Tessa whispers when they part. She dampens her flushed lips with her tongue. She rests a hand on Ardenal's chest before taking a step away. She sighs. "You can't erase all the lonely years with a kiss."

"But it can't hurt, can it? Sorry. I don't know how to say it differently. I wasn't present, but I didn't leave our marriage, Tess—is that better? I was trying to save Ella, to save us all from the heartbreak of losing her. I thought I could slip into this world, use my research to locate the antidote, and come back— that you wouldn't even know I was gone—because of the time. Time here, time there. It's wound differently."

"I now see that Jarr-Wya is real—that's undeniable—and I do hope, with all my heart, that Ella's cure is here, but presence is what makes a marriage. Presence and honesty. Why didn't you confide in me? It doesn't matter now. I can't forgive you for that, for the last two years of bitter absence. You are my Arden, but you are not my husband anymore." Tessa slowly shakes her head as she drops her hand from Ardenal's chest.

"That is not fair. Seriously, Tessa? If I told you what I had been up to, would you have believed me?"

Tessa is silent for a moment, considering it. "No. I would have thought you were nuts."

"Exactly! Like you thought Archie was demented and you were shopping for retirement homes, you would have shipped me off to the crazy-house."

"God, you make me sound like a monster."

"You're not, I know you are not. You're wonderful, that's why I love you. Why I will always love you. Your devotion to your family is fierce—but still, I couldn't tell you. You were carrying the weight of Ella's illness like a martyr, and I knew you would have died in her place if you could have. It consumed you, like my research did for me. If I came home one day and said I had coffee with a stone-headed creature or that I was tracking the appearances of a Steffanus—"

"A what?"

"A silver skinned, Amazon woman with wings. If I told you that I was hunting down a tool to take me to another world, you would have. . ."

"Yeah, I would have freaked. You're right."

"So, can you cut me a little slack, Tess? I never meant to hurt you. I thought I was protecting you."

"Thank you, Arden, for saving me in the blue forest, for cutting me free of the black flyer."

"You're welcome."

"But, despite all you have done, and your noble intentions, you still took off on your own. I know it doesn't make sense to you—maybe not to anyone—but I've felt abandoned all my life. That ache is like my own heartbeat. When you were gone, every day that slinked by, the constant thudding in my chest was a rude reminder: I'm easy to leave. Maybe I am harder now, as

Archie always tell me, but time changes people, even if it does move differently here. Look at you." Ardenal glances down at his red chest and the glowing veins beneath the skin of his hands. "I am not the same woman you married, Arden, and I cannot go back."

chapter 25

*A*rchie slides the leather envelope out of his shoulder bag as he crouches in the tall grass between two lanky trees in the white forest. He had tip-toed away from the company during a rest break taken at Lady Sophia's insistence, met with much grumbling from the Olearon brothers. Archie tasked Ardenal with watching Duggie-Sky, while also keeping an eye on Zeno, to satisfy the Bangol's outspoken demand that he not be left alone with Azkar, or "Scar" as the short creature now heckles his guard.

Archie lightly caresses his fingers across the smooth glass. He waits. "Blasted thing. Work!" he grumbles. A branch cracks underfoot to his right and the Olearon's secret history falls from Archie's hands onto the damp forest floor. He spins around and sees Duggie-Sky running toward him, followed closely by Ardenal. Thinking quickly, Archie tosses his bag onto the glass before the two approaching can notice.

"He wants you, Dad."

"I can see that," Archie huffs. "Wish I could have two minutes to myself. What's happening with Zeno? He's hollering. Go check, will ya? I'd like to relieve myself with some level of dignity." He waves his hands to shoo Ardenal away, who races off in the direction of the fitful Bangol, obviously spewing insults in whose direction Archie can only guess. Turning to Duggie-Sky, Archie continues, "You stand guard, over there," he points to a patch of dirt. "Help Grandpa Archie get some privacy." The boy side-steps into the place Archie had directed, within view of the resting company and near enough to Archie to appease the child, who turns his back to the squatting man and jumps up to pull leaves from low hanging branches.

"Alrighty, let's try this again," whispers Archie and he re-trieves the glass from beneath his bag. He polishes it with his coat sleeve, cleaning off dirt and checking for cracks. It is per-fect, without a chip. Archie leans his back against a tree and rests the glass on his knees, struggling to remember how he had brought forth the words in the citadel. Archie grazes his finger-tips along the perimeter of the jewels and then taps the surface once. Whether there was in fact a trick to activating the en-chantment, Archie is unsure, but he is thrilled that whatever combination of motions he had enacted prove effective.

The glass begins to move with angry looking clouds that darken like a dusk sky. Archie leans around the tree trunk and yells, "Duggie-Sky, you're a great guard! I may be a while— must've eaten somethin' funny." When Archie looks back, white words—which he immediately recognizes—have appeared and quiver on the glass. One by one, the words Archie hungrily con-sumes with his eyes disappear, with new ones curling into place or creeping up from below, so that Archie is ever searching and always connecting two wayward sentences. His vision adjusts to the peculiar patterns and he falls into the trance of the words.

The 22nd Lord of Olearon—born Devi—on the tenth year of his reign, commanded the capture of a Steffanus. His warriors extracted the following story of the alleged history of the Steffanus race, includ-ing their hypothesis on Jarr-Wya's magical origins.

*What truth can be gleaned from the following is doubtful. This ac-
count was first recorded by the 22nd Lord and was added to a secret
parchment by the 29th Lord—Telmakus—upon the public scorching of
the original testimony. Telmakus wished to prove his autonomy from
Laken, the sole remaining Steffanus, while continuing to search her
deceased sisters' words—the very memory of their lives—for clues.*

Thus, begins the transcribed record.

*Naiu—in its fullness of magic—began as a winged being with an
expansive, graceful serpent's tail. Its eyes were made of stars that sat
above its round, shadowy-black snout, and lips, which spilled sharp
teeth and piercing fangs. Its head was cloaked in equally black fur and
its body smoothed with oily, grey and amber features that wafted out
across its massive wingspan. It had no need for hind or forelegs as
there was no place to land.*

*Naiu was peaceful and content. It resided on the currents, only needing
the joy of flight. All at once—in a spark of curiosity which it had
never known before, nor from where it had now come—Naiu began to
create something out of its blissful, silky nothingness. What it made
was time. Naiu invented many variations of time and sprinkled them
into the velvety black, patient to see what would arise.*

*Those castoffs became the first moments of hundreds of worlds that
all continued to operate within their own unique time frames. In those
places, the magic flourished and blossomed into planets and sub-
planets, into plant life and races of cognizant beings, and all things
needed to sustain them. Those places were birthed of pure Naiu, but
they often split into unstable new systems, producing parallel dimensions with similar though fractured time to their mother-world. These
dimensions contained no magic, being lesser derivatives of the other.*

*The being—Naiu—had not realized that it gave away its power with
each creation. The worlds Naiu had formed collected its magic as they*

were carried by the currents to every corner of the dimly lit expanse, which was by then, indeed, a swelling collection of many worlds, dimensions, and constellations.

The human Earth was a derivative dimension—a parallel planet—formed from the world known as Jarr. Earth was void of all enchantment. It remained linked to its mother-world, though ignorant of it.

Winged Naiu, weak from its gift of magic, fell through and destroyed many planets. It crashed across the surface of Earth and into its mother-world. There, Naiu plummeted onto the island known as Jarr-Wya, finally resting in a cloud of rock-dust at the base of the mountain, Baluurwa, shaped from Naiu's impact with the land. Naiu could sense that its magic was strong on Jarr-Wya, but that it was not enough to save its form.

After crashing on Jarr-Wya, Naiu was surprised to see that a human child, one of the first in the parallel dimension of Earth—a baby girl—had stowed away on its giant wings. In Naiu's last breaths, it cared for the baby, teaching her to walk, to hunt and to kill. Then, Naiu fused with the girl, giving her its wings and tail, and its beauty. She retained the ability to plant herself at death and grow into a flower of many blossoms, of many sisters as Naiu foretold. The human girl and Naiu were the beginning of the Steffanus race.

The early time on Earth moved caterpillar-like at first, then much quicker than Jarr's sunsets. Humans evolved and changed rapidly, no longer budding and stretching forth from their fuchsia blossoms that covered their newborn land. They began to mate with each other, their roots and stems shriveling in disregard within their world and within their memory. The humans forgot how they began as a reflection where—in their impetus—their seed had expanded into blue and green and into everything they knew, including themselves.

The human part of the Steffanus was flawed, selfish, vengeful, and corrupt—separated from her own kind, never knowing family, but her promised sister-selves who would grow from her death. She was lonely. The gloom of Baluurwa shadowed her mind. It cut her skin with its rock. It did not shelter her from the elements. She grew icy cold in body and bitter in spirit. Crooked antlers sprouted from her skull. The first Steffanus chose darkness. The darkness of the caves where she burrowed into the mountain and also the darkness of her heart, though both dark and light did exist in her beginnings.

Tired of her isolation, she sought out the glow and warmth of the Olearons, but they feared her, and shunned her. They sent their flames to crisp her hair and scorch her feathers. They chased her back to the mountain and banished her there to die alone, or so they thought. The power of Naiu in the first Steffanus was powerful and she did not perish, but became something much worse than death. From her demise, grew a vine so deeply encroached that its roots cradled all Baluurwa.

The Olearons saw the Steffanus as a weed and wished to rid her from their land. One sunset, the vine—the flower—ceased its flourishing, appearing frozen from reaching its maturity. One thousand sunsets passed and the Olearons forgot the sole Steffanus—until, that is, her sisters bloomed.

Human time eventually slowed and became regular, counted in seconds, minutes, hours, days, weeks, months, years, decades, and centuries. Naiu had never intended for such rigorous recordkeeping and measuring of time—time beginning as a toy and as a happiness, not a burden.

Earth was a place the Steffanus yearned for and discovered within reach, with the help of the Tillastrion. Being part human and part Naiu, the Steffanus could form a Tillastrion in either world and venture between dimensions, in secret. They learned that their errand must be enacted with duality of spirit; one part drawing on the human in her, the other on Naiu.

On Earth, the Steffanus tucked their wings and coiled their tails, concealing them beneath clothing. Their beauty as women-kind allowed them many advantages. There they gathered knowledge. In the human world, the prophetic powers of the Steffanus grew. Their return to Jarr-Wya was always marked with oracles that the Steffanus would scratch with their silver daggers onto the glass of the Olearon's city by night. These were bleak words, only ever partially fulfilled, and most often of evil intent. Many instances, the prophesies the Steffanus—intended for destruction—would be realized in a way they had not hoped. What the Olearons knew with fire-certainty during that unsettling passage of time was that the blood that flowed through the veins of the Steffanus race had not forgotten the slight to their first sister.

Thus, concludes the transcribed testimony.

The record also notes that the Steffanus—who informed the 22nd Lord's warriors of such alleged origins—went on to coil her scaly tail around the neck of a guard to suffocate him. She flapped her mighty wings and sent two others falling backward out of the questioning room and into the training paddocks. The 22nd Lord deemed the Steffanus worthy of death.

"Archibald Wellsley, I have endured enough!" Zeno's raspy voice cuts into Archie's trance. Archie can hear the Bangol stomping his stubby feet and short legs in his direction.

"Do you wish me to bind your arms? Your legs? Perhaps gag your mouth?" Azkar's gruff words reply from a few paces behind the Bangol.

"This fire-brained imbecile does not give the respect my blood deserves. Archibald? Are you listening to me?"

"Yes, Zeno, a moment, will ya?" Archie retorts and shoves the glass back inside the envelope. He replaces it in his bag, slinging it over one shoulder, then stands and fiddles with his belt. He turns out into the open from behind the tree. "Really! Can a man not get ten minutes alone to do his business without babysitting one creature or another?" Duggie-Sky gives Archie a sly grin.

"I am no baby!" shrieks Zeno, a hand on his chest as though Archie's words have wounded him. "Fine, if you will not insulate me from this dimwit, I will take matters into my own hands." Zeno turns his back to Archie and snarls his pointed teeth at Azkar. The Olearon's flame grows. The Bangol begins to call the magic of Naiu into his palms where the dirt from around his feet floats up and forms into hard balls of earth. Archie remembers Zeno during his battle with Ardenal at the Olearon's pasture.

With speed, Archie closes the distance between him and the Bangol, knocks the filthy orbs out of Zeno's hands and says, "Ignore Azkar!" Archie bends one knee so he is on the same level as Zeno. "You are a king—or are meant to be at least," Archie whispers, "but do kings go around picking fights and name-calling?"

"They do on Jarr-Wya; look at Tuggeron!"

"And how much do you love Tuggeron? On Earth, the kings that are revered are fair, ruling with wisdom, strategy, and restraint, patient till the right moment to strike—you get me?"

Zeno nods thoughtfully. "You advise me well, Archibald. Maybe you are not the fool I had supposed. We must speak further about the kings of your world."

Archie nods to Zeno, who quiets the malice of his anger between his grey palms that he clasps together, his back suddenly straight as looks down on Azkar, though from his miniscule stature. Archie stands and addresses both Bangol and Olearon. "Good. Now, give it a rest, you two!"

chapter 26

*N*anjee and Luggie make sure I am with them when we take to the air again. Our dusty clay basket is one of the smaller ones, they tell me. I can't see much through the sack, which I'm told to stay in, at least until we get a little distance between us and the other balloons. I do trust them. Nanjee and Luggie. Maybe it's their age. Or the sketchbook. Nanjee tells me Luggie stole it from their dad's stuff. Their father is the king of the Bangols. I can't remember his name, so I call him Tuggs.

Nanjee continues, telling me that Tuggs has been documenting his reign as king, saying the Bangols need a written history like the Olearons. I, personally, have always found history a bore, but I guess if you think you're the best you'd want to get that down in writing. That's where the sketchbook came from. Tuggs had thousands of them made. Nanjee promises this one won't be missed.

The sketchbook is bound with string at its spine, needle-sewn through the thick pages in a fancy braided pattern. It's been stitched so securely that I'm sure the knots will outlive the paper. There is some rusty metal jewelry hammered onto its rectangular cover. The whole thing has a thin leather strap fastening it shut.

I make good use of my time in the sack, studying the

sketchbook. Enough light filters in through the loose weave of the burlap, though I apply my sense of touch more than anything. That's when I feel it. When I dig my fingers around at the inner spine of the back cover, there is a little flap hidden there. My fingernails feel like they're going to rip from my skin, but I claw it open. Inside there's a key! It is ornate and must have taken skill to make. It feels warm to the touch.

I pull out of my shirt the long chain I wear around my neck and thread the key onto it, beside my Grandma Suzie's locket. I re-tuck them both inside the collar of my shirt and slip it down beneath my clothes. I'm guessing Nanjee doesn't know about the secret pocket in the sketchbook, so she won't be looking for the key. Still, I don't want the Bangols catching me with it, even if they are my friends. And it is a good thing, because they rip off the sack so fast, I almost think they know. Thankfully, they don't mention the key.

The basket looks like the orangish terracotta pots Mom plants her annuals in at home, only bigger and flatter on the bottom. It's the perfect size for the three of us. I stay low so the Bangols in the other balloons don't spot me. Nanjee and Luggie encourage me to peek, though; they want to show me their island. It's a good distraction since I can't meet their eyes. I know I must keep my discovery a secret. That is easier to do than I expect.

Jarr-Wya is breathtaking. Oh, I wish I could capture this strange beauty in a photograph! It makes me sad that I'm not a better artist. Nanjee and Luggie, especially Luggie, love watching me draw. He is supposed to be learning to fly the balloon, though. I heard old Tuggs roar at Luggie from his airship ahead when we almost crashed into a tree—more than once.

"Draw me," Luggie begs. He stands as still as he's able while navigating the sky, guiding the balloon with ropes attached to the great sphere overhead. I look up and see that the huge fabric balloon is filled with orange butterflies.

When Nanjee and Luggie are occupied with the balloon, I also paint the key. I do it quickly, knowing my time is limited. I can feel the metal sit against my skin. It makes me tingle in some bizarre way that feels like love. It's weird. When Luggie looks down at me—to smile sheepishly through his crocodile teeth—I cover the sketch with black ink and smile back at him.

Ella

Ella

T he humans huddle close to the Olearons for heat as the temperature plummets and the air becomes icy. The Bangols' deserted camp is now four hours behind them. The company walk in silence for a time. Dusk descends swiftly, and all grow weary of the march.

A low rumble begins, first as a faint buzz that amplifies to a steady swoosh. A bubbling creek comes into view. Rocks glisten in the moonlight, which has already trounced the sun for juris- diction over the vast sky. The rocks along the riverbed sparkle with diamonds freckled across their smooth faces. Though the creek is clamorous, the water flows gracefully. The noise calms the humans, whose nerves have been frayed by the frightening snarls of Jarr-Wya's nocturnal creatures and the distant caws of the black flyers.

"We rest here tonight, in this clearing. Olearons, dampen your flames. We need not be a beacon to our enemies this night," Azkar orders, dropping his sack but holding fast to the stick. Zeno slinks away from him to stand on the far side of Ar- chie and Duggie-Sky.

Eek steps forward. "Are you sure it's safe to camp so close to the water?" he asks.

"All creatures will have drunk by now," replies Nameris. To the humans he adds, "They do not trust the water, as it is the stealer of their secrets." Lady Sophia covers her mouth with her plump fingers.

Eek nods, and warns, "Best maintain your distance. Keep your glass daggers and other weapons within arm's reach."

"Let us rest, company," Azkar says. "Eek, you take the first watch, Nameris the second, and Kameelo, the hours before dawn." They nod. In turn, each of the brothers embrace Eek and wish him alertness and bravery for the first watch.

Donna makes sure every member of the company is warm and their bellies full of the orange and green biscuits baked from the Olearon's harvest. The group huddles together, each one finding a smooth spot free of roots and the mysterious flowers that line the edge of the clearing.

Valarie rushes to Tessa's side. "May I sleep here?" she asks and Tessa nods, concealing her confusion. *Why does she want to lie beside me?* Tessa wonders. *Oh wait, I see.* Nate approaches behind Valarie, but the ground to Tessa's right is cut by a sharp rock. He purses his lips, then lies on the far side of his cruise director. Nate smiles faintly at Tessa before turning on his side, his back to Valarie, who inches closer to him.

"Lady Sophia," the Maiden begins, "Would you sing us to sleep? Sing good dreams into our heads?"

"I know just the thing. I will lull you with my favorite aria. This melody will carry you away, as it does for me when I'm on the stage."

"Only not too loud," Nameris interjects. Zeno scrapes dirt from the ground with his sharp nails. He shapes it into two small wedges that he shoves in his ear holes.

Lady Sophia's voice is velvety and tender.

Tessa shifts on the raw earth, hunting for a comfortable position. Her hands quiver with nervous energy and she tucks them beneath her head like a pillow. The pace on Jarr-Wya, while intensely physical, does not compare to the strenuousness of Tessa's life back home. On the magical island, her thoughts take her down perilous avenues that—as an emergency room nurse, single parent, breadwinner with every moment allocated to caring for one person or another—had been barricaded and nearly forgotten in the dark quadrants of her mind.

In part, it is the longing for companionship, which she alluded to with Archie on the *Odyssey*. With Ella's diagnosis, Tessa chose to shun her need for her own identity, for freedom, friendship, travel, and—with Arden's disappearance—romantic love, to focus on attending to the needs of her ailing child. Still, she is ravaged by the guilt of wanting more when her daughter will never know even half the life experiences Tessa cherishes, particularly those that followed her clumsy youth. Tessa lives in limbo, waiting for the inevitable, wishing it away, while simultaneously, terrifyingly eager for what lay beyond.

Now, despite being surrounded by people and magical creatures—and a man and an Olearon vying for her affection—a pit of loneliness lodges in Tessa's chest. All she has known for years is this role as mother-provider, yet, ironically, Tessa itches to return to the safety that identity affords her, with its comfortable, predictable martyrdom, as Ardenal had so astutely pinpointed. The tense muscles in Tessa's back scream against the hard earth. Her shoulders are tight and her thighs—still burning from the days spent running on uncleared trails—radiate pain throughout her body. Tessa's thoughts rage against each other, screaming so loud she is sure the others must hear. Despite all this, Tessa falls quickly into sleep.

TESSA sits up with a jolt. She cannot tell how much time has passed. It is bitterly cold. She curls her body into a ball but her exposed skin—her calves, arms, and neck—are stung by the moisture in the air, like the prick of a mosquito's needle-fine proboscis. Tessa rubs her goosebumps with both hands. She had been wearing a short-sleeved dress and light pink linen jacket when Archie and Zeno used the Tillastrion. She desperately wishes she had put on tights, like Ella, for Lady Sophia's concert that night. Tessa hopes that Ella is warm.

She scoots herself up to sitting and surveys the clearing. Donna and Harry cuddle together, their breathing synchronized. To Tessa's left, Valarie is curled up against Nate. He has not brushed off her arm, which drapes over him as he snores lightly. Lady Sophia has laid her head on a low mound and rests elegantly with one hand over her enormous chest. Her lips move as she still sings to the company, though now inaudibly, in her sleep. Zeno and the Olearons all rest, even Nameris, who dozes where he squats, failing to guard the sleeping company.

Tessa pushes herself to her feet. Her tongue sticks to the roof of her mouth. Taking careful, deliberate steps, she walks to the creek's edge and studies it under the moonlight. It appears to be an ordinary stream of clear water rolling over a rocky bed. *Harmless enough*, she reasons. Nameris's warning nags at her. *A creek stealing secrets*, Tessa scoffs. She crouches and scoops a handful of the icy flow. The water tingles on her tongue and she can feel every inch as it slips down her throat.

Many handfuls later, Tessa is full and satisfied. She wipes her trembling, cramping hand on her skirt as she stands and turns back toward her plot of earth—but her face crashes into a broad chest and she stumbles back, a small cry escaping her lips. A warm hand covers her mouth. Her feet slip on the wet rocks and Tessa senses herself falling. Another hand braces her back and cradles her weight until she finds her balance. Tessa looks up. It is Captain Nate.

He steadies her and whispers in her ear, "I'm sorry I startled you."

"It's fine. I didn't realize anyone else was awake." Tessa relaxes her shoulders. "Was I too loud?"

"Not at all. I'm a light sleeper. I actually think Lady Sophia's dream opera was the culprit."

Tessa muffles her giggle. She blushes. "Maybe we should wake him?" She tips her head in the direction of Nameris.

"Nah, let him sleep. Why don't you and I take up his post?"

"I guess I do feel strangely awake," Tessa admits.

They sit on a large rock on the edge of the creek and watch the slumbering company in silence. With his hands on his knees, Nate stretches a pinky finger toward Tessa, stroking the side of her leg. Goose bumps again ripple her skin, but this time not from the cold. She forgets how to breathe.

Nate leans over and cups Tessa's face in his hands. "Look at me," he urges when she drops her gaze. Their eyes lock, two green and two brown planets fixed within a hungry galaxy. Tessa feels Nate's breath on her lips, then his kiss, tender at first, then passionate, deep. His fingers tangle in her hair. Tessa remembers to breathe and it is audible and interwoven with longing.

Tessa pauses to whisper, "I don't know, I—"

Nate fills the space between them, interrupting Tessa's words. She finds herself pulling her hands through Nate's blond crew cut, longer on top. His muscular body throbs against hers and she can taste his scent. Slipping her fingers beneath his shirt, she traces the muscles of his back.

This isn't the first time she has touched his skin.

THE first day on the *Atlantic Odyssey*, when Archie took Ella for a walk on the deck, Tessa followed at a distance. She quickly became caught in a crowd of passengers touring the ship, and Archie and Ella slipped out of sight. Tessa reluctantly joined the tour group.

"Welcome to the bridge!" Captain Nathanial Billows said, smiling broadly, his arms outstretched with the same theatrics he'd used to greet the passengers at the port. "Come on in, there's room for everyone."

Tessa found herself on a level above the observation deck. The bridge was a floor unto itself, the highest point of the *Odyssey*. Floor to ceiling windows leaned outward, each with its own windshield wiper. Captain Nate sat on the worktable on the edge of a long bank of computer monitors, switches, and flashing lights.

"Many passengers ask me if the life of a captain is boring and I assure you, it's not. Imagine driving a twenty-thousand-ton vehicle, having control of every part of it as you stare down the horizon. It's the most gratifying job I've found."

A passenger raised her hand. "Who sails the ship while you are asleep? You do sleep, right?"

"Good question! The captain is like the CEO. I have three senior officers that report to me: the cruise director, whom you met—Valarie; the chief engineer; and the deputy captain. There's typically only one or two of us in here while at sea, but when we enter or leave a port, the bridge is a bustling place to be."

Tessa had let the other travelers pass her on their way to a different area of the *Odyssey*. She hung back and approached the large windows.

"Magnificent, isn't it?"

She turned to see the captain behind her. "I envy what you said about control," she replied. "There is little in my life that I can change."

The captain turned his head. "Sailors, can you grab those checklists we were talking about earlier?" He waited until the bridge door closed behind them with a click, then looked down at Tessa. "I know I'm a stranger, but I've got a listening ear. Want to talk?"

"My daughter is sick," Tessa blurted. "My husband left me. It's like I'm living a car crash in slow motion; I can see each thing I lose as I plummet toward the end. At least here, as I look out these windows, my problems feel small. I feel small. Like I don't need to be everything to everyone. I can just be."

For the next three hours, Nate and Tessa sat on the floor of the bridge and drank pinot noir retrieved from the captain's quarters. They watched the sun set sleepily over the North Atlantic Ocean. The on-duty deputy captain frequented the bridge to check the glowing buttons, adjust a dial here, or collect papers there. He rolled his eyes at the tipsy pair whose conversation was effortless and familiar as they told one story after another. They clinked their glasses each time the deputy exited. Tessa grew flushed and laughed until her ribs ached. She reminded Nate every few minutes that she needed to meet Archie and Ella in the dinning hall. Still, they continued well after their view was freckled with stars.

Tessa asked Nate if she was pretty. He said yes. She asked him if she seemed like the kind of woman that a man walks out on. He said no. She asked him if she deserved to be happy. He said yes.

Nate told her about his early days as a water transport worker, learning to be the quiet workhorse on the job, learning to respect the sea as if it were a woman. As he shared how he'd fought for his position, how he had to make his mark—sometimes in extreme weather and against all odds and more experienced sailors—Tessa began to see that Nate was the kind of man that didn't give up when life refused to be easy.

KISSING Nate felt natural on the *Odyssey*, like it does again at the creek's edge. Nate had promised to visit Tessa in Seattle. She had no doubt, by the look in his eyes, that he meant every word. *I deserve to be happy,* Tessa says to herself. She ignores the rocks digging into her legs. Her words slip out before she can censor them. "I'm scared to want you as much as I do . . ."

"I know it's fast, Tess, but I'm captivated by you. Breathless. You're beautiful . . ."

Tessa tips her head back and smiles up at the blinking stars. *I am not the mother of a sick child tonight,* Tessa thinks. *At this moment, I'm desired.* She sighs and lets her eyes slip closed. Nate kisses beneath her ears and along her collarbone. His lips grow fainter. A chill breeze brushes against Tessa's skin. When she looks back, Nate is gone.

chapter 28

Tessa is alone at the creek. Nate is asleep on the ground. Valarie's arm is over him. *Was it a dream?* *Strange,* she thinks, *the smell of his hair is still on my fingers.* Tessa stands and straightens her clothes. All the sleeping bodies are as they were when she first awoke.

"Young one," a deep voice says, making Tessa jump.

"Ardenal!" she yelps, but he does not stir.

"Over here," the voice calls. "Come to the water's edge."

She spins around, but all is still as she creeps over the rocks. Slowly, cautiously, she approaches the water, which continues to rush loudly by. All of a sudden, the clear water begins to cloud with white sediment. A drooping face carved with wrinkles appears beneath the surface of the current. Tessa gasps and stumbles backward, but the voice calls to her again.

"All is right, young one. You need not fear me," it rumbles deeply.

"Who are you?" Tessa's voice trembles. Long white hair falls from the old man's crown. His eyes are commanding.

"My name is Rolace," the deep baritone quakes beneath the rush of the creek.

"What do you want?"

"I see your secrets through the enchantment of the river. You hide many mysteries in your soul."

Tessa backs away, wrapping her arms around herself as if she wore her lifeline like a garment. Then she changes her mind. "What do you see?" she asks.

"I see an abandoned child."

"Ella?"

"No. Not your daughter."

"Me."

"You carry a heavy burden."

"I don't need parents. I don't need anyone."

"Why lie when I see you for who you really are?"

"You still have not told me what you want."

"I feel your fear for your child. You worry that if she is dead, your loneliness will overcome you."

Tessa quickly brushes a tear away, hoping the face does not notice.

"Your daughter is alive!" Rolace declares.

"Ella . . ." Tessa smiles without shame, beaming at the stream. "Where is she? How can I find her? Tell me—which way should we go?"

"Your daughter's whereabouts are not for me to see. I do know, however, that the Bangols have used their power over the stones to cause a landslide down the east side of Baluurwa. There the rocks pile high. You will not be able to find them in-land hugging the base of the mountain."

"What should I do?"

"Find me," Rolace instructs. "I will give you a gift, like I did Ardenal, and this will allow you to find your child."

"What kind of gift?" Tessa kneels on the stones, bending low, pleading to Rolace with clenched hands. "How do I find you?"

"The gift is a secret you will soon uncover, if your will is strong and your heart is brave. Ardenal knows the way." The face of Rolace begins to wash downstream in the roaring creek. "Bring me what I desire—let it pass untainted by cloth or wood or stone, from your skin to mine—and the gift will be yours."

"What do you desire?"

"Bring me the—"

Rolace's voice is drowned out by a large rock that plunks into the water, sinking immediately to the riverbed after sending an icy spray into Tessa's face. Her hands slip on the damp edge and she falls face-first into the glacial river. Instantly, the rushing current envelops her body and carries her along, her knees and arms banging against the jagged shadows beneath the stream. Her head smashes into something, and all is blackness.

Tessa's mind wanders in the endless void. There are whispers in the water, uttering words in high-pitched hisses: *"We know your secrets! We know your secrets!"* Tessa struggles to right herself and looks from side to side, but all is cloaked in gloom. *"We know where you come from! We know your origin!"* Tessa stretches out, but her feet find no solid ground, her hands find nothing to cling to.

I have always lived beneath the surface, she thinks, then abruptly shakes her head. *No, that's not true. How long have I been down here?*

"We know your deception! We know you, Orphan!"

Putting her hands to her face, Tessa scratches her eyelids, believing that something has blinded her, like the thin, slinking film-creature of the Olearons' lilac smoke. When she senses she has drawn blood by the sting of her skin, that she has clawed her own flesh, she stops and is still. Without knowing which way is up—if there even is an up in such a place—she surrenders to the whispering creek, revolving through the blackness, free of time and space.

"We heard the desire of Rolace! We know, Tessa! We know all your secrets, Sad One! Give yourself to us! We know your secrets! Open your

mouth! Yes, open your mouth! Do it and we will tell! Yes, the desire of Rolace! Open your mouth!"

Without hesitating, Tessa spreads her lips wide. Water floods into her mouth and down her throat. She tries to cough but the icy flow reaches forcefully through her lungs. She notices a lightness in her mind, though her body is pulled—toward what, she cannot tell. *What have I done?* As Tessa wonders this, a singular word, simple yet unfamiliar, lodges in her consciousness: *Banji.*

"Now you know," the water hisses. *"Die!"* The words cut like a blade of Olearon glass through her mind and even her ability to think fades to murky nothingness. At her last fleeting thought— *Ella*—Tessa becomes aware of pinpricks on her skin. They grow to stabbing, agonizing pain that increases like a thousand needles— until someone grabs her arm and hoists her by the elbow. The weight of the water falls away, but it is too late. All is carbon black.

chapter 29

I kissed Luggie. It wasn't anything fancy. I wanted to show him how I feel. We have been cooped up together since we took off from the south. He and I have talked—in our own way—non-stop. I'm happy in his company. He's not judging me like the guys at school. I feel normal, sort of—which is all I want. We are just a boy and a girl, getting to know each other. Sometimes I forget he is a Bangol. He's very attractive. Ugh, Mom is going to be so angry—and Dad too. I know what he thinks about the Bangols from what I read in his notebooks.

When Mom packed up all Dad's stuff, I'd go up there, to the attic. My favorite time was after classes were done for the day. Grandpa Archie would fall asleep on the couch in the afternoon sunshine. When I heard his snore, I'd drag over the step stool, climb up, pull the string to release and lower the wooden stairs, then ascend to the attic. I'd often wear one of Dad's sweatshirts. It made me feel better, though I know that's cliché.

I read all of Dad's notebooks—until the day that Grandpa Archie found them. He became protective of the attic, obsessed with it, though he thought I didn't notice. I was feeling worse by then. I would pretend to fall asleep on the couch and let Grandpa climb up the wooden stairs. He'd stay up there till we heard Mom's car door. I've never seen an old guy run so fast as

Grandpa did then. He'd slam the stairs up hard. I'm sure the mice in the attic thought it was the end of the world.

At first, I felt bad, going through Dad's stuff, as if he were dead and I was digging up his gravesite. But I knew something puzzling was going on. I still remember that last week before he left.

Dad started to come home for supper. He stuck around before work to walk me to school. That was a big contrast to how he had been for years—since my diagnosis. Right around the time the doctors told my parents to prepare themselves, that all the radiation and other treatments were not working, Dad started looking me in the eyes again. It made me nervous. It was like I wasn't a ghost anymore.

That was when he gave me the plant. Mom said Dad was in denial. "Why give her something that will outlive her?" she screamed at him. It was called Golden Creeping Jenny. I loved the name. He said he picked it because he knew I liked scary stuff. The plant was like a vine, growing leaves in green bowties. Already they were spilling over the side of the pot.

Mom called Dad a child. As if he believed in Santa. She had given up on me, but showed it by suffocating me with love. That last week, Dad repeated, over and over, "There's got to be a way."

Mom was exasperated. "Why are you torturing me with false hope?" she'd sob.

"There is always hope," Dad assured her, which perplexed me. I was listening from my room. They thought I was asleep. I was so confused! Was I dying or living? But when I heard Dad talking to Mom that night, after he gave me the Creeping Jenny, I decided I liked his fantasy. I felt horrible, but I kept thinking, *Dad had hope and so do I.*

Even after he left and Mom was deeply depressed and there

was nothing I could do. Even when throwing up corroded my teeth and I had to go to the dentist—a lot. Even when it would take me an hour to walk the two blocks home from school because, that day, my legs were so weak. Even when the headaches made learning anything in grade nine nearly impossible. Even when my body was polka-dotted with bruises because I couldn't avoid banging into stuff. Even when my first—and only—boyfriend broke up with me, his pity only lasting so long. Even then, I kept thinking, *Dad had hope and so do I.*

chapter 30

*A*rdenal beats Tessa's chest with his fists, pounding upon her bleach-white skin. "Oh god! I can't look!" Lady Sophia shrieks and turns away. Ardenal's flame is a whisper of smoke and his red jaw clenches, sharp like his cheekbones.

"Come on, Tess, come back to me!" he pleads.

"Out of the way," Nate barks. "You're doing it all wrong!" The captain crouches beside Tessa but Ardenal does not budge. Nate elbows him and reaches for Tessa. Ardenal lays a red hand on Nate's forehead and shoves the man away with one swift gesture that sends the human flying into a tree. Nate groans loudly and curses.

Ardenal presses his hot mouth against Tessa's blue lips and breathes into her the heat of his flame. Again, he pounds her chest, but this time water erupts from her bloated lungs. Coughing follows, then a wheezing suck of air, and she startles and stares wide-eyed at the faces blocking the light above her.

Nate joins the group expressing their relief. Rubbing the shoulder that slammed against the tree, he wears a happy, though reserved grin.

Lady Sophia pushes Valarie and Harry aside to get a better look. "Oh, good heavens! Tessa, you're alive! I—" she wails.

"*Banji,*" Tessa interrupts.

"What was that, dear?" asks Donna.

"Banji."

"How do you know that word?" Nameris demands.

"The water told me," Tessa blurts between coughs.

"The river is a liar," Azkar says slowly. "It lured you closer and would have risen to flood your lungs if I had not broken its hold."

"I thought you said the water could read a person's secrets," Tessa says, looking at Nameris, then the Maiden. "It knew things about me, things I have not told a soul."

"Truth and lies are indecipherable on the whisper of the water. It uses those secrets against you, to play on your weaknesses. What did it tell you?" asks the Maiden.

"That's not important." Tessa sits up and the humans and creatures take a step back. "What is important is that we find Ella—and stop the Bangols, right?" She rises and stands, shivering, her clothing drenched.

Ardenal detaches the belt of his blue jumpsuit and removes the vibrant fabric so that he is standing in a pair of soft muslin shorts. The Maiden turns away, but the *Odyssey* passengers stare at Ardenal's smooth, crimson skin and blooming muscles. "Please, Tess, take this," he says, passing her the jumpsuit.

Tessa accepts the garment and, accompanied by Donna, steps behind a wide tree to change. When they emerge, Tessa has fully rolled up the sleeves and legs of Ardenal's jumper to fit her petite figure.

Ardenal smiles at her. "You look cute."

"I'm drowning in this," she says, and Ardenal smirks.

"Give me your clothes." He holds out his hand and Tessa drops her wet dress and jacket over his arm. Ardenal drapes them loosely across his shoulders and says, "They'll be dry soon."

The company resume their march. "The Bangols have run

this route before," the Maiden says sadly as they pass through sections of hacked trees, the branches looking as if they've been sawed off with dull blades.

"These creatures destroyed every living thing in their path. Look at this," says Lady Sophia, pointing to a massive oak. "This tree must be a thousand years old, and now its bark is splintered. What did they do, use it as a scratching post?"

"Beasts," is the Maiden's only reply. Zeno tips up his nose.

The group divides into pairs as their path narrows, and Tessa finds herself walking beside the Maiden. "Do the Olearons have families like humans—you know, husbands and wives and children?" she asks the graceful creature at her side.

"Yes, we do," the Maiden replies. "Our couplings form life-long bonds that even death cannot destroy. When one partner passes, their spirit comes to inhabit the form of the living lover and the union is made even closer."

"So, what happens when the second partner dies?" Tessa stumbles on an exposed stone and the Maiden catches her. "Thank you."

"When both Olearons in the pairing are ready to begin their next journey, they find themselves in a new land, in new forms. Yet, no matter the separation, they always discover each other again. They may not know for what or for whom they search, but a yearning guides them. When together, they sense it. It is a perfect unity that binds them forever."

"That sounds . . . lovely." Tessa peers over her shoulder at Ardenal, who eyes the trees as they pass, alert for potential danger. He does not notice her gaze, and Tessa wonders—turning back to stare at the path ahead—if the kind of love the Maiden describes could exist for humans. *Or, are two people only meant for each other for one season in time?*

Tessa again peers behind her. Ardenal is talking with Archie and Zeno, beyond range of her hearing. Her father-in-law had promptly fogiven Ardenal, trusting him without suspicion. *Even if he is Arden—and as crazy as that is, I believe it—what does that mean?* Tessa wonders and clenches her fists. She's spent years scrubbing her heart clean of its attachments to Arden, hardening it against the very thought of him.

Nate catches her attention. He walks a few paces ahead of Ardenal and assumes she is gazing at him. He returns her probing expression. Tessa blushes sheepishly, remembering what happened—or what she imagined happened—by the creek. *Maybe it was the water I drank,* she reflects suspiciously, and her disappointment at that thought surprises her.

Then, Tessa sees Valarie. She walks beside Nate, glaring at Tessa with her jaw clenched, her lips compressed into a thin line, her eyes narrowed. Tessa's head snaps forward, but she can feel Valarie's loathing crawling up her spine. Nate had told Tessa, when they flirted and drank on the floor of the *Odyssey's* bridge, that he had a relationship—*if you'd call it that,* he had corrected himself—with his cruise director. A year had passed since he'd reciprocated her advances, but that didn't stop her from knocking on the door of his quarters during Nate's personal hours. *I should have stopped, and I feel terrible for it; I didn't intend to string her along,* he said.

"Look!" Azkar's voice snaps Tessa out of her wandering thoughts. "An avalanche!"

Ardenal runs to the front of the group and peers ahead. "The Bangols and their evil magic!" he spits. "They have destroyed a huge area of forest! If we walk around the wall of stones to venture north it will take us two extra days."

"A day and a half if we walk by night, the way ahead lit by our flames," the Maiden offers.

"I cannot keep up this pace," Lady Sophia groans, her forehead glistening with sweat and her clothing looking looser around her waist.

"We could go over," Nameris suggests.

Kameelo shakes his head. "It is too high and unsettled. We could inadvertently launch another avalanche and crush one or more of our company in the slide."

"One way or another, I am getting past it," Tessa blurts. "Even if that means I go alone. It breaks my heart to imagine Ella all by herself. Without her medication, the pill bottles drown on the ship, she must be in terrible pain . . ."

"I am a fool! I went back for the books, but not for Ella's meds," Archie curses.

Tessa takes a step toward the avalanche, "Onward and upward."

Nate steps forward, extending a protective arm to support Tessa. "What other options do we have? It's obvious there is little time to waste mulling it over. We need action."

Eek, who has been very quiet since they left the river, speaks up. "Pardon me, human," he says in a low, rumbling voice, staring down at Tessa. "We do not know for certain that the child is alive. I have survived the ruthlessness of the Bangols. It is unpredictable and bloodthirsty. They may wish us to believe they hold captives, to lure us to them—what reason do they have to feed them, to guard them from becoming prey in the night? We cannot proceed as a rescue party. Our mission is set out before us. Defeat our enemy. Purge the land."

"She is alive," Tessa retorts. "I know it. Ella is alive—but they'll kill her if we barge in and attack."

"You know something." Nameris's black eyes grow wide as he approaches Tessa. "What do you know? And who spoke it to you?"

"I feel it."

"Speak the truth!" Nameris barks at her, his flames roaring to life. Tessa cowers beneath his heat.

"Stand down, Nameris," Ardenal orders, covering the distance to Tessa in two long strides. "Never again speak to my wife like that!"

"Ardenal, you know my gift. It is as tangible as yours, though less visible. She is lying."

"What is your gift, Nameris?" Donna asks timidly from her place beside Harry on the edge of the group.

"There is a creature in our land that has the head of a man but the body of an enormous arachnid."

"A spider?" Duggie-Sky pipes up.

"How on earth do you know that word, little fella?" reels Archie, patting the boy on the shoulder.

"TV."

Nameris continues. "If your will is strong and your heart is brave, this creature will uncover your inherent gift. Mine is the ability to know the truth—or falsehood—of the spoken word." Nameris frowns at Tessa. "What are you hiding?"

The weathered face of a man in the current used the same words Nameris now utters. Tessa's palms grow sweaty. "What is the name of this creature you speak of?" she finally asks.

"You see? She knows something!" Nameris shrieks. "Out with it!" His flames roar inches from Ardenal, who stands between Tessa and the raging Olearon. Ardenal does not flinch.

"His name is Rolace," Ardenal answers coolly.

"Rolace." Tessa nods and so does Nameris, confirming Tessa's honesty. "I saw him," she confesses.

"Where?" Azkar demands. "Did he come to you?"

"Sort of." Tessa shrugs. "I saw his face. In the water."

The Olearons turn and whisper to each other.

"What? What is it?" Tessa asks.

"We are unsure of the trustworthiness of the one you perceived," the Maiden replies.

Nameris wonders aloud, "How can a message of truth come from the waters of corruption?"

Ardenal puts a warm hand on Tessa's back. "What did he say, Tess?"

"Well," Tessa fidgets with the belt loops of Ardenal's jumpsuit, "Rolace told me that Ella is alive, that I should not give up."

"What else?" Nameris probes. "There is more you are not sharing."

"Rolace told me I should find him. That if I bring him what he desires, he will give me a gift that will help me find Ella."

Lady Sophia snorts. "Is he going to make you like our fire-haired friends?" she asks with distain, then glances at the Olearons. "No offense!"

"He didn't say." Tessa pauses. "But if that is what must happen, then so be it." She gulps down an uncomfortable lump in her throat.

"It will be okay, whatever happens," Ardenal whispers to Tessa, but the Maiden's long hearing catches his words.

"You cannot guarantee that," the Maiden snaps at Ardenal.

Nate exhales sharply and declares, "I will protect you, Tessa. With my life."

Ardenal laughs once in response. Valarie crosses her arms.

"Rolace is mostly good, but there is a side to him that I cannot read," admits Nameris. "He opened me up to my gift; maybe that is why he is unreadable to me—and for that I fear him."

"The only thing I fear is losing my child. Without her, I will lose myself, my reason for breathing. There is something special about Ella. The world needs her. I am grateful you have all agreed to help thus far." Tessa balls her hands into fists. "So, let us finish what we set out to do."

"I am yet to have children of my own," the Maiden admits, "but I feel the love of a mother is deep with you. I will help you save your child, if indeed it is not too late."

"Us too," Harry vows.

Ardenal takes Tessa's hand. "You know I will do anything for you and Ella."

"I am sure we are all in agreement," says Kameelo impatiently. "Let us travel to Rolace. If he said he can offer this human a way to find her daughter, it will also assist us in reaching the Bangols much faster—to attend to our purposes concerning the Millia."

"And if it turns out the water assumed Rolace's face and spoke lies to the woman? What then?" Nameris challenges.

"Then we continue on. Zeno will help us find the Bangols," Tessa offers.

"Or," adds Eek, "Rolace's anger flares toward us for our intrusion. He captures us in his web and eats us, one limb at a time."

Lady Sophia gasps and faints onto Harry. Donna and Valarie roll her body aside and help the disheveled man stand.

Azkar turns to Tessa. "What did Rolace want in exchange?"

Tessa's eyes dart to Nameris. He studies her face's every twitch and crease. "He wants me to deliver to him—with my bare hands—the Banji flowers."

chapter 31

It seems like we have been flying forever. My shoulders and neck are angry at this hard clay basket. Thank goodness for the sack—I never thought I'd have felt that way, but it's been my only pillow, blanket, shade . . . everything. While I'm thankful to be out of it and breathing the fresh air, I wish I could stand and stretch. Our balloon is guarded by three others that float nearby, so I'm limited to lying or kneeling to avoid being seen. Maybe they're guarding me, but I think it's more about Luggie.

I drew a picture of an airplane to give Nanjee and Luggie an idea for faster transportation, but they didn't get it. They're attached to their butterflies, which I understand. They *are* really pretty.

Tuggs continues to holler over to Luggie from his balloon. He is grooming Luggie to be the next king. That old Bangol irritates me. Luggie does everything for Tuggs, but it's never enough. If my parents talked to me with Tuggs' tone, I'd scream—if I could scream like a normal person, that is.

Luggie told me how he killed an Olearon kid who was lost in the forest—his dad made him do it. That's dark. Luggie has bad dreams about it. Every night he sees the tiny flame, the fresh red skin. He hears the little voice. I cried. For the kid, yeah, but mostly for Luggie. He is kind. Sweet, actually . . .

Tuggs has got Luggie executing traitors, too, crushing his own kind with stones, then cleaning their blood off their rock amphitheater. Though Nanjee is older, Luggie is the favorite. But I think she has the better jobs. She is learning to write in their ancient language—not English—the history of the Bangols, at least the part where Tuggs came into power, which is a pretty horrible story.

Tuggs crushed the head-stones of the king before him. Instead of simply overthrowing that Bangol, and letting him run away in shame, Tuggs chased him. Tuggs skinned the old king and filled him up with pebbles. He brought the body out to the edge of a long dock, out over the ocean and in front of everyone. He pretended that the king gave him his throne, then made it look like the dead king jumped into the sea. There were some that knew, for sure. Nanjee and Luggie knew, though they were young.

Luggie is nothing like Tuggs. He's thoughtful; he shares his food with me. I love that spongy bread. I probably eat too much of it. Luggie really tries to figure out what I want to say. He doesn't read English, like Nanjee does, which is a shame, so I find my sign language coming in handy—at least my ability to do charades and mime. I guess I should have listened to Mom and studied harder. Still, I can make Luggie laugh. He's got the best smile.

When my hands and drawings fail to say what I mean, Luggie talks to me. He's teaching me about the Bangols. They didn't always hate the Olearons. It wasn't that long ago that they were like family, or close enough. Then the Millia showed up and messed with everything. It all comes back to the Star, he tells me.

The Olearons and the Millia are convinced that the Bangols are poisoning Jarr-Wya, but why would they, Nanjee and Luggie say. The Bangols came from the island, it is a part of them.

They love the clay and stones and soil. I believe them, though I'm keeping an open mind. Thanks to Tuggs's recordkeeping, the Bangols realized that the land grew sick after the Star crashed into their sea. *After*. Old Tuggs plans to defeat the Star and harness its power, though only his kids know that he has no idea how.

While Tuggs isn't all bad, he is all crazy. And paranoid. This other Bangol, named Winzun, one of the sons of the last king, was banished through a Tillastrion to another world, but—get this—he got back here somehow. He was all vengeful, which makes sense to me, but Tuggs got wind of it. He did the same thing to Winzun as he did to Winzun's dad. But this time, ugh, he left the body in their amphitheater until the skin was eaten away and all that was left was bloody pebbles.

Oh Luggie. I don't understand how someone so good can come from someone so bad.

I've been thinking about all that Luggie and Nanjee have told me. I've pieced it together. Winzun was Zeno's brother. That must have been how Dad got here. Tuggs has really messed up that family; killing them, banishing them. Luggie and Nanjee don't have good things to say about Zeno and Winzun, but I feel for them, though I'd never say that aloud, even if I could talk. I'm sure Zeno is furious, hence convincing Grandpa Archie to get here—at all costs.

I showed Luggie my scars from surgery. The small one on the back of my neck, below my hairline, was from the biopsy. The bigger one, the one that didn't heal as well, is called a hypertrophic scar. It's red. Raised. Ugly. That's why I never wear my hair up. It's from when the doctors cut me up to remove as much of the tumor as they could, to buy me more time. I could have gotten steroid injections to make the scar less grotesque, but Mom thought I was dying, so what's the point, right?

This bothers me because Mom should understand. When she was a kid, around three or four-years-old, she had bad scoliosis in her back. She told me that her spine was curved like a switchback highway. The doctors operated and straightened her out. She saved her money from then on, at first a penny here and a penny there, so that when she was eighteen-years-old she got her scars fixed, decreasing their purple puffiness. I'm sure if I got my scars fixed I would feel less paranoid about how I look—or maybe not. I'm thin and pale from the cancer, but Luggie doesn't know any different. Heck, his skin is grey!

It's hard to communicate cancer with a drawing but Nanjee and Luggie see the effects of my headaches and nausea; they see me get dizzy, even when Luggie is doing a good job of flying the balloon. Sometimes my hands don't work to hold the paintbrush. They quiver and spasm. I spilled ink on myself this morning. It looks like my shirt is bloodstained. At least it wasn't on the bomber jacket from Grandpa Archie.

Luggie touched my scar. No one outside of the hospital except Mom, not even Grandpa, has touched it. I'm so used to being prodded by the pediatric neurologist, the radiation and pediatric oncologists, and the endocrinologist—and all the nurses that I now know by name, who feel like my friends. But they don't touch me like Luggie touches me. He is not examining me. He is getting to know me. He looks into my eyes. He holds my hands when they tremble. Nanjee rolls her big yellow eyes at us and leans over the edge of the clay basket. I think she's giving us privacy. Luggie is like me. His life is not really a life. He is ruled by something. For me, it's cancer. For Luggie, it's Tuggs.

chapter 32

The company veers east around the towering avalanche. As they hike, they form a plan. Archie is content to listen as he and Duggie-Sky walk hand in hand. He does his best to answer the boy's questions, though they are incessant. "Let me listen, little fella. If you keep chattering, Grandpa Archie can't hear. I'll explain it to you once the grown-ups are finished, all right?" The boy nods and puffs his cheeks at Archie. The old man and little boy walk in silence for a time.

Finally, Archie turns to the child at his side. "Okay, here's the plan, Duggie-Sky. You ready? Good! So, the Banji flowers—which you are not allowed to touch—are magic, but not a good magic. They make people go loopy . . . they make people see things that aren't there, do things they shouldn't do, and go places where they shouldn't go. That's why we all can't pick the flowers willy-nilly—even if we want to. Only Tessa will pick them, since she's got to hand them over to the man-spider to get her gift—to help us find Ella. Got it so far? Good!

"They will prepare Tessa to hold the flowers. She's got to pick and carry them, skin to skin. They'll use Arden's belt to fasten tight around Tessa's grip of the Banji. So she doesn't drop them. That fabric from her skirt is to protect her hands from the belt—Tess, soon you're not going to have any skirt left—uh-oh, Duggie-Sky. That's what's called the 'wrath of a woman.' See her glare? Never mind.

"Tessa may feel lost, even with us, Duggie-Sky. You've had nightmares, right? Well, from what the Olearons said, it'll be like she's trapped in a nightmare. But she doesn't have to be scared— you don't have to be scared, ya' hear me? The captain here kindly volunteered to guide Tess, to keep her from falling. I would do it myself but I'm *your* guard. My son will protect Tessa and the captain—and we all will keep them at the center of our group."

"I missed you, Dad," Ardenal says as he passes Archie and Duggie-Sky on the path. Archie beams. For the moment, even though nothing is as he ever imagined it would be—and Ella is still a captive—Archie is content. The mysterious enchantment of Naiu has begun to work its way from his invigorated hands that clutched the Tillastrion to his elbows and shoulders.

When Archie carries Duggie-Sky—which is more frequent than he and the child had agreed on the stairs of the glass citadel— his arms do not tire. Even his heart drums forcefully in his chest. Its rhythm put Archie to sleep when they camped near the creek—after he secretly read more in the Olearons' cryptic records. Archie hadn't had time to study the words on the glass as thoroughly as he had hoped, because Tessa soon began to stir when Archie was only a dozen paragraphs in. Archie had quickly tucked the glass beneath his ribs and shut his eyes tight. He fell into a deep sleep not long after, though what he had read replayed in his mind all that night in contorted dreams.

The 29th Lord of Olearon was born as Telmakus of the sea guardians. He was exalted to the throne on the eve of the 28th Lord—his father—Teemun's passing. It was then that Telmakus was six-thousand sunsets young. As was his duty, in his birthright of royalty, Telmakus strove to unite with his sole companion.

Telmakus did not find his Maiden among the living Olearons during that obscure, murky season of history on Jarr-Wya. There were none Telmakus recognized from his last life. Thus, he abandoned his throne—and his guardianship of the Sea of Selfdom—to depart the city. He traveled inland and upwards, climbing high the great mountain: Baluurwa the Doomful, as it had been described for countless sunsets.

Every night, as Telmakus ascended, he reflected the moonlight from a shard of oval glass he fused to his left palm. The reflection caught in the glossed mirror mounted to a blue timber pedestal at the topmost step of the city's citadel. The Olearons of that time then rested deeply, safe in the comfort that their Lord was watching down on them from Baluurwa.

Their peace lasted twenty sunsets, until the moonbeam-beacon ceased. The night was smut-black. With fear of the loss of another Lord, the Olearons untied their flames, their city nearly molten in their blazing plea to Baluurwa. Even the day was grim in contrast to their light.

The kin of Telmakus recorded the sunsets of his absence—and of their grief—in burns across their chests. The warriors hastily raced to the foot of Baluurwa and climbed, where the Doomful crushed many Olearons beneath its vengeful stones. The warriors, however, were indeed successful; they discovered Telmakus wandering, his regal breastplate cracked and his traveling jumpsuit torn from his ruby flesh. Vines were coiled around his ankles and tangled in his hair. They reported his disorientation at the citadel, mentioning his claims of finding a clay pearly-painted opulus blossom—a formed and fired guilder-rose globe—inside a white-wooden case, secured with a brass bolt.

Telmakus ranted of using what he discovered was a device, and of a parallel place to Jarr-Wya, to the Olearon's land and the island surrounded by the lonely expanse of sea on every side. He recounted a world recorded in an outlandish measurement of time, like persistent, unbroken knocks; and of creatures, pale and powerless, and unreasonable in their fear. He returned with the proclamation that he had found his love, though she had perished, drowned, and was now present in his body.

The Lord was not the same after his journey. He grew fat in orders and in girth. One sunset, Telmakus disappeared once more. This time, the warriors did not hunt for him. There were rumors of his brother, Dillmus, rising to be the 30th Lord of Olearon. It was soon confirmed that his transformation was already a quarter complete when Telmakus returned, thin, and disagreeable. The Olearons questioned and examined their 29th Lord—something had left him, that was apparent, though he would not say what, only that he had met with a diviner who lived in the crooked tunnels of Baluurwa.

The Olearons condemned Telmakus, stating that the one he spoke of was Laken, the last of the evil she-race called the Steffanus. The Olearons had battled the Steffanus and defeated all but one that escaped: Laken. The Steffanus were striking with their rich amber mane and taunting blue-red eyes, with their smooth voices. Laken, like her departed sisters, could see through the veil of parallel sunsets, across Jarr-Wya's seas, and into future days.

There were some Olearons who begged to know Laken's vision, and others who silenced Telmakus before he could speak Laken's words in their company. Dillmus, who now lusted for his half-earned title, flared with his demands in the face of Telmakus, the one Olearons still hailed as their Lord. Dillmus hurled balls of fire at his eldest sibling and sent slithering coils of scorching chain around Telmakus' neck. The blood-incarnation of Telmakus as Lord of Olearon, and his bewitchment to the Steffanus, afforded the ruler immense power over the half-Lord.

Telmakus embraced Dillmus with hate, crushing his bones and rupturing his brother's control over his flame until it seared throughout the edifice of the gathering. Many wise Olearons perished that sunset. Dillmus was never spoken of again, and the memory of Telmakus—who grew so power-loving that, in the sunsets which followed, his flame tore him apart, severing his body into a hundred pieces—was altered in the public history of the Olearons. Telmakus's knowledge too, was declared forbidden from speaking, but was recorded in secret and discovered by the 30th Lord, now recorded in this black history so that Laken's oracles may be confirmed or disproven in time.

chapter 33

"Whhat is this? Sand?" Valarie asks nervously. At first no one pays any mind to her question. She repeats herself louder, a look of both annoyance and defeat across her scrunched forehead and she lets her brown hair fall over her eyes as she looks away.

Tessa gasps.

Archie turns from his conversation with Duggie-Sky to look in the direction Valarie gestured. It is true. The tree cover thins and the ground beneath their feet transitions from moss to granules of sand.

"Yes," Azkar eventually answers. "But do not worry; it is not the sand of the Millia." Valarie sighs, relieved. "This desert is like an island amidst the land. It is one of the ill effects of the Star, though harmless. There is no enchantment in these grains, only their sharp cut when the wind blows it into your eyes. We Olearons have not named this desert, or the others like it, as we hope for their impermanence. Alas, we must cross it to reach the great tree of Rolace." Valarie nods thoughtfully, staying close on the heels of Captain Nate, who walks beside Tessa.

"Wait!" Ardenal declares. "The desert—it has broadened since we were here last! Azkar, look! The Banji—they are disappearing! They grow sparse very quickly along our path."

Nameris examines the sky. "We still have a few hours' journey left this sunrise."

"If we travel to Rolace and do not find the Banji on his side of this desert, we lose time. We would be forced to return here, to this place," frets Eek.

The Maiden answers the worry with calmness. "We must collect the Banji now, but Tessa—" the Olearon regards the human, "that means many hours of holding the flowers. I have never known anyone to touch them for that long."

"I'll be fine."

Nameris clears his throat. "Your arrogance will not protect you—"

"Careful, Nameris!" Ardenal warns.

"She should know," Nameris shoots back. "The Banji are an offshoot of a magical, wicked race that grew from a flower themselves. They gave the Banji as a gift to impair their enemies so they could slice them in two with ease." Archie covers Duggie-Sky's ears. "The strength of their Naiu should not be taken lightly."

"I understand," Tessa responds evenly.

"I think we all understand, Nameris. Back to practical matters: Once we bind the Banji to Tessa's hands with fabric from her dress and my belt, we could then secure her hands to her body," Ardenal suggests, unfastening his belt. He and Tessa had changed back into their own clothing a mere half-hour after Tessa's dress and coat had hung to dry against Ardenal's skin.

The company test Ardenal's suggestion, but find his belt to be too short to bind both hands and body—the waist of an Olearon being quite narrow—and so Nameris offers up his belt as well and they loop the two together. The Olearons slip off the tops of their jumpsuits and wrap the arms around their waists. "See, this will work!" Ardenal beams. "She will be incapable of thrashing about and dropping them in her madness!"

Tessa nods nervously, though in agreement. Archie watches helplessly. He pictures Ella's blond hair and her freckled nose. In his mind, Ella remains Duggie-Sky's age: four, spirited and chatty. He again remembers her laugh, before the tumor stole it. "You are strong, Tess," he says. "You can do this."

"Thanks, Archie."

Ardenal stands on Tessa's left, Captain Nate on her right. Once Tessa plucks a bouquet of fuchsia Banji, the men enact their plan, careful not to disturb the pollen. Tessa's voice is small, "Oh no."

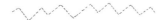

THE magic of the Banji is instantaneous. Tessa feels the discombobulation begin in her fingers; a prickling sensation on the inside of her skin. Her fingertips twitch on their own before the spasm morphs through her hands and wrists in a bolt of tingling energy. From her elbows to her shoulders, her chest to her core, Tessa's body hums in a writhing, twisting, tickling, unrelenting itch. The energy and power of Naiu works its way to her every ending points; her head and the tips of her hair, her toes, heels, ears, lips, eyelashes, and nose. The Banji's scent is deep and rich. The olive-green pollen wafts up into Tessa's nostrils. She sneezes loudly, blowing pollen squarely into Nate's face as he draws near to observe her reaction to the flowers. He staggers, his pupils dilating, his head bobbing side to side.

"He's been affected! Quick!" Azkar gestures to Kameelo, who stands nearby. Azkar's voice is like thunder in Tessa's ears and she turns away from its blast. Kameelo catches Nate around the waist as he tumbles backward.

"Let me go! Help!" Nate screams, thrashing his fists behind his head and at his sides to connect with Kameelo. "I've fallen

into the fire! I'm burning! Someone save me!" He wedges himself free, turning to his captor. With a look of confused terror—
with savage eyes that flit erratically back and forth, and exposed
teeth that he clenches hard—Nate attacks the flaming Olearon.
The instant Nate's fingers clench around Kameelo's neck, he
retracts them and wails, "I'm melting! I'm melting!"

Kameelo struggles with the fighting man, a hint of exas-
peration across his youthful red face. Eek runs to his brother's
aid. Valarie too sprints over to help, but Nate looks at her with
alarm. "A pale demon!" he shrieks, and punches Valarie square
in the nose. Blood sprays and she flops onto the sand.

Lady Sophia yelps at Valarie's blood, which sprayed across
her face and gown. Donna pushes Lady Sophia aside to kneel
with Valarie, tipping her head back and stroking her frazzled
hair.

"Not like that!" Harry barks. "Pinch her nose and lean her
forward."

The Maiden of Olearon swiftly approaches Nate from behind, moving soundlessly. She pulls off her belt and tosses it to
Eek, who nods, removes his own, and connects the two. The
Maiden meets eyes with Kameelo over Nate's shoulder, and he
tips his head in agreement with her when he perceives her intent. The Maiden hefts into the air a bulbous root, broken free
from a nearby tree, and strikes the captain squarely over the
head. Eek pounces and Kameelo turns. Eek straps Nate to
Kameelo's back. The Maiden drops the root to the ground with
a thud.

chapter 34

Tessa, under the spell of the Banji, discerns the fight within the company to be far from resolved and rages against Ardenal, laboring to free herself from his constraints. "Can't you see I have nothing?" she spits at him. "I have only lonely problems, that's all—and those I'd gladly give to you! I'm alone in this world—in every world—can't you see that?"

The Maiden steps forward. "Ardenal, deafen your ears to her," she warns. "It is the Banji. Tessa's thoughts are warped."

"No, Ardenal, take it all in," Zeno chides, standing at the edge of the group, watching with amusement. "You should have taken you wife with you when you came to Jarr-Wya many sunsets ago, and me as well, of course. We can all blame you for something."

"Silence!" Azkar growls at Zeno and wacks him on the head with the stick, which becomes hooked in the Bangol's head-stones.

"Must mind your manners when addressing a king—right Archibald," Zeno fumes, retracting his lips, exposing his fine-ground, spiky teeth, and snarling at Azkar. Zeno contorts his head sharply to one side, his stones snapping the stick into two splintering pieces.

"You know what will not break as easily?" Azkar charges forward, but Archie lunges between him and Zeno, blocking the flaming warrior. The Olearon takes a confused step back. Zeno, at first startled, unconsciously exposes gratitude—for a moment only—across his pinched face, before assuming an expression of nonchalance.

"Zeno is right!" hollers Tessa, startling Azkar, Archie—and Zeno himself.

"I am?"

"You should have brought me with you, Arden," she continues. "I would have found Ella's cure by now."

"Enough," the Maiden orders, but Tessa's revelation—amplified by the enchantment—causes her to resist Ardenal with maddening resolve. She sends sand spraying at her feet, forcing herself, and Ardenal, inches further into the desert, though Donna still tends to Valarie on the edge of the sand.

Tessa cracks her head against anything near. She thrashes with her legs as she continues to speak. "When my daughter dies, that will be it. The last love I have, sliced from my chest. Then what? Nothing! You—you fire-thief—you're robbing me, stealing Ella's cure and my hope for a future. . . Let me go!"

"There is truth in her words," Ardenal reflects sadly.

"As the Maiden said: Enough pandering to the Banji," Nameris grumbles. "If she will not walk willingly, you must carry her." Tessa, disgusted by Nameris' suggestion, sprints a few paces farther before Ardenal's firm grip slows her to a shifting, twisting shuffle. For a moment, she does not advance, though her limbs continue to quiver and her eyes dart erratically to and fro.

Meanwhile, an anxious Duggie-Sky runs to Archie's side, the old man lifting the child and carrying him out of the apex of the commotion. Archie shields the boy's eyes with his arm, though Duggie-Sky—still curious—yanks himself above it to watch the crazed human, impatient Olearons, amused Bangol, and the wounded on the messy, bloody path. Archie shifts from foot to foot, queasy at the sight of Valarie's mangled face. Finally, he abandons the effort of blocking Duggie-Sky's gaze. "You've witnessed worse things than this on the *Odyssey* and on the Millia's beach, little fella—though I hope for no more, for your sake."

Harry uses his golf shirt to wipe Valarie's blood from the distressed and quivering Lady Sophia. "Human, you must reserve your mighty voice for the appointed time," the Maiden cautions the lamenting singer. "We cannot know who has been alerted to our whereabouts after your theatrics."

In contract, Valarie whimpers quietly. She and Donna sit together. Valarie holds her nose, slowed from a profuse flow to a trickle, though the flesh around her eyes is already blotchy and swollen in raccoon-ovals of blood beneath her skin. Tessa stares at Valarie—as if Valarie's facial features have been reorganized in a hideous arrangement—and the cruise director glares back.

"And you two, are you fit to continue?" the Maiden asks Valarie and Donna. The women nod.

Nate droops, unconscious, against Kameelo. "Be careful to control your emotions," warns the Maiden as she marches past. "If you let them rule you, your new friend will be roasted." Blood from Nate's oozing wound drips onto Kameelo's flesh, where it simmers gently. Eek presses his finger to the place the root connected with Nate's skull and seals the cut.

"Let us be off. There is not a moment to waste," continues the Maiden, finally, as she starts trudging up the gradual hill of sand. One by one, the others follow in her long, agile footsteps. Ardenal directs Tessa, steering her by the shoulders with his large hands.

"I'll keep a watch out at the rear," Archie blurts. "The rest of you look like you've got your hands full." Zeno squints suspiciously.

Once the Olearons and humans have passed—along with Zeno, who is again prodded along by Azkar, despite the Bangol once more resorting to his rudest objections—Archie crouches quickly to look Duggie-Sky in the eyes. "Promise to keep a secret, little fella?"

"Yeah, Grandpa Archie!"

"Shh! I don't want the others knowing about this, all right?" Duggie-Sky nods. Archie yanks off one shoe and uncurls his sock from his ankle. He puts the sock over one hand. "Blech—is this the smell my Suzie complained about for years? I really should've helped her with the laundry!" Archie grimaces. Duggie-Sky watches Archie with a worried frown as the man kneels in the sandy dirt and—with his socked hand—collects a small bouquet of Banji. With his free hand, Archie pulls the collar of the sock down his wrist and over the flowers, making sure any jostled pollen drops at his feet, not on his skin.

"There," Archie says, pleased with himself. He holds the sock like a bag with the Banji contained inside. "Now, let me roll this up. Duggie-Sky, grab Grandpa Archie a few of those big leaves, like the ones you were jumping for earlier. Yes, those are the ones. They'll make a great barrier." Archie wraps the rolled flowers and sock inside a layer of foliage. "Hmm. This looks a tad suspicious. It needs a disguise. Can't be too careful. Aha!" He fetches his soiled handkerchief, encloses the leaf-wrapped sock within its folds, and tucks the bundle deep into one of his trouser pockets.

"Why do you want to go into a bad dream?" Duggie-Sky whispers, on the edge of tears.

"You never know when this stuff will come in handy," replies Archie as he pats his pocket. "A secret, remember? Now let's catch up before they notice!"

chapter 35

T he company trudges through the sand so that the comfort and protection of the forest is distant behind
them. Tessa watches her feet, a peculiar look on her face. "They
seem far away," she says. "How did they grow so small? Ah! My
legs! They're endless! Sucked deep into the sand!" She screams,
but Ardenal's fingers slip over her mouth. With the ever-
increasing enchantment of the Naiu-laced Banji, Tessa feels the
red muzzle convert her breath to steam, which scalds her lips.
She whips her head back and forth, fighting to be free.

"Be quiet and I'll take my hand away." Ardenal speaks
calmly, but Tessa follows the sound of his voice, cranking her
neck to look at him over her shoulder. Ardenal deliberately removes his fingers one by one.

Tessa smiles, pausing to turn her body to face Ardenal, then
she chokes on bile. "That one over dar; he wus right," she
moans as her eyes are locked with the Olearon's. "Youareade-
mon!" Her words slur together, and she arches her spine in an
uncomfortable dip away from Ardenal. His hands brace her hips
as her head plunks backward onto the sand. "Someone, save
me!" she howls from the bridge position.

"It's the Banji," Ardenal repeats. "Whatever apparitions you
see, they're your imagination only."

"Look! The sand! It's consuming me!" Tessa snaps back to upright and points to her feet, which are sucked down deep in the golden granules.

"It's all an illusion—" Archie starts to say as he catches up, then hesitates. He blinks. Tessa is, in fact, sinking farther than normal into the sand.

Ardenal hoists Tessa upward by her elbows, but, even once reset again on the surface, her feet, ankles and calves continue to submerge swiftly. "Do you see this?" Ardenal calls to the other Olearons.

Before they can answer, Tessa interrupts. "I see a ship!" she shouts and points, confusion and horror tightening across her face. "There! Its sails are crimson and its wood is black. It's coming this way!"

"Another delusion," grumbles Azkar—until he observes it as well.

The black-wood ship that has appeared in the clouds and sails through the dusty blue sky, crashes onto the golden hill with a splash of sand. It parts the desert as if it were warm butter. Its long flags ripple in an unfelt though raging breeze in the distance, billowing its sails toward the company, perhaps also summoning the newly arriving mist, slinking along in their direction.

The Maiden raises her voice, which for the first time is laced with dread. "It is the strength of the Banji! Whatever cursed hallucination Tessa conjures becomes our reality."

"It comes for us!" cries Tessa, as if in answer, and she attempts to run, but—like all in their company—she has sunk thigh-deep in the sand while watching the sky turn the sinister color of ink. The smoke-like clouds began with the mist, as far-off wisps, which grow and amalgamate into one jet-black tornado. The circling draft, now felt on the skin of the company, touches down on the sand a few hundred feet away and begins to suck it upward into the void. Tessa shelters her face from the pelting grit. "We are going to be torn apart!"

"She's remembering the Millia, the day we crashed on the island," Donna shouts above the wind, sand crunching between her teeth. The company is now waist-deep. Duggie-Sky climbs to Archie's shoulders and clings to his white hair—what is left of it—and his perspiring forehead.

The Maiden of Olearon strains and rips herself from the sand to slide along its surface on her chest, with her legs and arms fanning wide. She crawls to Ardenal and Tessa, cupping the human's face and insists, "Listen to me, Tessa Wellsley. If you want to save your Ella, look at me." She captures Tessa's wandering attention, fleetingly. "Imagine the storm retreating! Send it away, Tessa."

"It is too strong. I have no magic!" Tessa begins to weep.

"Fight it! Battle the storm!" Ardenal yells as he struggles to push the sand away from where it has risen to Tessa's shoulders.

As the ship approaches it catapults bloody cannonballs at them, which ricochet off the sand with a splash of gold. The first volley of cannon fire misses its mark, but the second is closer, revealing the cannonballs to be something much more menacing. As they roll closer, they prove to be skulls, scratched and broken but showing glimpses of white beneath the crimson that matches the ship's malevolent bloody sails. They leave a damp film on the sand.

"She's remembering your wretched ship," Zeno sneers, scowling at Azkar and Nameris.

"Picture it away!" yells Eek. "Human, please!"

Tessa ignores him, never breaking her fearful rapture with the scene before her. She screams, "The Millia! They've come for us!" As soon as the words leave her mouth, a huge quantity of sand between the company and the ship is sucked skyward, growing into a sparkling, shifting village.

"How did we get here?" Senior Karish demands. "A curse!"

The Millia leader, morphing into the form of a four-legged beast, leaps out of a wall and roars. The village transforms into two hundred similar seething, snarling forms. They scrape their clawed paws along the face of the desert, unaffected by its quickening drag.

With Tessa quivering at the sight of Senior Karish and the hungry pack behind him, the quicksand halts suddenly, leaving only the noses and foreheads of the humans, and the full heads and necks of the Olearons, above the surface. Zeno, who had scurried up the back of Archie, perches on one shoulder of the old man, while Duggie-Sky has shifted to sit on the other. Bangol and child feverously dig away the dusty grit at Archie's stubbly upper lip and chin, clearing space for the old man to breathe through his mouth. The Maiden, the only one free of the golden grip, still lies prostrate on the surface, as if weightless.

Senior Karish pounces toward them. "What is the meaning of this? How did you summon us from our shoreline? From our shoreline!" he roars.

"It is the Banji," the Maiden says as she stands upright to approach the glinting beast. She lights her body ablaze, turning the sand beneath her steps to glass, preventing her from slipping downward once more. "The flower's spell is strengthened by extended contact, altered on these wicked sands brought here by the Star."

As she speaks, the ship continues its advance, rippling the sand as it sends a third volley of skulls toward them. The Millia, between the company and the ship, burst apart as the skulls puncture their forms and continue rocketing onward. The sandy creatures turn to look behind them with vehement, shifting eyes.

One narrowly misses Valarie and Harry. All they can do is scrunch their eyes closed. Another skull connects. This time, it tears Eek's head and neck from his buried torso.

"NO!" screams Azkar. "BROTHER!" But his youngest sibling is mutilated beyond saving. Weeping hard, Azkar struggles to free himself of the sand's grip. He shifts his weight, dislodging enough sand for him to wedge out his shoulders, then his arms. Steam rises steadily from his eyelids as the fever of his flame evaporates his tears before they can fall.

"The ship!" Tessa yelps, her voice barely audible through the sand and above Azkar's grief-ridden moans. The Maiden and Senior Karish turn to look. "We'll be buried beneath it!"

"Millia! Destroy!" Senior Karish growls. The beasts run and jump together in a thunderclap of sand, momentarily fusing into one mammoth form before morphing into distinct shapes once more. They scale the side of the black ship as if it were a play structure and begin tearing its boards apart with thrashing fangs and piercing talons. The vessel is dismantled in a matter of breaths and the Millia mutate into tidal waves that repeatedly crash upon the enchanted black wood until only splinters and plasma remain.

The Millia shriek. With unquenchable hunger, they leech the blood from the sand, sucking it into themselves as Archie had witnessed them do once before, on the southern beach the day the *Atlantic Odyssey* shipwrecked there.

"Perhaps we stay, claim this desert, yes, claim this desert as our own," bellows Senior Karish.

"TESSA!" pleads the Maiden.

"The Millia are appeased," Tessa whispers through her silt-covered lips as Ardenal, who has freed his arms, beats back the sand encroaching further on her face. In a brilliant flash of light, the desert is once more unanimated, yet resumes its slippery suction; the voices of the Millia are replaced with the wheeze of the quicksand in its one long inhale.

"We are going to di——!" screams Tessa, but Ardenal shoves his fingers into her mouth so her tongue cannot form the prophetic words.

The Olearons wriggle free and, like the Maiden, fan their limbs wide on the sand's surface. They ignite their bodies. The tiny shards beneath them melt into firm glass an inch thick, allowing the Olearons to kneel, stand, and walk, unaffected by the quicksand. They frantically excavate the humans' heads, scooping away the sand before it clogs their nostrils. Kameelo rests Nate's body on a piece of glass and joins the others in the effort. Ardenal too shoves away large handfuls to expose Tessa's chin and soon she can drop her jaw to gulp in air—but the relief is fleeting.

"We cannot dig fast enough!" Nameris yells.

Tessa's eyes grow wide. "A tornado!" she whimpers.

"Here we go again," Zeno huffs as he slouches, exasperated, on Archie's shoulder. Duggie-Sky, too, looks weary of the onslaught and distressed at Eek's demise.

The windstorm that had inflated the sails of the black-blood ship was displaced once the vessel was destroyed. It languished here and there, unnoticed until now, as it picks up speed and spews sharp grit in every direction. The quicksand is no match for the volatile lust of the tornado; it grabs sand, humans, Olearons, and Bangol, lifting them toward the sun. Even Eek's body is freed and Azkar grabs ahold of it.

"Dampen your flames!" Kameelo orders through a coughing fit as his mouth brims with granules. "Our heat will turn the sand to daggers that will pierce us through!" The Olearons calm themselves, recoil their heat and expel coolness to their limbs. Their fire retreats beneath their dreadlocks.

All members of the company bash into each other as the group is spun higher into the sandstorm. Cries of pain swirl with them, though every voice is detached from its moaning lips.

Abruptly they are pulled to the center of the tornado, to float suspended among grains of sand in a pocket of peaceful air. "Tessa," the Maiden calls, her voice measured and calm, "you must imagine our safety. Bring us to the ground on the northeast side of this desert. You can do this. Do it for Ella. We must save her."

Tessa's dilated eyes whip around to each human and Olearon, and to Zeno as well, but she fails to focus—until she spots Azkar. The Olearon clutches the lifeless pieces of Eek; his body and severed neck and head. The Banji's effect is forceful, encompassing; and Tessa frets instead. "See? We are being pulled in two!" She points—and, at her unknowing command, the wind whirls faster, pelting them sharply with sand.

Harry cries out in agony. "Tessa! Save us," he wails as the sharp sandstorm eats away his shirt, stained with Valarie's blood.

"Imagine the forest on the far edge of the desert," Ardenal urges. "The milky-white trees are tall, only dwarfed by the mountain itself. They are robed in vines, like gowns that drape and fold. Picture them, Tessa. The sunshine illuminates their bark so that the forest glows and sparkles, so bright you must shield your eyes. This woodland on the east was once the home of the sprites, before the construction of the Bangols bridges. The trees still remember their magic. They call for us, Tess. Take us there."

"Yes! I see them through the storm!" marvels Tessa. "The forest is dense. Their branches reach, cradling the nests of fowl! The vines braid the trunks together. It's exquisite!"

"Good, Tessa. Wonderful!" Ardenal praises. "Now see their branches stretch farther, reaching out to us. Their trunks bow in our direction."

"They want us to live. They're trying to save us," Tessa sings, and the others finally see the trees and vines and nests as Tessa's words carry the forest's edge into view. The towering trunks arch before the spiteful gale.

Ardenal continues to guide Tessa's hallucinations. "Now see their viney-creepers unfurl from around them."

"They are! They creep like caterpillars up along the branches, and reach, stretching for us."

"Yes, Tessa, keep them coming! Now, shift the storm," Ardenal says. "Bring us close." The vines and the wind obey. The leafy creepers undulate through the sandy air and curl about the bodies of the company as they had around their trunks.

"Pull us—quickly—to the treetops so we don't plummet to the ground!" Ardenal yells. The company is snapped out of the raging wind and through the calm blue sky tinged with orange as the sun retreats into dusk.

"A net!" Ardenal yells as they fall toward the leafy canopy below. "The forest will save us!"

Tessa beams. The vines obligingly weave together to form a broad net as the group crashes through the upper leaves, startling birds and arboreal creatures that burst into the sky or scurry out of the way. The group hits the vines, bouncing and colliding until they finally stop, resting atop each other thirty feet above the forest floor, still tangled in the creepers.

The only sound is the weeping of Azkar, his thick scar pinched across is pained face. He clutches what is left of Eek. The deceased Olearon's blood drips to the leaf litter beneath them.

"Where are we?" Nate's voice startles them all. No one noticed when he regained consciousness.

"We are in the eastern forest. Rolace's dwelling is not far," Nameris answers faintly.

The Maiden ignites a flame in the palm of her hand and wraps it around one anchored vine after another. They drop, one jerky foot at a time, until they tumble onto the moist earth. The humans use their glass blades to hack off the remaining vines.

Ardenal had clutched tight to Tessa, chest to chest, as they had risen in the tornado and also as they were rescued by Tessa's vision of the bending forest. He now steps back as he and the company realize that the Banji had pressed against him as he hugged his wife. "I must be affected. Did Tessa cause the vines to save us—or did I? Disorientation . . . it's wafting through my senses." Ardenal steps aside willingly as Nate eagerly approaches to watch over Tessa.

"We must perform the scorching ceremony," the Maiden says gently to Azkar. "Will you honor Eek, or would you have Kameelo or Nameris do it? Or shall I?"

"I will," whispers Azkar through his flame. "He was my little brother. He was under my care. I should have saved him, taken the evil skull myself and died, but, at the very least, I will honor him now."

Azkar's fire burns over Eek, bright, blazing and elevated, just shy of the lowest dangling leaves overhead. The Olearon's skin morphs from the usual warm red to yellow, then to smoldering blue. Azkar's flame envelopes Eek's body, which radiates as a blinding white light. The humans are forced to look away.

"The forest is on fire!" Tessa screams. "The flames jump off Azkar! They burn the white bark to charcoal!"

"Get her away from here," demands the Maiden. Nate leads Tessa away from the memorial, calming her in a hushed voice, stroking her hair. Ardenal, lucid enough to walk, staggers over to throw dirt against the oxidizing bark.

Valarie chews her lips and folds her arms across her chest. "Nate, can I come with you?"

"Not now," he answers.

Valarie scowls at Nate's back while scratching dried blood from the outside of her nose, still pinching it closed. She stands alone on the perimeter of the group, then tiptoes into the trees.

The ash of Eek's body floats peacefully upward, swaying lazily from side to side. The Maiden begins to sing. Eek's brothers join her. Azkar's voice is low and lamenting: "Eek, your warrior spirit is invincible, from sunset to sunset, world to world, from this Star to the next. With every step, every breath, every laugh, we carry your bravery with us."

Archie clears his throat. "I'd like to pay my respects to someone who showed such kindness to my son. Thank you, Eek." Azkar nods at Archie with gratitude.

The Olearons—the Maiden, Nameris, Kameelo, and Ardenal—encircle Azkar, who looks up to the cinders and powdery remains. They link their bodies and walk in a circle around Azkar and what is left of Eek, the fixed points at their center. Their flames funnel together and swoop up through the leaves into the dull sky in a faultless column of fire.

chapter 36

"Nanjee lost her leg when our balloon crashed. It wasn't Luggie's fault! He was bringing us in for a nice landing when suddenly, whoosh! The wind sucked inland, back toward the patch of desert. We had a small area to set down in, on the rocky shore between the white forest and ocean. I think it was a hard landing for all the Bangols, but we were last. The rest of them were on the ground already, standing on large boulders strewn across the beach, watching us. That's a lot of pressure.

As our balloon jolted toward the tall white trees, I pulled the sack over my head. Even if I died, I didn't want Nanjee and Luggie getting into trouble because of me. Both were pulling the ropes but I'm guessing that together they weigh less that one adult Bangol. Our clay basket hit a tree and cracked open like a nut. We fell—I don't know how far. Rough hands hauled me away. Nanjee's screams were horrible. She kept yelling, "My leg! Where is my leg?"

Luggie didn't make a noise. I hollered for him, but it sounded all wrong, and the waves were loud. I tried to rip off the sack, but they pulled it over my body and dragged me. I hit my head against something solid and passed out. I woke up in this stone jail. It's fine, as far as cells go. I think only one day has passed, but I can't be sure.

Last night all the Bangols were muttering about some happening on Jarr-Wya. I could overhear them through the rocky walls, which are full of cracks. I can hear and see quite a bit in every direction. I found a small opening to shove my face against and could make out a streak of fire off in the distance. It rose taller than the trees, glowing in the almost night sky. It got the Bangols hustling.

A minute later they hauled my cellmate out by her foot. She was a school teacher, on her honeymoon. Deb was her name. She hadn't seen her husband since the first fireball hit the *Odyssey*. Deb talked a lot. She gave off the girlfriends-having-coffee vibe, even if we were sitting in a damp, eight-foot cell, surrounded by our own filth because there was nowhere else to relieve ourselves. Deb said when they were in her clay basket, the Bangols questioned her about purity.

Deb said they asked her repeatedly, "Are you pure?" She was like, "How do I answer that?" She told them that she was, hoping that they wouldn't hurt her if she was pure. I think this made Deb a little cocky. They treated her better than me, that's for sure. She wasn't all that scared when the Bangols came for her—but she should have been.

They dragged her to the end of a long stone bridge, where Tuggs was waiting. They had a big ceremony with amazing-smelling candles and flowers. Then they threw Deb into the ocean. She had a hundred stones tied to her ankles.

What's that sound? My name . . . Someone is whispering to me. Luggie! I stick my fingers through a crack and touch him. I get that giddy feeling in my stomach. Then I press my ear to the crack to listen.

"My father is sacrificing people," Luggie says. I feel cold suddenly, but I'm sweating. Luggie's words make my head dizzy. I realize that the voices of the screaming people, every night, are now dead bodies, floating like a garden planted at the bottom of the sea.

"My father believes that, because your kind are from another world and so is the Star, he can bribe it. But we Bangols are connected to the land. We can sense no change to the poison in Jarr-Wya's clay and soil after the first ten sacrifices—and our race are no more powerful. My dad and his warriors are getting desperate. They think the Olearons are hunting them.

"I told him that you are not a good sacrifice," Luggie continues. "I think you're great, Ella—but I said that you are broken, impure. I told him about your cut mark. I hope he trusts me. I'm trying to convince him that we should retreat to our fortress in the north and take the rest of the captives with us. That's inland, though. My dad is obsessed with the Star and everything happening above it. I hope he will listen to me. Once I get you to my home, then we can figure out what to do next.

"Here's something to eat." Luggie shoves the bread I love through the hole. It breaks apart and I catch every crumb.

"Oh no . . ." Luggie whispers. I press my eye back to the crack. It's Tuggs!

Tuggs punches Luggie across the face. Luggie falls to his knees. He's bleeding. Tuggs kicks him in the gut. Tuggs points at my cell and I crawl away from the opening. My heart hurts. I look back through the crack, but they are gone.

The door of my cell screams open on its salt-rusted hinges. I know I should be humble and beg for my life. I know I should cower and be broken, like Luggie told his dad about me—what everyone back home thinks about me as well. But when I see Luggie's big scared eyes, and his blood dripping, as he tries to get past Tuggs to reach me—because he wants to protect me—I feel bold all of a sudden. If I'm destined to die anyway, from cancer or as a sacrifice to the Star, I might as well go out fighting for someone I care about.

I glare at Tuggs, squinting so tightly he blurs between my eyelashes, and I take a purposeful step in his direction. He doesn't move, so I keep walking. Luggie tells me to stop, but I don't. I put my hand in my pocket and feel for the largest glass shard, all that is left of the dagger Olen gave me on the Millia's beach.

Tuggs reaches out to me slowly, without words. I wasn't expecting that. The gesture is not hostile. I freeze. With one finger he flicks crumbs from my shirt. Oh no. He knows! Tuggs turns and I grab him and slice his upper arm with the glass. He doesn't flinch. He rips the glass from my fingers and shatters it against the wall of the cell. I try to bowl him over, but he is solid. I let out all the things I want to say, and the noises scare even me, but Tuggs just shoves me down. The cell door slams shut.

Oh no, what have I done? I didn't help Luggie! I may have inadvertently killed him!

chapter 37

"My brother was too young. Barely a youth." Nameris beats his chest with a clenched fist. "He hadn't yet found his partner in this life."

"Maybe in the next," Ardenal offers. The lingering effect of the Banji had burnt off during the ceremony.

The Maiden addresses the brothers. "Your parents will be proud of your courage, Azkar, Nameris, and Kameelo. They will not blame you. I will explain upon our return."

"If we return," Nameris grumbles under his breath.

"I'm sorry about Eek," Ardenal says. "But I have faith—"

"Maybe it is easy for you to have faith because you were once as stupid as these." Nameris gestures to the humans. "How many of my brothers must die to fulfill your desires? Let's get on with meeting Rolace so he can rip our limbs from our bodies."

As the sun sets, the trees glow in the moonlight, which casts ominous crooked shadows across the earth. The company travels with care, as each branch and bush scratches at their legs and arms, and snags in their hair. The hoots and caws have been replaced with hisses and clicks. The company speaks in whispers. Nate carries a sleeping Tessa, exhausted though still plagued in dream by the Banji within her grasp. The Olearons lead ever onward with their light.

"I think it's time you told me the full story, son," says Archie, who matches Ardenal's pace. The Olearon carries a sleeping Duggie-Sky, keeping the child warm in the chill night air.

"Zeno had told me I needed someone from his world to travel with me to Jarr-Wya."

"Which is true," Zeno pipes up.

"My research had never pointed to that fact. What I had learned was that the Bangols are selfish and manipulative."

"Also, true," grins Zeno.

"I didn't believe what Zeno told me and, so I stole the Til-lastrion," Ardenal continues. "From what I had heard and read about the Bangols, I wanted to get as far away from Zeno as possible. When I was tucked down an unlit side alley of the market, I tried to activate the magic, but nothing happened. That's when Winzun arrived. He crept up behind me. I actually thought it was Zeno at first, hellbent on vengeance."

Archie scrunches his nose. "Who is Winzun?"

"My twin brother, Archibald," Zeno answers. "He stole my chance to get home."

Ardenal nods. "With Winzun, the magic—Naiu—came to life, and the Tillastrion glowed."

"Winzun and I—the only blood heirs—were banished to your world by Tuggeron," says Zeno. "When Arden arrived at *Treasures*, Winzun was not with me. I would have left him behind if Arden had not fled. I do not blame Winzun for doing the same to me. To be king was a dream we shared since the womb."

Ardenal continues, "Even before I met Zeno, and Winzun, my research in Seattle led me to believe that the Olearons were wicked and cruel. I read that they burned their way through Jarr-Wya to maintain dominion over it, but that was a lie. I had been searching around on my own here, on the island, lost because of the notebook I misplaced at home, wounded and starving. When I was about to step onto the Millia's shore, Olen tackled me."

"He was good at that," Archie says, remembering Olen take down Tessa and Ella on that same beach.

"As my friendship with the Olearons grew, I hoped they would reveal to me the secrets of this place. They knew nothing, however, about Ella's cure, but I kept searching and learning what I could. This is a dangerous place, Dad. I got into treacherous situations, with Bangols and other creatures, and the Olearons saved me—every time. I never did see a Steffanus, and of them the Olearons refuse to speak." The hair on Archie's arms prick upward at the mention of the women he had read about in the secret history of the Olearons. *Steffanus.* Archie shifts awkwardly from foot to foot, dropping his eyes from Ardenal's gaze.

"And for good reason," barks Nameris, who fails to notice the old man's sudden discomfort.

Ardenal dismisses Nameris' cantankerousness with a brush of his hand through the air, and continues, "One day, the Lord of Olearon called me to the glass citadel. He told me that he knew of a creature that would help me on my quest. The Lord told me that everyone has a distinctive gift, but only through magic can this power be brought forth. I asked him what my power was and how I could find this creature. It was then that I first learned of Rolace.

"So, I went on a pilgrimage with Azkar and Nameris to find the great tree of Rolace. When we found him, I begged for his help to reveal my gift. He told me that I had a choice; told me that I could not save Ella as a man—I needed to become of this world—and I believed him. I felt too deeply entwined in my mission to stop, that I had been gone from home for too long. I was afraid to go back without Ella's remedy. I was also afraid I would be too late even if I found it. I worried I would walk into our house and discover a place void of Ella's paintings and sketchbooks and novels; empty of ticket stubs to horror movies and of photos on the wall taken by Ella with her phone; and vacant of her smile . . .

"So, I surrendered myself to Rolace—Nameris, too—while Azkar stood guard. I soon discovered who—or what, I should say—I was to become."

"You are an Olearon now," the Maiden confirms. "In blood, bone, and mind."

Nate and Kameelo, who had been talking in low voices, stop suddenly. After carrying the captain on his back, the Olearon has grown fond of the man, but now their merry discussion is cut off without warning. They stand still. "A web!" Nate whispers over his shoulder to the rest of the company, as he gently wakes Tessa. Not all in the company hear his warning and the humans collide, bumping into the fiery Olearons, who quickly extinguish their flames to prevent a burning, and all beings knock into and trip over each other in the dark until they are thoroughly stuck in the semi-translucent silk web.

Ardenal is the first to speak. "We have found Rolace."

Already leaves are rustling overhead. "I would say Rolace has found us," Zeno retorts, more timidly than usual. He curls his stubby legs up to his chest where he hangs, now silent, listening.

"What do you have for me, Tessa?" Rolace's voice rumbles.

Tessa, who still sways under the spell of the Banji, looks to Nate and Kameelo, stuck in the maze of webbing beside her. They reach over and carefully unfasten the belt. Tessa's arms fall, but she never loses her grasp on the flowers. Kameelo burns her free so she can walk. Tessa takes a disoriented step farther into the maze, which connects one glowing white tree to another. Without a guiding word from the nervous company, Tessa relies on the perceptions of Naiu to find the face that had revealed itself to her in the creek, and now again in the shadows of the forest. Rolace's body is faintly illuminated by the Olearon's glow. The human eyes and wrinkled cheeks, his chin and forehead, are fused to the hairy arthropod abdomen and cephalothorax, but instead of eight legs, he has twelve.

"The Banji," Tessa says and holds out the flowers. "Now can you help me find my gift?" she manages to say.

Rolace tenderly collects the Banji and tucks them away in a pouch near his spinneret. "First, I'm hungry. Which of your friends do you care for the least?"

Tessa immediately grows more lucid under the stark absence of the enchantment. She retorts, "That was not part of our deal!"

"It was not *not* part of our deal, either," Rolace quips, and smiles craftily. "But have it as you wish," he sighs. "A flock of cradle birds is due to arrive in these parts tomorrow. I will fast until then. Now, shall we begin?"

"What are you going to do to me?"

"Oh, Tessa. I see your fear, but it is as I told you. If your will is strong and your heart is brave, you shall have no troubles with me."

"And if I am weak?"

"Weak, or wicked, then I may indeed taste warm flesh before the cradle birds turn up on their migration." He smirks. "I have helped many races of people. Even your own Ardenal, here. He came to me looking for a cure. I presume he never found it. Interesting. Nevertheless, I gave him the means. Now for you, Tessa, I do not know what your transformation will entail, but I will do my part and you must do yours. Do we agree?"

"Yes." Tessa nods passionately. "But first, cut loose my friends." She points to the others, stuck along different parts of the maze.

"Really, is there any harm in letting them hang around?" Rolace smiles. "I can deal with them later, if you wish."

A low sizzling startles the man-spider, who discovers that the Olearons are burning themselves free of the web and doing the same for Zeno and the humans. "Stop! I'll free you myself!" Rolace hisses, rushing over on his swift, harry legs. "I have worked too long to have this artistry burned with such heartless disregard."

The deed done, the company freed, Rolace turns back to Tessa. "So, now that we are all friends . . . Tessa, I will bind you in a cocoon of silk. My web is rich with Naiu, and there is also power from the spirit of this forest, the lingering magic of the long-departed sprites." Rolace gestures with a leg to the trees mostly concealed in blackness beyond the orange light of the Olearons' flames.

"Are you sure you want to do this?" Donna asks Tessa with motherly concern.

Tessa nods, squeezes Donna's hand. "So, you wrap me in a cocoon. Then what, Rolace?"

"Then the web will squeeze you until you have no breath left. It will creep into your mouth and nose and find its way through your veins to your heart. You must stay very still during this part or you may scare away the magic. It is mighty in this form, though timid. Whatever power is buried within you, Tessa, will emerge when you surrender. The web will search through your mind, behind your eyes, right down to the root of your toenails—and you must resist every inclination to fight. When the pain reaches the point where death is near, then that is the moment you must call life back to yourself. Bite. Fight to escape your smooth coffin. Once you stand before me again, your transformation will be complete."

"What if I die?" Tessa asks slowly.

"Then you die," Rolace replies. "And I eat."

"That will never happen, not on my watch," Nate growls, retrieving his knife from his boot. He flips it open.

Tessa thanks Nate through her gaze, but turns to Ardenal instead. "You did this," she begins. "Do you believe I can as well?"

"I know you can, Tess. You are strong and your love for Ella even stronger. It will not be easy, but never give up. You must fight." Ardenal leans in close to kiss Tessa and Rolace looks away, impatient. Nate purses his lips and grunts. Ardenal pecks her cheek, lingers, and whispers so that even Tessa strains to hear, "If you cannot break free, scream my name and I will burn you out."

Tessa faces Rolace, sighs, and says, "I'm ready."

"Finally!" Rolace groans. "But I would not be a good host if I did not also offer a cocoon to my other friends as well."

After a moment of silence, with the company frozen in contemplation, Kameelo steps forward boldly. "I wish for this as well."

Rolace's legs twitch with excitement. "Oh, wonderful! Anyone else?"

"We will," Donna and Harry say together.

Tessa turns to the elderly couple and worries aloud, "I can battle my way out, but you two—"

"Don't underestimate us, darling," Donna replies. "We may be old, but we're feisty."

"On one condition," Harry adds to Rolace. "We be bound in one cocoon, together."

"Strange," remarks Rolace. "I have never heard this request before today. I cannot promise the result. Why would you wish such a thing?"

"If we live, we live together. If we die, we do not face it alone. This—" Harry gestures around himself, to the land and those who stand at his side. "This has been the greatest adventure of our lives. We would not have it continue, or end, in any other way."

"Me too!" says a tiny voice.

Every member of the company turns to Duggie-Sky.

"No! No way, little fella." Archie shakes his head.

"You are the child's guardian, not his master," the Maiden corrects. "A brave spirit, despite its age, should never be under-estimated."

"I couldn't live with myself. No. What kind of person would that make me? No. Never," Archie whimpers and continues to shake his head, though more uncontrollably.

"This is not your world, Archibald," continues the Maiden. "The child is strong—and we may need his strength in the days to come."

"Aha! Now I get it," Archie snarls, stepping between Duggie-Sky and the Maiden. "You want to use the boy as a weapon! Sorry, lady, but you're way off base if you think I'll—"

A tiny hand taps Archie's leg.

"Grandpa Archie, I listened. I understand how scary it'll be. Right now, I'm a hero with no powers." The boy points to his T-shirt and the cartoon superhero riding the Douglas Skywarrior. "Please, I want to so badly."

"Listen to the child, Archibald," the Maiden urges.

Archie wipes away his emotion on his jacket sleeve and bends low, hugging Duggie-Sky tightly. They walk hand in hand toward the spider, where Archie allows the child's fingers to slip out of his wrinkled palm.

"The sunrise will be here soon enough. Line up before we waste the night," orders Rolace. Tessa, Kameelo, Donna, Harry, and Duggie-Sky face the enormous creature, who cackles through a mischievous grin. "See you all soon," he says, "in one form or another!"

Shiny threads of silk explode upward from Rolace's back-side. The threads first anchor in the trees, then fly at the line of waiting humans and Olearon to weave around their ankles. They are yanked sharply into the air, where they dangle upside down. Donna and Duggie-Sky cry out. Rolace regards them with hungry eyes—first with two human irises, before the pupils steal any color that surrounds them, and divide into four protruding spheres. Arthropod palpi emerge through the unnaturally stretched human mouth.

Archie looks on in dismay. "What have we done?"

chapter 38

Rolace climbs the first fine string attached to Harry and Donna's ankles. Tessa marvels that the nearly invisible thread can support his weight, but Rolace ascends effortlessly and the web barely flexes as he scurries across it. As silk spews from his spinneret, Rolace's many legs sew rapidly, feverishly spinning the couple. Harry clenches his eyes shut. The cocoon covers their feet and shins, then their knees and thighs, then their arms and torsos. The sticky silk fully envelops Donna and Harry and binds them together, cheek to cheek. Their cocoon sways in and out of the small pockets of moonlight that leak through the canopy. When Rolace is finished, only a few strands of Donna's white hair hang limply out of the glossy covering. They make no sound. The cocoon does, however, wriggle around, bending and arching. Every so often, the shape of two bodies is recognizable.

Rolace darts across the treetops, rustling flora and cracking twigs. Small leaves waft to the earth below. The man-spider drops down to spin and weave Kameelo's cocoon. Kameelo gives a quick smile to those below before the web covers his face. There is a weak hiss and a puff of smoke as the web quenches his flame.

Rolace cocoons Duggie-Sky in the same fashion—who looks tiny once obscured by the silk—before he approaches Tessa.

"Ready?" Rolace hisses, though he proceeds without waiting for her answer.

The web around her ankles wraps itself up her legs. Her feet tingle with a sensation between pain and fatigue. She covers her heart with her hands in time for the silver string to bind them there. Seconds later, her body is covered from her neck to her toes. In the instant before the webbing encases Tessa's ears, she hears Ardenal's voice call up to her, "I love you."

Tessa can sense the places on her back and head and feet where Rolace secures the cocoon—and the jab of pain at her scars where her crooked spine was snapped back into place as a child—before a swinging sensation catches her by surprise. She sees light all around her, where she had expected the darkness of confinement. The light is silver and painfully bright. Her eyes struggle to focus. In one instant, the light appears as far and expansive as a wide-open sky, then, in a matter of an instant, it feels as dim and close as a gray wall at the tip of her nose. Tessa's eyelashes stroke the web with every blink. Her breath bounces back into her mouth but carries with it a vulgar taste of moldy leaves.

The silver webbing starts to glow, defines itself with shadows, and slowly crawls on Tessa's skin. She takes a deep breath and tries to ready herself for what's to come. *If I turn into an Olearon, like Arden, will Ella still recognize me?* she wonders. Tessa thinks about Archie. He knew the Olearon was Arden almost immediately.

The web pries Tessa's lips wide and fills her mouth. She coughs and chokes on it as it slides into every available space, then creeps down her throat. Tessa's body shudders. Agony shoots through her as the web splinters into fine threads and traces the curves of her veins. She contorts back and forth as tears muddy the brilliance of the light.

Tessa mumbles Ella's name, although she cannot speak. Her jaw clicks and hangs loosely as more webbing inches in. *I am going to survive this,* she tells herself. *I will find Ella. Arden will find her cure. We are going to be okay. I am going to be okay. My family will not leave me. Not like my parents . . .* The thought interrupts the filling and the choking and the white.

Tessa becomes aware of floating in an endless galaxy. Her arms and legs stretch wide. There are stars all around her—and islands. Jarr-Wya. It is the size of her palm. She touches it and it spins away in an unpredictable rotation. She touches a star and it streaks through the expanse until it connects with another, which, like Newton's Cradle, maintains the momentum for infinity. Feeling sleepy, she lies back, displacing more stars and islands as she drifts from nowhere to nothing.

How heavenly! Would it be so bad to stay? she wonders. *In this flawless peace, away from all desire, with no worries, no one to take care of . . .*

Take care of! The though jars her. *I do have someone to take care of,* Tessa remembers. *Ella! I need to get out of here!* Tessa's thoughts race and she becomes aware of every bloated blood vessel in her body. Images flash before her eyes. Flames on sand. A sun in the sea. Ella. A child crying in a tree. Drowning in the clouds. Black. Silver. Hands around her neck. *I can't breathe!* Large yellow eyes. The words: "Hurry up!" A stone fortress on the edge of the sea. Rock cliffs. Flowers on water. A clay bowl, oats and water, poured out over stone. A strangely familiar yet unfamiliar voice. Chains jingling. Red spinning planets and blue dripping blood. The *Atlantic Odyssey,* eaten by caterpillars. They slice through the steel bearing the lettering Constellations Cruise Line, which lodges like slivers in their thousands of mouths. They fly off and scatter the memory into every corner of the world.

Tessa tries to scream for Arden, but no sound can escape her parched lips, gummed up as if with tree sap molted by the web as it evolves. *How am I going to get out of here?* She begins bashing at the emptiness and is relieved when her fingers dig deeply into something she cannot see. She claws it—and feels air fill her lungs, so she does not stop, even when her fingernails crack and her fingertips bleed.

Suddenly, a familiar yet unfamiliar voice speaks as clear as Tessa's own words in her head. The voice says, *"Hi, Mom."*

chapter 39

*E*lla?
    Yeah.

Is this a dream?

I think so.

Are you okay?

Okay enough.

Where are you?

Above the Star. Where are you?

In a cocoon.

Definitely a dream.

It's nice to hear your voice.

I've never stopped talking.

Did I stop listening?

Mom, you're in danger.

What do you mean?

Get out, Mom. Get out—

chapter 40

"*L*eave her alone, Valarie." Nate's voice is firm but pleading.

"Why should I? Because you love her? Well, you know what? You loved me once—me—but I never stopped loving you." The cruise director's mouth twists into a nasty snarl. Her shoulder-length brown hair is tangled with leaves and mud.

Valarie straddles Tessa's cocoon high above the forest floor. A rock with a lacerated edge is in her hand. Her other hand loops around the sticky thread above her. She leans forward and back, swinging the cocoon and kicking it with her heels.

"Valarie, climb down. You're going to fall," Archie calls.

Ardenal is already halfway up the nearest tree. "I don't want to burn you, Valarie, but I will," he warns.

"If you torch me, you'll also burn Tessa's thread and make her fall. Maybe that'd be perfect. The selfish beauty perishes and the one who no one noticed finally receives the attention she deserved all along. You see, I can tell. None of you care about me. No one has ever cared. Not my wretched self-absorbed mother. Not anyone at Constellations, though I rarely slept, making sure the passengers and staff were fed and entertained and massaged and catered to and their pets walked and their children contained so they could toss back bottles of champagne that I, of course, cleaned up. Did you ever really care about me, Nathaniel? Did you?"

"I did. I promise you, I did."

"Then what? Not blond enough for you? Not complicated enough? I didn't need saving?"

Lady Sophia fans herself with her hand. "Oh, good heavens!"

"Good heavens!" mocks Zeno.

"I . . . I didn't know what I wanted back then. I was lost, Valarie." Nate struggles for words. "You're great; really, it's my loss."

"Not good enough. Not even close." Valarie runs the rock against the strand of web beneath her. Tessa's cocoon bounces a foot lower in the air. "This will be easier than I thought."

"No, wait, Valarie! A part of me will always love you . . ." Nate begs, "please, come down and let's talk."

Ardenal sends a blade of burning grass shooting toward Valarie, but she leans, and Tessa's silky line is singed. Ardenal sends a fireball but Valarie ducks out of its way as well. The branch breaks under Ardenal's weight and he barely catches himself. Only a few boughs separate him from the place where Tessa's webbed thread is affixed. He continues to climb upward on the dangerously unstable branches.

"Oh, give up, Ardenal—Tessa will never love you, never forgive you, no matter how valiant you attempt to be. And Nate: I'm sick of your words. Empty promises. All of them! I'm sick of feeling this way. You made me like this, you know? You broke me." She slices the web, which comes apart with a snap. Valarie, holding fast to the sticky thread, is catapulted into the canopy above. Tessa, unaware in her cocoon, plummets.

"No!" screams Ardenal. He reaches for Tessa's cocoon, but his fingers narrowly miss.

Rolace—who had disappeared for a time, exhausted from the spinning—emerges from the darkness, leaps down, and surrounds Tessa's cocoon with legs like jewelry claws clutching a gem. His twelfth leg tows a new strand of web, which he affixes to the cocoon before scaling up its thin glowing line, in pursuit. Tessa sways, slower each time, until her cocoon hangs again unmoving. Those on the ground watch branches flutter where Valarie, hidden behind dense foliage, struggles to escape.

Valarie screams.

Rolace appears again. Pinched between the strong palpi that jut out of the man-spider's mouth is Valarie, fighting to free herself. He ejects a new thread, fastening it to a high branch and pulling it low to effortlessly bind Valarie's ankles. She shouts profanities at Rolace and lashes out at him with the rock that frayed Tessa's original line. Valarie slices one of his four spider eyes. The rock falls to the earth as Rolace weaves a cocoon around her.

"Her will is strong and her heart is brave—but also evil. I do not know what will become of her." Rolace shakes his head sadly while watching the fresh cocoon with Valarie inside quiver and quake. He sighs mightily and calls, "Maiden, would you please?"

The Maiden of Olearon approaches as Rolace lowers himself to crouch on the mossy earth. "Would you cauterize this eye for me? I'd rather lose its vision than let it sicken me slowly."

"As you wish." The Maiden lays her hands on the deep gash to the extreme left of the four spider-eyes, but before she ignites, she turns to the others. She gestures for the humans—Archie, Nate, and Lady Sophia—and the Olearons—Ardenal, Azkar, and Nameris—and Zeno too, if he is agreeable, to brace Rolace's nervous legs. Then, the Maiden's hands flare. Rolace makes no sound. It only lasts a moment.

chapter 41

While the humans and Kameelo hang from their co-coons—with Valarie's still fresh from Rolace's spinning—the great spider entertains his attentive audience with stories. He tells of his origin on Jarr-Wya, which he is not certain of himself, though he suspects his egg stowed away from some distant world. There, he presumes, are millions of his kind, compared to here, on the island, where he is both king and peasant, baker and cleaner, best friend and worst enemy. When Rolace laughs at his own plays on words, he winces in pain where Valarie destroyed his left-most eye. This does not, however, deter Rolace. He swings and climbs as he rattles on.

Archie begins to slink backward, away from the group, when he realizes that obtaining a magical gift is not a time-sensitive process. Rolace's stories remind him of the secret history of the Olearons, which he is eager to study. He slips from the clearing into the shrubbery at its perimeter.

Archie dances his fingers across the glass and takes a deep breath—smiling, though he doesn't realize it—ready to read. The surface of the glass is only beginning to cloud when Archie is torn from his hiding spot and roughly dragged by his jacket's collar back to the clearing. The firm hands that shove him down are Azkar's, but it is the Maiden who speaks.

"Give it to me now," she orders.

Archie looks for a place to conceal the glass, but it is in plain sight. Even the leather envelope is gone, dropped in the forest a moment past. Reluctantly, Archie rests the glass in the Maiden's hand.

"Azkar, burn him!"

"Wait, no!" Ardenal yells. He runs between his father and his comrade. Archie is surprised to see Zeno, as well, jump to his defense. It is not clear if the Bangol's gesture is one of self-preservation—loath to be with alone with the Olearons—or of genuine friendship.

"He is a traitor, Ardenal. He took something that does not belong to him. After all we have done for Archibald—I should have roasted him on their ship. I believed you when you said your father—your people—were worth saving. Was I wrong to trust you? Stand aside, warrior," the Maiden growls.

Ardenal does not budge. "What is it that he took? I'm sure it was a mistake." The Maiden conceals the glass in her jumpsuit.

"The concern is not what it is, but who it belongs to. The Lord will be furious to learn of this betrayal. I am confident he would order this human to be scorched."

"It was an accidental discovery," Archie pulls himself up from the dirt. "I meant no offence."

"Fine." The Maiden spreads her fingers and blades of grass and other forest debris rise and amalgamate into one long glowing band of fire. "I will not continue—my warriors will not continue—until this human is bound. We will wait to see how the Lord responds."

"That is very gracious of you, thank you, Maiden—but please," Ardenal begs, "my dad is old and our chords will burn him to the bone. What if we use the rope from Kameelo's supplies, then secure it in place with the lock from the bag of food rations? You will have your captive and he will remain un-harmed—for now."

Archie objects, "How can I be of help on our mission if I'm tied up?"

"True," Zeno agrees emphatically.

"I will not waste more breath on this matter. Here—" the Maiden retrieves Kameelo's rope and Azkar provides the lock. "You do it, Ardenal. Prove your loyalty."

chapter 42

Tessa claws harder against the invisible wall in the darkness of silver stars. She is unsure of the trustworthiness of the voice she heard. *More likely,* she reasons, *it is my own imagination. Maybe a lingering hallucination of the Banji. Either way, I need to break free of this.*

Tessa uses every muscle to jerk and tug against the cocoon, but her movements are limited. She can smell the iron in her blood and with every motion of her hands her fingertips burn. *What did Rolace say I must do?* She chokes on the webbing—and remembers. She jams her shoulder against her chin, snapping her jaw into place, chomping down and gnawing at the webbing with her teeth. She wiggles her forearms within their tight restraints, finally moving her hands up to her mouth. No matter how she yanks, the silver thread—interlaced and knotted within her veins—cannot be extracted. Instead, she swallows the webbing as her teeth finally slice the resilient silk.

Moments later, her fingers find a tear in the cocoon and poke their way through. A sliver of light shines in. Inch by inch, Tessa widens the hole until she can grab both sides and stretch it wide. Pressing her face against the hole, she sucks in air that wheezes down her throat. She forces her head out and then her shoulders. It is bright outside, maybe mid-morning, Tessa guesses.

"You did it, Tess!" Ardenal's voice rings up to her. "Let yourself fall. I've got you."

Too weary to argue, Tessa wrenches her hips and legs out of the cocoon, and drops.

On the ground, she mumbles, "Ouch!" at Ardenal's warm hands on her gaping jaw, forcing it wide. Tessa blinks to focus her eyes until she can make out the Olearon beside Ardenal. It is the Maiden. At first, Tessa is comforted to see her, but then confused. The Maiden takes a deep breath and exhales fire into Tessa's mouth. Tessa screams, but it's inaudible. The only sound is the hissing of the shriveling web inside her throat and clogged lungs, within her bloated belly and arteries.

As the hissing fades, Tessa's normal breathing returns. *I made it,* she celebrates. Then she asks aloud, "I am one of you, aren't I? That's why you can breathe fire into me and I'm not burned." It hurts to speak. Her jaw is sore with both fatigue and pain. She slouches in the moss.

Lady Sophia shoves Nameris and Zeno aside as she rushes to Tessa. "Oh, wonderful!" Her double chin bobbles as she speaks. "I'm so glad you're okay!"

Tessa tips to the side and expels a mound of slimy, bloody webbing.

"*¡Me cago en la mar!* My dear—that reeks to high heaven!"

"To high heaven," Zeno mocks.

"Oh, come here you!" Lady Sophia orders Zeno. She pulls him in close and surrounds him with her arms. "Do mothers of your kind give children affection? You lash out as if you're starved of it! This is what Valarie has taught me. That we all must give a little love."

"You are crushing me in your bosoms, woman!" Zeno sneers, but does not fight himself free.

"Tess—you look the same!" Ardenal says as Tessa frantically

examines her legs and hands and chest. "You look like you," he chuckles.

"I'm happy you're safe," Nate sighs, hanging back—an expression of somber reflection on his face—since Valarie's capture.

"If I look the same, then what is my power?" Tessa wonders. She tries jumping. She sings a few chords, though pitifully, Lady Sophia informs her. "Same skin, same voice, same limited athletic ability," Tessa notes. Every part of her body she touches feels familiar. She slows her racing mind and shuts her eyes. *Power,* she thinks, *come forth!* But nothing happens. She clears her mind, waiting for a vision, but all she conjures is a stronger headache.

Furious, Tessa turns to find Rolace to demand an answer. "Rolace!" she hollers.

"Not now, human," Nameris warns. "Leave the spider be."

"Wait—" Tessa crinkles her forehead. "I see four empty cocoons . . . so, who is in the fifth?"

"Valarie," Nate answers. "Tessa, I'm so sorry . . ."

"Valarie?"

"She tried to cut you down—Rolace saved you," says Ardenal.

"I never meant to put you in harm's way." Nate hangs his head. "It's my fault. I should have treated her better; at least drawn a hard line when our relationship ended."

"It's done now," Ardenal says. "I think we have all learned to be more observant."

"Tessa!" Harry and Donna call, fracturing their gloom. The couple joins them. They look the same at first, but when Tessa embraces the pair, their bodies feel peculiar. She investigates, taking Donna's hands in her own. Instead of wrinkled, pale, and loose skin, they are firm and smooth. It is the same for Harry.

"Are—are those . . . scales?" Tessa stammers. The couple

nod. Their bodies shine with subtle, but perfect staggered layers of cosmine and keratin. "What are you?"

"We don't know, exactly," Donna admits. Her smile lines are gone, though she still has her crackly old voice. "We also have gills." She points to her neck.

"I think this means we can breathe underwater." Harry chuckles. "I feel thirsty just thinking about it."

"And where is Duggie-Sky?" Tessa asks Archie, but her father-in-law is not there. "Archie?"

"Here, Tessa." Archie's voice is sad. He steps into the gathering.

"Why are you tied up? Who did this to you?"

"Ardenal did it," the Maiden answers. "Archibald betrayed my trust, the trust of the Lord. He stole something private and precious. Ardenal has demonstrated that he feels the same."

"That's ridiculous. Archie is not a thief; there must be a mistake. Here, let me help you." Tessa strains against the rope but it does not stretch.

"Back away, human, or you will be bound by the same fate." The tone of the Maiden's voice, its depth and quiver, convince Tessa to drop her hands.

"Leave it alone, Tess," whispers Ardenal. "I will explain later, but for now, let this go." Tessa studies Ardenal's face and recognizes the protectiveness of his manner. She nods and again inquires about Duggie-Sky's whereabouts.

"*Where* is exactly the right question," Archie replies weakly, as Duggie-Sky appears at Tessa's side. Then disappears. Then pops up twenty steps away. Then peeks from behind Archie once more. "He's having a rollicking good time. The Olearons speculate it's a relocation gift."

"Personal teleportation," the Maiden explains. "There are many benefits to this. Duggie-Sky may teleport away from danger— or into it, if our purposes require a spy, for example."

"Your purposes?" sneers Archie. "And you call me the traitor? Come here, Duggie-Sky, wherever you are." The child huddles beside Archie and swings the lock back and forth.

"Not at all, human. I was merely suggesting that there are many possibilities, some of which Duggie-Sky must discover on his own."

"And dare I ask about Kameelo?" Tessa sighs. The company point up to the blazing azure sky bursting with rotund, smoky-white clouds. There is a streak of red. Then another. "Is he flying?"

Kameelo's joyful hoot and "Yahoo!" reaches them on the breeze.

"I'm happy for you all, I really am—but I don't get it." grumbles Tessa. "I thought that this torturous process was to help me save Ella."

"Nothing is guaranteed." Rolace's voice startles Tessa. "I am sorry that I could not assist you on your mission. At least your friends discovered their gifts. Perhaps they will prove of great benefit in locating your daughter."

"Your eye," Tessa draws near to the spider's face. She touches him tenderly. Rolace folds closed his wounded eye, his complexion morphing; the nose and eyes and lips of the elderly man return. Tessa smiles with compassion at Rolace. "The others told me what you did for me. Thank you. I am so sorry you got hurt on my account."

"You may not have realized, Tessa, but you saved me first," Rolace says. "Since the Star fell, the Banji have begun to disappear. Especially here, in the white woodland where the soil is thin, thanks to the desert—the poison is dense. The Banji are fragile, though fierce, as you have discovered. Since I cannot cross the sand, I needed your help. It is the Banji, you see, that infuses my web with Naiu. I must rest now, please do excuse me. I wish you all safety and success on your journey."

"What about Valarie?" asks Nate. "Is she okay in there? We're not leaving without her, are we?"

Rolace scales his web and nudges her cocoon. "None have stayed in this long and survived."

chapter 43

"Now that this detour is complete, let us resume our travels north," Nameris grumbles impatiently and sets off. The Maiden nods her head of thick dreadlocks in agreement and—followed by the company of Olearons and humans, plus Zeno—begins to march through the whitewoods behind Nameris.

Tessa hesitates, then hurries to catch up. "I know we agreed to go north, but . . ." she trails off as the company give her their attention. Her voice sounds small in the dense, echoing wood, which gobbles up her protest. *They are going to think I'm crazy, like I would have of Arden if he came home ranting about such strangeness*, she scolds herself. She second guesses what she heard. She talks herself out of mentioning the voice, then back into it, convinced she must in fact share what transpired in secret while trapped inside the cocoon. Tessa straightens her back and wedges her way into the center of the group, to the side of the Maiden and Ardenal.

"Can this wait, human?" Nameris barks back. "We have spent precious time we will never make up at this sluggish pace. You are not familiar with Jarr-Wya. What can you possibly have to add?"

"Go on, Tess." Ardenal jumps in, glaring at Nameris.

Tessa clears her throat, mustering her courage. "I know I'm the stranger on your island, and I know this must sound mentally deranged, but while I was within Rolace's web—someone spoke to me."

"Who, dear?" Donna asks, coming near.

"I don't know, exactly . . ."

"Out with it, and let it be the truth!" Nameris demands, abruptly halting his irritable pacing, colliding with Lady Sophia who bounces into Azkar, causing Duggie-Sky to step on Zeno's heels.

"The voice, she—she called me Mom." The company fall silent on their makeshift path.

"Ella?" Ardenal exhales.

"Maybe. Or maybe it was the Banji. Or my desire projecting itself in my subconscious. Or, maybe I really am the nut job of the family—it's been me all along. That must be it. And, to that point, Ella can't talk!"

"But Ella can think," the Maiden retorts. Tessa's jaw snaps shut as this revelation creeps in and settles in her mind.

Lady Sophia, who pats Azkar's back in apology, bounds into the conversation beside Ardenal, and says, "If you were thinking, Tessa, then maybe Ella was too!"

"What did she say?" Nate asks, peering between the tall shoulders of the Olearons.

"Well, at the end, she told me I was in danger—and I was. Because of Valarie."

"That could be coincidence," Nameris dismisses.

The Maiden's flame grows and Donna steps away quickly. "Stand down, Nameris!" she orders. "Your suspicion has a place, but not in this instant. Please, Tessa, continue."

"I asked her where she was. She said: above the Star."

"We are all above the Star! All of Jarr-Wya floats six thousand fathoms above it," says Kameelo.

"Maybe this is your power," Ardenal suggests. "To communicate with others beyond place and time."

"Do it again," interjects Duggie-Sky, who appears all at once at the center of the circle.

"I wish I knew how."

"Powers are honed. Developed. Earned. Some come by their abilities more easily than others."

"You *are* pretty stubborn," chuckles Archie as he shrugs, accidentally jingling the lock against his belt buckle.

"And guarded," Ardenal adds.

"Thanks for the pep talk," Tessa huffs and stalks off.

Zeno crosses his arms. "The women of your kind, really!"

"Your determined resolve is a strong trait, a wonderful trait, Tess," Ardenal apologizes, following her. He reaches out for her hand, but Tessa pulls away before his fingers can graze her skin. He tips his head to the side, the expression he wears—which Tessa is beginning to regularly decipher, despite the unusual red skin and black eyes—is a mixture of frustration and yearning. He runs his pointer finger up the bridge of his nose readjusting the glasses he no longer wears.

"If I'm so miserable, why do you love me? Why do you pursue me?"

"You know," he whispers, wiping large tears from beneath Tessa's eyes. They sizzle and evaporate from his finger.

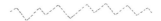

TESSA and Arden met at Brown Beans coffee shop, where they both worked while students at Seattle University. They bonded over American history and biology textbooks, and frothy macchiatos drizzled with caramel. Their friendship had been immediate. Tessa's breath grew shallow at the sight of Arden's hickory-colored hair and pale blue eyes. By the way he looked at her, she knew he felt the same.

Arden was completing his PhD in history and Tessa was in nursing school. While their schedules were rigid, they flirted behind the counter at Brown Beans and met for lunch at the university cafeteria, sometimes at odd hours when their courses allowed. Their love grew in the margins of their ambitious, early twenty-something lives.

Even then, Tessa was guarded. She had erected an inner stronghold around herself as a child that no one could demolish. When Arden asked to meet her parents, she told him they were traveling. When he informed her that he was planning to propose and wanted her father's blessing, she said she would never say yes to someone that old-fashioned. When two chairs were left unoccupied at their wedding reception, Arden did not mention it. He threw his suit jacket over the back of one, and pulled Tessa onto the dance floor.

There were many things left unsaid between them. Understood but never acknowledged. Arden accepted her—stronghold, secrets, and all—and for that, she had trusted him like no one else.

~\˄˅˄˅\˄˅˄˅~

FOR a moment, Tessa forgets where they are and who she and Arden have become. She smiles at the man before her, seeing in his frustrated yearning their better, simpler times. "Thank you," she says and does not explain. Tessa leads Ardenal back to the company where Nameris is arguing with Nate. She does not wait for them to stop before she speaks.

"Images flashed across my mind when I was in the cocoon. I saw someone drowning, surrounded by flowers. Fire burning on

a beach. A child crying in a tree. A bowl of oats and water spilling on a stone floor . . . Does this mean anything?"

"I'm not sure," breathes the Maiden.

"There were colors, hands around my neck, caterpillars
with wings, and—wait—I remember! A menacing fortress made
of boulders. Built on the edge of water. Rock cliffs."

"The Bangols' abandoned fortress in the east!" Ardenal
confirms. "You've described it vaguely, apart from the stone
arches which reach from the shore near its base—what was its
base—out over the sea. The fortress has been decimated, crushed
to rubble, for two-thousand sunsets now. It is the only place, on
all of Jarr-Wya, that resembles what you saw. I know this because I saw it once myself, only once, but I will never forget it."

"Nor will I, Arden," hisses Zeno. "The horrible, punishable
acts Tuggeron inflicted on my kin at that fortress. . . I hunger to
do the same to him and his offspring there one day soon." Zeno
grinds his teeth.

"It makes sense, in pondering it, that the Bangols would
retreat there," Nameris muses. "They know their scent will be
lost in the sea air, their crusts and bones washed away in the tide
and the roar of the waves drowning out their foolhardy yammering's."

"However, it is a thick-witted place for the king of the Bangols to venture," says the Maiden. "Those bridges are dangerous.
Deep in decay."

"I know the place well—so does Tuggeron," Zeno grimaces.
"The bridges are stronger than they may appear." He finishes
rolling a pasty ball of moss and mud between his grey hands
and lobs it at Lady Sophia, who shrieks and looks to the sky,
searching the clouds for where the blow originated. Zeno chuckles at what has become his favorite past time as they journey.

The Bangol's wicked smile fades. "Tuggeron held me there,

in a cell at the end of an archway—for more than twenty sun-sets—before banishing me to your world. I'd have rather been a prisoner on Jarr-Wya till my eyes rolled from my skull, rotten with age, than a castaway on earth."

"Come now, Zeno!" Archie chides. "It couldn't have been all bad. Your shop was quaint. You lived on an island paradise, some would say. Plus, if you were still holed up in a cell, you and I never would have met." Archie flashes a dazzling smile. Zeno rolls his yellow eyes and shuffles off into the woods, heading east.

Zeno hollers back, "Are you all coming?"

"It is a half-day's hike from here," the Maiden says, turning to Lady Sophia. "Are you ready?"

"Why do you look at me? I'm raring to go!" The large woman dances on the spot.

The corners of the Maiden's mouth twitch up for a brief moment. She outstretches her hand in the direction Zeno had trod and Lady Sophia prances forward. "Tessa," the Maiden continues, "as we journey, look within yourself for the voice. Call it out."

"I feel foolish talking to myself."

"The fool is the one who never tries."

The company hoist their sacks back over their shoulders and Archie herds Duggie-Sky, who howls with laughter as he zips in and out of the old man's view. They give Tessa space on her own, most walking a few long strides ahead, with Ardenal and Nate guarding Tessa a short distance behind her at the rear.

Okay, Tessa thinks. *Here it goes. Hello?* She waits. *Anyone there?* There is no voice beyond her own. *This is madness! I feel like an idiot.* Tessa clenches her fists.

Nate encourages her, observing her frustration. "Focus, Tess, don't give up. I believe you can do this, that you can do anything."

Tessa slows her breathing and relaxes her back, as she learned at yoga. She lines up her head above her shoulder blades above her hips above her feet as she proceeds carefully. She tunes out the conversations on her periphery. All Tessa hears is the rhythmic crunch of wilting leaves beneath her shoes. She takes an even deeper breath.

Hello? Ella? Can you hear me?

chapter 44

Shh, Mom! I'm trying to listen.

What are you listening to?

Shh! Give me a sec . . . It's Luggie. He's telling me the plan.

Who is Luggie?

My boyfriend. My friend. Oh whatever, it doesn't matter at this moment.

I am so confused.

Me too.

When did we take a family trip to Disney World?

What? Why? When I was eight.

I wanted to be sure it was you.

Of course, it's me! It rained in Florida the whole time. You and Grandpa Archie were miserable, but Dad and I had the best time on the rides, getting soaked. How could I forget?

It's been so long since I've heard your voice. I am so sorry, Ella. I knew you wanted to talk, but for some reason I felt you lived in a silent world, like me. I was so wrong.

Yeah, I understand, Mom. We're good. Save the mushy stuff for later, if there is a later.

What do you mean?

It's getting real here. Tuggs keeps killing people—humans—all for the Star. He's literally gone off the deep end.

Literally or figuratively?

Seriously?

Sorry.

Well, at least this proves to me that it's you. Even when we're talking telepathically, when we are in some alternate dimension, surrounded by the ultimate of ugly creatures, you still—STILL—feel the burning need to correct me.

A habit, Ell.

I first heard your voice after Tuggs beat me. I thought he scrambled my brain. He wanted information about the Star. Of course, I know nothing, but he thinks I poisoned Luggie against him, like the Star is to Jarr-Wya. I didn't give Tuggs anything; even if I wanted to, I couldn't. He thinks I'm choosing not to speak to him, so he kicked harder. I'm used to hurting, though. What's a few more bruises?

Are you bleeding?

I don't think so. Not on the outside at least.

Why have they kept you alive?

Tuggs got wind that I'm the daughter of an Olearon. Do I look red and flaming? I don't know who told him that, but I want to find out. Anyway, Luggie explained to me that Tuggs wants to use me for bartering with the Olearons. Seriously, he's crazy. Tuggs kept saying the name Ardenal. That's close to Arden, but Dad's human, obviously.

Was human.

What do you mean?

He's different now—on the outside. He saw you on the Millia's beach, but you didn't recognize him—I didn't recognize him. It has only been in the last day or two that I have let myself believe this Olearon is actually your father. He wanted to talk to you then, when he protected us from the sand storm of the Millia, but he was told to wait until we were all safe in the glass city. He went back to the Millia to save Grandpa. Azkar said his name, or at least what they call him here; Ardenal. Do you remember? Ardenal has been helping me, Ell. We are going to save you.

Silence.

Ella?

That's a lot to digest. And thanks, Mom. I appreciate you coming for me, but right now, I'd rather you keep yourself safe, please! I think Luggie's plan will work.

What's his plan?

Tuggs—who is Luggie's dad, that's the messed-up part—has been torturing Luggie since he discovered that his son was sneaking me food. He brought Luggie to the edge of the ocean and held his head under the water till Luggie choked. That's when Luggie got an idea. He started lying to Tuggs about hearing the Star. He told Tuggs that the Star was trying to communicate, that Luggie was slowly learning its language. Since then, Tuggs lets Luggie swim. When Tuggs gets bored watching Luggie dive, Luggie collects driftwood that's caught beneath the arches. He tows it out to the pier, the stone column beneath my cell. He's building a boat, Mom!

That doesn't sound very safe.

It's probably safer than what you're planning! This place is a nightmare, going by the small amount of it I can see through the cracks. Unless you have boats—and tell me if you do—you'd have to leave the forest and cross the beach. The Bangols are watching the shore day and night. You'd get stoned to death before you reached the water. The fortress is gone. Completely crumbled. The bridges still stand, though. I can see seven of them, but even those ones are falling apart. The bridges go up and down, like the McDonald's arches. The keystones at the tops of the arches are falling, crashing into the water. Bangols are constantly unsettling stones and wiping out into the sea.

So where are you, exactly?

I'm in a cell at the end of one bridge, way out over the sea. I think there are about five cells on each bridge from what I gather peeking out a handful of different cracks and holes. The cells are all connected by one landing area. Some of the cells have people in them, others are where the Bangols sleep, since their fortress on the shore is rubble.

How do you know you can trust Luggie? He's a Bangol. I don't even trust Zeno, even though he's doing a good job pretending to help us.

I don't know Zeno, but I know Luggie. He's my person, a true friend. I've never felt like this, Mom. It's real, even if it is weird.

Has he touched you?

I am not answering that. You have to trust me. I'm not just your sick little kid.

You are my kid, Ella. And you are sick.

God, I hate you some days. Go save yourself, Mom!

Ella? Ella!

chapter 45

"What is it, Tessa?" Archie asks. He notices the perspiration on his daughter-in-law's forehead and the way she clenches her fists and cracks her knuckles. They are mannerisms he is well acquainted with from their sixteen years as family.

Tessa had never spoken to Archie about her parents. He had many theories as to why, but early in their relationship Arden had told him not to mention the topic. It was clear, at least to Archie, that Tessa had no idea how to interact with him as a father. Instead, she treated him like a renter or a child, and on rare occasions as a friend—but never a dad. It made her uncomfortable when Archie asked her questions about the corner of Seattle where she grew up and what she was like at Ella's age. Tessa would frown at him in confusion and Archie could sense a fragment of fear beneath her controlled appearance.

"What is it, Tessa?" Archie asks again.

"I screwed up, Archie. Now, when I scream her name in my head, she won't answer."

"Did you talk to her? Was it Ella?" Ardenal asks as he approaches and matches the humans' pace.

"Yep, it was her."

Archie probes, "What happened, Tess?"

"I don't want to talk about it. All we need to know is where to find her and I'm certain of that now. We are heading in the right direction."

"They have fought a lot lately, Arden," Archie whispers to his son when Tessa stomps off in front of them. "Ella can't physically talk about it and Tessa, as you see, refuses. I have no idea where this pigheadedness comes from."

"Oh really, Dad? You have no idea?"

"Not a clue," Archie says as he tips up his chin and smirks.

The company trudges as fast as Lady Sophia can manage. Zeno continues to pester the woman and Nameris snaps at her for stopping to catch her breath. Kameelo heeds the Maiden's warning about the risks of flying near the Bangols' beach; they agree it is unwise to alert the yellow-eyes of their presence before their strategy is in place. Kameelo offers to carry Lady Sophia on his back, though he is remis to match the pace he walked with Nate through the desert. With their new arrangement—and Lady Sophia chattering merrily, like a tourist—the company cover ground swiftly. They see the sunset through the trees before the water's edge.

"This is close enough. Stop here. We need to plot our attack," Nameris orders.

"It's funny," Archie muses.

"What?" barks the grumpy Olearon.

"Where I'm from, my world, the sun rises in the east and sets in the west, which I learned from boy scouts when I was not much taller than Duggie-Sky—and I see that on Jarr-Wya, it is the opposite."

"I do not care about places I will never go." Nameris stomps off. *Never say never, that's what my parents always said*, Archie thinks, watching him go.

The company is famished and the Olearons rally for meat. Ardenal and Nameris creep off on one trajectory to hunt the cradle-bird Rolace had spoken of. Kameelo and Nate dash off on another. Donna collects purple and yellow barriers—approved by the Maiden—in the nearby brush. They are salty sweet, seasoned by the sea breeze, and are shaped like tiny dragon fruit with an edible skin. Not wanting to waste their water stores, Donna polishes them clean on her blouse. When the four return from the hunt, there is a bird for every member of their company— and eggs, too. Archie sees how the fowl received their name. The birds backs are curved in a U shape, dipping from their heads then rising equally high to the tips of their tails of violet-colored feathers. Their wings bend up on either side like a shrug. Between their heads, tails, and wings is a stringy, moss-covered feather-bed for the birds' offspring, where their eggs and babies are carried till maturity.

The Olearons begin skinning the fowl, but are interrupted by Nate, who teaches them an efficient and clean trick with his switchblade. The Olearons roast the meat on their palms and Donna seasons it with a berry rub while keeping an eye out that they do not overcook the eggs. The birds sizzle and pop, dripping savory smelling fat between red fingers. Archie drools at the aroma. When all have eaten, and Lady Sophia has devoured the leftovers, the company tiptoes to the brink of the forest.

"We are outnumbered," Nameris observes. "By many more than sixty."

"The short ones I count as half," Zeno answers.

"You're short," chirps Duggie-Sky.

"I am certainly not short—look at you!"

"I'm four." Duggie-Sky giggles and disappears.

Archie searches for the spot where the child will reappear. "Stay back, Duggie-Sky," he calls softly. "Out of sight!"

"Okay, Grandpa Archie." Duggie-Sky's answer echoes through the trees.

"Ella told me that the Bangols are rigorously guarding the beach," informs Tessa. "She said that approaching the cells at the ends of the arches would be better by boat."

"We cannot invade with a blatant attack, even by water if we did in fact have time to construct a raft, or multiple rafts," Nameris adds, glancing at Lady Sophia.

"You are right," the Maiden agrees. "We must use cunning, not force."

"What if we masquerade as renegades—deserters from the Lord of Olearon?" Azkar proposes. "We can claim that we have broken pledge and blood, and have come to join the Bangols."

"Why would they believe that?" Ardenal retorts. "The Bangols will see right through us."

"We would need to demonstrate our change of heart, our evil intentions," reflects Azkar. "Maybe we feel that the Millia are too strong and that the Lord has grown weak, bending to the will of Senior Karish. We suggest an alliance to overthrow the Lord and the Millia together."

Zeno nods. "The Bangols do hunger for the lands of the Olearons—and the southern shores. Their lust may cripple them till your true intentions are revealed. Tuggeron must die. That is the only way."

The Maiden steps forward. "I will lead in this deception."

"No, Maiden!" snaps Azkar.

"Remember your place," she growls.

"Forgive me, my concern is only for your safety." Azkar bows his head. "We have nothing here to create a suitable disguise."

"I will not require a disguise, Azkar."

"How will you convince them you have forsaken your soul-partner?" Kameelo asks the Maiden.

"A plan is forming in my mind. Leave that detail to me," she answers, deep in thought.

"We must be convincing," Ardenal says. "Even if they accept our story, they will search for a crack in our façade."

"I don't know how you will convince them, Maiden, but if

you can, your presence may actually work in our favor," reflects Azkar, meeting the eyes of his brothers and Ardenal.

Archie leans toward his son. "About what they said," he whispers. "I'm surprised they would want their queen involved in this plan at all."

"The Maiden refuses to lie. The Bangols know this. It is against her nature," Ardenal replies quietly. "The Maiden and the Lord are joined; they are like one spirit in two bodies. The Maiden must convince the Bangols that her desire for dominion of Jarr-Wya is more precious to her than the sacred bond shared between Olearon rulers since the creation of their race. If she fails to sway the Bangols to this thinking, at the very least they will still welcome her in as a charade, waiting for the moment to take her captive."

"If speaking the truth is her nature, how's this all going to work?"

"I see what you're saying, Dad, which is why she must express herself. It's the only way we can trick them. She will have to demonstrate that her nature is no longer upright."

"How's she going to do that?"

"Strength of will," the Maiden answers, interrupting the side conversation between Archie and Ardenal. "I love the Lord as I love myself. He has chased me through history, through countless worlds. He has always found me. This is our love story.

"I am born mortal in whatever race my spirit inhabits next, after our deaths. Then, when found by the Lord in his new form, I undergo the shift from common to royal. It was painful at first, when my spirit was newly birthed by Naiu, but now I welcome it, the stretch of growing pains from girl to the fullness of my nature. That nature, for me and every other Maiden before and after, is linked like eternal chains to truthfulness and loyalty—to the Lord. It's the goodness of Naui, its purity.

"Yet, the 30th Lord is not as he seems—" The Maiden grabs her stomach, as if bracing herself after a mighty blow. She doubles over, beginning to choke. Her warriors draw their glass blades and their shoulders and hair ignite in flame. The Maiden gasps painfully, then slowly rises to her full height, and deeply inhales.

"The Lord can feel me speaking ill of him," she says weakly. "He does not know my words but only the intent and manner in which I have said them. The blood in my veins runs cold, white, if I lie, but I have been practicing—in secret—to be dishonest in tone and without a change to my spirit and body; to lie even to the one I hold most dear. It is a torturous exercise that I hope will one day save both he and I."

"Save you from what, Maiden?" Kameelo asks.

"I cannot speak it. Not now. Or he will know. The other will know—" The Maiden is knocked over by something the company cannot see. Nameris and Kameelo are first to her side. Her flame is small and weak, a mere breath of smoke around her, concealing her already difficult to read emotions.

Again, the Maiden rises. "Please, no more questions. Please. Let us focus on what we can affect now, on our mission, that we might be successful. The plan to defeat Tuggeron has fully formed in my mind," she announces. "And I will share it with each member of our company in private. There are many parts, some of which must remain a secret. Who knows what magic, like Tessa's telepathy, the Bangols have conjured in their paranoia. It is best that we all contain a distinct knowledge of the plan, in case one in our company is captured. Much sacrifice is required. And we must hurry. The dawn is awaking."

chapter 46

The Maiden weaves through the group, whispering to each Olearon, human, and Zeno in turn. When she speaks with an Olearon, her flame grows to envelop them both in secrecy. To the humans, the Maiden talks in hushed tones.

"This is ridiculous—suspicious! That's what it is!" Tessa vents to Nate as they watch Zeno form a clay ball. The Bangol lightly tosses it to Duggie-Sky, where it slips between the child's arms and cracks apart at his feet. Duggie-Sky howls with laughter.

"Like this, like this!" Zeno demonstrates, exasperated. "I don't know how many times we must practice this, Duggie-Sky." Zeno calls forth more clay and molds a new sphere. The Bangol again slowly pitches it to the child who, this time, plucks it from the air. "Ah, that is much better. Now let us practice so you become proficient. One catch out of forty is hardly enjoyable." Duggie-Sky dances on the spot and whips the ball back to the yellow-eyed creature. Archie, who leans on a nearby tree, his arms still fastened tight in front of him, praises the boy.

Nate shakes his head in response to Tessa's annoyance as he watches the game. "I don't know, Tess. How the Maiden responded to Archie and that glass thing he stole . . . It's got me thinking. There is more going on here than everyone's letting on, do you know what I mean?"

"I do. I don't get it and I don't like it."

"At the same time," Nate continues to whisper. "After all we have been through, and with all that we have coming, I don't know if we have any other choice but to trust her. The Maiden has spoken to me. I can't share with you what I've been told, but I think this plan could work."

"*Could* work? Not *will work?*" Tessa bites her lip.

"Listen, Tessa. I do believe this is our best shot—for now—and if it fails, trust me. You and I will figure out a way."

"She's my daughter. This is my mission. I want to know what's going on!"

"The Olearons have a lot at stake here too, Tess."

"Oh, look! The Maiden pulled Lady Sophia aside. If I crouch by that fallen tree over there, on the far side of it, they'll never see me."

"Are you sure you want to do that? What if you get caught and the Maiden lassos you with fiery grass? Or ties you up like poor old Archie? Or maybe worse, what if you hear something you don't want to hear?"

"That's exactly why I'm going. Don't follow me."

Tessa leaves Nate and slinks toward the Olearon and opera singer, finally crawling in low to kneel by the collapsed trunk and splintered stump.

"Your role is simple," the Maiden tells Lady Sophia. "Stay by my side. I will protect you. You have nothing to fear."

Tessa frowns. *Why would the Maiden honor Lady Sophia as her attendant?* she wonders. *Why protect her? Of all the members of our company, she is the most useless!* As Tessa is about to stand and confront the Maiden, Ardenal interrupts her.

"You must feel relieved," he says as he crouches beside her.

"Shh!" Tessa scrunches her nose and glances quickly over the stump. She turns back to Ardenal. "What are you talking about?"

"To talk to Ella. That's amazing. You must be relieved that she's okay," Ardenal clarifies. "Yours is not the gift of flight or fins, but in my opinion, it's way better."

"She's ignoring me. Just like at home. And if it's not that, Ella is silent for some other reason, which is what has me worried."

"I'm worried too, Tess. She's all I can think about."

Ardenal's love for Ella is enough to erase any lingering doubt Tessa has about his identity. She feels her heart softening for the man huddled low beside her. "It must have been hard for you to be here, away from us," Tessa acknowledges for the first time.

"It was the worst. Lonely. Confusing. I missed you and Ell every day, every second. But . . ."

"But what?"

"Over the last few days, I have forced myself to accept the fact that you will never forgive me. I see you with Nate. You come alive. You blush. Your smile is genuine. I do hope we can stay friends after this—even worlds apart."

"It sounds like you are breaking up with me."

"Not at all, Tess. I love you. I'm releasing you."

"Releasing me?"

"I want you to find happiness and love."

Tessa had been furious for years that she could never move on because a tiny part of her, a part that she would never have admitted to, still hoped Arden would show up on their front steps. Her life had been in limbo and there were countless days when she wished she had heard the words Ardenal had spoken to her now. *So why do they sound so terribly wrong?* she wonders. Aloud, Tessa manages to eke out, "I don't know what to say." Tessa had cursed Arden and wished he was dead, but now her feelings for him—as she is still unwilling to admit—make her mind spin with confusion.

"You are the only woman I have ever loved, but I know loving you means letting you go." Ardenal adds, "If you choose Nate, I understand. He is a good man. I hate him for the way he looks at you, but—"

"How long have you two been there?" the Maiden roars.

"We were uh, only talking—sorry!" Tessa grimaces and jumps to her feet. Her eyes burn with tears. She runs away from the Maiden, Lady Sophia, and Ardenal—into the forest.

A warm hand grabs her by the shoulder. "I was starting to love you again," Tessa blurts—but it is not Ardenal.

"May I talk to you, Tessa? We do not have much time," breathes the Maiden. Tessa nods, her cheeks hot with embarrassment. "Tessa, I know you want to lead the charge to find your daughter, but you must trust me," the Maiden continues. "I will lead the Olearons onto one of the bridges. We will win the Bangol's confidence only to slaughter the stone heads the moment they are most vulnerable, then we will rescue your daughter. You, Tessa, will wait with Ardenal, who will protect you on the shore, hidden at the forest's edge." Tessa begins to protest but the Maiden holds up a hand to silence her. "You must do this. If the Bangols see you, or Ardenal, they will know it is an ambush. If our plan is to succeed, you must play your role and let me play mine."

"Why can't I know more? What are you keeping from me?"

"Your perspective must change, human. I do not withhold to harm you, but to help you. Imagine the Bangols recognized your ability to connect your mind to Ella's; what greater danger would we have then placed her in? I will not mention the lengths the Bangols would take to probe that connection, to uncover our plans, perhaps even to use Ella—or you—against us."

"I see," Tessa folds her arms across her chest, her thoughts suddenly plagued by tragic scenarios. "I have no say in the matter then, do I? I must trust you."

The Maiden nods her head slowly. "Have faith in me." The Maiden leans forward and kisses Tessa on the forehead, her hot lips leaving a warmth that lasts for a moment after she pulls away.

"What was that for?" Tessa asks, blushing.

"You have taught me the power of a mother's love. When I birth life myself, I will be even more passionate in my devotion because of your example."

Kameelo surprises Tessa and the Maiden as he swoops down from the sky. "Gather around," he calls to the company. "Reconnaissance complete, no Bangol the wiser. Here's what I saw: The ruins of the fortress are unguarded, but what Ella told Tessa is correct. The beach, beyond the rubble, is patrolled by watchmen on the arches, with stores of weapons to defend from their elevated positions. In addition, five Bangols guard each of the seven bridges."

Donna cannot stand still. "And which bridge do you plan to enter by?" she asks. The Maiden looks to Kameelo.

"Tuggeron keeps to the southernmost," he answers.

The Maiden looks Donna in the eye. "You and Harry must depart, immediately. Kameelo will guide you to the tree line. Creep out as close to the sea as possible under the cover of the rubble. From there, adhere to the plan and know that our thoughts will be with you." Harry rubs his hands together eagerly.

"Kameelo," the Maiden continues, "we will await your return. Fly back to us swiftly. Now go!"

Kameelo leads Donna and Harry in a sprint through the dark forest. Tessa marvels at the fluidity and stamina of the elderly couple, who run parallel to the Olearon.

The Maiden turns to Ardenal. "Are you ready?" He nods and tears off a piece of his jumpsuit at the breast. As he passes it to the Maiden, she retrieves her glass dagger from its sheath on her belt and slices open Ardenal's palm. His steaming blood begins to pool and drizzle onto the ground.

Tessa shoves Ardenal back and screams, "Stop! What's the matter with you?"

The Maiden does not flinch. "Calm yourself, Tessa," she says evenly.

"Don't tell me to calm myself! You said Arden's role was to protect me, to remain unseen, not that you would leave him injured. I don't like surprises, Maiden. What is your *real* plan?"

"My plan is your plan, Tessa."

Ardenal lays his uncut hand on Tessa's shoulder. "They need my blood to convince the Bangols they have killed me. We need them to believe that I am dead." The Maiden shakes her head as Ardenal divulges his part of the plan. He extends his dripping palm to the Maiden, who wraps it with the fabric from Ardenal's jumpsuit. Once it is drenched, she folds it inside a large waxy leaf and tucks it into her pocket. Ardenal silently cauterizes his own hand with a scowl of agony.

"This will work, Tessa," is all the Maiden says before hailing the Olearons to her side.

Nameris, Azkar, and Kameelo, as if cued from the shadowy forest, join the Maiden, who addresses Ardenal one last time. "Remember who you serve. Upon my return, I expect to find your father bound and the lock secure. Loyalty is proven every day." The Maiden pats her pocket where Ardenal can see the shape of the key to Archie's lock. She and her warriors set off into the fading night. Lady Sophia rushes along behind them.

"I get it Arden, don't feel bad," says the old man once the Maiden is out of earshot. The lock again clanks against Archie belt.

"I'm sorry, Dad. This is killing me inside. I feel both human and Olearon, yet I'm forced to choose. If the Maiden finds you free, that will be it, her trust in me will be broken."

"Whine later," Zeno snaps. "I don't want to miss the show!"

Ardenal nods. "Let's make sure we've got everyone. Archie, Tessa, Nate, Zeno . . . Where's Duggie-Sky?"

"Hi!" Duggie-Sky says as he appears with a gush of wind. "I have a present for you, Grandpa Archie."

"What is it, little fella?"

"This—" Duggie-Sky hands Ardenal a rusty metal key. "Unlock him," the boy says to the Olearon. Ardenal hesitates, his brow creased, then forces the key within the lock, which snaps open with a click. Ardenal unfurls the rope which reveals clammy white and purple skin on Archie's forearms.

"Oh, Dad—"

"Look, the circulation is already flowing back. I'm all right. We'll simply carry this rope and lock—and the key—along with us. The second we see the Maiden approach, we'll bind me up again. Toss the key into the grass as if she dropped it. Our secret."

"Thanks Dad."

"Thank you, son—and thank you, Duggie-Sky!" Archie grins and flexes his wrists and shakes his hands at his hips. "Now," Archie continues, "we've got somewhere to be. Stay close, little fella. Hold Grandpa Archie's hand, now that I'm able. There's a good sport!"

The six take a southeastern trajectory. "We will wait farther south than the battered fortress, hidden in the trees, away from danger," Ardenal explains. "That position is downwind from the bridges. The breeze will carry every word into our ears."

As they near the spot Ardenal describes, a heavy rain begins to clatter on the shore.

"Why am I not wet?" Zeno mutters.

"Because it's not rain . . ." Nate's voice trails off.

They arrive in time to see stones dropping from the sky above the heads of the Olearons and Lady Sophia.

chapter 47

The Maiden pulls Lady Sophia against her chest and the brothers form a triad around them. They emit a powerful dome of orange light, a shield that crumbles and deflects the stones dropping from the sky to pummel them.

"We wish to speak!" the Maiden calls through the quivering barricade of flame.

"Look out!" Lady Sophia shrieks, and yanks Nameris back as a boulder effortlessly slices through the shield and compacts the ground where he had stood.

"Thank you," he breathes without his usual cantankerous edge. Nameris returns to discharging his flame above and in front.

"We mean you no harm. We have come to join forces!" the Maiden continues.

The five shuffle across the rocky beach beneath their shield to the foot of the southernmost bridge. Only seven stone arches remain of the thirty that once stood. At one time, they extended far out over the sea and connected to each other in erratically placed arcs. Age and war had crumbled the bridges and pathways, and they had collapsed into the hungry sea to form breakwaters visible above the ocean surface.

The easing night still clings to darkness, though Bangol torches illuminate cells and their bridges, and the water below them that batters against the piers with angry sprays of foam.

Zeno whispers to the small company tucked into the darkness of the forest, "This place was once busy and happy, when the Bangols and the Olearons worked together to defend Jarr-Wya against the Steffanus. Together we held every shore and hunted those wicked women up Baluurwa. Once the Steffanus were wiped out, or so we thought, the Bangols broke the alliance and invaded Olearon territory, desiring their fertile pasturelands. The red bodies were waiting, however, and drove us clear across the island. To this fortress, which was lost. It is a mystery to this day how the Olearons knew we were coming. The bloodshed was excessive. After the battle, this place was abandoned, with the focus on preserving our hold on the northern shore. Many evils entered the east by way of this deserted fortress."

When Zeno begins a rant about his banishment, Ardenal leans to Tessa and whispers, "Has Ella spoken?"

"No."

"Try again."

Ella? Ella, can you hear me?

I can't talk now, Mom. Something is happening on the bridges. Oh no, the Bangol at my door . . . he's got the rope and the stones . . .

"She spoke!" Tessa nearly sings. "Ella knows something is going on—she's in danger!"

"Look," interrupts Archie. "The Olearons and Lady Sophia are being allowed onto the southern arch!"

The Maiden, swiftly followed by Lady Sophia, is first to scale the stone walkway, which has no rails and is no more than six feet wide. They are followed by Azkar and Nameris, and finally Kameelo. Their flames are intentionally modest.

The Maiden announces loudly, her voice carrying, "I am the Maiden of Olearon. I have come, with these, to make an alliance with the Bangols."

A single stone soars through the air and nearly bashes the

Maiden's head, but she gracefully ducks to the side. The stone whooshes by and splashes loudly into the water. "Is that any way to greet one who offers you what you desire?" she asks calmly.

"How can you possibly know what we desire?" sneers a little creature halfway across the bridge.

"You want an end to the reign of the Lord of Olearon— and to inhabit his lands—do you not? And, possibly greater still, you crave the Star."

The Bangol guard blinks with surprise, his yellow eyes flashing like the warning beacon on a lighthouse. "Well, yes, that's right—but all know of our intentions; we are not subtle in their execution," he says gruffly.

"We are renegades, breaking pact with our birthright. We wish for an audience with your king."

"It makes no sense. What kind of a trap is this?" demands the guard, lifting a stone mallet.

"What is your name?"

"I am Chergrin, lead guard."

"Let me speak with Tuggeron. I waste no further breath on you," the Maiden answers.

Chergrin scowls, then turns on his heel to scurry into one of the cells at the end of his bridge. "Wait there!" he orders over his shoulder before disappearing through a heavy door of weathered wood. There is silence for a time. The Olearons are still, but Lady Sophia shuffles back and forth on her stout legs and nervously fusses with her clothing.

Finally, the wooden door creaks open and the guard exits, followed by a much taller, fatter Bangol. "Who addresses me?" he asks.

"The Maiden of Olearon."

"Have you not known enough bloodshed from our swift stones in the blue forest, or the decimation on the Millia's shore five sunsets past?" he asks proudly. "Have you come here to die?"

"We have come to join you," answers the Maiden. "Are you the king?"

"I am Tuggeron, yes—and I don't trust a word from your red lips."

"If you know who I am, which I believe you do," the Maiden responds calmly, "you know that I do not lie. I have done that which no other Maiden has before: severed souls with her Lord. The Lord of Olearon is cowardly and bends to the will of the Millia—while I yearn for conquest. In that, I believe our interests are aligned."

"Your race is pathetic, of that we agree," sneers Tuggeron. "We Bangols have known as much for many generations. Thank you for this information. You may go now." Tuggeron begins tromping back to the cells.

"Wait—" calls the Maiden. Tuggeron moves no farther. "—let our races unify once more in shared control of Jarr-Wya. Many Olearons feel as I do, some of whom stand behind me. We know many valuable secrets. Together we will overthrow the Lord, drive the Millia back into the sea from where they came, and harness the power of the Star."

"Your offer is enticing," Tuggeron says as he swivels to again face the Maiden. "Our two races would own all shores of Jarr-Wya. You could remain in the fields at the glass city, since you are the better farmers, while giving us three-quarters of the harvest. There are many more of us to feed." Tuggeron laughs and grabs his paunch.

"We are agreeable to that condition," the Maiden replies. "With the Millia gone from the south, we might also cultivate that region—its pastures and blue forest. There will be more than enough to eat for both Bangol and Olearon."

"You are forgetting one thing." Tuggeron exhales deeply. "What good are all the lands on Jarr-Wya if they rot the crops before ripening? If they are laced with sickness that wipes us out? It is the Star that I desire most. And for that, I have no need of the Olearons. I will harness its power alone and then all of the island will be mine."

"Impossible," the Maiden retorts.

"Impossible?"

"Yes. Do you remember I mentioned secrets? Over the last three-hundred sunsets, one of our own, Ardenal, has trained me in how I might break the wildness of the Star to my will. It was birthed in his world. Ardenal came to Jarr-Wya with the ruse of saving his child, but truly, he sought the Star for himself."

"So why teach *you* how to lord over it?"

"Ardenal had not foreseen how many fathoms beneath the sea the Star would come to rest. He needed me, and the Olearons, to retrieve it from the depths. We have, in fact, discovered a way."

"But surely Ardenal desires the Star only for himself."

"He was greedy. I am not." The Maiden pulls out the folded leaf and throws it to Tuggeron.

"What is this?" Tuggeron unfolds the foliage. He smiles at the bloodied fabric. He buries his nose in its wetness and inhales. "I know this blood. Ardenal came looking for knowledge. We battled. He was an untrained but unrelenting adversary. And you have killed him?"

"With my own hands."

"Inspiring."

"Thank you. And I have even more proof of my trustworthiness—for you, Tuggeron."

His eyes brighten. "Oh please, let's see! I am beginning to enjoy this quite unexpected meeting!"

"Azkar. Nameris." The Maiden orders them forward and they grab Lady Sophia by her arms.

"Hey! Ouch! What's the meaning of this? The Maiden told me I would not be hurt. Get your hands off me!" the singer screeches.

"This human," the Maiden says, "is their leader. She directed the vessel to Jarr-Wya, hunting the Star. My companions and I here, we have roasted the others that came with her, the ones that outlived the Millia and your attack from above."

"And why keep this one alive? She doesn't look powerful," Tuggeron growls, studying Lady Sophia.

"Appearances can be deceiving. The best of a race are most always the fattest, wouldn't you agree, Tuggeron? She possessed many powers, one of which could gut us all where we stand."

Tuggeron shifts uncomfortably. He exchanges a glance with Chergrin. "Well then, why have you not destroyed her? Do you bring her here to undermine me?"

"I have brought her here so that you may watch."

Azkar recovers a belt from his sack. He and Nameris wrap it around Lady Sophia, who struggles against them, objecting loudly. She begins to weep.

The Maiden continues her story as they work. "I stole her powers by way of Rolace, from whom we have just now come. Together, Tuggeron, we shall use them to our mutual benefit." The Maiden smiles wickedly. She steps aside so Tuggeron can appreciate the work of Azkar and Nameris. The belt, which Lady Sophia tears at hysterically, is decorated with heavy stones.

The Maiden grabs Lady Sophia by the neck and thrusts her off the bridge. The woman descends quickly and crashes into the water. She does not reemerge.

chapter 48

"**D**id you know about this?" Tessa demands, her face close to Ardenal's. She whirls. "Did you know, Archie?" Fat tears drop from her eyes.

Zeno interrupts. "The Maiden alluded to me that Lady Sophia may play such a role. It's quite delicious!" He shows his sharp teeth in a wide grin.

The voices on the bridge begin again and the company in the woods fall quiet to listen.

Chergrin waves forward the Olearons. "Come," Tuggeron says. "Let us share our secrets, away from the ears of the wind— the breeze has been different, have you noticed? Since the Star arrived? It speaks no tongue of this island, at least none I know." Chergrin follows close behind them. They disappear into a cell.

"What now?" Tessa asks anxiously.

Archie replies, "We wait."

All of a sudden, a child begins to cry high up in the branches of the white trees.

"Duggie-Sky!" Archie frets, straining his vision upward.

"I'll find him," Nate says, and runs off into the darkness.

Suddenly—there is a click. Only one. It interrupts all conversation. It dissects normal sound and arrests the small segment of the company, as if they are frozen in word and gesture.

Silence, pause—just long enough for the heart to cling to the hope that the noise was a reflux of memory—then another click startles them. And another. The sounds begin at first faint—disparate and distant—then grow, like an approaching thunder storm.

"Arden, I know that clicking . . ." Archie whispers.

Tessa huddles close. "What is it?" she asks.

Ardenal clenches his jaw. "Carakwas."

"Was this in the Maiden's plan?" Tessa asks. Ardenal shakes his head, *no*.

"What about Duggie-Sky?" Archie whispers.

"And Nate?" Tessa grimaces, biting her lip.

"Shut your bright eyes, Zeno. Turn your face to the ground," Ardenal orders, ignoring the questions of his family. "We do not need them attracted to your light."

"I am going for Ella!" Tessa grits her teeth and jumps to her feet—but Ardenal swiftly wraps his arms around her waist and drags her to the forest floor.

"You are not going anywhere. That is my only mission. The Olearons stand a chance against the carakwas. You do not. I will let go when it is over."

The clicking grows so loud that everyone, but Ardenal, covers their ears—even Zeno, who wears an expression of anxious dread across his wincing face. Through his grey skin, Zeno's dulled yellow eyes can be seen, darting this way and that. The group can no longer hear each other or even their own thoughts. The clicks are sharp, piercing, deafening, impending. They do not slow and give no time for the company to catch their breath or a quiet moment for them to discuss a plan. Ardenal pulls Tessa away—with Archie and Zeno following helplessly. They crouch low in the tall grass on the forest's edge a mere moment before the carakwas—thousands of them, intent and focused—scurry through the white forest twenty feet away, heading in the direction of the sea.

"Oh no, oh no, oh no . . ." Archie wheezes. Ardenal reads his father's lips and makes a shushing gesture.

The carakwas easily scale the rubble of the Bangol's decimated beach fortress with their muscular reptilian legs. They tip their beetle heads up at the sky and screech—a sound so full bodied and malicious that Zeno quivers and clings to Archie like a child, like Duggie-Sky would have done if he had been with them. The salty air carries far the carakwa's wicked howls and their pincher's throaty clicks. The entire eastern beach hangs in stillness, as if holding its breath, waiting for the first casualty in the imminent onslaught.

The creatures cross the beach and reach the edge of the sand, where the water laps gently. At first, they pause, then advance with a scraping sound from their claws against the stone bridges. The carakwas rise on the bridges, or float on the water's surface. They continue to pour out of the forest. The beach, earth, stones, and sea are completely obscured beneath the carakwa's dusty rainbow shells.

The Bangols flood out from the cells and scream to each other across the expanses between the arches, over the carakwas on the water below. Some Bangols rush to their projectile cannons and send chiseled, razor-sharp stones raining down on the nearest lizard-beetles. Others plant their feet on the bridges and set their fierce buttery eyes to the beach. These Bangols spread their hands wide and speak to the earth beneath the sand in their curt language. The shore begins to quiver. Catching many carakwas unaware, spears of hard clay shoot up with the power of Naiu, directed by the Bangols. The stabbing motions of the sandy clay skewer many of the creatures that continue to thrash recklessly, lacerating others nearest to them. Still, the hungry mob is undeterred. Carakwas climb over their deceased counterparts and leave tracks of their oily blood on the bridges.

Tuggeron and Chergrin race out of the cell. They holler orders and point directions to their fellow Bangols. Tuggeron fans his hulky fingers and piercing grey claws toward the beach and chants, his bellowing voice confident in its enchantment. Large sections of earth rise at his command and slap down onto the water's face, crushing and drowning many carakwas, pulling their bodies to the sea floor as the dirt and sand and debris swiftly sink at the command.

Chergrin howls into the white woodland and, in response, pebbles, stones and the remnants of the Bangol's fortress from the beach begin to roll out, thwarting many carakwas as they charge the bridges. Adding to the cantankerous roar of clicking and screeching is the crunch of shells and wail of murdered Bangols, whose control of the earth and wielding of their stone weapons proves useless to the sheer number of possessed creatures. All effort is in vain.

Tuggeron staggers backward. He turns with a flash of desperation to the Olearons. The Maiden and three brothers—who had watched from the crooked doorway of Tuggeron's chamber at the end of the bridge—stand unmoving.

"Your fire!" screams Tuggeron as the carakwas continue to pour out of the forest at his back. The lizard-beetle's sharp nails can be heard and their vibrations felt against the stone bridge as they scurry nearer. "Burn them alive! Burn them now!" he commands.

The Olearons burst into flame and the corners of Tuggeron's chapped lips turn upward and he nods—but his satisfaction is fleeting. The Maiden and her warriors do not advance beyond the landing. Tuggeron's circular eyes narrow to a bloodthirsty squint. He scrunches his lips beneath his grey nose and grinds his teeth.

"Your truth has been revealed," Tuggeron spits. He orders Chergrin forward. The guard charges past them and raises his stone mallet above his head. He wields it with such force that five carakwas crunch beneath his blow. Their blood paints the sea with rainbows of oily gloss. Chergrin kicks the lizard-beetle's carcasses into the sea, out of his way, as he once more wields his mallet, and again connects.

"When should we step in?" Nameris asks the Maiden.

"Not yet," she answers without flinching.

Kameelo's voice rises swiftly, "Look out, Maiden! At your side!" A carakwa—which had swum out to the barrel pier supporting the cells—scales the stones and approaches the Maiden quietly. Without shifting her eyes from the beach, the female Olearon points one hand at the thousand eyes on the nearing creature and they instantly melt. The carakwa screeches in agony and whips its beetle-head against the stones. The Maiden continues to send her flame upon the creature. It's hard shell curls and whitens, then rises, weightless, as ash. It only takes a second for the flesh of the lizard to be incinerated.

"Where did Tuggeron slink off to?" Askar asks, when the carakwa at their heels crumbles into charred pieces. His words snap the Maiden's eyes away from the shore.

"I saw him duck behind a cell," she answers, stepping forward. "Is he not there?"

Azkar growls, "No, Maiden."

"Search!" she commands and she jolts forward, her black gaze relentless.

A raspy, deep-throated laugh cackles above their heads. Their eyes follow the sound. Tuggeron—waiving with his own stone mallet—is soaring rapidly, lifting-off in a balloon that had been concealed nearby, out of sight behind the rearmost cell.

"Good luck down there," the Bangol king bellows. "If you

make it out alive, I promise—as I too do not lie—that I will hunt you down with my dying breath. I will use your bones to pick the cradle bird's flesh from between my teeth. And your glass city, well! I will take much pride in seeing it shatter!"

"And," the Bangol king continues slowly, drawing out his words, "since Ardenal is dead, I won't be needing this one." He yanks Ella from inside his balloon, her feet bound with rope and stones, and drops her over the lip of the clay basket. Tessa, watching with held-breath, gasps loudly and weeps at the sight of Ella and the deep blood stain on her bomber jacket.

"Kameelo, go!" the Maiden yells. The Olearon darts to the edge of the bridge.

"The child has been saved," Kameelo stutters, "by a young Bangol—they look to be friends."

Tuggeron growls. "You spiteful traitor—"

"Leave Ella for now," whispers the Maiden. "We soon will face the infestation."

Chergrin, weary and drenched in carakwa blood, appears near the Olearons. "Wait!" he pleads to his king.

"Sorry, old friend." Tuggeron shrugs as he exerts force upon the ropes. His balloon jolts higher and disappears into the emerging dawn.

"Show us mercy, please! Help us!" Chergrin begs the Olearons. Again, the Maiden does not advance. Not even when Chergrin screams in pain, does she move an inch in his direction. Chergrin shrieks again as a carakwa leaps onto his back and hooks its claws into the flesh of his neck. The clicking is piercing. Kameelo covers his ears.

"Go in peace, Bangol," says the Maiden as she nods and touches her heart.

"The vengeance of the Bangols be upon you!" Sickly smelling blood bubbles out of Chergrin's neck as the carakwa slices it open with its forelegs. The creature begins to feast on the Bangol's jugular, tearing his muscles apart with its pinchers. Chergrin's radiant yellow eyes dull to gray and his body collapses.

The Bangols along the other bridges also scream out in horror as they desperately stab and hack at carakwas with their stone spears and axes. Catapults launch boulders from the wider platforms near the cells. More clay daggers rise from the earth. The broken foundation of the fortress quivers and dislodges, pieces flipping through the air on the breath of Naiu. Other Bangols shoot stones with slings. Some lift the·carakwas to their mouths and bite down, burying their blade-like teeth deep into the creatures' insect-skulls. It is not enough. They weary under the incessant attack. When the Bangols raise their hands to summon Naiu, carakwas invariably leap forth to gnaw off their fingers.

The Bangols calm themselves, out stretch their arms to each other—as if they reach across the sea between bridges—and close their bright eyes, focusing intently as one unit. A white wind begins to weave around them. A rumble, like thunder, shakes the arches and causes many of the remaining keystones and other pieces of the abutment and parapet to dislodge—but not to fall. They hang in the air. Boulders and stones, too, from beneath the surface of the water, slowly rise, but before the rubble can rocket forward—one by one—the carakwas slice and pinch away the lives of the Bangols, so that finally every shard of stone and piece of earth tumble helplessly back from where they came.

The Olearons hold fast, standing together, burning as one bonfire that summons the cherry light of the new day. They watch, stoic and solid, as every Bangol is consumed by the carakwas. All that remains of the yellow-eyed creatures are the stones that had jutted through their skin, which now cover the bridges and wash up on the shore. The huge black flyers plunge from above and scrape through the headstones with their protracted claws that grow from the tips of their wings, scavenging for flesh.

The Maiden—remaining ablaze to ward off the carakwas that continue to pursue them on the landing—retreats to search the cells at the end of the southern bridge. Azkar, Nameris, and Kameelo form fireballs between their palms and hurl them toward the arches and beach, where large numbers of the lizard-beetles burst into flame. Carakwas that venture too close to the Olearons are singed and scuttle backward. A great sizzling noise rises in the air.

The furious clicks and screeches of the creatures follow the Maiden at her heels as she darts in and out of cells, though the carakwas maintain their distance from her heat. She finds human clothing, excrement, and a bowl of oats shattered on the floor. An ornate, bloodstained book leans against a wall in a tiny vacant cell. It catches the Maiden's eye. She punts a carakwa back and slams the cell door shut. Her flame is withdrawn into the nape of her neck. She unlatches the book. It is filled with drawings, all signed *Ella*. As the Maiden flips through to the back, she discovers a secret pocket sewn into the inner cover along the seam of the binding. The pocket is empty.

chapter 49

"Ohhhh, Tessaaaaa!" a familiar, yet warped, voice calls out. "Naaaaate! Arrrrrrchie!"

Tessa stiffens in the tall grass. "Who is that?"

"Not an Olearon," answers Ardenal.

"Not a Bangol," Zeno adds. "Obviously. They are all dead, except for Tuggeron."

"Or a human," Archie says, "though it does remind me of the cruise director, Valarie . . . Look! Something is happening to the carakwas!" Archie points.

The carakwas withdraw from the bridges and water, gathering on the shore. They start to climb over themselves, stepping up on their rainbow shells, hooking their curled claws together, building, expanding, growing taller and taller, and rising in two columns that join twenty feet above the beach, then rise as one. Two offshoots develop on either side and droop. The top forms a head and face. The clicking grows quiet but never ceases.

"Hello down there! Come out, come out! It's time to play!" booms a female voice from the massive carakwa figure.

"Who are you?" the Maiden demands, having joined the other warriors on the bridge.

"Aww, don't you recognize me? Should I help you remember?" The monster of carakwas takes a lunging step toward the bridges. Sand quivers at its heavy footfall.

"Nate: I loved you. Olearons: I obeyed you. Tessa: I followed you across an island, so you could save your precious little Ella. Archie: I listened to all your long-winded stories. Did you ever ask about me? Did any of you even care if I lived or died?"

Archie whispers, "It believes that all of our company is on the bridges, that the rest of us are hiding in the cells."

"Valarie—" begins the Maiden, but she is not allowed to continue.

"I have a gift for you all." The four-story-tall carakwa shape takes another long step forward. Its scaly, shimmering arm—formed of hundreds of obedient carakwas—tosses something round into the water, where it bobs and is illuminated by the climbing sun. "You didn't recognize me at first—but what about him? He's not all that scary without all his legs, now is he?"

Rolace's head rocks in the gentle swell. His eyes are vacant. His neck has been roughly mutilated from his body. The water darkens with his blood.

"He thought I was dead. You all thought I was dead. Why didn't you have a scorching ceremony for me, like you did for Olen? Or for Eek? Didn't I too deserve to be burned? To have my ashes float up into the sky? When Rolace cut open my cocoon, he had a nice surprise. Not a feast, unfortunately. Too bad he could barely see me coming for him."

"What do you want, Valarie?" asks the Maiden coolly.

"What, no begging for my forgiveness?"

"I doubt you would change your mind if I did."

"Speaking of mind—" Valarie chuckles "—each one of my pets here has my brain. My thoughts. My feelings. My memories. My love. My hate. It is our collective knowledge. Hurt a part of me, we will reform. Slight one of us, and the whole hive grows angry." Valarie laughs wickedly.

"You see," she continues, "I have spent my whole life trying to be good. Be the perfect student, Valarie. Be the best friend, even if they don't deserve it. Be the most attentive lover, Valarie. The perfect host for Constellations. The compliant follower through these wretched forests . . . I have spent my life trying to be good, but only in dying have I discovered that I actually have a different fate—and that I have a huge debt of heartless neglect to repay."

"No! Kameelo, wait—" the Maiden pleads, but it is too late.

The young Olearon soars into the sky and flings a fireball at Valarie. Her carakwa head falls to the sand with a mighty crash. The remainder of her form staggers but does not break, even headless. The carakwas that had once shaped Valarie's neck, hair, eyes, and nose sizzle and quiver, and finally grow still on the sand.

"Now that wasn't very friendly of you," the rest of the carakwas bellow through their pinchers, clicking vehemently. "But I guess we never really were friends."

The lizard-beetles hurriedly unhook their claws and scurry around each other. For a moment, they make one iridescent, lustrous silhouette. They swiftly reform Valarie's head, but as they do so—with all black eyes focused there—one arm rises suddenly and strikes Kameelo out of the air. His body—still aflame—soars onto the dense canopy of the white trees. Above the clicks, there comes the sound of snapping branches and the crackle of incinerated leaves.

"You can scorch me ten carakwas at a time, a hundred at a time, but there are millions of me and only thirteen of you, if my math is right. I have only lost eighty-seven to Kameelo's flame. Does that put it into perspective for you? Now, where were we?" Valarie says, her tone shifting. "Come out, come out, wherever you are, Ella! Since all of this—and I mean every part—has come about because of you, I thought it only fitting that you should be the first to die. Where are you hiding?" Valarie takes another step forward and the sand leaps into the air.

"This can't be happening," Tessa whispers. "We are so close . . . This is my last chance."

"No," Ardenal squeezes tighter. "Never! I have lost you before but not again. Not today."

"You told me you release me, don't you remember?"

"To live again! Not to die!"

"I can't live with myself if I don't go now."

"Arden, don't let her," Archie orders.

Ardenal loosens his grip and strokes Tessa's hair. He runs his fingers across her cheeks and brushes his lips against her forehead. "You are the bravest woman I know, Tessa Wellsley."

"Arden, no!" grunts Arche, panicking.

Tessa sighs. "Thank you, Arden." She turns and runs.

"Come out here, Ella! I want to meet you! Oh, did I say meet? My mistake. I meant eat. I can hardly wait to crunch your bones between my shells!" Valarie takes a monstrous step and then another. She is in the water. The carakwas click impatiently. The creatures that form her feet send bubbles up from beneath the tide. "We are ever so hungry . . ."

The Maiden grabs the hands of Azkar and Nameris. "Come close," she commands in a whisper. "I wish time allowed for me to explain more, though you will surely see, soon enough. Many regrets do I have. Alas, we will see each other at the glass city. I am going now—to be with my love." Without another word, the Maiden pushes Azkar and Nameris over the edge of the bridge. Their expressions betray confusion and fear as they fall, their flames extinguishing as they plummet and the water splashes over their faces.

"That was unexpected," Valarie snarls and wades a step closer to the Maiden.

The Maiden turns her eyes upward to the screeching creature, and says, "I hope this will be as well . . ."

chapter 50

om, I'm sorry. I should have listened. This has gotten way worse than I ever imagined.

Ella, I saw you bleeding, are you okay? Where are you?

It's only ink, Mom. I'm in the boat. If you'd call it a boat. I'm with Luggie. He pulled me from the water, cut the stones from my ankles. We were trying to save his sister, Nanjee. She was recovering from our balloon crash in a cell on the next bridge over. We heard her screams when the bug-things came. Then her screams stopped. That's when Luggie dropped the paddle. It floated far, then sank.

I've reached the beach, Ella. I will swim out and find you.

I think two Olearons just jumped into the water, Mom. Why would they do that?

I saw it, too. Now only the Maiden is on the bridge. I have never seen her flame that big, that blue . . . Oh, Ella! Get in the water!

Valarie swings forward a thick arm with outstretched fingers of linked, ravenous carakwas. They reach for the sole Olearon and shred the air just shy of her face. As Valarie wades closer, the Maiden closes her rosy eyelids and places a quivering hand over her heart. When she reopens her eyes, their twinned blackness glints like the depths of the sea beyond the cells at her back. Tears spill onto her flushed cheeks.

As Valarie closes her fist of lizard-beetles around the

Maiden—and the carakwas pierce her deeply with a thousand claws—the Olearon's red skin tears apart and white-hot light blasts out. As the heat radiates, the gashes in the Maiden's flesh curl and burn, and are disintegrated in blue flames. Her lips part and fire rockets out in a smoldering beam, which bends her back sharply between the carakwas' grasp. Flames project out her fingertips until all the Maiden's body is engulfed in white-blue heat. As the creatures that form Valarie's hand wail and sizzle—the arm still raising the Maiden to its gaping, laughing void of a mouth—the female Olearon erupts in a final blinding flash that paints the landscape in white.

The sound of the Maiden's explosion follows a moment after. Its vibration rattles the island. The stone bridges remain as skeletons of their former shapes. The trees burn. The sky is obscured by smoke. The Maiden's body is no more, but for the fireworks of consuming sparks that continue to explode up high, illuminating the lower atmosphere, and trailed by sweeping lines of lavender billows. The screeches and clicks of the lizard-beetles turn into one unified scream. The carakwa figure is ablaze and is instantly consumed, reduced to molten rainbows that crumble and are blown in every direction from impact. The sea, too, is displaced; downward and out, with sprays that reach high into the dawn sky.

MOM? *Mom! MOM!*

I'm here, Ell. I guess I don't know where here is . . . I hit my head.

The Olearon—the Maiden—she blew up!

The light was so bright. I saw her sacrifice herself. Then the fire and a wave of heat—it threw me back into the forest. Ella, are you burned?

I tipped the boat so Luggie and I were in the water. But my throat—

it's raw. I can barely swallow through the blisters. My ears are ringing but I can tell the clicking has stopped. Luggie's right ear is gone. The air is full of ash. I can't see anything. It's like a snowstorm.

I'm coming, Ella.

Wait—there is someone here. An Olearon. I didn't know they could fly!

Kameelo!

Can I trust him, Mom?

Yes! He can airlift you out. I will figure out where I am—keep talking to me. Sign and gesture to Kameelo. He will try to understand.

Luggie doesn't want to go with us. What do I do, Mom?

Where does he want to go?

He wants to drown. He's angry the Olearons let his sister be killed. He's biting Kameelo . . . Kameelo is bleeding!

Punch him, Ella!

Kameelo?

No, Luggie! Knock him out so Kameelo can get you two out of there . . . Ella?

I did it, Mom! He's going to be mad.

Better mad than dead.

Kameelo wants me to tell you something. He says the beach is on fire. He can't land there. The forest too along the shore. It's raging. He wants you to run inland—as fast as you can. He says we'll meet you at the glass city.

chapter 51

a rchie feels the enchantment of Naiu in his every step. It started with the glass sphere of the Tillastrion, which had strengthened his hands—that was immediate—but it did not stop there. Now, his shoulders are thrust back and square. His spine is erect and strong. His steps are springy as he strides through the white woodland, keeping pace.

The smell of Jarr-Wya—the same fragrance that Archie first experienced in Zeno's shop, Treasures, on Lanzarote in the Canary Islands—is thick and intoxicating in Archie's nostrils. It feeds him with an energy he hasn't known since his youth. He had sensed this subtle, euphoric enchantment since the day the *Atlantic Odyssey* was captured by the Olearons and ran aground on the Millia's beach. None of the humans in his company, not even Tessa, had mentioned the smell, which had lingered in the air even after the lilac smoke of the flaming ship had been carried away by the sea breeze. No human had voiced even one good or ill effect on them from the peculiar fragrance, so undeniably laced with Naiu.

Maybe they're keeping it to themselves, Archie wonders. *Or, maybe this reaction is mine alone?* Archie struggles to place the aroma and its undertones. He spent the countless days on the exhausting journey east, from the glass city to the Bangol's beach, attempting to find the vocabulary to name it, to no satisfying conclusion.

What Archie is certain of, however, is that the fragrance—the very perfume of the parallel-world, what small amount of it he knows from his time on Jarr-Wya—smells like home. *Home.* The word now confuses Archie. He does not speak this revelation to anyone, not even Ardenal, afraid of what it may mean. Archie's gradual acceptance of the fragrance's bizarre tingling sensation on his skin, sweeping through his veins, causes one thrilling yet terrifying question to bounce around in his skull:

When someone from this world constructs a Tillastrion to transport Tessa and Ella back to Earth, do I go with them? Maybe instead I build a new life here on Jarr-Wya, with Arden . . . He cannot help but think of his late wife, Suzie. *I have no one to go back for,* Archie laments.

Archie clears his throat and re-centers his intentions back to the present moment. Duggie-Sky sits on his shoulders. The boy's face is tight with scabs and his tiny hands cling to the old man's chin which has blossomed into a full white beard since arriving on the island. Nate is beside Archie, weaving between the silvery trunks.

WHEN the captain ran to find Duggie-Sky, before the Maiden's blast, he eventually spotted the boy farther north, perched high overhead along the tree line of the Bangols' beach. Wrapped around a branch, gripping it tightly and shivering, Duggie-Sky had watched wide-eyed, fighting panic, as the thousands of carakwas gathered on the shore. He squeezed his eyes tightly shut at the heart-stopping sound of Valarie's devilish laugh.

Nate had climbed the tree and there, in the leafy canopy, the two had safely watched as Valarie instigated her vengeance. Nate had told Archie—when they were reunited—that he had sensed what would happen next when the Maiden turned blue.

It was then that Nate had torn Duggie-Sky from the limb and dropped from branch to branch down the tree, seeking escape, but not swiftly enough. When the Maiden released the full heat of her flame, when her black eyes crumbled like exhausted embers, the force of the explosion had rocketed the humans out of the tree and inland through the whitewood. They counted their wounds from the fall as new bruises among many. Moments later, they discovered Tessa, disoriented in the smoke, running frantically a few yards in one direction, then another.

When Archie and Ardenal found the three, they were rushing southwest on the route their company had traversed less than a day before. Nate was carrying Duggie-Sky on his muscular back and holding Tessa's hand, their fingers entwined. The captain failed to mask his irritation upon crossing paths with Ardenal.

Tessa wore the same expression of wild determination then, at the company's unexpected meeting, that she wears now, as she leads their smaller, tired group toward the glass city of the Olearons. At their backs, climbing above the sea, is the foreign sun—but instead of bursting with yellow light, it cuts the sky as a shimmering red orb. The bloody daylight and the shadows it creates are the company's only navigational markers in the dense smoke that billows inland, the choked sunshine hinting at the eastern shore behind them. They feel the caress of the morning's diffused heat as they flee its presence.

Tessa mumbles under her breath, talking with Ella, and only speaks loudly to update the group on her daughter's whereabouts. Archie wishes Tessa offered more frequent updates, that he too could communicate with Ella, even if only to hear in his own ears her broken speech as confirmation of her safety. The near silence proves necessary, however, on their treacherous hike. The company walk with outstretched arms and leery steps through the smoke, careful not to lunge forward into a tree or onto unstable footing through the sandy patch of desert where Tessa had carried the Banji. No one mentions Rolace as they leave his web behind them, the misery of his murder a lump in the throat, the clenching of fists and the gritting of teeth. The man-spider who, at first sight, made Archie's heart arrest between beats, had proved tremendously invaluable on their mission to find Ella.

A day into their journey west, Tessa confirms that Kameelo has safely delivered Ella and Luggie to the Lord of Olearon, though there is a commotion there with the red beings in the glass city that Ella does not understand. Archie looks uncomfortable at the news, though Ella's safety renews Tessa's pace and, as politely as she can, Tessa warns Lady Sophia that there will be no more frequent rest breaks. The singer shrugs, but offers no promises.

THE Maiden's plan for Lady Sophia had unfolded flawlessly. When the plump singer plummeted into the sea with a loud splash and had not resurfaced, the Olearons had earned, however guarded, the trust of the Bangols. They had acquired precious information within Tuggeron's chamber—such as a secret ore mine in the north—that they hoped would ripen to their advantage in the sunrises to come. Little did the stone-heads know, however, that Harry and Donna had been waiting. The transformed humans relished the chance to use their gills, to inhale water and swim through the sea as every cell in their Naiu-lined bodies had ached to do since Rolace's web. They rescued Lady Sophia and lugged her to safety, concealing her in a dip in the beach to the south, behind a boulder from the long-gone fortress, though still within view to watch the happenings on the arching stone bridges.

Harry and Donna had also swum to the aid of Azkar and Nameris, though their fall had not been part of the Maiden's strategy. The two Olearon warriors were carried away from the shore on a fitful wave caused by the Maiden's explosive combustion. Donna and Harry had breathed air into their lungs and towed them to where Lady Sophia sat, peeping at the scene, coughing in smoke, and fruitlessly cleaning ash from her gown.

When the Olearon brothers and Lady Sophia were about to depart the eastern beach, heading inland, Donna and Harry announced that they had decided to remain with the sea. Donna kissed their cheeks in a tearful goodbye, though Harry was all smiles. "I've spent my life measuring and calculating at my job, recording golf scores, paying off my car and house—really, I've had enough! Beneath the water, the sound is different. It's peaceful. It feels wrong now to breathe this thin, dry air."

The Olearon brothers had bowed their heads to Donna and Harry, in gratitude for saving them, and in respect at their parting. Lady Sophia curtsied. The couple had turned and sprinted into the rip tide with a triumphant splash at their heels before diving, disappearing for a moment, then waving goodbye above the water with their scaly, webbed hands.

The brothers—and Lady Sophia, who they happily carried in favor of trekking more quickly—were homebound when they caught up to the other half of their company on the path back to the glass city. Azkar and Nameris confirmed the demise of the Maiden—and of the carakwa incarnation of Valarie.

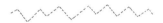

DESPITE the joyful surprise reunion, Azkar and Nameris have been in mourning since the Maiden's death. They tell the humans, and Ardenal, of the Maiden's final words.

I wish time allowed for me to explain more, though you will surely see, soon enough. Many regrets do I have. Alas, we will see each other at the glass city. I am going now—to be with my love.

"Her spirit will be with the Lord," Nameris says before reigniting his flame with Ardenal's help. Azkar does the same.

The three red-skinned beings follow Tessa on the journey back to their home, striding shoulder to shoulder, harmonizing in the Olearon lament of the dead.

Even three full days away from the eastern beach—where Kameelo's flame set the white forest ablaze—the smoke is dense. The company find themselves still within a sheet of white, claustrophobic and even, without variance in its pervasiveness. It brings the company to the edge of oblivion, nearly erasing the landscape so that they march through a purgatory of nothingness. Before that expedition west, Archie had thought of white as pure and clean and clear. The white of the smoke from the now ash forest, on the other hand, is suffocating and hopeless.

"There! Home!" Azkar calls suddenly and points to the glimmering grey and gold glass, to the crystaliths, and the Olearons' gentle hill.

The company had not noticed the break between days and nights. Their eyes had not perceived the change of color which marked the ending of the whitewood and the beginning of the blue. Nor even did they comprehend the thinning of the smoke, or that their noses were free of the stench of it—until now. Now as they find themselves on the edge of the field that spans the land between the blue forest and the glass city.

"Almost there, Ella," Tessa whispers.

Mom! I'm coming!

They dash across the uneven field where Zeno and Ardenal had battled and the Bangol ripped root from earth. They avoid the chasm to the south. There, on the outskirts of the city, a group of red-skinned beings gathers with tall, black-eyed children at their knees. At their center, stands the Lord of Olearon. He wears iron-lined, beveled glass armor with a cape of champagne-gold silk affixed to each pointed epaulet that drapes down his back. His sleeves are fitted and long, like the corrugated folds of his robes that fall from his waist to the earth. The Lord of Olearon shows no skin—unlike when he and his warriors, in matching blue jumpsuits, laid siege to the *Odyssey*—but for his stern red face.

Suddenly, an awkward shriek splits the air. Ella squeezes through the crowd and darts toward Tessa.

Archie's heart soars and—despite the pain and the sacrifices, and the loss of lives which he will never forgive himself for—he feels that his singular mission of finding Arden and reuniting his family is complete. His granddaughter's smile is brilliant as she sprints toward them, though her face has thinned and her boney fingers quiver. Ella's illness is never far from his mind. In that moment, however, Archie refuses to wonder how long their closeness will endure.

chapter 52

"Oh, Ella! I am so glad you're safe, and that your arm is healing well."

You too, Mom . . . Who's this?

Ardenal approaches to stand at Tessa's side, with a beaming Archie close behind. Tessa pauses to look at the Olearon before speaking. "Well, Ella, this is . . ."

Wait! I know. It's Dad!

Ella's blue eyes lock on the black ones that stare down at her. She walks up to Ardenal and takes his hands. She pulls him toward her, where Ardenal kneels so they are on the same level. Ella touches the smooth rosy skin of his cheeks before lunging toward him in an embrace that sends out a burst of fire from Ardenal's hair. Archie rests his hands on Ella's and Ardenal's shoulders. The old man looks at his family, speechless, tears glinting between his wrinkly lids.

Tell him I love him, Mom. Tell Dad I've missed him and that I love him.

"She wants you to know—" Tessa's voice quivers "—Ella says she missed you and she loves you."

"I love you, my sweet Ell. And I have missed you—with an ache in my heart that nearly tore me in two. I never meant to leave you. I came to Jarr-Wya for you."

"She knows, Arden. I've told her what you told me," says Tessa gently.

Ardenal nods. "But I'm sorry, Ella. I haven't found your cure. I forgot the notebook. Grandpa Archie had it when he came to Jarr-Wya, but—but the notes . . . in the half-sunken cruise ship, my research washed away." Hot tears stream from his black eyes. Ella cups her father's face once more.

The Lord of Olearon approaches the haggard company. He gestures with his long graceful hands and his attendants step from behind him and advance toward Tessa, Archie, Duggie-Sky, Nate, Ardenal, Azkar, Nameris, and Lady Sophia. Some attendants carry tall, sparkling crystal goblets filled with a pearly serum, which they encourage the humans and warriors to drink. Other attendants examine the company for injuries with their hot, probing fingers.

"Despite succeeding at your charge of hunting and decimating the Bangol troop in the east, your actions have failed in eliminating their king or purifying the land," the Lord begins, his words rich with disappointment, "I do join with you in remembering the perished, and their bravery—" He pauses. "But—wait! There is one unaccounted for. Where is the Bangol, Zeno?" The Lord's flame surges behind him. Tessa pulls Ella in close, moving a few paces away from the livid Olearon who strides to and fro before them.

"Zeno deserted us," Archie steps forward and answers. "He cheered when the Bangols loyal to Tuggeron, his own kind, were wiped out by the carakwas. He stole away not long after, headed north I'm sure. He didn't reveal his plan to me, but I bet it involves the stone-head king. Zeno didn't even say goodbye. He just up and ran, right after the Maiden—"

"You do not need to speak it, human. I know, and she is with me now," the Lord interrupts, touching his chest. "Her bravery, her sacrifice, will be remembered in our written history, in every age of the Olearons, in every sunset, and as the very blood within my veins until the day I too die, and she and I begin again."

Azkar, Nameris, and Ardenal bow low. "Our Lord, our Maiden," they say together.

"When the Maiden came to me after her fire devoured the carakwas, she told me of all things. Of Eek's demise . . ." the Lord shakes his head, "of the Bangols' plans. Of your thievery, Archibald, which we will discuss in private. And Ella, tell me the truth: do you know anything of a secret compartment? No? Fine. I saw all things through the Maiden's eyes. I felt her pain in my skin. Her knowledge is now my wisdom. Still, with everything that has transpired, there is no change to Jarr-Wya, no lessening of the poison or lifting of the curse, what your company was halfhearted in accomplishing."

Tessa realizes that her initial instinct was right; that saving Ella was never the intention of the Lord. She grits her teeth, loathing the smug, towering Olearon, but stops her tongue. *There will come a time when I'll speak my mind*, she muses. She clutches Ella tightly, though her daughter does not appear afraid. Tessa looks to Archie. The forehead of the old man is copiously perspiring. He keeps one hand tucked in his pocket, looking ready to pounce in defense at a moment's notice.

"The poison must continue to be conjured and leeched into the land from the north, at the stone fortress of the Bangols," Azkar reflects. "Where Tuggeron fled when the carakwas—Valarie—descended upon us." He spits onto the soil.

"Before disappearing, Zeno told me Tuggeron's weakness," offers Archie. "It is his ambition for immortality. This motivates him in everything, even to do what is evil."

"Especially that which is evil," Azkar barks.

"Tuggeron is bloodthirsty and unpredictable," Ardenal adds, "but I believe this lust must also blind him. We can use

Tuggeron's weakness to our advantage. Still, he is crafty. We must never take him for a wild-stone king."

Nameris steps forward. "The Bangols will expect an attack from the east, from our company," he says. "Or that the seven-sunset scorching ceremony in the Maiden's honor will occupy us, perhaps distract us from our pursuit entirely."

"The incense for the Maiden burns ever in our city and within our warriors, whether present or in spirit." The Lord gestures behind him, where teal clouds of sweet-smelling smoke waft into the sapphire abyss. "We do not wait to pursue the Bangols, to wipe them out, king and all. Even their dust I will grind between my teeth."

The Lord calls forward his warriors to join him; Azkar, Nameris, and Kameelo—who had swooped in moments be-fore—and others Tessa does not recognize that had hung back upon the company's return, guarding the Lord. "We must form a new, more capable contingent," the Lord of Olearon declares, "and shall map a route to pass along the western coast, through the fairy vineyards, to lay siege to the north."

"What about Ella's cure?" Tessa asks, as much to Ardenal as to the Lord.

"It will be discussed," the Lord answers curtly. Ardenal nods ever so subtly to Tessa.

Tessa opens her mouth to continue but Azkar interrupts. "And what of our ship?" he inquires.

"We will leave it for the Millia to toy with—for now. A ship is of no use if the Bangol's poison makes our kind too weak to sail it. We will return for it or rebuild when our strength is re-newed. For now, we have the rafts, though their speed is no match. Our focus, our mission, must be turned to our home, our land, and our health." An attendant produces a map. "Ah yes, let us chart our course. Warriors, gather."

"Where is Luggie?" Tessa whispers to Ella, keeping an eye on the Lord. She adds, *Is he safe here?*

The Lord told me how the Maiden showed him what she saw: Tuggeron beating Luggie before he slipped away to our boat, before he saved me. I think the Lord understands that Luggie is different—different from the other Bangols, I mean. The Olearons have been nice to him, Mom. But Luggie won't talk, not even to me. Even when he was forced to sit still as the Olearon nurse stitched the place where his ear was blown off, I couldn't get him to tell me what I could do to help. He won't look me in the eyes. He only lays there on the bed, tucked beneath the blankets in his glass room. I'm scared. I don't know if he's eating . . . Why is Captain Nate looking at you like that? What's going on, Mom?

Tessa turns and notices Nate's protective gaze. Ardenal also stares at Tessa over his shoulder—distracted from the warriors' huddle—with equal, though dejected affection. She mouths the words *not now* to them both. "I feel . . ." Tessa admits in a whisper as she looks back to Ella ". . . so confused." Ella squints. "But that's not important now. All that matters is you. I want us to cherish every moment we have together."

Sheesh, Mom. You're so fatalistic. I'm not dead yet. Plus, I think I know something that may help with my mortality problem. Can you tell Dad?

"Arden, Archie," says Tessa, interrupting the Lord and warriors, and Archie, who was informing an Olearon attendant of Duggie-Sky's wounds. "Arden, Ella just told me that she read your notebooks."

"What? When?" Archie blurts.

"When you were supposedly on grandpa-duty, watching her after school." Tessa raises an eyebrow at Archie, who shrugs guiltily.

"Ella told me she read about a cure, but didn't know that it was for her. She doesn't remember the words, only the pictures.

She said that she can draw them for us. Ella agrees with the Bangols, with Luggie; they are not the ones poisoning the island. It's the Star! That's what has changed here, on Jarr-Wya. That's what created the Millia in the first place and crazed the Bangols and destroyed the soil. It's the Star! Ella wants to show us what she remembers. I believe her, Arden, Archie. Lord—" Tessa turns to the Lord of Olearon, who has halted the deliberations with his warriors, who now all listen intently as she relays Ella's message. "I believe you are fighting the wrong enemy," Tessa finishes, convinced that she cannot trust the Lord as she had the Maiden, though for the time she must pretend.

"Get her paper! A pen! A paintbrush!" Ardenal beseeches the attendants. At first, they do not budge. Then the Lord—after pausing reflectively, as if looking inward—nods and gestures to the glass city and the attendants speed toward it.

"The Maiden agrees," the Lord answers. "She found the human child's sketchbook. Such perceptive beauty, the Maiden tells me, was painted on its pages. At this very moment, I am flipping through the book in my mind, seeing the artwork for myself through her memories. A shame it was destroyed in the Maiden's flame. In whatever way the cure for this young one, this Ella, may be connected with the Star, with Jarr-Wya—we must waste no time in finding out!"

Tessa is startled and speechless at first. She had not anticipated the Lord's willingness to listen. "Thank you," she mumbles. *Maybe he will be an ally, not an adversary, moving forward,* Tessa hopes.

The swiftest of the attendants produces thick, fibrous paper and a flask dripping with ink. Also thrust into Ella's pale hands are round-tip and flat-bristle paint brushes with ferrules of polished iron crimped to blue-wood handles.

"Ella, show us what you remember," Tessa urges, holding her breath as her daughter begins to paint.

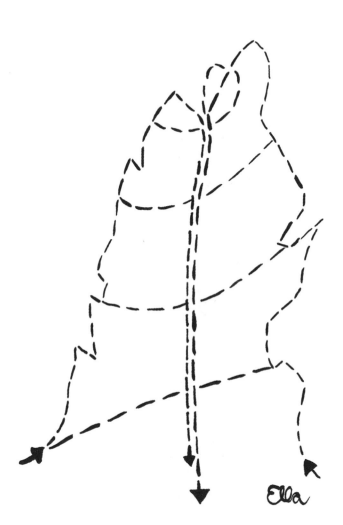

Ella

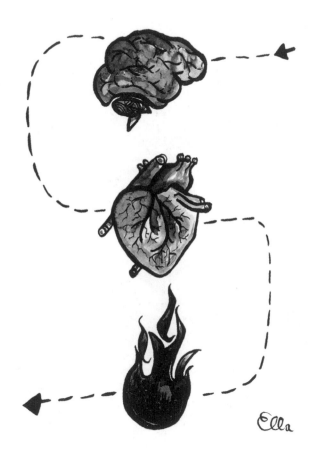

*A*t that very instant—while Ella draws with ink the clues to finding the cure for both her and the island—Luggie pulls his silky sheet further over his head. It diffuses enough sunlight that shines down on him through the glass roof of his chamber, allowing him to gaze at the object he clings to dearly. His fingers stroke the edge of a glass shard he cradles carefully in his hands. It slices the thinnest top layer of his skin, but Luggie is too engrossed—too focused on reading—to notice the blood. His large eyes grow even broader and brighter.

WHEN the Maiden was devoured by her fire, she threw the secret history of the Olearons back, behind her, toward the rising sun and out to sea. While she had hoped that it would sink and be forgotten forever, the Naiu in the object rebelled. It rose to the surface in the place it had fell, popping up above the unsettled water where Luggie and Ella were treading tiredly with dying effort.

To Luggie's right—in the direction of the cell where his sister, Nanjee, had been tended to, where she had been consumed alive by the carakwas—he noticed an unusual reflection on the water. When Luggie outstretched his arm, his hand caught hold of the piece of glass. It was hot to his touch in the tepid sea. He kicked hard, struggling to propel his body upward in the water, while curling his long arms behind him, endeavoring to tuck the glass within the folds of his garments. While he kicked, the task was impossible. Luggie knew he desired the glass—that it wanted to be saved by him—and so he let his legs grow still and his body sink beneath the waves that thrust him and Ella deeper and further out to sea, as the fire of the Maiden blinded him and burned the side of his face.

Under the water, Luggie was successful in securing the glass, just as Ella pulled him up by his shoulder. She had found and clung to a wooden board, part of their disheveled boat, dragging onto it the weight of Luggie's body. She cared for him—in that moment Luggie had no doubt of that. By the look on her face and the way she kissed his lips despite the salt water, Ella wordlessly begged him not to give up, not to drown himself. He was strangely glad that she assumed this and did not know what he concealed, when he didn't even know himself. Suddenly a flying Olearon arrived. Luggie hated the red being and fought hard, but then—without warning—Ella punched him between his wide eyes and he slipped beneath consciousness.

Since awaking to the sight of a horde of hot red bodies— and Ella—Luggie was despondent. He was homesick for his sister, for familiar grey faces, but most of all, for the shard of glass. Even Ella and her constant care were bothersome, as all Luggie wished to do was tickle the magic from the smooth shiny surface. Luggie knew Ella would want to see what he had found. For now, Luggie wished to protect Ella, in part; the other part of him wished to protect himself. Ella's blow to his face had so greatly startled Luggie that he began to question her affection for him. In the days he studied the glass, he began to question everything.

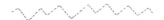

LUGGIE listens for sounds beyond the sunlit sheet. When he hears nothing, he dances his sharp fingernails across the glass in the way in which he learned calls forth the storm clouds and the words, in his own language. His senses cause his skin to goose-bump. His heart bangs the insides of his ribs. The churning, unsettling sensations that course through Luggie's body cue him that what he is about to read will be something of significance, something that may change everything on Jarr-Wya—for better or for ill.

This is the record of the forbidden oracle of the Steffanus—Laken—told to the 29th Lord of Olearon, and relayed to his most trusted councilors before his form was dismantled in his madness and collected in secret, to be preserved within the hidden compartment beneath the glass throne.

Laken's Oracle:

"A half-blood Olearon will return to Jarr and the race of Olearons will cease as they have been known since the first sunrise and their first spark. With this knowledge, the Steffanus sisters will come forth once more to the Olearons, but this time not for help—for vengeance."

epilogue

The Star looks up from beneath the sea and observes all the happenings above it. It senses that Ella is near. *Finally,* it thinks, *the child has come to die.*

glossary

of Characters, Creatures, Plants, and Places

ARCHIBALD "ARCHIE" WELLSLEY

A white-haired senior citizen and retired roofer from Seattle, Washington. He is father to Arden, father-in-law to Tessa, grandfather to Ella, and widower to his late wife, Suzie. He moved in with Arden and his family after Suzie's death, when Ella was seven years old.

ARDEN WELLSLEY

A professor of Ancient Egyptian Dynasties at Seattle University. He is the adult son of Archie, husband to Tessa, and father to Ella. He has dark brown hair, blue eyes, and chunky glasses. He disappeared without a trace when Ella was twelve years old.

ARRECIFE (PRONOUNCED: ARH-AY-SEE-FAY)

A real-life port city on the island of Lanzarote in the Canary Islands, in the North Atlantic Ocean. The city faces the African continent and the country of Morocco.

ATLANTIC ODYSSEY

The name of the cruise ship that sails through the Canary Islands in the North Atlantic Ocean, captained by Nathanial Billows.

AWAKINS (PRONOUNCED: A-WHAY-KINS)

Large magical butterflies with two sets of wings: By night, they are airborne with a purple pair, and by day, with a yellow-orangish pair. They never land. The Bangols capture them for use in their air-transportation balloons.

AZKAR (PRONOUNCED: AZ-CAR)

An Olearon warrior and the eldest brother to Olen, Eek, Nameris, and Kameelo. Incredibly strong and often gruff, he is known for his scowl, bravery, and the jagged black scar stretching from below his left eye to his collarbone.

BALUURWA THE DOOMFUL (PRONOUNCED: BAL-OO-R-WHA)

A mountain that rises sharply at the center of Jarr-Wya, created when Naiu crashed onto the island. The mountain is carved out by tunnels and has many small fragments of land jutting out at its side, connected by rock chutes, vines, or simply floating on their own. It is home to the Steffanus.

BANGOL (PRONOUNCED: BANG-GUL)

A race originating from the rock, clay, and earth of Jarr-Wya. They possess power from Naiu, the magic in the world of Jarr, to manipulate earthen materials at their will. They have large, glowing yellow eyes, grey skin, and stones growing out of their cheekbones and bald heads.

BANJI (PRONOUNCED: BAN-GEE)

A magical flower that contains strong quantities of Naiu. It has the power to distort perceptions and is often used as a weapon. In the presence of the Star, the growth of the flowers wane.

CANARY ISLANDS

Real-life Spanish islands of volcanic origins, which are connected in a chain called archipelago. The islands are located off the coast of Africa in the North Atlantic Ocean. The seven main landmasses include Lanzarote, Fuerteventura, Gran Canaria, Tenerife, La Palma, La Gomera, and El Hierro.

CAPTAIN NATHANIAL "NATE" BILLOWS

A brown-eyed, blond-haired, tattooed sailor who captains the ship named the *Atlantic Odyssey*. Theatrical in his gestures, he loves to tell stories. He is young, brave, and flirtatious.

CARAKWA (PRONOUNCED: KA-RACK-WA)

A clicking, screeching creature the size of a small dog. It has the body of a lizard with the hard shell and head of a beetle. It has fly-like compound eyes, half-moon claws, and sharp lacerating forelegs. It has no soul and thus is easily possessed by evil spirits.

CHERGRIN (PRONOUNCED: CHAIR-GRIN)

A faithful Bangol warrior, loyal to King Tuggeron, and leader of the Bangol's defense.

CONSTELLATIONS CRUISE LINE

The name of the business that offers passengers tourist voyages through the Canary Island on the *Atlantic Odyssey* cruise liner.

CRYSTALITHS (PRONOUNCED: KRIS-TALL-LITHS)

Light-transferring prism-shaped columns made of crystal that channel the sunshine, converting it to Naiu. The columns aid in disbursing the magic through the soil to nourish the crops that grow in the Olearon fields.

DONNA

A senior citizen and passenger on the *Atlantic Odyssey*. She is married to Harry and has a passion for gardening and baking.

DUGGIE-SKY

A four-year-old, African American passenger on the *Atlantic Odyssey*. A good-spirited boy with a love of aviation and superhero-themed clothing. His nickname, Duggie-Sky, refers to the Douglas A-3 Skywarrior airplane, designed by Ed Heinemann, introduced in the 1950s. Duggie-Sky traveled on the cruise with his father.

EEK (PRONOUNCED: EE-K)

An Olearon warrior and the youngest brother to Azkar, Olen, Nameris, and Kameelo. He is youthful and inexperienced, but strong and appreciated for his critical thinking.

ELLA WELLSLEY

The blond, blue-eyed fourteen-year-old daughter to Arden and Tessa Wellsley, and granddaughter to Archie. She is a considerate, creative young woman with a quick wit and a humorous approach to life. When she was ten, doctors discovered a cancerous tumor at the base of her brain and wrapped around the top of her spinal cord. She lost her ability to speak six months before boarding the *Atlantic Odyssey*.

HARRY

A senior citizen and passenger on the *Atlantic Odyssey*. He is married to Donna and, on earth, was an accountant and avid golfer.

JARR (PRONOUNCED: JA-RR)

A world formed by and filled with magic (known as Naiu), and connected to the derivative dimension of Earth. On Jarr, days are measured in sunsets.

JARR-WYA (PRONOUNCED: JA-RR-WHY-AH)

The magical island in the world called Jarr. The island has long been ruled over by three dominant races: the Olearons, Bangols, and the sea creatures, turned into the Millia after the arrival of the Star. None of these, the Jarrwian, know what lies beyond the island. In the past five thousand sunsets, the magic on Jarr-Wya has changed, with all creatures feeling the effect.

JUNIN (PRONOUNCED: JOO-NIN)

A female Olearon, mother, and warrior in the contingent tasked with protecting the surface of the sea at Jarr-Wya's southern shore, next to the Millia's beach.

KAMEELO (PRONOUNCED: CAM-EE-LOW)

An Olearon warrior and brother to Azkar, Olen, Nameris, and Eek. He is known for his eagerness and free spirit.

LADY SOPHIA

A portly Spanish opera singer and the entertainer on Constellations Cruise Line. She is a loud talker, flamboyant and self-centered, though not unkind.

LAKEN (PRONOUNCED: LAY-KEN)

She is the last of the she-race called the Steffanus. She has rich auburn hair, blue-red eyes, silvery skin, and horns wrapped in gold growing out of her skull. She flies on large wings. She is prophetic in nature, though her visions do not always unfold as expected.

LANZAROTE (PRONOUNCED: LAN-ZA-ROW-TAY)

A real-life island, one of the seven in the Canary Islands, located off the western coast of Africa in the North Atlantic Ocean. One popular tourist destination on the island is Timanfaya National Park. The capital city is Arrecife.

LORD AND MAIDEN OF OLEARON

Titles given to the male and female rulers of the Olearons. The Lord and Maiden must find each other in every age as their souls are always connected. As with all Olearons, when one dies, the other inhabits the living one's body until his or her final demise. The Maiden stands approximately eight feet tall and the Lord approximately ten feet tall, a full foot above his male warriors.

LUGGIE (PRONOUNCED: LUG-EE)

A five-thousand-eight-hundred-sunset-old Bangol (roughly sixteen human years), son to the current king, Tuggeron, and brother to Nanjee. He is next in line to rule after Tuggeron, and is tasked with learning to lead the Bangols, including inflicting punishment and flying their transport balloons.

MILLIA (PRONOUNCED: MILL-EE-AH)

A race on Jarr-Wya formed of crushed seashells, their name meaning 'soul of the shell.' The sea creatures desire the Star beneath the island, but they cannot reach it. Thus, the shells crash on the shore and break into millions of pieces that make up the Millia on the southern beach. The sand contains all the bitter unfulfillment of its past masters. They can change to any shape, though remain one solid material.

NAIU (PRONOUNCED: NY-UU)

The magic in the world of Jarr and on the island of Jarr-Wya. According to the secret history of the Olearons, as told by a Steffanus, Naiu was a flying being and created all worlds and all time, which expended its power to each of its creations. Naiu crashed onto Jarr-Wya and, before it died, fused with a human child, creating a new race called the Steffanus.

NAMERIS (PRONOUNCED: NA-MER-IS)

An Olearon warrior and brother to Azkar, Olen, Kameelo, and Eek. He discovered his power—the ability to tell if someone speaks the truth—after visiting Rolace. His personality is often grumpy and skeptical.

NANJEE (PRONOUNCED: NAN-GEE)

A six-thousand-two-hundred-sunset-old Bangol (roughly seventeen human years), daughter to the current king, Tuggeron, and sister to Luggie. She is tasked with recording the history of the Bangols, particularly that of her father.

OLEARON (PRONOUNCED: OH-LEE-AIR-ON)

A race of creatures on Jarr-Wya with red skin, full black eyes, and dark dreadlocks. They can release fire from the backs of their necks, and envelope their whole bodies in flame. Their warriors wear royal blue jumpsuits and, in addition to their fire, wield weapons made of glass. Their race is ruled over by the Lord and Maiden of Olearon.

OLEN (PRONOUNCED: OH-LEN)

An Olearon warrior and brother to Azkar, Nameris, Kameelo, and Eek. He is known for his bravery and kindness.

ROLACE (PRONOUNCED: ROW-LIS)

A huge spider with twelve hairy legs and the head of an elderly man. He uses the enchantment of Naiu, found in the Banji flowers, to spin a cocoon-web around an individual to expose his or her unique powers, but only if the will is strong and the heart is brave.

STAR

Five thousand sunsets past, it flew through the sky, heading for Jarr-Wya, which it chose to spare. Instead it crashed into the ocean, coming to rest beneath the island. It crazed the Bangols. The shell creature's love of it turned them evil, forming the Millia sands. Much plant life and many creatures have been altered. The island has not been the same since.

SEA OF SELFDOM

The mysterious ocean off the west coast of Jarr-Wya, near the Olearon's glass city. Those that venture far on its waters never return.

SENIOR KARISH (PRONOUNCED: KA-RISH)

The leader of the Millia sands and spokesman on behalf of the evil race. He wears a crown and breastplate made of shells, still inhabited by their sea creatures. Selfish and consumed with desire for the Star, he strikes deals that bend in his favor.

STEFFANUS (PRONOUNCED: STEFF-AN-US)

A race created by the fusion of a human girl and a magical being, Naiu, at its death. They have large wings that extend out from their backs, antlers from their heads, and skin that shines silver. Their weapons are long daggers with gold-coiling handles. They collect gold and silver and have a fascination with traveling to Earth, which they do by building their own Tillastrions.

TESSA WELLSLEY

A Seattle nurse with long blond hair, green eyes, and a feminine style. Wife to Arden, mother to Ella, and daughter-in-law to Archie. She is the sole breadwinner and caregiver since Arden's disappearance. She is stubborn and passionate, with a quick tongue and an unbreakable motherly-love, though often gives off an air of suspicion.

TILLASTRION (PRONOUNCED: TILL-ASS-TREE-ON)

A portal jumper between one magic-filled world to its connecting, derivative dimension. Two beings are required for the device to function: one to build it and the other to operate it. The one who builds must be from the world the pair wish to reach; the one who operates must be from the world they wish to depart.

TREASURES

The Bangol Zeno's shop in Mercado Artesanal Plaza Haria, on the island of Lanzarote. The shop sells antique jewelry, bobbles, lamps, and furniture.

TUGGERON "TUGGS" (PRONOUNCED: TUG-ER-ON)

The murderous current king of the Bangols, and father to Luggie and Nanjee. A fat, selfish Bangol that wields a stone mallet and desires dominion over Jarr-Wya. He wears a sleeveless outfit of brown and grey fabrics, decorated with animal hides.

VALARIE

The spunky brunette cruise director of Constellations Cruise Line on the *Atlantic Odyssey*. She is in love with Captain Nathanial Billows. After a challenging youth, she has grown jaded and spiteful.

WINZUN (PRONOUNCED: WIN-ZUHN)

The twin brother to Zeno and co-blood heir to the Bangol kingship.

ZENO (PRONOUNCED: ZEE-NO)

A Bangol and rightful co-heir to the throne. He and his twin brother, Winzun, were banished to Earth by Tuggeron, a wicked Bangol who killed the twins' father to become king himself. Zeno owned a shop on the island of Lanzarote called Treasures.

The Olearon Alphabet

The Bangol Alphabet

A		N			
B		O			
C		P			
D		Q			
E		R			
F		S			
G		T			
H		U			
I		V			
J		W			
K		X			
L		Y			
M		Z			

Decoder Challenge

Decipher the language and the words. Email the decoded message to secret@abovethestar.com to receive a secret clue to an important revelation for books two and three in The 8th Island Trilogy.

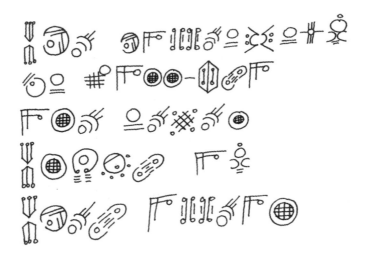

Acknowledgments

To Aaron Chute, for always believing in my wildest dreams and supporting my harebrained plans. You are my rock and my home. I hope to be as tireless a cheerleader for you, as you are for me. I dedicate this book to you and to our adventures together.

To Hannah, Zachary, Eden, and Luca—thank you for lending your mom to the magical world of Jarr-Wya. You four are my inspirations and my joy. Your love of reading gives me hope for the future.

To my parents: Charlotte Robb, Robert Duke, Doug Robb, and Nancy Reid. Mom, you are my hero. Thank you for your pep talks, kicks in the butt, and unconditional friendship. Dad, thank you for instilling in me a passion for fantasy, storytelling, and the arts. When you shaved your head to play Tuggeron in the book trailer, I felt incredibly loved. Bob and Nancy, I couldn't wish for better stepparents. To me, you two are simply *Dad* and *Mom*. Thank you all for babysitting and taking such great care of my family while I am away on tour.

To my fabulous publishing and publicity team, thank you for your creativity, hard work, and continual faith in my stories. Gratitude to Brooke Warner, Lauren Wise, Crystal Patriarche, Morgan Rath, Savannah Harrelson, Rebecca Lown, and Stacey Aaronson. Thank you also to Marg Gilks and Megan Hannum, my keen-eyed editors, and to Warren Sheffer, one of the most badass lawyers I know.

To my early readers—I kiss the ground you walk on. Your

feedback blew my mind and improved my story. Bountiful thanks to Charlotte Robb, Aaron Chute, Jeff Alberda, Melysa West, Naomi Maharaj, Maya Breen, Marlin Ehrenholz, Rick Cummings, Ashley Schiefer, Brooke Gander, and Cassidy Richlard.

To the *Above the Star* book trailer cast and crew . . . You signed on when you had little idea of the fantastical visual world we would create together, and yet your enthusiasm brought the Maiden, Tuggeron, Senior Karish, and Laken to life. Gratitude to Aaron Chute, Tom Lim, Maya Breen, Perry Medina, Evan Crawford, Janelle Snow, Doug Robb, and Brooke Gander— Brooke, your creativity and tireless work are immensely appreciated.

To my creative friends—writers, artists, photographers, musicians, curators, publishers, educators, and beyond—around the world, and online: I hold dear your encouragement, accountability, and community. Thank you to my Lesley University friends, advisors, and dearly loved mentors; Rachel Manley, Pam Petro, and Jane Brox.

As well, a special thanks to NaNoWriMo, otherwise known as the National Novel Writing Month. The challenge of penning a fifty-thousand-word novel in thirty days was the perfect distraction I needed at the end of a tragic season. Tessa, Ella, and Archie thank you as well.

Finally, to my readers. Thank you for your emails, reviews, and social love. You make the often solitary life of a writer and artist that much friendlier. Keep reading. Words are precious and powerful.

A Note from the Author

Dear Reader,

Thank you for portal-jumping with me to Jarr-Wya! If you enjoyed the journey we have taken together, please send a note to info@alexismariechute.com, as I would love to hear from you. For free downloads of Ella's drawings, wallpapers for your phone and computer, discount codes, secret chapters, character profiles, book tour info, and more, please visit:

www.AlexisMarieChute.com
and subscribe to the e-newsletter at
www.AlexisMarieChute.com/contact

Thank you!
Alexis Marie Chute

About the Author

Alexis Marie Chute is an award-winning author, artist, filmmaker, and inspirational speaker. *Above the Star* is her second book. Her memoir, *Expecting Sunshine: A Journey of Grief, Healing and Pregnancy After Loss*, was a Kirkus Best Book of 2017, and received many other literary awards. *Expecting Sunshine* is also a highly acclaimed feature documentary film produced and directed by the author. Alexis Marie received her Bachelors of Fine Art in Art and Design and her Masters of Fine Art in Creative Writing. She is an internationally exhibited painter and photographer, curator of InFocus Photography Exhibition, and a widely published writer of fiction, non-fiction, and poetry. Alexis Marie is passionate about creative living and coined the term, "The Healthy Grief Movement." She is a highly sought-after keynote speaker and teacher across all her artistic and healing disciplines. In her spare time, she loves traveling, canoeing, and paddle-boarding, sharing thoughtful conversations with friends—old and new—and spending time with her family. Alexis Marie lives in snowy Edmonton, Alberta, Canada with her husband Aaron and their children.

Connect with Alexis Marie Chute

WEB: AlexisMarieChute.com

EMAIL: info@alexismariechute.com

E-NEWS SUBSCRIBE: AlexisMarieChute.com/contact

INSTAGRAM: @alexismariechute

TWITTER: @_Alexis_Marie

YOUTUBE: youtube.com/alexismariechute

FACEBOOK: facebook.com/AlexisMarieProductionsInc

PINTEREST: pinterest.com/alexismarieart/

When sharing on social, please use these hashtags:

#alexismariechute, #abovethestar, #8thislandtrilogy

Help Spread the Word

Please join with readers around the world in spreading the word about *Above the Star* and *The 8th Island Trilogy*!

HERE ARE 10 IDEAS:

1. Write a review of the book on Amazon and Goodreads.
   Review on Amazon: bit.ly/ats-amazon
   Review on Goodreads: bit.ly/ats-goodreads

2. Recommend the book through word of mouth to your friends and family.

3. Share the book on your social media accounts—and post a photo of you and your copy on Instagram and Twitter to be in the running for a special prize.
   Social Sharing Hashtags: #abovethestar #8thislandtrilogy #alexismariechute

4. Read the book at your book club (email the author info@alexismariechute.com for the club study guide, using the words "ATS Study Guide" in the subject line).

5. Order the book from your local bookstore and request it at your local library.

6. Purchase a copy for the waiting room of your doctor or dentist, or leave a copy for strangers to pass along on the train.

7. Invite Alexis Marie Chute to speak at your organization or community event, or to teach an art or writing class.

8. Write about the book on your blog or talk about it on your podcast or YouTube channel.

9. Invite people to the book launch events—and if there isn't an event near you, join with the author in planning one.

10. Subscribe to the e-newsletter at www.AlexisMarieChute.com/contact for more ideas and ways to connect.

BONUS: Email the author at info@alexismariechute.com to share how the story has impacted you.

Thank you!

With gratitude,
Alexis Marie Chute

Other Books by Alexis Marie Chute

Expecting Sunshine:
A Journey of Grief, Healing and Pregnancy After Loss
(She Writes Press, 2017)

Follow the adventures of your favorite characters
from Above the Star:

Book 2 in *The 8th Island Trilogy* coming 2019
Book 3 in *The 8th Island Trilogy* coming 2020

SELECTED TITLES FROM SPARKPRESS

SparkPress is an independent boutique publisher delivering high-quality, entertaining, and engaging content that enhances readers' lives, with a special focus on female-driven work. Visit us at
www.gosparkpress.com

Ocean's Fire, Stacey Tucker, $16.95, 978-1-943006-28-1. Once the Greeks forced their male gods upon the world, the belief in the power of women was severed. For centuries it has been thought that the wisdom of the high priestesses perished at the hand of the patriarchs—but now the ancient Book of Sophia has surfaced. Its pages contain the truths hidden by history, and the sacred knowledge for the coming age. And it is looking for Skylar Southmartin.

The Infinite Now, Mindy Tarquini, $16.95, 978-1-943006-34-2. In flu-ravaged 1918 Philadelphia, the newly-orphaned daughter of the local fortune teller panics and casts her entire neighborhood into a bubble of stagnant time in order to save the life of the mysterious shoe-maker who has taken her in. As the complications of the time bubble multiply, this forward-thinking young woman must find the courage to face an uncertain future, so she can find a way to break the spell.

Hindsight, Mindy Tarquini, $16.95, 978-1943006014. A thirty-three-year-old Chaucer professor who remembers all her past lives is desperate to change her future—because if she doesn't, she will never live the life of her dreams.

Tree Dreams, Kristin Kaye, $16.95, 9781943006465. In the often-violent battle between loggers and environmentalists that plagues seventeen-year-old Jade's hometown in Northern California, she must decide whose side she's on—but choosing sides only makes matters worse.

The Raven God, Alane Adams, $16.95, 978-1-943006-36-6. As an army of fire giants amasses in the south, prepared to launch all-out war on the defenseless Orkney, Sam embarks on a rescue mission to bring Odin back from the dark underworld of Helva—but the menacing Loki is pulling all the strings.

But Not Forever, Jan Von Scleh, $16.95, 978-1-943006-58-8. When identical fifteen-year-old girls are mysteriously switched in time, they discover the love that's been missing in their lives. Torn, both want to go home, but neither wants to give up what they now have.